A VISION OF SHADOWS

WARRIORS

THE RAGING
STORM

WARRIORS

THE PROPHECIES BEGIN

Book One: *Into the Wild*

Book Two: *Fire and Ice*

Book Three: *Forest of Secrets*

Book Four: *Rising Storm*

Book Five: *A Dangerous Path*

Book Six: *The Darkest Hour*

THE NEW PROPHECY

Book One: *Midnight*

Book Two: *Moonrise*

Book Three: *Dawn*

Book Four: *Starlight*

Book Five: *Twilight*

Book Six: *Sunset*

POWER OF THREE

Book One: *The Sight*

Book Two: *Dark River*

Book Three: *Outcast*

Book Four: *Eclipse*

Book Five: *Long Shadows*

Book Six: *Sunrise*

OMEN OF THE STARS

Book One: *The Fourth Apprentice*

Book Two: *Fading Echoes*

Book Three: *Night Whispers*

Book Four: *Sign of the Moon*

Book Five: *The Forgotten Warrior*

Book Six: *The Last Hope*

DAWN OF THE CLANS

Book One: *The Sun Trail*
Book Two: *Thunder Rising*
Book Three: *The First Battle*
Book Four: *The Blazing Star*
Book Five: *A Forest Divided*
Book Six: *Path of Stars*

A VISION OF SHADOWS

Book One: *The Apprentice's Quest*
Book Two: *Thunder and Shadow*
Book Three: *Shattered Sky*
Book Four: *Darkest Night*
Book Five: *River of Fire*
Book Six: *The Raging Storm*

EXPLORE THE WARRIORS WORLD

Warriors Super Edition: Firestar's Quest
Warriors Super Edition: Bluestar's Prophecy
Warriors Super Edition: SkyClan's Destiny
Warriors Super Edition: Crookedstar's Promise
Warriors Super Edition: Yellowfang's Secret
Warriors Super Edition: Tallstar's Revenge
Warriors Super Edition: Bramblestar's Storm
Warriors Super Edition: Moth Flight's Vision
Warriors Super Edition: Hawkwing's Journey
Warriors Super Edition: Tigerheart's Shadow
Warriors Super Edition: Crowfeather's Trial
Warriors Field Guide: Secrets of the Clans

Warriors: Cats of the Clans
Warriors: Code of the Clans
Warriors: Battles of the Clans
Warriors: Enter the Clans
Warriors: The Ultimate Guide
Warriors: The Untold Stories
Warriors: Tales from the Clans
Warriors: Shadows of the Clans
Warriors: Legends of the Clans

MANGA
The Lost Warrior
Warrior's Refuge
Warrior's Return
The Rise of Scourge
Tigerstar and Sasha #1: Into the Woods
Tigerstar and Sasha #2: Escape from the Forest
Tigerstar and Sasha #3: Return to the Clans
Ravenpaw's Path #1: Shattered Peace
Ravenpaw's Path #2: A Clan in Need
Ravenpaw's Path #3: The Heart of a Warrior
SkyClan and the Stranger #1: The Rescue
SkyClan and the Stranger #2: Beyond the Code
SkyClan and the Stranger #3: After the Flood

NOVELLAS
Hollyleaf's Story *Mapleshade's Vengeance*
Mistystar's Omen *Goosefeather's Curse*
Cloudstar's Journey *Ravenpaw's Farewell*
Tigerclaw's Fury *Spottedleaf's Heart*
Leafpool's Wish *Pinestar's Choice*
Dovewing's Silence *Thunderstar's Echo*

Also by Erin Hunter

SEEKERS

Book One: *The Quest Begins*
Book Two: *Great Bear Lake*
Book Three: *Smoke Mountain*
Book Four: *The Last Wilderness*
Book Five: *Fire in the Sky*
Book Six: *Spirits in the Stars*

RETURN TO THE WILD

Book One: *Island of Shadows*
Book Two: *The Melting Sea*
Book Three: *River of Lost Bears*
Book Four: *Forest of Wolves*
Book Five: *The Burning Horizon*
Book Six: *The Longest Day*

MANGA

Toklo's Story
Kallik's Adventure

SURVIVORS

Book One: The Empty City
Book Two: A Hidden Enemy
Book Three: Darkness Falls
Book Four: The Broken Path
Book Five: The Endless Lake
Book Six: Storm of Dogs

THE GATHERING DARKNESS

Book One: A Pack Divided
Book Two: Dead of Night
Book Three: Into the Shadows
Book Four: Red Moon Rising
Book Five: The Exile's Journey

Survivors: Tales from the Packs

NOVELLAS

Alpha's Tale
Sweet's Journey
Moon's Choice

BRAVELANDS

Book One: Broken Pride
Book Two: Code of Honor
Book Three: Blood and Bone

A VISION OF SHADOWS

WARRIORS

THE RAGING STORM

ERIN HUNTER

X

HARPER

An Imprint of HarperCollinsPublishers

Special thanks to Kate Cary

The Raging Storm
Copyright © 2018 by Working Partners Limited
Series created by Working Partners Limited
Map art © 2018 by Dave Stevenson
Interior art © 2018 by Allen Douglas

www.harpercollinschildrens.com
ISBN 978-0-06-238657-1 (trade bdg.) — ISBN 978-0-06-238658-8 (lib. bdg.)
Typography by Ellice M. Lee
18 19 20 21 22   CG/LSCH   10 9 8 7 6 5 4 3 2 1
❖
First Edition

ALLEGIANCES

THUNDERCLAN

LEADER   **BRAMBLESTAR**—dark brown tabby tom with amber eyes

DEPUTY   **SQUIRRELFLIGHT**—dark ginger she-cat with green eyes and one white paw

MEDICINE CATS   **LEAFPOOL**—light brown tabby she-cat with amber eyes, white paws and chest

JAYFEATHER—gray tabby tom with blind blue eyes

ALDERHEART—dark ginger tom with amber eyes

WARRIORS   (toms and she-cats without kits)

BRACKENFUR—golden-brown tabby tom

CLOUDTAIL—long-haired white tom with blue eyes

BRIGHTHEART—white she-cat with ginger patches

THORNCLAW—golden-brown tabby tom

WHITEWING—white she-cat with green eyes

BIRCHFALL—light brown tabby tom

BERRYNOSE—cream-colored tom with a stump for a tail

MOUSEWHISKER—gray-and-white tom
APPRENTICE, PLUMPAW (black-and-ginger she-cat)

POPPYFROST—pale tortoiseshell-and-white she-cat

LIONBLAZE—golden tabby tom with amber eyes

ROSEPETAL—dark cream she-cat
APPRENTICE, STEMPAW (white-and-orange tom)

LILYHEART—small, dark tabby she-cat with white patches and blue eyes

BUMBLESTRIPE—very pale gray tom with black stripes
APPRENTICE, SHELLPAW (tortoiseshell tom)

CHERRYFALL—ginger she-cat

MOLEWHISKER—brown-and-cream tom

AMBERMOON—pale ginger she-cat
APPRENTICE, EAGLEPAW (ginger she-cat)

DEWNOSE—gray-and-white tom

STORMCLOUD—gray tabby tom

HOLLYTUFT—black she-cat

FERNSONG—yellow tabby tom

SORRELSTRIPE—dark brown she-cat

LEAFSHADE—tortoiseshell she-cat
APPRENTICE, SPOTPAW (spotted tabby she-cat)

LARKSONG—black tom

HONEYFUR—white she-cat with yellow splotches

SPARKPELT—orange tabby she-cat

TWIGBRANCH—gray she-cat with green eyes
APPRENTICE, FLYPAW (striped gray tabby she-cat)

FINLEAP—brown tom
APPRENTICE, SNAPPAW (golden tabby tom)

CINDERHEART—gray tabby she-cat

BLOSSOMFALL—tortoiseshell-and-white she-cat with petal-shaped white patches

QUEENS   (she-cats expecting or nursing kits)

DAISY—cream long-furred cat from the horseplace

IVYPOOL—silver-and-white tabby she-cat with dark blue eyes (mother to Bristlekit, a pale gray she-kit; Thriftkit, a dark gray she-kit; and Flipkit, a tabby tom)

ELDERS   (former warriors and queens, now retired)

GRAYSTRIPE—long-haired gray tom

MILLIE—striped silver tabby she-cat with blue eyes

SHADOWCLAN

LEADER   **TIGERSTAR**—dark brown tabby tom

DEPUTY   **TAWNYPELT**—tortoiseshell she-cat with green eyes
APPRENTICE, CONEPAW (white-and-gray tom)

MEDICINE CAT **PUDDLESHINE**—brown tom with white splotches

WARRIORS	**JUNIPERCLAW**—black tom
	WHORLPELT—gray-and-white tom
	STRIKESTONE—brown tabby tom **APPRENTICE, BLAZEPAW** (white-and-ginger tom)
	STONEWING—white tom **APPRENTICE, ANTPAW** (tom with a brown-and-black splotched pelt)
	GRASSHEART—pale brown tabby she-cat **APPRENTICE, GULLPAW** (white she-cat)
	SCORCHFUR—dark gray tom with slashed ears
	FLOWERSTEM—silver she-cat
	SNAKETOOTH—honey-colored tabby she-cat
	SLATEFUR—sleek gray tom **APPRENTICE, FRONDPAW** (gray tabby she-cat)
	CLOVERFOOT—gray tabby she-cat
	SPARROWTAIL—large brown tabby tom **APPRENTICE, CINNAMONPAW** (brown tabby she-cat with white paws)
	SNOWBIRD—pure white she-cat with green eyes
QUEENS	**DOVEWING**—pale gray she-cat with green eyes (mother to Pouncekit, a gray she-kit; Lightkit, a brown tabby she-kit; and Shadowkit, a gray tabby tom)
	BERRYHEART—black-and-white she-cat (mother to Hollowkit, a black tom; Sunkit, a brown-and-white tabby she-kit; and Spirekit, a black-and-white tom)
	YARROWLEAF—ginger she-cat with yellow eyes (mother to Hopkit, a calico she-kit; and Flaxkit, a brown tabby tom)
ELDERS	**OAKFUR**—small brown tom
	RATSCAR—scarred, skinny dark brown tom

SKYCLAN

LEADER   **LEAFSTAR**—brown-and-cream tabby she-cat with amber eyes

DEPUTY   **HAWKWING**—dark gray tom with yellow eyes

MEDICINE CATS **FRECKLEWISH**—mottled light brown tabby she-cat with spotted legs

FIDGETFLAKE—black-and-white tom

MEDIATOR   **TREE**—yellow tom with amber eyes

WARRIORS   **SPARROWPELT**—dark brown tabby tom
APPRENTICE, NECTARPAW (brown she-cat)

MACGYVER—black-and-white tom

DEWSPRING—sturdy gray tom

PLUMWILLOW—dark gray she-cat
APPRENTICE, SUNNYPAW (ginger she-cat)

SAGENOSE—pale gray tom
APPRENTICE, GRAVELPAW (tan tom)

HARRYBROOK—gray tom
APPRENTICE, FRINGEPAW (white she-cat with brown splotches)

BLOSSOMHEART—ginger-and-white she-cat
APPRENTICE, PIGEONPAW (gray-and-white she-cat)

SANDYNOSE—stocky light brown tom with ginger legs
APPRENTICE, QUAILPAW (white tom with crow-black ears)

RABBITLEAP—brown tom
APPRENTICE, PALEPAW (black-and-white she-cat)

BELLALEAF—pale orange she-cat with green eyes

REEDCLAW—small pale tabby she-cat

VIOLETSHINE—black-and-white she-cat with yellow eyes

MINTFUR—gray tabby she-cat with blue eyes

NETTLESPLASH—pale brown tom

TINYCLOUD—small white she-cat

ELDERS **FALLOWFERN**—pale brown she-cat who has lost her hearing

WINDCLAN

LEADER **HARESTAR**—brown-and-white tom

DEPUTY **CROWFEATHER**—dark gray tom

MEDICINE CAT **KESTRELFLIGHT**—mottled gray tom with white splotches like kestrel feathers

WARRIORS **NIGHTCLOUD**—black she-cat

BRINDLEWING—mottled brown she-cat

GORSETAIL—very pale gray-and-white she-cat with blue eyes

LEAFTAIL—dark tabby tom with amber eyes

EMBERFOOT—gray tom with two dark paws

SMOKEHAZE—gray she-cat

BREEZEPELT—black tom with amber eyes

CROUCHFOOT—ginger tom

LARKWING—pale brown tabby she-cat

SEDGEWHISKER—light brown tabby she-cat

SLIGHTFOOT—black tom with white flash on his chest

OATCLAW—pale brown tabby tom

FEATHERPELT—gray tabby she-cat

HOOTWHISKER—dark gray tom

HEATHERTAIL—light brown tabby she-cat with blue eyes

FERNSTRIPE—gray tabby she-cat

ELDERS   **WHISKERNOSE**—light brown tom

WHITETAIL—small white she-cat

RIVERCLAN

LEADER   **MISTYSTAR**—gray she-cat with blue eyes

DEPUTY   **REEDWHISKER**—black tom

MEDICINE CATS   **MOTHWING**—dappled golden she-cat

WILLOWSHINE—gray tabby she-cat

WARRIORS   **MINTFUR**—light gray tabby tom
APPRENTICE, SOFTPAW (gray she-cat)

DUSKFUR—brown tabby she-cat
APPRENTICE, DAPPLEPAW (gray-and-white tom)

MINNOWTAIL—dark gray-and-white she-cat
APPRENTICE, BREEZEPAW (brown-and-white she-cat)

MALLOWNOSE—light brown tabby tom

BEETLEWHISKER—brown-and-white tabby tom
APPRENTICE, HAREPAW (white tom)

CURLFEATHER—pale brown she-cat

PODLIGHT—gray-and-white tom

HERONWING—dark gray-and-black tom

SHIMMERPELT—silver she-cat
APPRENTICE, NIGHTPAW (dark gray she-cat with blue eyes)

LIZARDTAIL—light brown tom

HAVENPELT—black-and-white she-cat

SNEEZECLOUD—gray-and-white tom

BRACKENPELT—tortoiseshell she-cat
APPRENTICE, GORSEPAW (white tom with gray ears)

JAYCLAW—gray tom

OWLNOSE—brown tabby tom

ICEWING—white she-cat with blue eyes

ELDERS   **MOSSPELT**—tortoiseshell-and-white she-cat

A VISION OF SHADOWS

WARRIORS

THE RAGING STORM

GREENLEAF
TWOLEGPLAC
TWOLEG NEST
TWOLEG PATH
TWOLEG PATH
CLEARI
SHADOWCLAN
CAMP
SKYCLA
CAMP
SMALL
THUNDERPATH
HALFBRIDGE
GREENLEAF
TWOLEGPLACE
HALFBRIDGE
CAT VIE
ISLAND
STREAM
RIVERCLAN
CAMP
HORSEPLACE

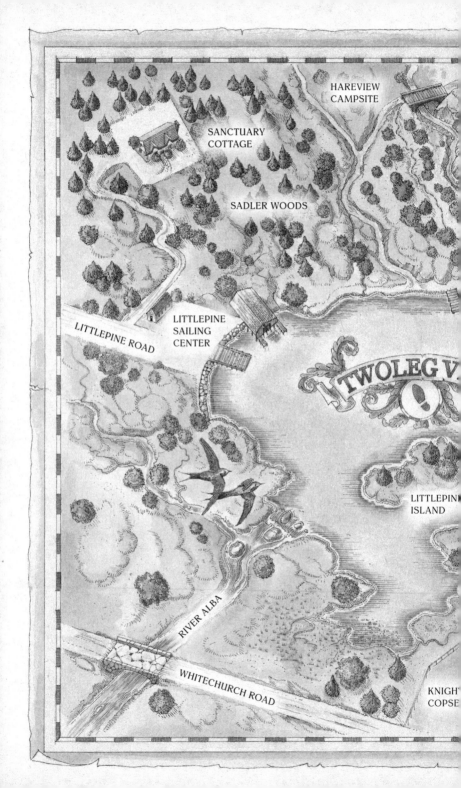

PROLOGUE

As darkness shrouded the valley, the lake glittered with broken moonlight. Firestar paced the island, watching from the shore. He could smell newleaf on the wind and, with it, the promise of seasons the Clans might never see.

Blackstar shivered a few tail-lengths away as the ghostly leaders of other Clans stood around him, stars shimmering in their pelts. "Why bring us here?"

Tallstar fluffed out his thick black-and-white fur. "What needs to be said here that couldn't be said in StarClan? It's warm there."

Firestar didn't answer. Longing pulled at his belly as he saw the oak forest, covering the shore like a pelt.

Bluestar touched her tail-tip to his flank. "Tell us why we're here," she meowed gently.

"It's pointless rushing him." Crookedstar sat at the water's edge and tucked his paws beneath his tail. "Firestar likes to think before he speaks."

"He should have done his thinking before he brought us here," Tallstar grumbled.

Blackstar flicked his tail impatiently. "We don't need to

stand here in the dark to know what's waiting for the Clans."

Firestar turned on him. "We know what is coming. But I don't think we've understood how ill-prepared the Clans are to face it. They sleep while we worry." As he spoke, a shadow moved among the pines near the shoreline. Firestar jerked his muzzle toward it. "Rowanclaw? What are you doing here?"

The ShadowClan cat's eyes flashed in the darkness as he padded toward the others. Stars glittered in his fur. "If you came here to discuss the future of the Clans, I have a right to be part of it."

"You're not a leader anymore." Reproach hardened Blackstar's mew.

Rowanclaw growled. "I gave up my nine lives so that my Clan could survive."

"You gave up your Clan so that *you* could survive," Blackstar hissed.

"That's not true." Rowanclaw flattened his ears. "*I* died! But my Clan is a Clan once more. My son has returned. Tigerstar will lead them to greatness."

"At what cost?" Bluestar shifted her paws. "If there's one thing I know about ShadowClan cats, it's that they always have their eyes on another Clan's land."

Rowanclaw's eyes narrowed. "ShadowClan must never face extinction again. It needs its territory back."

"But SkyClan cannot lose its land." Firestar's emerald eyes reflected starlight. His gaze seemed to see beyond the starry pelts of the other cats, and drifted toward the distant trees that marked SkyClan's territory. "They belong beside the lake."

"Of course they belong beside the lake," Tallstar grunted.

Bluestar eyed Rowanclaw. "Will your son let them stay?"

"Tigerstar must do whatever it takes to make ShadowClan strong," Rowanclaw shot back.

Firestar flicked his tail. "Rowanclaw is right about one thing: ShadowClan must grow strong. We can't risk losing them again. *Every* Clan must grow strong, but not by stealing another's territory. They must learn to live together. If the five Clans cannot live as one, the coming darkness will destroy them all."

"We've survived darkness before," Crookedstar argued.

"Not like this," Firestar insisted. "These young cats don't understand the danger. They've fought invaders, they've survived hardship, but they don't yet realize how fear can weave its way like a shadow between the Clans and how greed can drive them apart." The stars in Firestar's pelt shimmered as his fur prickled anxiously.

Blackstar snorted. "Do you think the Clans learned nothing from Darktail?"

"I don't think they learned enough." Firestar met his gaze. "Look how Darktail split them. RiverClan withdrew. ShadowClan collapsed. At a time when they needed to work together, they drew apart."

"But RiverClan has rejoined the Clans now," Crookedstar pointed out.

"And ShadowClan has a new leader," Rowanclaw argued.

"A strong leader, who will guide his warriors well."

"A *young* leader," Firestar cautioned, "who wants above all to prove his strength and the strength of his Clan. This is no time for battles. SkyClan is still finding its paws here. Their return has tested everyone. And the test isn't over. They must be fully accepted. If the Clans can't learn to live peacefully together, how will they face what is to come?" His eyes darkened. Bluestar looked away. The others glanced nervously at one another, as though sharing knowledge too dreadful to speak. Firestar went on. "Together, the Clans are like a paw with five claws reaching deep into the earth. If each claw is strong, the paw will hold fast. But if just one claw releases its grip, all will be swept away by the coming storm."

"It won't only be the lake Clans that are lost." Bluestar closed her eyes as the newleaf wind rippled her fur. "With no one to remember us, StarClan will disappear too."

"So we must warn them." Tallstar whisked his tail agitatedly from side to side.

"We can't warn them more than we have." Bluestar sighed. "How many times have we told them that they must face the future together?"

Firestar narrowed his eyes. "We can only point out the path. We can't make them follow it."

Bluestar looked across the lake. "Let's hope they find the way. If they don't, there will be nothing of us left, not even the warrior code."

CHAPTER 1

"Why do we have to clear all this mess?" Flypaw sat back on her haunches. Her tabby pelt twitched as she stared at the twigs littering the clearing. "We've been working at it for days."

Twigbranch let go of the stick she'd been dragging and blinked impatiently at her apprentice. "We have to clear the training ground if you want to practice battle moves here."

"Why can't Spotpaw and Stempaw help?" Flypaw complained. "They'll be training here too. And Plumpaw's stronger than me. She'd be better at dragging sticks."

"Plumpaw's hunting with Eaglepaw and Shellpaw, and their mentors, today," Twigbranch said, fighting back irritation. *Did I complain this much when I was an apprentice?*

"Why can't *we* hunt?" Flypaw grumbled.

"You don't know enough hunting moves."

Flypaw flicked her tail. "I'd know some if you let me train instead of making me clear sticks."

If you spent less time arguing and more time working, we'd be finished by now. Twigbranch swallowed back the words. "Bramblestar wants the training ground cleared. The storm left a mess and he asked us to do it." She glanced at Snappaw, who was helping

5

Finleap haul a branch to the edge of the clearing. "Your lit-termate isn't complaining."

Snappaw dropped the stick. "Finleap told me that moving sticks would make me strong." He puffed out his chest. "I want to be the strongest apprentice in ThunderClan."

Flypaw scowled. "Don't get *too* strong or Bramblestar will make you clear every branch from the forest."

Finleap blinked at her sympathetically. "You've worked hard all morning." He caught Twigbranch's eye. "Why don't we teach them a few battle moves?"

Snappaw pricked his ears. "Really?"

"Please!" Flypaw bounced past the sticks and crouched excitedly. Sticking her hindquarters in the air, she bared her teeth and lashed her tail. "Look! I'm ready to attack."

With a purr, Snappaw rushed to join her.

Exasperated, Twigbranch closed her eyes. At this rate, they'd never clear the training ground. What would Bramble-star think if she couldn't even make her apprentice do the simplest of tasks? Would he regret making her a mentor so soon?

Fur brushed her cheek. Finleap was weaving around her. "We can finish clearing the rest of the sticks later," he meowed. "There's no harm in taking some time out to go over some battle skills." He looked so eager that she didn't want to disappoint him. But she hadn't planned to teach battle skills today. She hadn't practiced.

"I don't know." She frowned.

"What are you worried about?" Finleap blinked at her.

"We're mentors! We're not breaking any rules by training our apprentices."

Twigbranch lowered her voice. "What if I do it wrong?"

Finleap's eyes widened. "How could you do anything wrong? You were an apprentice for the longest time. You must know everything there is to know about training." Admiration shone clearly in his wide yellow eyes.

Twigbranch purred softly, feeling comforted. It was hard not to love Finleap. He was clumsy and tactless at times, but his heart was always in the right place.

Everyone expected they would be mates soon, especially Finleap. He hardly left her side, he purred at all her jokes, and he brought her prey from the fresh-kill pile every evening. She was lucky to have him.

And yet she wasn't sure she was ready to become mates. She had not been a warrior for very long, and she had an apprentice who needed training. *Lots of training!*

More than anything, she wanted to prove she was worthy of ThunderClan. She had changed her mind so many times as an apprentice, leaving for SkyClan and returning again. She wanted ThunderClan to know she was loyal. And she was determined to earn the Clan's respect. She didn't have *time* to worry about a mate yet.

"Come on!" Finleap padded toward Snappaw and Flypaw. Snappaw had flattened his belly to the earth and was enthusiastically hissing at Flypaw. Flypaw lashed her tail and pretended to hiss back. Finleap stepped between them and beckoned them to their paws with a flick of his tail. "You won't win any battles by making faces," he purred.

"We weren't making faces," Snappaw mewed indignantly. "We were being fierce."

"I've seen fiercer hedgehogs." Twigbranch stepped over the scattered sticks and joined them.

Flypaw blinked at her eagerly. "What are you going to teach us?"

"Follow me." Twigbranch led her apprentice away from Finleap and Snappaw. She didn't want anyone watching her first attempt at battle training. Stopping at the edge of the clearing, she brushed away twigs with her paws. "Let's see how you react to an ambush."

Flypaw's ears twitched nervously. "An ambush?"

"Walk along the edge of the clearing. I'm going to attack you from the side. Keep your balance. Don't let me knock you off your paws." It seemed to Twigbranch like an easy lesson. Why did Flypaw look so worried?

"Will you tell me when you're about to attack?" the striped tabby asked.

Twigbranch blinked. "The whole point of an ambush is surprise."

"But I'm still learning."

"This is the best way to learn." Twigbranch shifted her paws and hoped she was right. Before Flypaw could ask any more questions, she pushed through the bracken surrounding the small clearing and ducked behind the stems. She waited for Flypaw to start walking. But Flypaw was watching Finleap and Snappaw train. They tumbled over the sandy earth.

Snappaw struggled free of his mentor and leaped clumsily to his paws. "Let me try again!"

"Flypaw!" Irritably, Twigbranch twitched her tail.

Flypaw snapped her gaze guiltily toward the bracken and began pacing along the edge of the clearing. Keeping low, Twigbranch shadowed her. She was pleased to see Flypaw's ears pricked and her tail centered. The apprentice was clearly alert. Tensing, Twigbranch prepared to pounce. As she bunched her muscles, a bird gave a warning cry overhead. Flypaw looked up at it just as Twigbranch leaped. Twigbranch slammed into her. With a startled yelp, Flypaw lost her balance and rolled onto the ground.

Twigbranch leaped to her paws. "That was easier than tumbling a sparrow!" She glared down at Flypaw, not giving her a chance to answer. "You knew I was going to ambush you! Your legs should have been braced for the attack!"

"The bird distracted me!" Indignantly, Flypaw scrambled to her paws.

"You live in a *forest*! If you get distracted every time you hear a bird, you're never going to learn how to fight, or hunt!" Twigbranch shook out her pelt crossly. Flypaw was so unfocused! How would she teach her anything? While Snappaw, Spotpaw, and the others were earning their warrior names, she'd still be trying to teach Flypaw how to stalk butterflies! *I'll look like the worst mentor ever.*

"Let's try it again," Flypaw mewed. "I'll be ready next time."

"Try saying that to a ShadowClan patrol when they steal your prey." Twigbranch pushed her way through the bracken once more and waited for Flypaw to start pacing. "Keep low, and push your weight through your paws as you walk," she called through the stems.

Flypaw dropped her belly and padded awkwardly around the clearing. Twigbranch sighed. *She looks like a duck.* Shadowing her, she followed her apprentice for a few tail-lengths, then leaped. Exploding from the bracken, she slammed into Flypaw's flank. Flypaw shrieked with surprise, threw her forepaws into the air, and twisted before losing her balance and thumping onto the earth.

Twigbranch stared at her. "That was the worst defensive move I've ever seen."

Flypaw found her paws and shook the dust from her fur. Her eyes were round. "I didn't expect you to hit me so hard."

"I was ambushing you!" Twigbranch snapped. "This isn't the nursery. You're not play-fighting now."

Flypaw glared at her. "You *want* me to fail," she accused. "That's why you're making it so hard. How am I meant to know what to do if you just keep knocking me off my paws?"

Twigbranch pressed back her frustration and tried to remember what it had been like when she'd first started training. It seemed such a long time ago. "Okay." Forcing her mew to be gentle, she looked at Flypaw. "Place your paws like this." Reaching out, she adjusted each of Flypaw's legs until the young tabby was standing square and firm. "Now sink down into your pads, as though you're as heavy as a badger." She watched as Flypaw flexed, finding strength in her stance. "This time, I won't come out of the bracken. You'll see me leap. Just try to keep your balance."

Flypaw nodded, her eyes dark with concentration.

At least she's trying. Twigbranch took a few steps back, then leaped at Flypaw's flank. It was a soft attack, but firm, and she pushed hard against Flypaw, relieved to feel resistance as she threw her weight against the young she-cat. Flypaw staggered, but kept low and didn't fall.

Twigbranch dropped lightly back onto all fours. "Not bad," she conceded. "Considering you knew the attack was coming. I'm not sure there's enough strength in your legs to withstand a surprise attack, but we can work on that."

"I thought she did well." Finleap's mew took Twigbranch by surprise. The brown tom padded toward them, Snappaw bouncing at his side. "She has a firm stance. And she's smaller than you. But she still managed to stay on her paws."

Twigbranch frowned at him. "I'm not sure she deserves *that* much praise," she cautioned. "She's got a lot to learn."

"We've both got loads to learn." Snappaw wove happily around his littermate. "It's going to be fun! Finleap has already taught me how to dive under a cat's belly. You should teach Flypaw how to do that. Finleap says it's a useful technique for smaller cats. He says I'm a natural."

"I'm not sure *I'm* a natural." Flypaw's ears twitched crossly.

"Of course you are!" Finleap reassured her. "With Lionblaze and Cinderheart as parents, how could you be anything else?"

Flypaw's eyes brightened, and Twigbranch felt a twinge of irritation. If Finleap spoiled Flypaw with praise, would she even try to improve her skills? "There's no such thing as a natural warrior," she meowed curtly. "Skill comes with hard work and training."

"*You* must be very skilled. You trained for *moons*," Flypaw muttered.

The apprentice's words stung. Twigbranch flattened her ears. She had only trained for so long because she had gone from one Clan to another. It wasn't that she hadn't been *ready*. "The first thing a warrior must learn is *respect*!"

Flypaw stared at the ground.

Finleap whisked his tail. "Why don't you two clear the last few sticks?" He nodded to Flypaw and Snappaw. "Twigbranch and I are going to check the border. Meet us there when you're done. We can show you how to lay markers. Is that okay with you, Twigbranch?" He didn't give her a chance to agree, but nudged her out of the clearing and along the rabbit track that led to the ShadowClan border.

"Did you hear what she said to me?" Twigbranch was indignant. "That's what you get when you praise them too much. Cheeky fox! I should have clawed her ears."

"Do you want her to be scared of you?" Finleap didn't look at Twigbranch as he padded at her side.

"She might listen to me more, if she were."

"You don't believe that, do you?"

"She has the mind of a butterfly! Always distracted. Always wishing she were doing something else."

"You've only been training her for three days," Finleap reasoned. "She probably has strengths you haven't seen yet."

"I'll never see them if you keep telling her she's a natural!" Twigbranch huffed. "She won't bother to learn."

"I just wanted to encourage her."

"Encourage your *own* apprentice," Twigbranch snapped. "Leave mine alone."

Finleap stopped and gazed solemnly at Twigbranch. "I'm just worried you're being too sharp with her. You don't want to discourage Flypaw before she's learned anything. Don't you remember how unhappy you were when Sparkpelt was hard on you?"

"That was different." Twigbranch's pelt pricked uncomfortably. Sparkpelt had been judgmental and unforgiving as a mentor when Twigbranch had rejoined ThunderClan. It had made her miserable. "Sparkpelt was just testing my loyalty."

"Did your loyalty need testing?"

"No!" Twigbranch turned away. Mentoring was challenging enough without Finleap criticizing her. "I'm just doing what I think is right!"

"I know." Finleap spoke softly. "It's scary having so much responsibility. And these are our first apprentices. But it's okay for us to make mistakes and it's okay for them to make mistakes. We're learning together."

"But I'm supposed to know what to do." A lump sat in Twigbranch's throat like a stone.

"Why?" Finleap wove around her and stopped as he caught her eye. "You're a great warrior, Twigbranch. And you're kind. You don't have to stop being kind just because you're a mentor. Trust your instincts. Push Flypaw when she needs pushing, but encourage her too. You must know how good a little encouragement can feel when you're facing something new and difficult."

There was warmth in his gaze that touched Twigbranch's heart. He really cared whether she'd be a good mentor. He wanted her to succeed. She purred and touched her nose to his.

"Besides," he went on, "mentoring will teach us patience. Imagine what good parents we'll be when we have kits."

When we have kits! Twigbranch pulled away. Finleap's gaze was misty. Was he really thinking about having kits already? They weren't even mates yet. Twigbranch wasn't ready to be tied to the nursery. She was barely ready to think about having a mate.

She changed the subject. "Let's check the border." She didn't want to hurt Finleap's feelings. "Flypaw! Snappaw! This way!" she called to the apprentices, scanning the bracken until they appeared, then turned and headed along the trail toward ShadowClan's territory.

Flypaw caught up to her as she reached the scent line. "Is this the border?"

"Can't you smell it?" Twigbranch opened her mouth and tasted the stench of ShadowClan mingling with Thunder-Clan scent.

Flypaw copied her, frowning with concentration. "Is that musky smell ShadowClan?"

"Yes." Twigbranch followed the scent line. The markers were fresh. She stopped beside the root of a pine and left her own marker. "Leave your scent on the next tree," she told Flypaw.

As Flypaw crouched beside the trunk, Finleap and Snappaw sniffed the trees a few tail-lengths away.

Finleap wrinkled his nose. "It smells like ShadowClan cats have been leaving scent marks twice a day."

Twigbranch shrugged. "They're probably just pleased to have their territory back."

"I guess." As Finleap padded to her side, Snappaw hurried ahead with Flypaw.

"Can we mark every tree?" Snappaw asked.

"It's a long border," Finleap told him. "Save some scent for farther along."

Flypaw was sniffing a fern clump. Curled fronds poked up from the moist earth. "There are so many scents out here." She turned to sniff between the roots of a tree where fresh grass was sprouting. Then she dug through a heap of rotting leaf mold and sniffed until she sneezed. "What does a mouse smell like?" she asked.

Snappaw padded past her. "You've smelled mouse before!" he meowed. "We've eaten them in camp."

"I've never smelled a *live* mouse." Flypaw blinked at Twigbranch. "Do they smell different from dead mice?"

"That's a good question!" Finleap commented before Twigbranch could answer.

She shot him a look. *Let me train my own apprentice.* "Live mice smell sharper than dead ones," she told Flypaw.

"Sharper?" Flypaw looked puzzled.

"They have a . . ." Twigbranch searched for the word. "A tang. You'll understand when you smell one."

But Flypaw had turned away. Twigbranch flexed her claws with irritation. Was it always going to be hard to keep Flypaw's attention?

The striped tabby's ears were pricked. "I can smell something else," Flypaw mewed.

"Is it tangy?" Snappaw lifted his muzzle. "Are there mice around?"

Twigbranch tasted the air. The scent markers were so strong here it was hard to detect another scent. But Flypaw was right. A musky smell tainted the air.

"It smells like a ShadowClan cat," Finleap meowed.

Twigbranch's pelt prickled. Was a patrol approaching the border?

Finleap stalked along the border. "This way," he breathed. "Follow me, but be quiet."

Snappaw and Flypaw hurried behind him, bumping into each other as they tried to stay close. Twigbranch followed. Another scent was mingled with the ShadowClan smell. *Blood.* She quickened her pace. Skirting past Finleap, Flypaw, and Snappaw, she took the lead. She strained to see between the tree trunks and, pricking her ears, heard a groan. Breaking into a run, she hurried toward the sound.

A large bundle of silver mesh was caught between two trees. Beneath the mass of thorny twine was a brown-and-white pelt. Puddleshine, the ShadowClan medicine cat, was struggling underneath it, groaning with pain. The scent of blood was strong.

"Puddleshine!" She hurried toward him, careful not to touch the vines, which massed like brambles between the trees. Borage sprouted around him. Was that what he'd been reaching for? She could see that his pelt was caught on the sharp thorns of the vines. Blood welled at every wound.

"Don't move. You'll make it worse." Panic fluttered in her chest as she met the ShadowClan medicine cat's agonized gaze. "We'll get you out," she promised. "Just lie still."

Finleap caught up, Flypaw and Snappaw at his heels.

"What is this?" Flypaw stared at the mesh, her eyes wide with horror.

"It's silverthorn. A Twoleg vine," Finleap explained. "They use it to make barriers around their land. The thorns keep animals trapped in their meadows. Only StarClan knows why they left a bundle of it here."

"I can reach him." Snappaw dropped onto his belly and squirmed beneath the silverthorn.

"Be careful!" Finleap warned.

Snappaw wriggled toward Puddleshine. "We'll get you out," he told the medicine cat.

"Every time I move, I get more tangled." Puddleshine sounded weary with pain.

Finleap looked at Flypaw. "Can you find your way back to camp?"

Flypaw nodded.

"Run home and fetch help. Tell Bramblestar that we'll need many paws to get Puddleshine out. And we'll need a medicine cat. He's bleeding badly."

Twigbranch called to Snappaw. "Go with her. We'll stay with Puddleshine." She didn't trust Flypaw to fetch help alone. What if she forgot the message or got distracted along the way?

Snappaw wriggled from underneath the silverthorn, and the two apprentices hared away between the trees, urging each other to run as fast as they could.

Twigbranch flattened herself to the ground and peered at Puddleshine through the silverthorn. "They'll be back with help soon."

Puddleshine looked at her, his eyes glittering with pain. "The thorns are sticking in everywhere," he meowed weakly.

The borage leaves around him were stained with his blood. Twigbranch could see where the thorns jabbed through his pelt, tearing his fur on both flanks and along his spine. One had snagged the back of his neck, forcing his chin to the earth. She fought back a shudder and blinked at him encouragingly. "Our warriors will find a way to get you out."

Finleap padded around the edge of the tangled mass, sniffing at the vines, as though looking for a gap that might let him reach Puddleshine. He poked his paw beneath a vine and lifted it gently. The whole bundle shivered, and Puddleshine grunted with pain. Finleap frowned. "It's going to be hard not to hurt him."

"With many paws working together, we can do it." Twig-branch didn't take her eyes from Puddleshine.

Overhead, birds chattered excitedly. The newleaf sun reached warm claws through the canopy and made the budding leaves glow so that the forest seemed swathed in an emerald haze. Twigbranch grew stiff as she held Puddleshine's gaze. Finleap circled the silverthorn. At last, the thrumming of paw steps sounded through the earth.

"They're coming!" Finleap lifted his head toward the swish of leaves as Bramblestar burst first from the bracken. Blossomfall, Thornclaw, and Bumblestripe slewed to a halt beside him. Behind them, Alderheart was carrying a thick wad of cobwebs between his jaws. He dropped them on the ground as Molewhisker and Larksong caught up.

Bramblestar padded around the tangled silverthorn, anger sparking in his gaze. "Don't Twolegs have enough territory where they can dump their rot without leaving it on our land?" Even as he spoke, his gaze was darting over the silverthorn. Twigbranch guessed he was looking for the best way to lift it from the ShadowClan medicine cat.

Alderheart ducked down and blinked at Puddleshine. "Do you know how many wounds you have?"

"I've lost count. It hurts too much." Puddleshine stared back desperately.

"I've brought you poppy seed." Alderheart reached for the wad of cobweb and picked poppy seeds from the sticky strands with his teeth. He flattened himself beside Twigbranch, spat the poppy seeds onto his paw and reached beneath the vines. With a groan, Puddleshine stretched forward and lapped them up.

Bramblestar beckoned to Thornclaw with his tail. "You lift here. Larksong, lift there." He nodded the black tom toward a vine farther along, then padded around the silverthorn. "Bumblestripe, take this vine. Blossomfall, take that one, and Molewhisker, can you reach through that gap and lift the vine on Puddleshine's back?"

Molewhisker nodded and poked his paw through the gap Bramblestar had gestured to.

When the patrol was in position, Bramblestar hooked his paw beneath the vine that twisted in front of Puddleshine's nose. He looked at Finleap. "When I give the word, we're going to lift the silverthorn. Can you pull Puddleshine out?"

Finleap nodded. Twigbranch saw determination in the young tom's gaze. Wasn't he scared? She felt queasy at the thought of tearing the medicine cat free. Bramblestar turned to her. "I want you to unhook any thorns catching in Puddleshine's fur as Finleap pulls him."

Twigbranch swallowed. "Okay." She felt sick.

"Alderheart, get cobwebs ready," Bramblestar ordered.

Alderheart scrambled to his pile and began tearing it into strips.

"When I say *now*, lift." Bramblestar glanced at his warriors. They nodded. "Now!"

Growling with effort, Bramblestar lifted the vine with his

paw. Around the silverthorn, the other warriors lifted too. The tangled mass shivered as they moved it. Puddleshine shrieked. "Grab him!" Bramblestar ordered.

Finleap shot into the gap the warriors had created. Twigbranch wriggled after him, her gaze darting over Puddleshine's pelt as Finleap grabbed the medicine cat's shoulders between his forepaws and tugged. Twigbranch saw a thorn lift Puddleshine's pelt. She reached out with her paw and quickly unhooked it. Another thorn snagged him and she knocked it away. Slowly, Finleap hauled Puddleshine out. Twigbranch freed barb after barb as they caught in the medicine cat's pelt. She could see the strain on the warriors' faces as they held the silverthorn clear.

"Is he free?" Bramblestar's mew was taut.

"Yes!" Finleap dragged Puddleshine away from the vines.

Twigbranch wriggled out, her heart racing.

"Let it go!" Bramblestar yowled. The tangle of vines dropped as the warriors released their grip and landed, trembling, on the ground. A vine broke free and unfurled beside Bumblestripe, slapping the earth a whisker away.

"Is everyone okay?" Bramblestar glanced around at the warriors.

Molewhisker nodded. Larksong licked his paw urgently, as though soothing a scratch.

Thornclaw's ears twitched. "No injuries here."

Bumblestripe looked at Puddleshine. "He's the only one hurt."

Alderheart was already pressing cobweb into a wound on the medicine cat's flank. He balled up another strip in his paws and pressed it into a cut on Puddleshine's neck. Twigbranch stiffened as she saw the blood oozing from the tom's fur. There were too many injuries to count.

Bramblestar gazed anxiously at Puddleshine. "Will he be okay?"

Alderheart swabbed another wound. "None of the cuts are deep, but there are a lot of them and there's always the chance of infection. We need to get him to a medicine den so I can treat them properly."

Bramblestar looked across the border. "There's no point taking him to ShadowClan. He's the only medicine cat they have. There will be no one to treat him there."

"We'd better take him to our camp." Alderheart pressed another wad of cobweb into a wound.

Puddleshine's eyes were glazed. He lay limply as Alderheart worked on him.

"Is he really okay?" Twigbranch asked anxiously. "He's hardly moving."

"That's the poppy seeds working," Alderheart told her. "I gave him plenty."

"Tell me when he's ready to be carried back to camp," Bramblestar meowed.

Alderheart nodded, not pausing his work.

"We should tell Tigerstar what's happened," Finleap meowed.

"Yes." Bramblestar nodded. "Take Twigbranch and go to the ShadowClan camp."

Finleap glanced at the border. "Should we wait for a ShadowClan patrol to escort us?"

"No." Bramblestar twitched his tail. "Cross the border. Tigerstar will understand why you're on ShadowClan land once he hears the news. Tell him we'll take care of Puddleshine until he is well enough to return. He is welcome to send a patrol to check on him."

Twigbranch glanced at Finleap. What if a ShadowClan patrol attacked them before they had time to explain why they were there?

He blinked at her. "Come on." Leaping away, he skirted the silverthorn and headed across the border.

Twigbranch followed him. Her heart quickened as she crossed the scent line. "Do you know the way to the Shadow-Clan camp?"

"No, but you do." Finleap slowed and let her take the lead.

She hurried past him and led the way up a rise. She knew this trail well. She had traveled to the ShadowClan camp many times—usually in secret—to visit her sister, Violetshine, when they'd been kits. She'd been scared then, but she felt more anxious now. Since Tigerstar had returned, no cat had heard much from ShadowClan. Who knew what sort of leader he'd become? She glanced nervously between the pines. "What if Tigerstar is angry that we've taken Puddleshine to our camp?" she asked Finleap in a hushed mew.

Finleap fell in beside her, matching her stride. "How can he be angry when we're trying to help?"

His confidence soothed her. He seemed so sure of himself. Even when he'd been pulling Puddleshine free, he'd known he could do it. He was sure they'd be mates too and that they'd have kits one day. And the thought didn't scare him. Anxiety wormed beneath Twigbranch's pelt. *Then why does it scare me?*

♣

CHAPTER 2

Violetshine padded into a glade, where newleaf sun dappled white patches of snowdrops. Mintfur walked beside her while, ahead of them, Sandynose sniffed the air, his whiskers twitching as a mild wind carried the scent of the lake through the forest.

"Look here, Fidgetflake!" Frecklewish stopped beside a patch of dark green leaves sprouting between the roots of an alder.

The younger medicine cat hurried toward her, his black-and-white pelt prickling eagerly. "Is that some kind of comfrey?"

"It's wood sorrel," Frecklewish told him, plucking out a few leaves with her claws. She held it out for him to sniff.

Fidgetflake wrinkled his nose, backing away. "I know what it smells like. Horrible and sour."

"It tastes even worse," Frecklewish murmured. "But it makes a good poultice for boils and abscesses. It draws out infection and dries the wound."

She stripped a leaf from a nearby bramble stem and began to roll the sorrel leaves into it. "We'll take this back for the herb store." She purred happily. Frecklewish had been eager to join the border patrol. The herb store had been depleted by the long, cold leaf-bare, and she wanted to collect fresh supplies. "The newest growth is the strongest," she'd told Fidgetflake as they'd followed Sandynose, Violetshine, and Mintfur out of camp.

Now Violetshine halted at the bottom of the glade, relishing the feel of sunshine on her fur. As she waited for Frecklewish and Fidgetflake to bundle up the wood sorrel, Sandynose padded around her, scanning the trees.

Mintfur lay down and rolled in the warm dry leaf litter, clearly enjoying the fresh scents of newleaf. "It's good to have our territory to ourselves again," she meowed, sitting up and shaking the dust from her gray fur.

"It's good to have our *camp* to ourselves," Sandynose grunted. "I don't know how Leafstar ever thought Shadow-Clan could fit in. They're too different."

"Not *so* different." Frecklewish looked up from her herbs. "They're still warriors, after all. They follow the warrior code. And they eat and sleep and hunt just like us."

"They hunt like foxes and snore like badgers," Sandynose grunted.

Mintfur licked her paw and drew it over her ear. "Well, they're gone now, and we don't have to worry about tripping over them anymore."

"It was good of Leafstar to return their land without a fight," Sandynose meowed. "After all, ShadowClan gave it to us. And then slept in our dens and ate our prey for a moon."

"Tigerstar thanked her for our kindness," Violetshine reminded him.

"They owed us more than thanks," Sandynose sniffed.

Frecklewish padded to Mintfur's side. "Everything's back to how it should be," she mewed. "Five Clans living beside the lake. It's best for everyone this way."

Sandynose narrowed his eyes. "I just hope Tigerstar agrees."

The warrior's suspicion made Violetshine uneasy. "Why wouldn't he?"

"Tigerstar only cares about what's best for Tigerstar." Sandynose looked up the slope, his ears pricked. "He abandoned his Clan and his kin when they needed him. Then he came back when it suited him. And his mate is no better. Dovewing broke the warrior code and had kits with a warrior from another Clan, then left her own Clan to be with him and took her kits with her." The light brown tom blinked at Violetshine. "A leader is supposed to set an example for their Clan. What kind of example has Tigerstar set?"

Frecklewish shook out her fur. "He made mistakes. But StarClan guided his paws back to ShadowClan and made him its leader. He must understand how important it is that there be five Clans beside the lake."

"He might just think it's important for *ShadowClan* to be beside the lake," Sandynose meowed darkly.

Mintfur got to her paws and headed up the slope toward the stretch of pines where a ditch stretched toward the Shadow-Clan border. "It's no use worrying. We've been through enough trouble over the past few moons without wishing for more."

Violetshine padded after her, comforted by her easy tone. They'd survived the storm. Surely there couldn't be more trouble waiting for the Clans?

Leaves rustled behind her as Frecklewish and Fidgetflake followed.

"I wasn't *wishing* for trouble," Sandynose grumbled as he joined them. "But ignoring the rain doesn't stop it from falling."

At the top of the rise, Mintfur stopped. She stiffened and lifted her muzzle.

Violetshine could see her tasting the air. Alarm pricked beneath her pelt. "What is it?"

Mintfur's eyes shone. "Can't you smell it? Mouse!"

Sandynose had already dropped into a hunting crouch and was creeping toward a ditch that cut the forest floor like a claw mark.

Violetshine pricked her ears. She heard leaves rustle at the bottom of the ditch. The tangy scent of mouse touched her nose. She licked her lips. She hadn't eaten yet, and even though she knew this catch would be taken back to camp for the fresh-kill pile, she was pleased to know that prey was returning after the leaf-bare chill. She hung back with Frecklewish and Fidgetflake, letting the others take the prey. Sandynose was already stalking along the top of the ditch. Mintfur had hopped over it lightly and was crouching farther along, her gaze fixed intently on the leaves at the bottom. As they rustled, Sandynose pounced. Landing in the ditch, he slapped his paws down. Mintfur dropped in front of him, blocking the mouse's escape. But she needn't have worried. Sandynose caught it cleanly and killed it with a quick bite.

"Thank you, StarClan, for this prey," Frecklewish whispered beside Violetshine.

Sandynose hopped out of the ditch, the fat mouse dangling from his jaws.

Fidgetflake dropped the herb bundle he'd been holding between his teeth and sniffed the mouse. "That's even bigger than the one that Macgyver brought back yesterday."

Mintfur scrambled up beside Sandynose, purring. "It's good to see the fresh-kill pile well-stocked again. There's enough food for everyone."

Sandynose dropped the mouse. "Even now that we've got an extra mouth to feed." He swapped glances with Mintfur.

The gray she-cat rolled her eyes. "You mean Tree."

"He was supposed to help out with patrols, but I notice that Leafstar never asks him to join and he never offers." Sandynose looked indignant.

"He doesn't mind sharing what's on the fresh-kill pile, though," Mintfur mewed meaningfully.

Violetshine bristled. "He can take what he wants from the fresh-kill pile. He's part of the Clan now."

"How can he be?" Mintfur asked. "He doesn't even know the warrior code."

"He didn't join as a *warrior*," Violetshine meowed defensively. "He joined as a mediator."

"I've never seen him mediate," Mintfur shot back.

"That's because there's been nothing to mediate yet." Violetshine glared at her.

Frecklewish padded along the top of the ditch, looking thoughtful. "It is strange having a cat in the Clan who doesn't act like a warrior. But his role is new and he's still finding his paws. I think Leafstar was right to ask him to join us. Tree has a way with other cats that puts them at ease."

"He'd put *me* at ease if he spent less time lying around camp and more time helping out," Sandynose muttered. "If he doesn't want to patrol, he could help repair the dens instead. There are still walls and roofs that need patching after the storm. And with so many apprentices, we could do with more space in the apprentices' den."

Anger flared through Violetshine. She lifted her chin. "If you've got a problem with Tree, why don't you talk to him instead of complaining about him?"

"Don't think I haven't tried," Sandynose answered. "But you know how he is. Always so easygoing and friendly. It's hard to criticize him. He always has an answer. He says he 'doesn't want to get in the way,' or he's 'learning by watching.' And he seems so genuine, it's hard to argue."

Violetshine puffed out her chest. "He *is* genuine. He's got a good heart, and just because he doesn't act like a warrior doesn't mean he isn't important to the Clan. You wait and see. Frecklewish is right. He does have a way with other cats. Sometimes words are more powerful than claws, and they cause far less bloodshed."

Mintfur's whiskers twitched with amusement. "It sounds like you're fond of him, Violetshine."

Violetshine felt hot beneath her pelt. "So what if I am?" She and Tree had a special bond. She'd found him, and he was closer to her than he was to any other cat in SkyClan. Her paws prickled with happiness at the thought.

"Sandynose." Fidgetflake's anxious mew made the cats turn. The apprentice medicine cat had crossed the ditch and was sniffing the ground beyond. "Come and smell this."

Sandynose leaped the ditch and sniffed the ground beside Fidgetflake.

"Do you smell ShadowClan?" Fidgetflake asked.

"Yes." Sandynose's fur lifted along his spine. He padded quickly forward and sniffed the ground again. He paced one way then the other, sniffing as he went. "ShadowClan cats have been here."

As Mintfur hurried to join him, Violetshine followed, her belly tightening. ShadowClan scent hung in the air. "They've crossed the border into our territory," she breathed.

Sandynose was already following the scent trail to the border. He stopped beside a bush and flattened his ears. "They crossed here."

"Do you recognize the scents?" Mintfur asked.

He shook his head. "They don't smell like any of the cats who stayed in our camp."

Violetshine pushed back the fear that was pressing in her throat. "ShadowClan does have some cats who grew up outside the territories," she murmured, remembering the gossip she'd heard about an adventure Tigerstar and Dovewing had once had, far away from the lake. "Those cats could have strayed over the scent line without realizing. They haven't lived here that long, so maybe they don't recognize the borders yet."

Mintfur snorted. "Even *those* cats must know what a scent marker means."

Sandynose's pelt bristled. "Let's head back to camp. Leaf-star should hear about this."

Sunshine filtered between the pine and alder branches crisscrossing above the SkyClan camp.

"You're sure the scents were on our side of the border?" Leafstar's amber eyes narrowed.

"I know where the border is even if ShadowClan doesn't," Sandynose snapped.

Leafstar shifted her hindquarters. The returning patrol had woken the SkyClan leader from a nap. Beside Sandynose, Violetshine felt her belly tighten. The warrior had worked himself into a rage on the journey back to camp, and Mint-fur agreed with him that ShadowClan had crossed SkyClan's border on purpose. Frecklewish and Fidgetflake had tried to reason with them. It might have been an accident. But Sandy-nose was convinced that a ShadowClan patrol had left its scent on SkyClan land deliberately.

Hawkwing, who was clearing weed from the small stream that cut through the camp, kept working but pricked his ears as Leafstar considered her response. Tree, lying stretched in a pool of sunlight, lifted his head sleepily and watched.

Macgyver, Nettlesplash, and Bellaleaf left their work patching holes in the elders' den and padded closer, while Blossomheart and Harrybrook looked up from the mouse they were sharing beside the fresh-kill pile. Pigeonpaw and Nectarpaw paused from practicing battle moves in the clearing to watch as well.

"I don't think we should jump to any conclusions," Leafstar said at last.

Plumwillow poked her head out of the warriors' den. "Conclusions about what?"

Pigeonpaw blinked at her. "ShadowClan cats invading our territory."

"They didn't invade," Nectarpaw mewed.

"Their scent is on our land," Sandynose snapped.

Plumwillow slid from the den, her pelt bristling. "What are ShadowClan cats doing on our land?"

Leafstar stood up. "That's what we're trying to decide."

"It can't have been anything good," Macgyver meowed. Nettlesplash and Bellaleaf muttered in agreement.

"It was probably an accident." Blossomheart left her mouse and padded closer.

Harrybrook got to his paws. "Perhaps it was a clumsy apprentice with a bad sense of direction."

"That's what I said." Violetshine was eager to avoid conflict. StarClan wanted all of them to live peacefully around the lake, didn't they? "Don't forget they have new warriors who aren't Clanborn."

"Exactly," Blossomheart agreed. "One of them could have strayed across the border without realizing."

"Nonsense!" Mintfur snorted. "The border was clearly marked. Any cat would have smelled it. Even one who's not Clanborn."

"Silence." Leafstar flicked her tail sharply. "We don't know why ShadowClan crossed the border. But I'm not willing to accuse them of aggression when we don't have the facts."

"You should be protecting SkyClan, not defending ShadowClan," Sandynose muttered.

Violetshine saw Leafstar's hackles lift. The SkyClan leader was clearly irritated by Sandynose's challenge. "I *will* protect SkyClan. We'll re-mark the border." She nodded to Hawkwing. "Organize three border patrols tomorrow instead of two."

"Okay." Hawkwing lifted a clump of dripping weed from the stream and dropped it onto the pile he'd collected. He met Leafstar's gaze. "And I'll make sure the border is marked again before sundown today."

"Good." Leafstar looked satisfied.

Sandynose's pelt twitched. "If ShadowClan doesn't respect our borders, re-marking them won't make a difference."

Leafstar frowned at him. "ShadowClan is rebuilding. Have you considered that Tigerstar might not be fully in control of his warriors yet? They may be crossing the border without his knowledge. I'm not going to risk undermining him by making an issue out of a single incident. We should leave ShadowClan alone until we know they are strong again."

Macgyver's gaze had darkened. "What if they're already strong? This could be the first sign that they're a threat. Are you going to ignore it?"

"He's got a point." Hawkwing shook the water from his paws and padded closer. He stopped in front of Leafstar. "We have no idea of Tigerstar's intentions. Who knows how he's changed since that time he left the Clans? Just because he once supported our claim to this territory doesn't mean he still supports it. He's leader now, and ShadowClan is stronger than it's been since we arrived at the lake. It might be sensible to find out what he is thinking before we let this incident pass."

Leafstar's gaze flicked around the watching Clan. Violetshine could see from her frown that she was thinking. Bellaleaf and Macgyver exchanged glances. Harrybrook whispered something in Blossomheart's ear. Hawkwing watched his leader, his expression unreadable.

"Tree." Leafstar's gaze reached the yellow tom. "You're here to mediate between the Clans. What do you think?"

Violetshine leaned forward as Tree got to his paws. He'd know what to do. He always seemed to instinctively sense what cats were thinking.

Tree padded toward the SkyClan leader, his gaze thoughtful. As he reached her, he cleared his throat. "I think you're right to be cautious," he mewed. "I have no doubt that Tigerstar is already a strong leader. That doesn't mean he's dangerous, but if these scents are the first sign of ShadowClan aggression, he might be hoping you'll react. It would give him an excuse to escalate this incident into a conflict."

Violetshine stared at Tree. *He's so smart.* Perhaps all the time he spent lying in the sun wasn't wasted. Perhaps he was thinking instead of dozing.

Leafstar narrowed her eyes. "So you agree that we shouldn't react."

"I agree that you need more information before you do," Tree told her.

"Will you go to ShadowClan and speak with Tigerstar?" Leafstar asked.

Tree shook his head. "That would be too direct. It's best for the moment if Tigerstar doesn't know you're worried. After all, the scent marks may be unintended. There's no point antagonizing Tigerstar with our suspicions if they are."

Sandynose grunted impatiently. "Then what exactly do you suggest?"

"I could wander over to ShadowClan territory," Tree proposed. "Hang around the border until I bump into a ShadowClan warrior and then we could just chat. It's not hard to find out information through a bit of harmless small talk."

Leafstar's eyes brightened. "Good idea." She glanced at Sandynose.

The tom was nodding. "It sounds like it might work."

Mintfur's ears twitched crossly. "I think we should send a patrol there. We should start with a show of strength, so Tigerstar knows what he's up against."

"We'll show strength when we have to," Leafstar told her. "For now, Tree will find out what he can." Her gaze swung toward Violetshine. Violetshine's heart lurched. "You can go with him," Leafstar told her. "You were raised in Shadow-Clan. You'll be able to tell what they're thinking."

Will I? Violetshine wasn't sure, but she wasn't going to argue. She was excited to be part of Tree's mission to investigate ShadowClan. She dipped her head to Leafstar. "I'll do my best."

Leafstar stretched, signaling an end to the matter. Padding across the camp, she stopped at the stream and glanced along the bank. "Good work on the weed clearing, Hawkwing."

Violetshine blinked at Tree. The yellow tom was already heading toward her. His eyes were bright as he neared. "Are you ready?"

"Yes." Violetshine purred.

"Good." He brushed against her as they headed out of camp, and she wondered if it was intentional. His fur felt soft against her flank, and as she ducked through the entrance tunnel, her paws pricked with pleasure.

Outside, Tree paused and glanced around the forest. "Where were the ShadowClan scent marks?"

Violetshine nodded in the direction of the ditch. Tree turned and headed in the opposite direction. She hurried after him. "Why are we going this way?"

"If we want to avoid arousing suspicion, it's best we don't start a conversation with a ShadowClan cat while standing next to their scent trail."

Violetshine looked at him. "Of course! We don't want them to realize we've noticed their scent on our land."

He nudged his shoulder teasingly against hers as they walked. "You're smarter than you look."

"Hey!" She nudged him back. "I look as smart as you."

"Almost." He glanced at her out of the corner of his eye, then broke into a run.

She charged after Tree, happy to be out in the forest alone with him. The warm breeze streamed through her fur as she followed him, zigzagging between trees and leaping branches that had fallen during the storm. He was heading toward the border that led to the lake. As they neared it, she waited for him to slow down. But he kept running, clearly enjoying the fresh air as much as she did.

"Watch out!" She could smell the scent markers ahead.

He glanced back without slowing. "What for?"

"The border!" Alarm sparked beneath her pelt. If they crossed into ShadowClan territory, they could make the situation worse. "Stop!"

Tree pulled up a tail-length from the scent line. He tasted the air, his pelt pricking in surprise. "I didn't realize we were so close."

"Couldn't you smell it?"

"Not till now." Tree whisked his tail. "I'm still learning the different Clan scents. All Clan cats smell the same to me."

"But you knew the border was here, right?" She knew her Clan's borders with her eyes closed.

"I do now."

"I guess you haven't been on many patrols like I have." She glanced at him. "Maybe you should start going on them." If he joined in with Clan patrols, her Clanmates might accept him more easily.

He shrugged. "I guess. But it seems a lot of effort. It's like you're looking for trouble. I always think you should wait to see if trouble finds you, not go searching for it."

"It does no harm to be prepared." Would Tree ever settle into Clan life? With a jolt, Violetshine wondered if he even intended to. Perhaps he was just staying with SkyClan temporarily before he moved on to somewhere new. The thought sent hedgehog prickles through her heart. Should she ask him what his intentions were? She glanced at her paws, feeling hot. He might make fun of her for caring.

"Look." His hushed mew made her lift her head. She followed his gaze. Cloverfoot, a ShadowClan warrior, was padding between the brambles on the other side of the border. The gray tabby's gaze flitted intently from one bush to another. Her ears were pricked expectantly. She was clearly looking for prey.

Tree turned his gaze to Violetshine. "I told Hawkwing that the best prey is always closer to the lake. But he said that in newleaf prey is good everywhere." He spoke loudly; Violetshine guessed that he was trying to attract Cloverfoot's attention.

"It's better in greenleaf." She matched his tone, glancing at Cloverfoot. The ShadowClan warrior had heard them and was heading toward the border.

"Why are you yowling so loudly?" she growled across the scent line. "I'm trying to hunt. You'll scare the prey away."

Tree turned to her, his eyes wide with innocence. "I'm sorry." He sounded contrite. "If I'd seen you I'd have kept my voice down."

"Yeah, sorry," Violetshine mumbled.

Tree gazed admiringly at the ShadowClan warrior as though he were unaware of her bristling fur. "I doubt a warrior as fit as you will have any trouble catching prey. We'll leave you in peace. Sorry for the disturbance." He turned to walk away, then paused. "Prey must be running well in ShadowClan, too," he mewed breezily. "Our fresh-kill pile is so well-stocked that our apprentices grow faster than nettles."

Cloverfoot swished her tail. "We've got plenty of prey."

"Good." Tree blinked at her. "Is ShadowClan doing okay? It must be good to be back in your real home."

"It is." Cloverfoot's fur smoothed. "We've rebuilt the dens and reinforced the barrier wall. The camp is better than ever."

Tree was gazing eagerly at Cloverfoot, his ears pricked as though he relished her every word. Violetshine felt a twinge of jealousy. "Tigerstar seems like a good leader," Tree purred.

Cloverfoot puffed out her chest. "He's a *great* leader."

"Tougher than his father, eh?"

"Much tougher than Rowanclaw. All the cats respect him. He makes sure everyone's belly is full, that the camp is kept in order, and that the apprentices are getting proper training. He says ShadowClan will be great again. We were strong in the past and we'll be strong in the future."

"That must be good to hear after all ShadowClan has been through." Tree rounded his eyes sympathetically.

"It feels right," Cloverfoot purred.

"Hawkwing says you're keeping the borders well-marked," Tree mewed. "He says strong borders make strong neighbors."

He caught Violetshine's eye as though prompting her.

She hesitated. What did he want her to say? "It's hard to stray across a well-marked border," she mewed uncertainly. Had she guessed right?

"I guess." Cloverfoot tipped her head, as though wondering what Violetshine was getting at.

Tree changed the subject quickly. "How are the cats from the Twolegplace settling in? It must be a big change for them."

"They love warrior life. Especially Blazepaw. It's like he was born to be a warrior." Cloverfoot's eyes shone as she spoke of him.

"They must find it hard getting used to all the new scents," Violetshine chimed in. "Border scents, for example. They must be confused by all the scent markers."

Suspicion flashed in Cloverfoot's eye. "They seem to do okay."

Tree scratched his ear nonchalantly. "I was just saying to Violetshine how hard I still find it to spot borders. I nearly ran across this one without noticing it. Fortunately, Violetshine called out to me in time. I know Clan cats take border crossing very seriously." He met Cloverfoot's gaze, suddenly earnest. "No ShadowClan cat would want to cross into another Clan's territory if they didn't have to, would they?"

"No." Cloverfoot stared at him, her eyes glittering with sudden distrust. She backed away. "I'd better get back to hunting. I promised Blazepaw I'd bring him a shrew if I could find one." She turned away and disappeared between the brambles.

Violetshine looked at Tree anxiously. "Did we give too

much away?" ShadowClan wasn't supposed to realize they knew about the border crossing. Had they been too heavy-pawed?

Tree lifted his tail. "I think we gave away just the right amount." He headed back toward camp. "We know that Tigerstar is a strong leader, and that he has plans for Shadow-Clan. We had to let him know that we found ShadowClan scent on our land, without directly accusing him of anything. He should know that SkyClan won't be caught off guard."

Violetshine hurried after him. "Do you think ShadowClan is a threat?"

Tree hesitated. His silence made her paws prick with fore-boding. Then he glanced over his shoulder at her. "I don't know. But SkyClan must face the future with open eyes."

CHAPTER 3

Alderheart sat down heavily beside Puddleshine's nest. Two sunrises had passed since Bramblestar's patrol had carried the ShadowClan cat to ThunderClan's medicine den, and he had not improved. He frowned. Puddleshine was sick. Many of his wounds were still infected despite the careful cleaning and the marigold poultices Alderheart had applied day and night. It made no sense.

"I can't seem to clear the infection," he murmured.

Puddleshine lifted his head stiffly and blinked at him, his eyes clouded with pain. "You've treated my wounds the same way I would have. I don't know why they're not healing, either."

"How is the pain today?"

"The poppy seeds you gave me have eased it a little."

Alderheart touched his nose to Puddleshine's ear. Heat pulsed from it. "You're running a fever too."

"It must be the infection," Puddleshine mewed.

"Perhaps you have some other illness that is making you vulnerable to the infection. You smell weird."

"I felt fine before I got tangled in the silverthorn."

Puddleshine's eyes darkened. "How could I have been so foolish? I should have stayed clear."

"There's no point growling about it." Alderheart was more concerned with dealing with Puddleshine's wounds than with worrying how he got them. "Do you have any other symptoms? A sore throat? A bellyache?"

"No." Puddleshine shifted wearily in his nest. "Only my wounds hurt."

Alderheart glanced toward the den entrance. He felt out of his depth. He wasn't used to not knowing the cause of a cat's sickness. It was no comfort that Leafpool and Jayfeather were baffled too. "Do what you can," Jayfeather had told him. "You'll figure something out." The blind medicine cat was checking on Ivypool's kits in the nursery now. Leafpool had been out since dawn collecting herbs. Alderheart turned back to Puddleshine. "Can you think of another herb we could try?"

"Frecklewish mentioned wood sorrel at the last Moonpool meeting," Puddleshine told him. "It's just starting to sprout now."

"I don't know if it grows in ThunderClan territory."

"There's some around the ShadowClan border." Puddleshine winced. "It's dark green and has a sour smell."

"I'll find some. Let's hope it works."

As he spoke, voices sounded in the clearing. He pricked his ears. They sounded like ShadowClan. His heart lurched. Tigerstar had told Twigbranch that he'd be sending a patrol to fetch Puddleshine in a few days. Was this it? Alderheart shifted his paws. How would he explain that Puddleshine was in no fit state to travel home? He noticed Puddleshine's gaze flick anxiously to the medicine-den entrance. "You rest," Alderheart mewed. "I'll go and see what's happening." He hurried out of the den.

Tawnypelt and Scorchfur stood in the clearing, flanked by Brackenfur and Fernsong.

"We found them waiting on the border," Fernsong was explaining to his Clanmates, who were watching the Shadow-Clan cats warily as Bramblestar scrambled down the rock tumble.

For the first time, Alderheart noticed Dovewing standing behind Tawnypelt. The former ThunderClan warrior's pale gray fur was bristling anxiously.

Alderheart narrowed his eyes. Why had she come? Dovewing had visited the camp when she'd first returned with Tigerstar. Every cat had been so relieved to see she was safe, they'd barely reproached her for her decision to abandon her Clan and take her kits to live with their father in Shadow-Clan. But that had been more than a moon ago. He wondered how ThunderClan felt now, seeing Dovewing as part of a ShadowClan patrol.

Squirrelflight padded forward to greet her, but a warning look from Scorchfur made her hesitate. Lionblaze frowned from beside the fresh-kill pile. Graystripe and Millie slipped from the elders' den and exchanged looks as they saw Dove-wing. Cherryfall and Bumblestripe glared at their former Clanmate, their hostility plain as Bramblestar reached the ShadowClan cats.

"You've come for Puddleshine?" the ThunderClan leader asked.

Tawnypelt met his gaze stiffly. "Tigerstar told the two youngsters you sent that we'd fetch him in two days. Is he ready?"

Scorchfur scanned the camp, clearly looking for the ShadowClan medicine cat. Dovewing's gaze had drifted to the nursery.

"Well?" Tawnypelt pressed when Bramblestar didn't answer. The ThunderClan leader was staring at Dovewing.

"I'm surprised you brought her here," he meowed. "Feelings are running high about her decision to leave." He glanced uneasily at Cherryfall and Bumblestripe. The pale gray tom's hackles were up.

"She's a member of ShadowClan now," Tawnypelt meowed simply. "She joins our patrols whether they're hunting or escorting Clan members home."

Bramblestar narrowed his eyes. "Surely she should be in the nursery taking care of her kits?"

Dovewing padded forward. "I asked to come," she mewed softly. "I was hoping to see Ivypool."

Bumblestripe lashed his tail. "You visited with Ivypool and her kits a moon ago. Before you went to ShadowClan. When you left your Clan, you left your kin. I thought you understood that."

"I did what I thought was best for every cat," Dovewing told him.

Alderheart's pelt prickled uneasily. Bumblestripe's feelings had clearly hardened since he'd last seen Dovewing. He looked toward the nursery.

Ivypool hung back in the shadows at the entrance, her gaze uncertain.

Bristlekit pushed past her mother, pale gray pelt fluffed with excitement. "Is that her?" she asked, bouncing into the clearing and staring at Dovewing.

Flipkit and Thriftkit crowded between Ivypool's forelegs, their heads pressing against her chest. Their eyes were wide with curiosity.

"Are we allowed to talk to her?" Thriftkit asked.

"Why wouldn't we be allowed?" Bristlekit padded closer to Dovewing and stared at her boldly. "Ivypool says you came to visit us before. But I don't remember you. We'd only just opened our eyes. You look like Ivypool except you don't have white splotches."

Dovewing looked past the kit toward Ivypool, her gaze shimmering with hope. Ivypool didn't move.

Daisy emerged from the nursery, pushing past the silver-and-white queen. "I don't know what all the fuss is about. Kin is kin no matter the Clan."

"Clan is more important than kin!" Cherryfall moved closer to Bumblestripe.

Lionblaze flicked his ears. "Loyalty is more important than anything," he growled. "Bumblestripe's right. When you leave your Clan, you leave your kin."

Alderheart thought he caught a flicker of movement from the elders' den. Graystripe was shifting uneasily, trying to look like he wasn't listening to the discussion. Long before Alder-heart was born, Graystripe had briefly left ThunderClan to be with kits he'd had with a RiverClan warrior. ThunderClan had eventually welcomed him back, though Alderheart had heard that not all of his Clanmates had trusted him right away.

Jayfeather stomped from the nursery and headed for the medicine den, his pelt twitching with irritation. "If warriors didn't keep falling in love with the wrong cats, a lot of trouble could be avoided." His blind blue gaze flashed toward Squir-relflight as though he could see her.

Squirrelflight bristled. "Don't blame me for what your mother did," she mewed sharply. "I only tried to help her."

"So, that worked out well, didn't it?" With a sniff, he pushed past Alderheart and disappeared into the medicine den.

Alderheart's chest ached with sympathy for Dovewing. She was gazing at Ivypool with such longing he wondered how Ivypool could hesitate. But the ThunderClan queen returned her sister's gaze blankly, her eyes round with indecision.

Flipkit padded into the clearing and stopped beside Bris-tlekit. He glanced shyly at Dovewing. "Ivypool says you have kits too. Do they look like us?"

"Shadowkit does, a little." Emotion thickened Dovewing's mew. "Lightkit and Pouncekit look more like their father."

Graystripe padded toward Dovewing. Sympathy filled his warm amber gaze. "They must be very handsome," he meowed softly.

"They are." Dovewing blinked at him gratefully, then looked back to Ivypool, her tail drooping. "Won't you come and greet me? I thought you'd understand. I made the best choice I could."

Ivypool's eyes glittered with pity. The two sisters stared at each other a moment, before Ivypool dipped her head and hurried to Dovewing, pressing her muzzle against her cheek. "Of course I understand," she murmured. "It's just so strange to think that you live with another Clan now, and our kits will grow up without ever knowing one another." She pulled away. "How are your kits?"

"They're well," Dovewing purred. "I wish you could come and see them."

Scorchfur flicked his tail. "That's not going to happen anytime soon. Tigerstar doesn't welcome visitors from other Clans."

Alderheart shifted uneasily. That explained the frosty reception Twigbranch had reported when she and Finleap had returned from ShadowClan.

Scorchfur was glaring at Bramblestar. "Where is Puddleshine?"

Alderheart's belly tightened. He stepped forward. "He's too sick to travel."

Scorchfur bristled. "Haven't you treated his wounds?"

"Of course he has." Bramblestar gazed evenly at the ShadowClan warrior. "But Puddleshine's injuries are healing more slowly than expected."

"I've dressed them with marigold and horsetail, but infection has taken hold," Alderheart fought back anxiety as he tried to explain. "I don't know how. I'm trying to clear it, but

I haven't found the right herb yet."

Tawnypelt's gaze sharpened. "You have three medicine cats!" she snapped. "Surely one of you is skillful enough to cure a silverthorn scratch?" She didn't wait for an answer but marched toward the medicine den. Bramblestar hurried after her as she pushed past Alderheart and into the den. Scorchfur sat down in the clearing, his gaze mistrustful. Dovewing was admiring Ivypool's kits, her whiskers twitching fondly as they slid beneath her belly, purring while their mother watched happily.

Alderheart squared his shoulders and followed Tawnypelt and Bramblestar into the den.

Tawnypelt was already sniffing Puddleshine while Jayfeather busied himself soaking nettles in the shallow pool at the back of the den. "He smells terrible. Haven't you been taking care of him?"

Puddleshine looked at her through fever-hazed eyes. "Alderheart has done everything I would have done," he meowed.

"The smell is something to do with the wounds." Alderheart hurried to Puddleshine's nest. "It's not an infection I've seen before."

"An infection is an infection," Tawnypelt snapped.

Puddleshine shifted with a grimace. "Alderheart's doing his best."

Jayfeather looked up from his work. "Not everything is curable with a poultice and a prayer to StarClan," he told Tawnypelt. "And getting angry isn't going to help. Puddleshine clearly can't walk home, and besides, there's no one there to treat his wounds."

"Alderheart can go with him," Tawnypelt meowed.

"I'm not taking Alderheart away from his Clan," Puddleshine meowed firmly. "I'll stay here another few days until Alderheart has managed to treat the infection, and then I'll return."

"Who's going to look after ShadowClan in the meantime?" Tawnypelt demanded.

"Is some cat sick?" Puddleshine asked, anxiety sparking in his gaze.

"No," Tawnypelt admitted.

Bramblestar steered the ShadowClan warrior gently away from Puddleshine's nest. "Let him rest," he meowed softly, laying his tail across her back comfortingly. Tawnypelt relaxed a little beneath his touch, and for a moment, Alderheart thought how strange it was that he sometimes forgot his father had a sister in ShadowClan. "We'll escort him home as soon as he's well enough. We know he is needed back in your camp, but in the meantime, if there are illnesses or injuries in ShadowClan, send for us and I will gladly spare Alderheart or Leafpool to help."

Tawnypelt frowned and then nodded curtly. "Okay." Her gaze softened as she looked back at Puddleshine. "Get well," she told him. "We miss you."

Puddleshine blinked at her gratefully and she headed out of the den.

Jayfeather left the nettles soaking in the pool as Tawnypelt and Bramblestar disappeared. He padded to Puddleshine's nest. "This is an infection I've never seen before," he mewed thoughtfully. "And that smell!" He wrinkled his nose.

Alderheart could smell it too. It had grown worse day by day and now carried the putrid scent of decay. Fear wormed beneath his fur. "It must be the pus," he mewed anxiously.

Jayfeather sniffed Puddleshine. "It's all of him," he mewed. "As if the infection has spread right into his fur. It's even on his breath."

"We need to find an herb that will fight the infection from the inside," Alderheart speculated.

Jayfeather narrowed his eyes. "Have you tried marigold and goldenrod?"

"In poultices," Alderheart told him.

"He could swallow some," Jayfeather suggested.

"Won't they make him sick?" Alderheart frowned.

"What about horsetail?" Puddleshine looked toward the crack where the herbs were stored. "That's good for infections."

"But we only use it in ointments," Alderheart reminded him.

Puddleshine's ear twitched. "Jayfeather could be right. I might have to swallow the herbs to make them work. Putting them directly on the wound isn't helping."

"Okay." Jayfeather headed toward the store. "Let's start with marigold. I'm certain that won't make you sick."

"Puddleshine mentioned an herb I wasn't familiar with that could dry up the wounds. It's called wood sorrel. He told me what it smells like. I could go out and find some," Alder-heart offered.

"Do it now while I try this." Jayfeather reached into the crack and pulled out a bundle of dried marigold.

Alderheart blinked at Puddleshine. "Don't worry," he told him. "We're going to find out what's wrong and how to cure it."

Puddleshine purred weakly.

"I'll be back as soon as I can." Alderheart turned to the den entrance. He'd bring back wood sorrel, but he had a second plan in mind. He wanted to return to the silverthorn where Puddleshine had been injured. He might find a clue there about what had made the ShadowClan medicine cat so ill. Had something strange gotten into Puddleshine's wound? If he could study what had infected Puddleshine, it might help him work out how to cure him.

Quickly, he crossed the clearing. Dovewing had left with her Clanmates. He could smell the ShadowClan patrol's scent still strong at the camp entrance. Ivypool's kits were chatting excitedly.

"We have ShadowClan kin!" Bristlekit sounded proud.

"Can we go and live in ShadowClan one day too?" Flipkit asked his mother.

"Hush!" Ivypool's pelt bristled with alarm. She glanced around nervously. "You must never say that again. A warrior is loyal to the Clan they were born in."

"But Dovewing wasn't loyal," Bristlekit mewed.

Alderheart ducked out of camp, his heart aching with pity for Ivypool. How could she defend her sister while teaching her kits that, without loyalty, the warrior code was hollow? He followed the route the ShadowClan cats had taken to the border, but peeled away from it as he reached a dip in the forest floor. He crossed it and headed deeper into the oak forest, following a long swath of nettles that flourished where the canopy opened in a slit overhead. This trail would take him straight to the silverthorn. He could investigate it thoroughly, and find the wood sorrel on his way back to camp.

Sunshine glittered through the leaves overhead. Fresh scents filled the air. Alderheart wondered if Leafpool had gathered many herbs. It would be good to have fresh leaves to work with again. He crossed the clearing the apprentices trained on. The sticks that had littered it had been cleared neatly to one side. As he pushed through the bracken on the far side, he tasted ShadowClan scents drifting from the border. The markers were fresh. He leaped the twining roots of an oak and ran up the short slope that led to the scent line. The silverthorn glinted in the shafts of sunlight piercing the canopy. Alderheart pulled up a few tail-lengths away and sniffed the air. There were no strange scents here, nothing that would explain Puddleshine's infection. He could smell rabbit. One must have a burrow nearby. Sniffing the earth, he padded closer to the silverthorn, his gaze flicking ahead of him, scanning for clues. A deathberry bush sprouted beneath a rowan a few trees away. The berries that had survived leaf-bare clustered on the tips of the branches. Alderheart frowned.

Could the juice of a deathberry be the cause of Puddleshine's infection? He scanned the earth where the medicine cat had been trapped. There was no sign of berries there. He reached gingerly through the silver vine and rubbed the ground with his paw, then sniffed it. He could smell nothing but forest scents and a faint trace of Puddleshine's blood.

Paw steps thrummed behind him. Undergrowth swished. He turned as the scents of Sparkpelt, Berrynose, and Amber-moon washed over him. The three ThunderClan warriors slewed to a halt on the path ahead. They'd left camp this morning to hunt. Berrynose was carrying two dead shrews by the tail while Ambermoon held a squirrel between her jaws.

"Hey, Alderheart!" Sparkpelt greeted him with a purr. "What are you doing here?"

"I'm looking for clues about what's making Puddleshine so sick," Alderheart told her.

Ambermoon dropped the squirrel. "Is he worse?"

"Yes." Alderheart glanced toward the silverthorn. "I wondered if he picked up an infection here that is making it hard for his wounds to heal."

Sparkpelt flicked her tail angrily at the silverthorn. "Who knows what Twolegs use to make that stuff? I wouldn't be surprised if it's poisonous."

Berrynose laid the shrews on the ground. "We wondered whether to try to use sticks to cover it up. But I think it's better to leave it in plain sight so cats can see to avoid it."

"It's too big for us to move." Ambermoon blinked at the

silverthorn. "Besides, where would we move it to? It'll be dangerous wherever we leave it."

Alderheart sniffed the vine once more. "If it is Twoleg poison making Puddleshine sick, herbs might not be enough to cure him." Worry jabbed in his belly.

"You'll find a way," Sparkpelt mewed encouragingly.

"I hope so." As he spoke, movement caught Alderheart's eye. A rabbit hopped clumsily from beneath a bramble a few tail-lengths away. Hadn't it scented the cats?

Sparkpelt had already seen the prey. She'd dropped into a hunting crouch, and her gaze was fixed on the rabbit as it stumbled into the open.

"It's injured," Alderheart whispered. He could see dried blood on its swollen hind leg.

"So it'll be easier to catch." Sparkpelt's tail quivered with excitement as Berrynose and Ambermoon stood as still as rocks behind her.

"Wait!" Alderheart detected a familiar scent wafting from the rabbit—the same sweet scent of decay that clung to Puddleshine. "It's not just wounded; it's infected."

Sparkpelt looked at him questioningly. "Are you sure?"

"Can't you smell it?"

Ambermoon's nose was twitching. "He's right. It smells sour. Let's leave it. We don't want to poison the Clan."

Sparkpelt straightened, disappointment in her eyes. "I guess we'll have to try elsewhere."

Berrynose nodded toward the rabbit as it lolloped heavily toward the deathberry bush, eyes dull with pain. "Look, it's so sick, it can't even tell we're here."

"Come on." Sparkpelt jerked her head toward the slope. "Let's head for the beeches. There will be healthy rabbits there." Berrynose picked up the shrews again and Ambermoon grabbed the squirrel. "Will you be okay?" Sparkpelt asked Alderheart.

"Sure," he told her. "I'm about to head back to camp. There are herbs I want to pick on the way."

Sparkpelt dipped her head politely before heading away. Berrynose and Ambermoon followed, nodding as they passed.

Alderheart glanced back at the rabbit. Why was it snuffling around the deathberry bush? Alarm sparked through him as the rabbit paused and reached up with its teeth to pluck a deathberry from the tip of a branch. *What's it doing?* Alderheart watched in horror as the rabbit dropped the berry at its paws and began to nibble delicately at the flesh. *Doesn't it know that it's poisonous?* He thought *all* woodland creatures knew to stay away from deathberries. Their bitter tang betrayed the poison they carried. *Perhaps it knows it's dying and wants to end its suffering.* It must be in a lot of pain to choose death. For the first time, Alderheart felt a twinge of sympathy for prey. Perhaps he should kill it himself. It would die quickly. But Alderheart didn't trust his skills. He'd begun training as a warrior before he'd become a medicine-cat apprentice, but he'd never been very good. He could hunt if he had to, but he couldn't be sure his killing bite would be as quick or as painless as it should be. And the thought of biting into infected prey made him hesitate.

He turned away. If the rabbit wanted to die, he'd leave it in peace. Besides, he'd promised Puddleshine he'd fetch the wood sorrel as quickly as he could.

Heading away from the silverthorn, he tried not to think of the rabbit's suffering. Whatever poison the silverthorn carried, it was clearly deadly. He quickened his step. The sooner he treated Puddleshine the better. He just hoped that the wood sorrel would be enough to cure the stricken medicine cat.

CHAPTER 4

❧

Alderheart dreamed that he was padding through unfamiliar woods. His paws caught on sticks that littered the ground. Cracks scarred the uneven earth and he had to weave around them. Trees crowded close, their branches twisted, their bark gnarled. Hazy light filtered between them and the air felt too thick to breathe. Alderheart's pelt prickled uneasily and he glanced over his shoulder, sensing danger behind him. He quickened his pace.

Behind him, a faint growl lifted to a roar like wind rushing toward him. His heart lurched as he broke into a run. Shadow pursued him, swallowing the light until darkness pressed at his heels. Fear surged in his chest as he smelled a deadly scent. *Smoke!* Acrid clouds blasted over him, and he felt heat on his tail. Looking over his shoulder, he saw fire pierce the smoke. It was chasing him down like a fox driving prey. Alderheart dashed between trees, leaping fissures and branches. Terror scorched beneath his pelt as the roar of the flames drowned out the pounding of blood in his ears.

He saw rocks ahead. A steep cliff rose from the forest floor, its rough face lined by ledges and cracks. He could climb it.

Hope sparking in his chest, he leaped for the lowest ledge and scrambled upward, blindly reaching for paw hold after paw hold until he felt fresh air around him. He heaved himself onto the top of the cliff. Flames tore through the trees below. Smoke swirled and billowed as the fire howled past. Safe on the rocks, Alderheart watched for the smoke to clear. The forest would be charred. Nothing could have survived such a fire.

A breeze caught the thinning smoke and stirred it into thin mist. As it dissolved, Alderheart blinked in surprise. Where blackened stumps should have been, he saw a vibrant meadow. Lush green grass trembled with life, brilliant in the sunshine. The tang of its freshness bathed Alderheart, so strong that it woke him. He blinked open his eyes, the dream still fresh, and stared from his nest into the shadows of the medicine den.

Dawn light was filtering through the entrance and reaching down through the gap where fresh water dripped into the pool. Leafpool's nest was empty. So was Jayfeather's. Alderheart lifted his head. Anxiety jabbed his belly. Something was wrong.

"Jayfeather?" As he called through the half-light, he saw the blind medicine cat crouching beside Puddleshine's nest. Leafpool was beside him, bent over the ShadowClan medicine cat. Panic sparked through his pelt as he scrambled from his nest. "Is he okay?"

Jayfeather turned his blind blue gaze on him. "He's having a seizure."

Leafpool was pressing Puddleshine into his nest while the tom thrashed violently beneath her paws.

"Hold his hind legs still," Jayfeather ordered.

Alderheart thrust his paws into Puddleshine's nest. The tom's legs flailed stiffly. He struggled to hold them still as Jayfeather grasped the unconscious tom's jerking head between his forepaws. Leafpool pressed down on the tom's shoulders as he convulsed.

Please, StarClan! Don't let him die! Alderheart had brought wood sorrel back to camp the day before. He'd chewed it into poultices and applied it carefully it to every wound. He'd nursed the semiconscious medicine cat through the long afternoon and had gone to his nest hoping that the sorrel would fight the infection. Clearly it had done nothing to help.

Slowly Puddleshine's seizure weakened. His legs fell limp beneath Alderheart's paws. "Is he alive?" Alderheart looked at Jayfeather, his throat tight.

"He's still breathing." Jayfeather laid Puddleshine's head gently on the side of his nest.

Leafpool sat back on her haunches. "We should tell Tigerstar."

"No!" Alderheart stiffened. "We can still cure him." They were acting like there was no hope.

"Tigerstar should be warned," Jayfeather murmured.

"Not yet." Alderheart headed for the entrance. "We're going to save Puddleshine. Give him feverfew to cool him down and thyme to calm his seizures. I'll be back as soon as I can."

"Where are you going?" Leafpool blinked at him.

"Out." Alderheart left the den and hurried across the

clearing. The answer to Puddleshine's illness *must* lie with the silverthorn. Alderheart would have to go back to it.

The camp was blue in the dawn light. Squirrelflight was stretching beneath the Highledge. Alderheart guessed she was getting ready to organize the day's patrols. Graystripe was washing outside the elders' den. Molewhisker was poking through the remains of the fresh-kill pile, while Cherryfall yawned sleepily in the clearing.

Alderheart nodded to them but didn't speak. He walked with purpose, and no cat asked where he was going. He padded through the entrance and headed into the woods. Instinct carried him, as though StarClan were guiding his paws. He remembered his dream. The shock of Puddleshine's seizure had driven it from his thoughts, but now it returned. He could smell the smoke from the fire and see the lushness of the meadow that had blossomed after it had passed. Was it a sign from StarClan? Were they trying to show him the answer?

He shook out his pelt. *Don't be dumb.* What did a forest fire have to do with Puddleshine's illness? It was just a dream. Not every dream held a message.

He followed the trail across the apprentices' training ground and through the forest to the slope that led to the silverthorn. The sun had lifted above the horizon by the time he arrived, and its light was slicing between the trees.

Alderheart stopped beside the silverthorn. He padded in circles, tasting the air and sniffing the ground. If the silverthorn carried Twoleg poison, how would smelling it help? Frustrated, he lashed his tail. He had to think of something!

As he paced, he saw the deathberry bush shiver. A rabbit hopped from beneath it. Alderheart blinked in surprise. It was the wounded rabbit he'd seen yesterday. It was still limping, but its eyes had brightened. The stench of its infection had lost its bitter tang. It hopped into the sunlight and, lifting its ears in alarm, looked at Alderheart. Panic lit its eyes and it turned and fled.

Alderheart stared after it. Yesterday it could barely hop. Hope flared in his chest. If the rabbit had begun to recover from its infected wound, then so could Puddleshine. Alderheart remembered with a jolt that the rabbit had nibbled deathberries. *It should be dead!* He padded to the bush, careful not to tread on any fallen berries. He didn't want poison on his paws. Peering beneath the low branches, he saw that the rabbit had left a makeshift nest in the dried leaves underneath. Leaning in, he examined it. Deathberry seeds were piled in a small heap beneath the bush.

Ducking out, Alderheart's thoughts quickened. Had the deathberries cured the rabbit? Perhaps eating the flesh and leaving the seeds had given it just enough poison to kill the infection without killing the rabbit. Could it be true?

His dream flashed in his mind once more. The fire hadn't killed the forest; a meadow had blossomed in its path. *It was a sign!* Alderheart stiffened with excitement. *If I feed deathberries to Puddleshine, they won't kill him. They'll save him!*

Quickly, Alderheart searched for a dock plant. He found one sprouting at the foot of an oak. Tearing off the largest leaf, he carried it back to the deathberry bush. He plucked berries gingerly with his claws and dropped them onto the leaf. Then he rolled up the leaf, folding the edges in so that the deathberries were safely wrapped. Carrying the bundle gently between his jaws, he headed back to camp. How was he going to persuade Jayfeather and Leafpool that such a desperate cure would work? His heart pounded. He would have to. These deadly berries could be Puddleshine's only hope.

CHAPTER 5

❧

Twigbranch brushed past an oak trunk, enjoying the tug of the rough bark against her fur. It soothed her.

"Stop dawdling!" Ahead of her, Finleap padded cheerfully between the trees. "We came out here to hunt, not to scratch."

"I'm coming." Twigbranch hurried after him.

She had taken Flypaw out at dawn to practice finding prey, but the apprentice had been so sleepy she'd hardly listened to a word Twigbranch had said. She'd yawned when she was meant to be sniffing for rabbit tracks and kept falling behind when Twigbranch was trying to hurry her to the next mouse nest. When Twigbranch had scolded her, Flypaw had moved even more slowly, as though Twigbranch's criticism had injured her rather than helped her.

Eventually she'd sent Flypaw back to camp to clean out the elders' den. Early morning training seemed wasted on her apprentice. Instead she'd asked Finleap if he wanted to hunt. They were heading into the forest now. Gentle sunlight dappled the trees. Finleap padded beside her as they climbed the rise where beech grew between the oaks. Twigbranch glanced at him. "Did you find it hard to get up early to train when you were an apprentice?" she asked.

"No." He blinked at her. "I couldn't wait to get started."

"Me neither." Twigbranch flicked her tail happily as she remembered. "Some mornings I was already waiting outside Ivypool's den when she woke up. I wanted to be a warrior more than anything else."

Finleap slowed. "Are you still having trouble with Flypaw?"

"Her heart's just not in it," Twigbranch worried. "Or perhaps it is. Perhaps I expect too much from her."

"She's just begun training," Finleap pointed out. "Give her time to find her paws."

"I'm trying to give her time, but we just don't seem to connect." Anxiety pricked in Twigbranch's belly. "When I correct her or criticize her technique, she takes it personally, like I'm criticizing *her*." Her pelt twitched with frustration. "I feel like I can't tell her anything in case I upset her. I have to tiptoe around her like I'm stalking prey. Sometimes I wonder if I'm training her to be a warrior or she's training me to be a mouse."

"You'll figure it out," he meowed. "Relationships take time to build."

"Do you get along with Snappaw?"

Finleap purred. "He's fun. He can be slow, but he listens and he works hard. He's going to make a good warrior."

Twigbranch fought back a twinge of jealousy. How had Finleap gotten the easy apprentice? *Perhaps I'm just a bad mentor.* Should she try harder to adapt to her apprentice, or simply be tougher and expect more of her?

Finleap whisked his tail. "I smell squirrel."

Twigbranch froze as he stopped and scanned the forest. She saw a gray tail bobbing over the forest floor a tree-length away. "There!" She dropped into a hunting crouch. Finleap dropped beside her. Together they watched the squirrel stop at the roots of a beech. It rummaged through the leaves caught between the roots and began picking out beechnuts.

Finleap padded forward, moving noiselessly over the forest floor. Twigbranch crept after him, keeping her belly a whisker above the ground so it didn't brush the leaves. Silently they advanced on the squirrel. It was intent on the beechnuts, nimbly cracking the shells and pulling out their seeds before stuffing them into its mouth. As Twigbranch neared, she glanced at Finleap, looking for a signal to pounce. He caught her eye and nodded her to one side. They split up and, ducking lower, moved to flank the squirrel.

Twigbranch paused and waited for Finleap's signal. His eyes shone with excitement. He looked at her and flicked his tail. *Go!* They leaped at the same moment. But the squirrel was fast. Quick as a bird, it shot upward, gripping the bark of the beech and skittering toward the branches. Twigbranch stared after it, but Finleap didn't hesitate. He leaped up the trunk, hooking in his claws, and hauled himself after the squirrel. "Come on!" he called down.

Twigbranch followed, pushing clumsily upward with her hind legs. Bark crumbled beneath her claws and showered past her. It felt strange to hunt above the ground, despite her SkyClan training. Finleap was swarming after the squirrel as though he'd been born in a tree. The squirrel hopped onto a branch and raced along it. Finleap followed, balancing easily as he chased the squirrel to the branch's end.

Twigbranch reached the branch, panting, and watched as the squirrel leaped from its end to the next tree. Her heart seemed to stop as Finleap leaped after it. He landed in the next tree, wobbling dangerously as he found his paws. His stumpy tail flicked one way, then the other, as he fought to stay upright. Twigbranch glanced at the forest floor below. *Don't fall!*

In a moment Finleap had regained his balance and was pelting after the squirrel. He caught it as it tried to leap up to the next branch, rearing and hooking it with his claws before it could escape.

Twigbranch felt a rush of pride. Even with a short tail, Finleap could keep his balance and hunt at the same time. Would he pass his SkyClan hunting skills on to their ThunderClan kits? She stiffened. *Kits!* What was she thinking? They were both too young to have a family yet.

She shook out her fur and slithered to the ground. Hurrying to Finleap's tree, she waited for him as he scrambled tail first down the trunk, the dead squirrel dangling from his jaws.

He dropped it on the ground. "It feels good to hunt in the trees again," he mewed happily.

Twigbranch brushed her muzzle against his cheek. "Great catch!"

He purred. "Let's take it back to camp." He grabbed the squirrel and headed away.

Twigbranch followed, pleased both by the good catch and at seeing Finleap so happy.

When they reached camp, Finleap headed to the fresh-kill pile to drop his catch. Twigbranch began to follow, but raised voices in the medicine den made her stop. An angry yowl sounded from the entrance.

"Have you got bees in your brain?" Jayfeather hissed.

"But I've seen it work! Nothing else is helping." Alderheart sounded desperate.

Alarmed, Twigbranch hurried to the medicine den and nosed her way through the brambles that trailed at the entrance. No one seemed to notice her. Jayfeather was cringing from a small pile of dark berries, which lay on a dock leaf at Alderheart's paws. Leafpool's pelt was bristling as she pressed protectively against the nest where Puddleshine lay. The ShadowClan cat's eyes were glazed and dull.

"How could you bring deathberries into camp?" Leafpool stared at them. "What if a kit finds one?"

"I'll hide them where no kit can find them," Alderheart promised.

"What if you get juice on your paws and walk it through camp?" Jayfeather argued. "A kit might pick up some poison without anyone realizing."

"That's not going to happen!" Alderheart's hackles lifted. "I know the dangers. I'm not going to risk any cat's life."

"Except Puddleshine's!" Jayfeather lashed his tail.

Twigbranch's eyes widened. Was Alderheart really planning to give Puddleshine deathberries?

Leafpool flicked her ears. "How did you get such a crazy idea?"

"I told you! I saw the rabbit," Alderheart mewed urgently. "One day it was sick with the same smell as Puddleshine, and the next it was recovering. I saw it eating the berries."

"Are you sure it was eating *deathberries*?" Leafpool asked.

"They were berries from the same bush where I gathered these," Alderheart told her.

Jayfeather's blind blue eyes were hard with rage. "You're not feeding those to Puddleshine." Twigbranch stiffened. She knew Jayfeather could be bad-tempered, but she'd never seen him this angry.

Alderheart met Jayfeather's gaze unflinchingly. "I have to try it. If I don't, he will die."

Twigbranch looked at the nest where Puddleshine lay. Could he hear this? Did he know he was dying? The Shadow-Clan medicine cat shifted. She saw his gaze focus for a moment, and he groaned as he tried to lift his head.

"Let him try it," Puddleshine grunted.

Jayfeather turned his head toward the sick tom. "It will *kill* you."

"I'm already dying." Pain showed in Puddleshine's gaze. "If Alderheart is wrong about the rabbit, then at least I'll die quickly. If he's right, then I have a chance." He fell limp with a groan.

Alderheart stared urgently at Jayfeather. "It's the only choice we have."

Jayfeather curled his lip. "It's *your* choice, then. Do it if you must." With a growl he stalked past Twigbranch and pushed his way through the trailing brambles out of the den.

Leafpool glanced anxiously at Alderheart. "Do what you think is best," she mewed. "But be careful. If this harms Puddleshine, you'll never forgive yourself." Frowning anxiously, she followed Jayfeather out.

Twigbranch stared at Alderheart. "Are you really going to do it?"

"Of course I am." He crouched and began carefully tearing open the flesh of a berry.

"What if he dies?" Twigbranch breathed, her heart pounding in her throat.

"Then I'll know at least I tried everything." Squinting in the gloom of the den, he picked out the seeds and dropped them onto the dock leaf. "I'll feel worse if he dies without me having tried." He didn't look up but, intent on his work, slit open another berry.

Twigbranch slid out through the brambles and paused at the edge of the clearing. Jayfeather was disappearing into the elders' den. Leafpool was crouched beside the fresh-kill pile, gazing anxiously ahead. *Alderheart trusts his instincts.*

Energy pulsed through Twigbranch's paws. *I must do the same with Flypaw.* She wanted to make the young she-cat understand how important training was. These moons mustn't be wasted. Flypaw could learn so much. She was young and quick, and the techniques she learned now would form the bedrock on which all her future skills would rest. It was no time to ease up on her. Twigbranch knew she had to be tough. *What if I'm wrong?* It was a risk worth taking. She knew suddenly that, like Alderheart, she must follow her instinct.

She hurried to the elders' den and stuck her head in. Flypaw was supposed to be cleaning out the bedding, but all she saw was Jayfeather, sniffing Millie's ear while Graystripe watched anxiously. The medicine cat pulled away. "Can you hear birdsong in the morning?" he asked.

"Yes," Millie answered.

"Can you hear Graystripe snoring?" Jayfeather asked.

"*Everyone* can hear Graystripe snoring," Millie purred.

Graystripe grunted, a sparkle in his eyes.

"In that case, your hearing is okay," Jayfeather pronounced. "Maybe not as sharp as it once was. That might be a blessing. You say you can't hear the kits mewling in the nursery anymore. Enjoy the peace." He turned his head toward Twigbranch as though he could see her. "Are you going to follow me into every den today?"

Her ears grew hot. "I'm looking for Flypaw."

"She's not here," Jayfeather mewed curtly. "Try someplace else."

"Did she clean out your bedding this morning?" Twigbranch asked Graystripe.

"She took half of it away," Graystripe plucked sadly at his nest's thin pile of bracken with a paw. "We haven't seen her since."

"She's probably collecting fresh moss," Millie suggested.

Twigbranch's pelt pricked irritably. "She's probably watching thistledown floating between the trees and imagining she's leader of SleepyClan." She saw Graystripe and Millie exchange looks as she ducked out of the den and scanned the camp. Flypaw couldn't even clean out bedding without getting distracted. With a grunt, Twigbranch decided that she'd better go and find her apprentice. She headed for the camp entrance.

"Twigbranch!" Finleap called to her from beside the warriors' den, where Rosepetal and Blossomfall were sharing a mouse.

Twigbranch glanced at him. "Not now," she called. "I'm busy."

Finleap hurried toward her. Frustration clawed Twigbranch's belly. She wanted to find Flypaw. They'd wasted enough training time already. Reluctantly she waited for Finleap to reach her. "What?" she snapped.

He blinked at her, hurt flashing in his eyes. "I'm sorry to hold you up, but it's important."

"Sorry." Twigbranch tried to push back impatience, but it wormed beneath her pelt. "What is it?"

"Reedclaw is sick. Rosepetal just told me. She and Blossomfall met Plumwillow at the border while they were patrolling. It's only greencough, but when she was a kit, greencough always made it hard for her to breathe. I'm worried about her."

"I'm sorry to hear that." The thorn barrier shivered, and Twigbranch glanced at it, hoping that Flypaw had returned. Her heart sank as she saw Molewhisker pad into camp. "Have you seen Flypaw in the forest?" she asked him.

"No," Molewhisker told her as he passed. "Is she okay? Do

you want help finding her?"

"No, thanks. I'll find her myself." Twigbranch shifted her paws. How far from camp had Flypaw wandered?

"Listen!" Finleap was still gazing at her.

"What?" Twigbranch dragged her attention back.

"Reedclaw's my littermate," Finleap mewed urgently.

"I know that." What did he want from her?

"I need to visit her." Finleap searched her gaze.

Twigbranch stared at him. "She's in SkyClan."

"So?"

"You're a ThunderClan warrior now," she reminded him. "You can't just visit SkyClan whenever you feel like it."

"You used to visit Violetshine."

"When we were apprentices," she mewed. "We were young. We didn't care so much about rules."

"But Reedclaw's *sick*."

"I know." This conversation was taking too long. Flypaw could be on the other side of ThunderClan territory by now. "And I'm sorry. But SkyClan has a medicine cat. Frecklewish will take care of her. She'll be fine."

"What if she's not?"

"You have to stop worrying about your kin in SkyClan," Twigbranch told him. "There's nothing you can do to help them. You left them when you joined ThunderClan."

Anger sparked in Finleap's eyes. "I only joined Thunder-Clan to be with you."

Twigbranch bristled. "Are you regretting it?"

"No!" Finleap's eyes glistened. "But I thought we'd be

mates by now. I thought we'd be starting a family."

Twigbranch's chest tightened. She fought to steady her breathing. Was he going to press her into a relationship before she was ready? "What's the rush?"

"There's no *rush*," he meowed pointedly. "I thought it's what you *wanted*. That's why I left SkyClan. I thought it's what we *both* wanted, but I guess you need more time to be sure."

Guilt hollowed her belly as he marched away. *I should go after him and tell him that I am sure. I don't need more time.* Shame washed her pelt as she stood rooted to the spot and watched him go. *I am sure, aren't I?*

CHAPTER 6

♣

Violetshine's heart quickened as she followed Tree across the bridge to
the island. Would Twigbranch be at the Gathering? It would
be good to share tongues with her sister again. The smooth
bark was cold beneath her paws. Moonlight shimmered on the
water below her. Ahead, her Clanmates were already swishing through the tall grass toward the clearing. She could smell
ShadowClan scents. Tigerstar and his warriors must already
be here. ThunderClan cats were pacing on the shore behind,
waiting for SkyClan to cross. She glanced back and spied her
sister's pelt, pale in the moonlight. Twigbranch didn't see her.
She seemed distracted, frowning at the young tabby at her
side.

"Hurry up!" Sagenose pressed at Violetshine's heels. His
apprentice, Gravelpaw, was trying to squeeze past.

"Sorry!" Violetshine ran along the log and leaped onto the
far shore.

She caught up to Tree as he shouldered his way into the
long grass. "Are you nervous?"

"Why should I be?" Tree padded beside her.

"What if they ask you to mediate?"

He shrugged. "Then I'll mediate," he meowed. "That's what I'm here for, right?"

She wondered how he could be so calm at the thought of addressing the Clans. Did he realize how many cats would be there?

As she nosed her way out of the grass, her Clanmates were already streaming across the moonlit clearing. The scent of ShadowClan was stronger here, and Violetshine's pelt prickled with alarm as she saw the Clan shifting beneath the trees. Moonlight dappled their thick pelts. They moved with confidence, muscles rippling beneath their fur. And there were so many of them! She remembered the last time she'd seen ShadowClan cats at a Gathering. They'd bowed their heads and hardly spoken, avoiding the gaze of the other Clans. How different they seemed now.

Violetshine caught Tawnypelt's eye without meaning to. The tortoiseshell stared back coldly, as though she had no memory that they'd shared a camp a moon ago. Grassheart and Strikestone watched the arriving Clans, their gazes betraying nothing. Unnerved, Violetshine shivered and moved closer to her Clanmates.

As ThunderClan padded into the clearing, they nodded friendly greetings to ShadowClan and SkyClan. Only SkyClan returned them.

"Hi!" Pigeonpaw called out to a ThunderClan apprentice. The black-and-ginger apprentice blinked back excitedly. Violetshine guessed it must be her first Gathering.

Leafpool and Jayfeather padded to the Great Oak and sat

down without speaking. When Frecklewish and Fidgetflake joined them, the ThunderClan medicine cats greeted them with a curt nod but barely returned their gazes. Violetshine narrowed her eyes. They seemed anxious. Was there sickness in ThunderClan?

WindClan and RiverClan entered the clearing. Their apprentices hurried to greet the apprentices from Thunder-Clan and began showing off battle moves.

Gravelpaw glanced hopefully at Sagenose. "Can we join them?"

"I don't know." Sagenose looked at Blossomheart. Gravelpaw and the other apprentices, Pigeonpaw, Quailpaw, and Sunnypaw, were fidgeting at her side. "Should they mix with other 'paws?"

"I don't see why not." Blossomheart flicked her tail, and the young cats bound over to the others.

Around the clearing, warriors stopped to talk to one another, or nodded polite greetings. Hawkwing was talking with Squirrelflight and Berrynose. Plumwillow was chatting with Sandynose and Podlight while Harrybrook exchanged gossip with Emberfoot and Oatclaw. Only ShadowClan hung back. Their apprentices stayed at their mentors' sides and watched through narrowed eyes. Violetshine shifted her paws uneasily. Twigbranch was with Lionblaze as he talked with Reedwhisker and Minnowtail. Her sister's gaze flitted away from the RiverClan cats and caught Violetshine's eye.

Violetshine blinked at her, happy as their old connection sparked anew. She began to cross the clearing, wondering what news her sister had to share. Were she and Finleap mates now? As she neared, the Clans grew still. A hush fell over the clearing. She glanced around. Tigerstar was heading toward the Great Oak. Bramblestar followed. Harestar, Mistystar, and Leafstar padded after him. As Tigerstar leaped onto the lowest branch, Tawnypelt, Hawkwing, Reedwhisker, Squirrelflight, and Crowfeather took their places on the arching roots below.

Violetshine looked at Twigbranch. Her sister dipped her head apologetically and turned back to her Clan. Disappointed, Violetshine returned to her own Clanmates and looked up at the Great Oak as Bramblestar cleared his throat.

"Newleaf has brought fresh prey to ThunderClan." He gazed out over the Clans. "Our bellies are full, and the warmer weather has given us chance to strengthen our dens and begin to restock our herb store." He turned to Tigerstar. "Alderheart is currently taking care of Puddleshine. ShadowClan's medicine cat was injured by some Twoleg silverthorn and is being treated for infection in the ThunderClan camp."

"I trust he will be ready to return home soon." Tigerstar met Bramblestar's gaze.

"Of course." Bramblestar didn't hesitate, but Violetshine saw Leafpool glance nervously at Jayfeather. Was there more to Puddleshine's illness than either leader was giving away?

Tigerstar lifted his muzzle. "We have nearly finished restoring our camp. And we have new apprentices training under experienced ShadowClan warriors. They will be taking their warrior names soon." He nodded toward a white-and-ginger tom, one of the cats Tigerstar had brought back with him from his journey beyond the territories. "Blazepaw"—the young tom puffed out his chest—"Cinnamonpaw, and Antpaw." *Cinnamonpaw.* The name sounded strange to Violetshine. *It must be a Twoleg word.* She followed Tigerstar's gaze as it flicked to the other cats with him. They looked too old to be apprentices, but pride shone in their eyes as their leader acknowledged them. "We have more news." As Tigerstar spoke, Violetshine saw Juniperclaw slide from among his Clanmates and push his way to the front of the gathered cats. Tawnypelt hopped down from the roots of the Great Oak, and Juniperclaw took her place. Tigerstar blinked at the black tom approvingly before addressing the Clans once more. "Tawnypelt is stepping down as our deputy. Our new deputy will be Juniperclaw."

Murmurs of surprise rippled through the watching cats.

"Didn't Juniperclaw abandon ShadowClan to follow Darktail?" Brackenfur called from among the ThunderClan cats.

Macgyver stared up at Tigerstar. "Why would you trust a cat who once betrayed your Clan?"

"A deputy must be loyal!" Sandynose called.

"He might be your leader one day!" Brackenfur's pelt bristled indignantly.

Tigerstar silenced the Clans with a sharp flick of his tail. "I choose my deputy, and my choice concerns no Clan but ShadowClan!"

Strikestone raised his voice in support of his leader. "ShadowClan makes its own decisions!"

Sparrowtail chimed in. "No one dictates to ShadowClan!"

Tigerstar's gaze blazed across the gathered cats. "Shadow-Clan is born again. Past mistakes have been forgotten."

The ShadowClan cats yowled in loud agreement.

Violetshine shrank beneath her pelt. How had Shadow-Clan grown so sure of itself in a single moon? She noticed Tree watching Tigerstar, interest sparking in his amber eyes.

"Prey is running well—"

"So well that sometimes they have to follow it onto Sky-Clan land!" Sandynose's hackles lifted as he interrupted the ShadowClan leader.

Tigerstar returned the SkyClan warrior's gaze coolly. "No borders have been crossed," he meowed slowly. "My warriors have assured me of that."

Leafstar's tail twitched irritably. "If that's true, then why have *my* warriors reported finding ShadowClan scents on SkyClan territory?"

"Perhaps they're not sure where the borders lie." Tigerstar met her gaze evenly.

"They are very sure," Leafstar growled.

Tigerstar didn't respond. Instead he turned away and addressed the Clans once more. "ShadowClan was weak when Rowanclaw gave up territory to SkyClan. My father had many noble qualities, but not every leader would have made the decisions he made. When he surrendered our land to Sky-Clan, he was protecting the Clan that we were *then*. He wasn't thinking of the Clan we'd become."

Bramblestar blinked in surprise. "It was *your* suggestion that ShadowClan give territory to SkyClan!"

Tigerstar ignored him. "ShadowClan is strong now. We need more territory to feed a growing Clan." The Shadow-Clan leader's tone was ominous. Violetshine looked anxiously at Hawkwing. She wanted reassurance. But her father's eyes were dark with worry. Violetshine's pelt prickled as Tigerstar went on. "We will let SkyClan keep the territory Rowanclaw gave them if they agree to let our warriors hunt on it."

Harrybrook growled. Sagenose's ears flattened. Plumwillow and Macgyver showed their teeth. On the Great Oak, Leafstar stared incredulously at Tigerstar. "Have you decided which part of our land you wish to hunt on?" she mewed sarcastically.

Tigerstar blinked at her. "All of it. It was once our land, after all."

"And now it's *ours!*" Leafstar bristled. "We won't share it."

"ShadowClan is strong now."

Violetshine shuddered as Tigerstar repeated the phrase. It sounded like a threat.

"*Strong!*" Leafstar hissed. "Perhaps ShadowClan would never have been weak if you hadn't abandoned them!"

"StarClan guided my paws," Tigerstar meowed solemnly. "They led me to where I stand now." He faced Leafstar, muscles twitching in his wide shoulders.

Dread hollowed Violetshine's belly. Were the leaders going to fight at a Gathering? She glanced at the sky. Clouds drifted around the bright, round moon.

"There must be a way to solve this."

Violetshine jerked in surprise as Tree called out from

beside her. She grew hot as Tigerstar ignored him, his dark amber eyes glaring at Leafstar. "Do you reject the will of Star-Clan?"

"We don't know this was StarClan," Leafstar hissed back at him.

Harestar shifted on the branch. "This must be settled. Tigerstar's claim should be heard. Rowanclaw surrendered the land when ShadowClan was too weak to patrol it. But ShadowClan has been restored since then."

Leafstar glared at the WindClan leader. "Are you saying we should give our territory to ShadowClan?"

"No." Harestar's gaze flicked from Leafstar to Tigerstar. "There must be five Clans beside the lake, and a Clan needs territory. But this dispute must be settled."

Tigerstar eyed Leafstar threateningly. "I'm happy to settle it right here."

Bramblestar slid past Leafstar and stood between the leaders. "This is not an issue that can be decided quickly or easily." The Clans watched him in silence, their eyes round. "Star-Clan did not lead SkyClan to the lake for fresh blood to be shed."

Tigerstar let his fur smooth. His gaze suddenly softened. "It seems strange that StarClan would lead a Clan to the lake and yet ask only one of the Clans to sacrifice territory to keep them here. Surely StarClan meant for every Clan to give up land, not just ShadowClan. What is stopping us from shifting all the borders to accommodate SkyClan? Why should ShadowClan be alone in giving up prey to feed other cats?"

The gathered cats murmured to one another. Violetshine watched them. Did they agree with Tigerstar? After all, the ShadowClan leader's argument sounded reasonable.

"What use would RiverClan territory be to SkyClan? Or to any of you?" Mistystar's mew took Violetshine by surprise. "Who could make use of the marsh or the river but us? No other Clan likes getting their paws wet."

"And no other Clan knows how to hunt the moor," Harestar chimed in. "Would SkyClan want to endure the snow and ice up there come leaf-bare?"

"They could learn," Tigerstar argued. "They've learned to live in a gorge and in a pine forest. Why not learn to live in a marsh or on a moor?"

Leafstar bristled. "You talk about us as if we're a bunch of loners with no rightful home!" Her gaze flashed over the other leaders. "We're meant to be here. StarClan brought us. Why should we have to move our home every time one of you thinks you need more territory?"

Mistystar shook out her fur. "It's ShadowClan's problem, not ours. They want their territory back, let them fight over it."

"Let ShadowClan and SkyClan settle this between themselves," Harestar meowed.

Violetshine felt a pang of sadness. The Clans weren't even going to consider giving up land. Her heart sank as Bramblestar nodded in agreement.

"We shouldn't let this dispute lead to conflict among all the Clans." The ThunderClan leader looked at Tree. "We agreed under StarClan that you would be mediator, the cat who seeks compromise when none can be found. Perhaps you could meet with Tigerstar and Leafstar and come up with a solution before we all get dragged into a battle over territory. I'm sure there must be a solution that suits both SkyClan and ShadowClan."

Leafstar grunted. "I'm not sure any solution will suit ShadowClan," she snarled. "First the rogues, then Rowanclaw, now this. ShadowClan seems destined to cause trouble for the rest of us."

Tree blinked calmly. "Let me try to help." He wove his way to the front. "A meeting between the leaders of SkyClan and ShadowClan might help us find out what each Clan needs. There must be enough land to share, because no cat has starved so far. I will help find a solution."

Bramblestar dipped his head. "Thank you, Tree. We will leave this matter in your paws for now." He looked at Mistystar. "Perhaps it's time we moved on with the Gathering and heard news from RiverClan and WindClan."

Mistystar sniffed. "It seems the longer we stay, the more chance there is that the rest of you will come up for an excuse to take our land." Swishing her tail, she leaped down from the Great Oak and headed for the long grass. As her Clanmates hurried after her, Harestar spoke.

"It looks like this Gathering is over." He nodded to Bramblestar, Tigerstar, and Leafstar and then jumped into the clearing.

Violetshine watched WindClan leave. ThunderClan followed. They were muttering as they headed into the long grass. Violetshine blinked at Twigbranch as she passed. Twig-branch dipped her head apologetically. They weren't going to get a chance to share tongues tonight. Tree waited for Leafstar as the SkyClan leader scrambled down the oak. Was he sure he could help Leafstar and Tigerstar come to an agreement? How would talking solve Tigerstar's hunger for territory?

Violetshine hurried to meet her father, unease pricking in her belly. "Will Tigerstar make Leafstar let him hunt on our land?" The thought of ShadowClan warriors sharing their forest made her nervous.

"Let's hope Tree comes up with a solution." Hawkwing glanced at the yellow tom, looking unconvinced.

Her chest tightened. "Do you think we'll have to leave the lake?" What else could they do if Tigerstar wouldn't give up his claim to their land?

Hawkwing touched his nose to her head. "It will be okay," he promised softly. "StarClan led me here so that you, Twig-branch, and I could be close to one another. They won't make us leave."

As he spoke, a hiss sounded from the edge of the clearing. Macgyver and Strikestone stood face-to-face, their hackles up. Both cats had tried to take the same trail through the grass. They held their ground, growls in their throats.

"Let him pass," Leafstar called across the clearing. "We can wait."

Macgyver flattened his ears and stepped back. Strikestone barged past him, Blazepaw at his heels. The ShadowClan cats streamed past SkyClan, heads high. Sagenose and Nettlesplash showed their teeth but let them pass.

As ShadowClan disappeared into the long grass, a shiver rippled Violetshine's fur. Was this how it would be now? Must SkyClan give way to ShadowClan to avoid a fight? Her paws felt heavy. She'd believed StarClan had led SkyClan home by guiding them to the lake. But would it ever be a real home if the other Clans were always threatening to take it away?

CHAPTER 7

Fear gnawed at Alderheart's belly as he watched Cloudtail and Mole-whisker race from the camp. He wished they were carrying better news.

Bramblestar shifted beside him. "Let's pray Tigerstar doesn't overreact when they tell him." The ThunderClan leader's eyes were dark. With a curt nod, he turned and bounded back onto the Highledge.

Alderheart pushed his way heavily into the medicine den, feeling the tug of the brambles along his spine as he slid into the shadowy cave.

Jayfeather looked up as he entered. "Well?" His milky blue gaze seemed to reach for Alderheart. "What did Bramblestar say?"

"What do you *think* he said?" Irritation flashed beneath Alderheart's pelt. *Why do I have to keep explaining myself? I'm doing my best!*

"Did you tell him about the deathberries?" Jayfeather's gaze was unwavering.

"Yes." Doubt shifted like a stone in Alderheart's belly. After all he'd gone through to convince his denmates that this treatment was Puddleshine's only hope, the berries didn't seem to have made a difference. Puddleshine was still sick, slipping in and out of consciousness, racked by a high fever that threatened to send him into spasms once more.

His uncertainty had worsened when he'd told Bramblestar about his radical treatment for the sick tom. As his father's eyes had widened with disbelief, Alderheart had shrunk beneath his pelt. "You should have consulted me *before* you gave him the berries," Bramblestar had growled.

"I consulted with Leafpool and Jayfeather," Alderheart defended himself.

Bramblestar's fur bristled. "They're not your Clan leader!"

"You're not a medicine cat," Alderheart snapped back.

"I'm the one who told Tigerstar last night that Puddleshine would be ready to return home soon."

"I had to do *something*." Alderheart felt helpless. How could Bramblestar ever understand the life-and-death decisions a medicine cat had to make?

"It could kill him."

"He was already dying." He looked miserably into Bramblestar's angry gaze. "This is the only thing that might save him."

"You say a dream told you to use the berries," Bramblestar grunted. "Are you sure it was from StarClan?"

"As sure as I can be. And I saw the rabbit eat the berries and recover. That was *real*. Not a dream."

Bramblestar twitched his tail impatiently. "ShadowClan must be told."

Alderheart had felt dread welling in his belly as the

ThunderClan leader gave Molewhisker and Cloudtail orders to travel to the ShadowClan camp and inform Tigerstar that Puddleshine's condition was critical.

A whimper from Puddleshine's nest jerked Alderheart back to the present. He hurried to where Jayfeather was already crouching beside the sick medicine cat and touched his nose to Puddleshine's head. The fever had still not broken, despite the berries Alderheart had fed him through the night, hoping with each morsel that this would be the one that brought the tom back from the brink of death. *It helped the rabbit.* Trembling with exhaustion, Alderheart sat down. "I felt sure it would work," he murmured.

"It hasn't killed him," Jayfeather conceded. "And where there's life—"

"There's hope. I know! You keep saying."

"There's no hope in death, and he's not dead yet." Jayfeather sounded encouraging, but Alderheart could tell by the pricking of the blind tom's pelt that he was still not convinced the deathberries could cure Puddleshine. *At least he's trying to be supportive.* Alderheart felt a glimmer of gratitude toward his former mentor.

Jayfeather got to his paws. "Leafpool will be back soon with more feverfew. We must at least be grateful that newleaf has brought fresh herbs." Alderheart stiffened as Jayfeather's gaze flicked toward the den entrance. "It sounds like we've got visitors," he mewed ominously.

Alarm spiked through Alderheart's pelt. "ShadowClan?

Already?" Molewhisker and Cloudtail had only just left with the message.

"Go look for yourself." Jayfeather nodded toward the trailing brambles.

Alderheart hurried toward them and slid through, narrowing his eyes against the glare of the sun. He smelled ShadowClan and, as his eyes adjusted to the brightness, saw Tigerstar in the clearing with Juniperclaw and Sparrowtail. Molewhisker and Cloudtail flanked the ShadowClan cats.

His heart lurched.

Ivypool was watching from outside the nursery as her kits clambered over her. Whitewing and Birchfall blinked from the shadows beside the warriors' den while their Clanmates shifted uneasily at the edges of the camp.

"They were waiting at the scent line," Molewhisker called to Bramblestar.

The ThunderClan leader looked down from Highledge, and then jumped into the clearing. "Tigerstar." He nodded to the broad-shouldered tabby.

Alderheart's breath grew shallow. Tigerstar's pelt gleamed in the sunlight. A frown shadowed his wide forehead as he dipped his head politely to Bramblestar.

Cloudtail caught Bramblestar's eye. "Tigerstar wants to speak with you in private."

Alderheart saw pelts prickle around the camp. Bramblestar blinked slowly at Cloudtail, a question in his gaze. Alderheart saw the white tom shift his paws, his blue eyes staring at the ground. "We haven't spoken to him," he mewed quickly.

Molewhisker nodded. "We found them at the border wait-ing for a patrol to escort them, so we brought them *straight* here."

Alderheart's tail twitched nervously, as he realized what the two warriors were telling their leader. *They haven't told Tiger-star about how sick Puddleshine is.*

Should he feel relieved? The ShadowClan leader was going to find out eventually.

"Let's speak over here." Bramblestar guided Tigerstar toward the shade of the Highledge, leaving Sparrowtail and Juniperclaw in the clearing. His sharpening gaze warned his Clanmates to return to whatever they'd been doing. As the warriors busied themselves, Tigerstar narrowed his eyes at Alderheart distrustfully, his gaze like ice cutting through Alderheart's pelt. "Do ThunderClan medicine cats have to hear everything their leader says?"

Alderheart's legs twitched, and just for a moment he thought he should go back to his den, but from the way Bramblestar pointedly ignored Tigerstar's question, he knew that his leader thought he should stay. *He will need a medicine cat to explain some things. . . .*

"What do you wish to discuss?" Bramblestar asked Tiger-star.

The ShadowClan leader's gaze was cool. "I'm supposed to be meeting with Leafstar soon to settle the question of ter-ritory. I want to have something to offer her, but I don't see what I can."

"What does that have to do with me?" Bramblestar's muscles hardened defensively beneath his pelt.

Tigerstar's tail flicked irritably. "Do you really expect ShadowClan and SkyClan to settle their border dispute alone? I know you believe this cat Tree can help, but what does a loner understand of Clan borders?"

"He understands how cats think," Bramblestar shot back.

Tigerstar narrowed his eyes. "Does he understand how *Clan* cats think?"

Bramblestar shifted his paws impatiently. "Why come to *me*, Tigerstar? I'm not taking sides."

"I come to you because we share a border. I come because you can help. If SkyClan and ShadowClan are left to settle the dispute alone, there are only two outcomes. SkyClan can either give us back our land peacefully"—Tigerstar fixed his dark gaze on Bramblestar—"or they can fight to keep it."

Bramblestar did not flinch. "Would you really drive SkyClan from the lake after all we have suffered to bring them here?"

"We won't drive them from the lake." Tigerstar meowed evenly. "But we *will* drive them away from *our* land."

"The pine forest is huge," Bramblestar reasoned. "Surely there is enough territory for two Clans?"

Tigerstar gazed toward the camp wall, as though seeing the forest beyond. "Yes, you might be right—*if* other Clans were to give up some land as well. It shouldn't just be SkyClan that moves its border. If ThunderClan were to also move its border, then there might be more than enough room for—"

Bramblestar cut him off. "We decided at the Gathering that Tree would mediate between you and SkyClan to settle this dispute. It has nothing to do with the other Clans. And Leafstar won't be happy if she hears you have been talking behind her back. She will see it as a lack of respect." There was a warning in his gaze.

Tigerstar frowned. Foreboding prickled through Alderheart's pelt as the dark tabby tom stared at Bramblestar.

"Fine." Tigerstar swished his tail. "But don't say that I never came in peace." He glanced around the camp. "Since I'm here, I may as well take my medicine cat home."

Alderheart stiffened. "He's not well enough to travel." Fear jabbed his pelt.

"*Still?*" Tigerstar swung his incredulous gaze toward Alderheart.

Alderheart looked at the ground. "We're having trouble curing the infection from the Twoleg thorns."

Suspicion glittered in the ShadowClan leader's eyes. "Let me see for myself." Tigerstar pushed passed him and shouldered his way into the medicine den.

Alderheart hurried after him.

Inside, Tigerstar had stopped. He was staring in horror at Puddleshine's nest. "He looks half dead!"

"Keep your voice down!" Jayfeather bristled. "If yowling helped, we could have cured him already."

"What's wrong with him?" Tigerstar demanded.

"I told you." Alderheart darted between Tigerstar and Puddleshine's nest. "We can't cure his infection."

"Why not?" Tigerstar was bristling. "You've had more than a quarter moon."

"None of our herbs are working." As he spoke, Alderheart caught sight of the deathberries he'd left on a dock leaf beside Puddleshine's nest. Dread froze like ice in his belly as Tigerstar followed his gaze.

Tigerstar stared at the berries. Slowly he padded across the den and sniffed them. "Are these deathberries?" Disbelief clouded his gaze as he looked at Alderheart. "In a *medicine* den?"

Alderheart nodded, his heart lurching as Tigerstar's gaze hardened with rage.

"Are you trying to poison him?" His rage seemed to howl like a storm through the den.

Bramblestar pushed through the entrance. "No cat is trying to poison any cat." He nudged Alderheart to one side and stood facing the ShadowClan leader. "In fact, I was sending Molewhisker and Cloudtail to warn you that Puddleshine is gravely ill. But you intercepted them at our border. Alderheart, Jayfeather, and Leafpool have been doing everything they can to heal Puddleshine. Alderheart's barely slept in days. Look!" He nodded toward Puddleshine's nest. "He's washed and he's lying on fresh bedding. We've taken the best possible care of him. But we can't fight Twoleg poison."

Tigerstar's gaze was still fixed on Alderheart. "So you decided to put him out of his misery instead!" His yowl dripped with anger.

Alderheart stiffened against the trembling in his legs. Was

his plan to save Puddleshine going to cause war between ThunderClan and ShadowClan?

Jayfeather lifted his muzzle. "Puddleshine was close to death," he meowed calmly. "Alderheart saw a rabbit cured from the same infection by eating deathberry flesh. He wanted to see if the cure would work on Puddleshine. We'd tried everything else. It was our only chance to save him."

Tigerstar glared at Jayfeather. "It doesn't seem to have worked." He narrowed his eyes accusingly. "But I know how little you value ShadowClan lives."

Jayfeather seemed to recoil.

Alderheart frowned. "What do you mean? Jayfeather values every life."

"What about Flametail, my littermate?" Tigerstar showed his teeth.

Bramblestar lashed his tail. "No cat ever believed Jayfeather killed your brother. No cat except Dawnpelt, and she was out of her mind with grief!"

Tigerstar's gaze stayed on Jayfeather. "You didn't manage to save him, though, did you?"

Guilt flashed in Jayfeather's blind blue gaze. "I had to let him go," he whispered.

"And now you're trying to let Puddleshine go too," Tigerstar growled.

"No!" Anger flared in Alderheart's chest as he faced the ShadowClan leader. "We're not letting him go. We're going to keep treating him until he's well. StarClan showed me a vision of flowers returning to the land after a fire. They were telling me that deathberries could cure Puddleshine, that they could make him stronger. I'm only feeding him the flesh, not the seeds. It will cleanse the Twoleg poison from his body, I know it will!" Conviction surged beneath his pelt, stronger than it had since he began the potentially deadly treatment. He held Tigerstar's gaze, his paws shaking as the ShadowClan leader glared back at him.

"Puddleshine agreed to the treatment," Jayfeather whispered. "We all knew how dangerous it was, but nothing else worked, and Puddleshine was willing to try."

Tigerstar turned his head. "Puddleshine agreed?"

Jayfeather nodded. "He knew we meant to give him deathberries and he understood why. He told Alderheart to go ahead."

Tigerstar eyed Puddleshine's limp body for a moment; then he narrowed his eyes. "Is the treatment working?"

"He hasn't died," Jayfeather growled.

"But he might?" Tigerstar gaze flashed with uncertainty.

"He might," Jayfeather conceded.

Tigerstar paused. His tail swished slowly behind him. "Then I will take him home," he meowed at last. "If he is to die, he should be among his Clanmates."

"But he's too sick to walk," Jayfeather pointed out.

"Juniperclaw and Sparrowtail can carry him," Tigerstar shot back.

Alderheart's paws pricked with fear. "But who will look after him once he's home?"

Tigerstar's eyes rounded with mock innocence. "Surely

you'll want to come with us to care for your patient?"

Alderheart hesitated. What if Puddleshine died? *I'd be alone, in a hostile camp.* His belly churned with fear.

"Alderheart stays here." Bramblestar lifted his muzzle defiantly.

"But Alderheart has already pointed out that Puddleshine will need treatment," Tigerstar meowed smoothly.

"Then Puddleshine will have to stay too," Bramblestar growled.

The leaders held each other's gaze. Neither moved, but Alderheart could see their muscles hardening beneath their pelts. Bramblestar's fur began to bristle. Were they going to fight? *I chose to use the deathberries.* Alderheart swallowed. *My choice mustn't cause a war.* "I'll go," he murmured softly. Foreboding hollowed his chest.

"It's good to see you have such faith in your treatment," Tigerstar meowed. "If Puddleshine recovers, all will be well."

Bramblestar's ears twitched. "And if he doesn't?"

Tigerstar met the ThunderClan leader's gaze. "In that case, an argument could be made that Alderheart poisoned him. Surely a cat who kills another cat should be punished?"

"Don't be rabbit-brained!" Jayfeather snapped. "Alderheart is trying to save him!"

"If that's true, then he'll be happy to travel to ShadowClan to see him through his recovery." Tigerstar stared challengingly at Jayfeather.

"You want to hold him hostage," Bramblestar growled.

"I don't intend to discuss this further." Tigerstar flicked

his tail. "We're taking Puddleshine home and Alderheart will join us. Unless, of course, you have no faith in your medicine cat. Perhaps you want to keep Alderheart here where you can protect him, because you know this treatment is a sham."

Anger surged beneath Alderheart's pelt. "It's not a sham. Feeding him deathberries is the best hope he has. I'll come with you and I'll prove it."

"Alderheart, are you sure?" Bramblestar stared at him, worry clouding his gaze.

"I'm sure." Alderheart lifted his chin. "It was my decision to use the deathberries. I stand by it. No other cat is going to suffer because of it."

Tigerstar moved to the entrance and called to his Clanmates. "Juniperclaw! Sparrowtail! Come here." He nodded to Bramblestar. "If Puddleshine recovers, I'll send Alderheart home, unharmed."

Alderheart's chest tightened. *And if he doesn't?*

CHAPTER 8

"Keep your muzzle down." Twigbranch tugged Flypaw closer to the earth, praying that the young cat would be quiet. A log hid them from a plump chaffinch, which was rummaging through leaf litter for bugs. "Birds are the hardest prey to catch," she whispered. Her whiskers brushed the damp moss. "They are sensitive to any movement, and they'll fly away at the slightest noise. You need to be fast."

"If they're so hard to catch, why don't we just hunt mice and squirrels instead?" Flypaw whispered back.

Twigbranch blinked at her. "Because warriors need to be able to catch birds as well."

"Why?"

Twigbranch swallowed back frustration. "Because we're *warriors!*" Flypaw was missing the point again. Twigbranch could hear the chaffinch pecking at the leaves. Her paws itched impatiently. She jerked her nose toward the rise. Flypaw lifted her head above the log to follow her gaze as she went on. "When you stalk a bird, you need to be patient. You must wait until it's distracted and only pounce when you're sure you're—"

Flypaw didn't wait to hear the rest. With a *mrrow* of excitement, she scrambled over the log and hurled herself at the chaffinch. Twigbranch stared after her as the chaffinch exploded upward in a flurry of feathers. Flypaw twisted in the air, reaching for the escaping bird, and fell back to earth with a thump.

"What did I tell you?" Anger scorched beneath Twigbranch's pelt as she leaped the log and marched to where Flypaw was shaking out her ruffled pelt.

Flypaw blinked at her. "You said I had to be fast."

"I said you had to be patient!" Why did Flypaw always grasp the wrong end of the worm?

"But you said I had to be fast too." She held up a paw where feathers snagged between her claws. "Look. I nearly got it."

"*Nearly* doesn't feed the Clan! If you'd waited until the chaffinch was focused more on the bugs and less on the forest, you'd have caught it." Twigbranch's pelt rippled along her spine. She was following her instinct and being tough on Flypaw, but the young tabby was still messing up. *Perhaps it's me.* Doubt pricked in Twigbranch's belly. *I did tell her to be quick.* She growled crossly to herself. *Why do I need to be so precise all the time?* Flypaw was staring at her like a crestfallen kit. Twigbranch's annoyance hardened. "Why can't you understand what's important and what's *not* important? Perhaps if you paid more attention, you wouldn't make so many mistakes."

"I like to follow my instinct," Flypaw mewed dejectedly.

"Instinct is not enough!" Twigbranch glared at her. "If it were, kittypets and loners would rule the forest. You need

skills that have been learned and honed by cats for genera-
tions. Instinct is where you begin. Training is what will make
you a warrior."

"But there's so much to learn." Flypaw's tail drooped.

"You only have to learn it *once!*" Was that too much to ask?
"These moons of training will teach you everything you need
to know to be a warrior. Once you've learned what you need
to, then you can fill your time however you like. But for now, I
expect you to put in some effort. I'm not going to be the first
mentor in moons to have her apprentice fail their assessment!"

Flypaw's eyes rounded. "Do you think I'll fail?"

"You will if you carry on like this!" Exasperated, Twigbranch turned her tail on her apprentice and headed back to
camp.

"Aren't we going to stalk another bird?" Flypaw called after
her.

"No." Twigbranch couldn't bear to watch Flypaw fail again
today. "We're going home. You can spend the rest of the afternoon practicing your hunting moves in the clearing. You can
think about what sort of warrior you want to become. It might
make you more attentive tomorrow."

Twigbranch stalked between the trees, her belly tight with
rage. She heard Flypaw trailing after her, keeping a few paw
steps behind. Twigbranch didn't look back. She could feel Flypaw's hurt in the silence that sat between them. Guilt began
to worm beneath her pelt as her anger faded. Flypaw wasn't a
bad cat. She just seemed to find it hard to focus on what was
important. *Perhaps I should be more patient. Perhaps toughness isn't*

enough. Her paws felt heavy with defeat as she reached camp and ducked through the entrance.

Flypaw slid past her, catching her eye. "I'm sorry I didn't catch the chaffinch," she mumbled. "I'll try harder tomorrow." She hurried away before Twigbranch could respond and scurried across the clearing to where her mother, Cinderheart, was patching the elders' den. Cinderheart dropped the honeysuckle vine she'd been weaving into the den wall and blinked in surprise as Flypaw pressed against her. Twigbranch's ears grew hot as Cinderheart looked across the clearing and caught her eye anxiously before wrapping her tail protectively over Flypaw's spine.

Twigbranch turned away. *It must feel good to have a mother to run to for comfort.* She pressed back bitterness. Lilyheart had fostered Twigbranch when she'd first been brought to ThunderClan as a kit. Lilyheart had been kind and gentle, but Twigbranch had always been aware that she wasn't one of Lilyheart's true kits. What would her life have been like if Pebbleshine had lived? With a real mother to raise her, she might have known where she belonged instead of switching between SkyClan and ThunderClan in search of a home that felt right. And with the tough but gentle love of her own mother, she might have learned how to be a better mentor.

"Do you think Tigerstar *will* kill him if Puddleshine dies?" Daisy's mew jerked Twigbranch from her thoughts. The queen was sitting beside Ivypool while the silver-and-white she-cat washed Bristlekit between the ears.

Bristlekit ducked from beneath her mother's tongue.

"Graystripe says that the old Tigerstar murdered Firestar. Perhaps *all* Tigerstars are murderers."

"Don't be silly." Ivypool tugged the kit closer and carried on washing her. "Tigerstar and Firestar died in the same battle, that's all," she mewed between licks. "And this Tigerstar is nothing like the old Tigerstar."

"How do you know? You never met the old Tigerstar." Bristlekit blinked up at her. "Graystripe knew him since he was a kit."

"Graystripe likes to make an adventure out of every story," Ivypool mewed dismissively, but she glanced uneasily at Daisy.

Who was Tigerstar going to kill? Twigbranch hurried toward the nursery and blinked at the queens as she reached them. "What are you talking about?"

Ivypool shooed Bristlekit away. "Go and play with Thriftkit and Flipkit." The kit scampered away, and Ivypool met Twigbranch's gaze solemnly. "Tigerstar brought a patrol to the camp while you were out. They took Puddleshine back to ShadowClan and made Alderheart go with them."

Twigbranch had known that Puddleshine would have to return to ShadowClan at some point. She supposed it made sense for Alderheart to go with him, to nurse him and provide a medicine cat for the rest of ShadowClan while Puddleshine was sick. "Didn't Alderheart want to go?"

Daisy's eyes were wide with worry. "Bramblestar said he volunteered, but you could see Alderheart was scared."

"But Bramblestar wouldn't let him go if he thought he was in danger," Ivypool reasoned.

"It sounds like he had no choice," Daisy mewed. "Mole-whisker said he overheard the whole conversation. Alderheart has been feeding Puddleshine deathberries."

Ivypool's tail twitched nervously. "Tigerstar found out and accused Alderheart of trying to poison Puddleshine, and now he's made him go to ShadowClan to prove the treatment will work."

Twigbranch glanced toward the camp entrance, her heart quickening as she thought of Alderheart alone in Shadow-Clan. "And you think Tigerstar will kill him if Puddleshine dies?"

"He said as much," Daisy breathed.

"He said Alderheart will be *punished*," Ivypool corrected. "But there's no way he can believe Alderheart would really try to hurt Puddleshine. He was just talking like a fox-heart to get Bramblestar to send Alderheart to his camp. They must need a medicine cat there, and Tigerstar's too much of a Shadow-Clan cat to ask politely. ShadowClan cats love to feel they're in charge. They think manners are for rabbits."

A plaintive mewl sounded from behind the nursery. Flipkit was complaining. "I want to be the hunter this time. I was the prey last time!"

Ivypool got to her paws.

"I'll go." Twigbranch flicked her tail to signal to the queen that she should stay where she was. "You relax for a bit. I'll show them some hunting moves."

Ivypool blinked at her gratefully. "Don't let them wear you out."

"I won't." Twigbranch padded around the nursery. The news of Alderheart had been alarming, but it hadn't pushed her worries about Flypaw away. Perhaps teaching the kits how to stalk would cheer her up. She might discover she wasn't such a bad mentor after all.

Moonlight seeped through the brambles and pooled around Twigbranch's nest. Her paws ached from playing with the kits. Her attempt to teach them hunting moves had quickly turned into more exciting games, and she'd spent the afternoon chasing them around the camp or giving them badger rides across the clearing. Perhaps all young cats were easily distracted. *Or perhaps I'm just no good at teaching.* She tried to push the thought away. If only Finleap were here to talk to. She glanced at his empty nest. He hadn't come back to camp with Snappaw after training. Snappaw had told her there was something Finleap wanted to do before he returned to camp. Twigbranch had waited for him as the rest of the Clan settled down at dusk to share tongues. She'd saved him a shrew from the fresh-kill pile, and had sat beside the mouse she'd taken for herself, staring hopefully at the entrance, expecting him to walk in at any moment. But he'd never appeared, and she'd eaten her mouse alone and returned the shrew to the pile. Now his nest was empty, and as the other warriors began to snore around her, she wondered where he could be. Worry pricked in her paws. Perhaps he was hurt and couldn't come home. Should she report his absence to Squirrelflight or Bramblestar? Her chest tightened. What if he was staying out on purpose? Perhaps he wanted to try night hunting. Or he might be on his own secret mission to spy on ShadowClan. Finleap was still quite new to ThunderClan. She didn't want to get him in trouble.

But if he has gone hunting or spying, why didn't he tell me? It seemed strange that Finleap would go off alone without asking Twigbranch to join him. They did everything together. *He'll be back soon,* she told herself. *StarClan will be watching over him.*

She pressed her nose between her paws and closed her eyes. Slowly, weariness quieted the anxiety in her belly and she slid into sleep.

Birdsong woke her at dawn.

"Finleap?" She breathed his name before she opened her eyes. Her dreams had been filled with him—some had brought him home safely; others had shown him alone in the forest, danger lurking behind every bush. Pale light glowed at the den entrance as she lifted her head. She turned to his nest, alarm spiking beneath her fur as she saw it was still empty. She sniffed it quickly. *Cold!* He hadn't come home. Panic gripped her heart. He'd never stayed out all night before.

Where is he?

CHAPTER 9

Violetshine stopped at the edge of the meadow and breathed the cold, fresh air. As the sun slid behind the dark moor, it sent long shadows across the grass. She could see the lake from up here, where the land lifted toward the mountains and the forests parted and left a space for Twolegs to build their pelt dens during greenleaf. There were no dens here yet, but the scent of Twolegs was fresh, and she guessed they still came even without dens, although she couldn't imagine why. Did they patrol their borders like the Clans, or was there prey here they hoped to find? She could feel the chill of the coming night. Her paws were damp with dew. Why had Tree arranged the meeting so far from camp?

The yellow tom paced the meadow while Leafstar kept to the shelter of the trees. The SkyClan leader's eyes sparked, half-anxious, half-defiant. Was she nervous about meeting Tigerstar, or about what this meeting might lead to?

"Couldn't we have met closer to camp?" Leafstar asked testily.

Tree stopped and looked at her. "This is neutral territory. Neither ShadowClan nor SkyClan has claims here."

"We could have met on the lakeshore," Leafstar grumbled as she fluffed out her fur against the cold.

Violetshine shook dew from her pelt. "I guess it's private here." She knew how hard Tree had worked, racing from one camp to another, to get the leaders of SkyClan and Shadow-Clan to meet. "There's no chance of cats from other Clans butting in."

Leafstar snorted. "Why would they? The other Clans have made it clear they want nothing to do with this dispute. They've left us to deal with ShadowClan alone."

"At least they're avoiding taking sides." Tree gazed into the forest, clearly searching for signs of Tigerstar's patrol. Violet-shine wondered how many warriors the ShadowClan leader would bring. She was proud that Leafstar had chosen her to join this patrol with Bellaleaf, Sandynose, Harrybrook, and Sagenose. The older warriors clustered together a little far-ther up the hill, as though unsure what to do with themselves. They'd been trained to fight for their Clan, not to negotiate for it. Leafstar looked at them impatiently. "Can you spread out a little? You look like a bunch of apprentices at their first Gathering."

Bellaleaf and Sandynose swapped glances before fanning out self-consciously beside Harrybrook and Sagenose.

"Can you see him?" Leafstar asked Tree.

"No sign yet." Tree twitched his tail.

"He's late." Leafstar sat down and stared stiffly across the meadow. "I don't know what we can discuss anyway. I'm not giving up SkyClan's land. It's *our* right to hunt on it."

"Perhaps, if we can work out what each Clan needs, we can come to a compromise," Tree meowed gently.

"I'm not letting ShadowClan warriors cross our border whenever they feel like it." Leafstar glared at him.

"If I can make ShadowClan understand that this could be the first step toward another Great Battle, Tigerstar might back down," Tree reasoned. "After all, SkyClan was led back here by StarClan. Surely even Tigerstar wouldn't go against their will."

A sharp wind gusting from the hill above reminded Violetshine that newleaf had only claimed the lowest parts of the valley. She pressed back a shiver, not wanting to appear nervous.

Harrybrook pricked his ears. Bellaleaf's gaze flicked toward the shadowy forest.

A bramble shivered between the trees, and Leafstar turned expectantly.

Tigerstar? Violetshine strained to see as a dark tom slid out from the forest.

"Juniperclaw!" Leafstar looked puzzled. Her gaze slid from the ShadowClan deputy to the empty space behind him. "Where's Tigerstar?"

Juniperclaw didn't answer. Instead he eyed Harrybrook, Bellaleaf, Sagenose, and Sandynose. "Is this an ambush?" he growled.

Tree hurried forward. "Of course not."

Juniperclaw curled his lip. "But it is a show of strength." He glanced accusingly at Leafstar. "Were you hoping to intimidate ShadowClan into agreeing to your demands?"

"We're not the ones making demands," Leafstar shot back.

Tree padded between them. "Where is Tigerstar?" he asked politely.

"Tigerstar had other duties to attend to."

Leafstar bristled. "More important than this?"

"I'm his deputy." Juniperclaw lifted his muzzle. "I speak for Tigerstar in Clan matters."

"I didn't come here to speak to a deputy!" Leafstar glared at him scornfully.

"Aren't I important enough for you?" Juniperclaw growled.

Violetshine shifted her paws anxiously. Would the meeting end before it had even begun? She looked hopefully at Tree.

The yellow tom was already circling Leafstar and Juniperclaw, his tail high and his pelt smooth. "Every cat is important," he meowed evenly. "While we are all here, it would be a waste not to discuss the matter that is troubling you both."

Juniperclaw narrowed his eyes and looked at Leafstar. Leafstar flexed her claws.

"There's no harm in talking," Tree pressed.

"What is there to say?" Leafstar snapped. "Except to remind ShadowClan that trespassing on another Clan's land is against the warrior code." She glared at Juniperclaw. "You can report that to Tigerstar, although he should know it already. But perhaps he forgot the rules while he was away from his Clan."

Tree's eyes widened. "I'm sure he still knows the warrior—"

Juniperclaw cut him off, glowering back at Leafstar. "I knew you'd be unreasonable!"

"Is it unreasonable to expect to keep land that was given to us fairly?"

"*Fairly?*" Juniperclaw's ears twitched. "ShadowClan had been weakened by invaders and by treachery. Some might say you took advantage of the situation to strengthen your Clan at the cost of ours."

"SkyClan didn't intend—" Tree tried to object.

Leafstar ignored him. "It was Tigerstar's idea to offer us the land," she spat at Juniperclaw. "He wasn't even your leader then, but he fought to convince his Clanmates that it was the right thing to do. And now he decides he wants it back?"

"ShadowClan has more cats now." Juniperclaw stood his ground. "We need more land."

"SkyClan has more cats too!"

Tree opened his mouth but, this time, no words came out. *He doesn't know what to do!* Violetshine held her breath, willing Tree to say anything that might defuse the growing anger. The yellow tom caught her eye. Alarm showed in his gaze. He was clearly taken aback by Leafstar's and Juniperclaw's vehemence. He held Violetshine's gaze for a moment, then seemed to pull himself together. Puffing out his chest, he turned back to Leafstar and Juniperclaw. "It's clear that both Clans are larger than they used to be, and both Clans need land. The pine forest might be big enough to provide for every cat. Why not mark new boundaries?"

Leafstar eyed Juniperclaw warily, as though waiting for his reaction before she gave hers.

"New boundaries?" Juniperclaw swished his tail. "Shadow-Clan has already conceded more than any Clan. It has given up land that belonged to it for moons before we even knew there was a SkyClan. Why should we alone make sacrifices to keep SkyClan beside the lake?"

"Why should we be driven from our new home?" As Leafstar hissed at the ShadowClan deputy, an excited yelp sounded at the top of the meadow.

A dog raced over the crest of the hill. Violetshine's pelt bushed as she saw three Twoleg kits racing after it, their eyes as bright as the dog's.

Sagenose flattened his ears. "We need to get out of here before it picks up our scent." Bellaleaf and Sandynose had already turned to face the dog as it bounded down the hill. Their hackles lifted as they took up defensive stances.

Leafstar stared at Juniperclaw through narrowed eyes for a moment longer, then lashed her tail. "Let's get back to camp." She beckoned her Clanmates with a nod and stalked past Juniperclaw. "We're wasting our time here."

Violetshine hurried after her. She was relieved to slip into the shadows of the forest. Behind her the dog's bark rang over the field. Sagenose, Bellaleaf, and Sandynose quickened their pace as Leafstar pushed her way past brambles and disappeared into the undergrowth. As she followed, Violetshine saw Juniperclaw from the corner of her eye. The black tom was moving like a shadow downhill, weaving between the pines as he followed his own route. As she lost sight of him, she felt Tree's pelt brush her flank.

He padded at her side, his gaze heavy. "I can't believe that went so badly."

"It was always going to be hard." Violetshine's heart pricked with pity for him.

"But I hardly got a word in." Tree frowned. "I wanted them to begin to understand each other's point of view, but they've come away more divided than ever."

"I think they both came to the meeting determined to be angrier than the other one," Violetshine soothed. "There was nothing you could do."

"I should have made them listen to me."

"How could you when both sides are so stubborn?" Violetshine moved closer to the yellow tom, hoping that the warmth of her flank against his would give him comfort, but he seemed lost in his own thoughts.

Voices sounded over the rise ahead. Leafstar and the other warriors had stopped and were talking heatedly. Violetshine hurried up the slope to join them.

"The time for talking is over." Leafstar paced in front of Bellaleaf and Sandynose, while Harrybrook and Sagenose watched. The warriors' gazes were hard with indignation.

"Imagine sending his deputy to such an important meeting!" Sagenose growled.

Harrybrook's hackles lifted. "He had no intention of trying to settle the dispute."

Leafstar flexed her claws. "There'll be no more talking. I want border patrols doubled, and if any ShadowClan cat crosses the border, we retaliate immediately."

Tree stopped beside Violetshine and stared at the warriors. "Give me more time. I'm sure we can settle this without claws," he meowed.

Leafstar met his gaze fiercely. "We don't have time. Every ShadowClan patrol that crosses our border makes us look weaker."

Tree's ears flicked with frustration. "It was your idea to make me mediator for the Clans," he reminded her sharply. "Why give me the role if you won't let me mediate?"

"I overestimated the other Clans," Leafstar growled. "They're so used to fighting, they've forgotten how to talk. Tigerstar clearly wants a battle. When we first came to the lake, I thought that the other Clans just gossiped about Shadow-Clan out of spite. . . . But I see now that ShadowClan cats are fox-hearts. I can see why Rowanclaw gave up on them. And why some of their warriors chose to follow Darktail. They are natural troublemakers. Well, if they want war, they'll get one."

"Fighting isn't the answer," Tree insisted.

Leafstar shook her head. "Can't you see that it is? Fighting is the way things are done around here, Tree. It's not just ShadowClan—*none* of the lake Clans think like us. They train their warriors to fight, not to talk. If we want to keep our territory, we have to be like them. If we don't fight for what we believe in, the other Clans won't ever respect us, and it won't just be ShadowClan pushing us around, don't you see?"

Violetshine felt Tree slump with disappointment beside her. "What about the plan Tigerstar suggested at the Gathering?"

she mewed quickly. "Where each Clan gives up a smaller part of their territory, instead of just ShadowClan." She gazed hopefully at Leafstar.

Leafstar grunted. "Didn't you notice how the other Clans responded to that idea? They couldn't get off the island quickly enough."

Sandynose blinked sympathetically at Violetshine. "We just have to accept that the other Clans don't want to help us."

Bellaleaf sat down heavily. "We're on our own, just as we've always been."

Tree flicked his tail angrily. "Then why am I wasting my time here?" Ears twitching, the yellow tom stalked away.

Violetshine could see how hurt he was. His pelt rippled spikily over his shoulders as he slumped down beside the roots of a pine with his back to the SkyClan cats. *Is he wondering whether he made a mistake? Perhaps he's wishing he'd never stayed with us.* The thought sent alarm prickling through Violetshine's pelt. Tree had given up his solitary life to offer help that wasn't wanted. Tree wasn't a proud cat, but the Clans' rejection of his skills must sting even him. Would he decide to return to his life as a loner?

Leafstar beckoned to Violetshine with a flick of her tail. "Leave him." The SkyClan leader must have noticed her watching the yellow tom. "He looks like he needs space. He'll realize soon enough that we have no other choice."

Violetshine blinked at the SkyClan leader, her heart aching for Tree. He wouldn't give up on his beliefs so easily. And yet, even though she felt sorry for Tree, she understood Leafstar's point of view. Tigerstar had offered nothing but insults to SkyClan, and the other Clans hadn't defended them. It looked like SkyClan was as isolated here as it had been at the gorge, and that if they wanted to keep their territory beside the lake, they'd have to fight for it.

"Come on." Leafstar headed downhill. "Let's go home."

Violetshine followed Harrybrook and Bellaleaf into camp. The sun had set, and twilight darkened the shadows beneath the camp walls. Their Clanmates were sharing tongues around the clearing. Suddenly she smelled the faint scent of ThunderClan. She pricked her ears, thinking instantly of Twigbranch. Had her sister found an excuse to visit?

Leafstar clearly caught the scent too. As Sagenose and Sandynose headed toward the fresh-kill pile, the SkyClan leader stopped and looked around the camp, her nose twitching.

Hawkwing padded from the fresh-kill pile to meet her. "How did it go?" His voice was low. Leafstar hadn't told the whole Clan about the meeting.

Leafstar flicked her tail. "Tigerstar didn't come."

"He sent Juniperclaw." Bellaleaf stopped beside the leader.

Harrybrook swished his tail. "He wasn't interested in talking. He just wanted to repeat what Tigerstar had said at the Gathering."

Hawkwing frowned. "Tigerstar is determined to make our lives difficult."

"It's disrespectful! Especially after the kindness we've

shown to ShadowClan. We let them live with us, for Star-Clan's sake!" Irritation rippled through Leafstar's pelt. Her nose twitched again and she glanced toward the medicine den. "Is a ThunderClan cat here?"

Violetshine followed her gaze eagerly. The Thunder-Clan scent was definitely stronger there. Her heart began to quicken hopefully, but as she tasted the air she realized that the scent didn't smell like Twigbranch.

"Finleap is back," Hawkwing told her.

Violetshine widened her eyes. "Back?" Had he left ThunderClan for good?

"He's come to visit Reedclaw," Hawkwing explained. "He'd heard she was sick."

As he spoke, the medicine den trembled and Finleap squeezed out. His eyes brightened as he saw Violetshine. "Hi!"

Leafstar glowered at the young tom as he trotted to meet the patrol. "How's Reedclaw?" she asked curtly.

Finleap seemed taken aback by her sharp tone. He stopped, his ears twitching. "She's almost well again," he told her.

"Did Bramblestar say you could come?" Leafstar's fur bristled.

He dropped his gaze, "He doesn't know I'm here."

"You slipped away without telling your leader *and* crossed the border into another Clan's territory?" Leafstar sounded angry.

Violetshine moved closer to Finleap. "He's only come to visit his kin."

"He left his kin when he left SkyClan," Leafstar snapped.

As Harrybrook and Bellaleaf exchanged glances, indignation surged in Violetshine's chest. "He can't stop caring about them just because he lives somewhere else now!" Did Leafstar think she and Hawkwing had stopped caring about Twigbranch? She blinked at Hawkwing, hoping he'd support her.

Hawkwing retuned her gaze sympathetically. "Of course he stills cares for them. But he lives in a different Clan now. He must respect his new leader and our borders."

Hurt sharpened Finleap's gaze. "I do respect Bramblestar." He blinked at Leafstar. "And I'll always respect you. But I was worried about Reedclaw. I've never been away while she was ill before."

Leafstar seemed unmoved by his plea. "Being worried is no excuse for breaking the warrior code."

Finleap's shoulders sagged. "I'll go home, then."

"Not now, you won't," Leafstar meowed firmly. "You can wait until morning, when a patrol will escort you back to ThunderClan and explain what happened."

Violetshine's belly tightened. Why did Leafstar have to make such a fuss? If a patrol escorted him home and reported him to Bramblestar, Finleap would be in trouble with his new Clanmates. "I can take him across the border now," she offered quietly. "He can slip back without anyone knowing."

Leafstar glared at her. "Do you want to deceive ThunderClan too? What if you're caught by a patrol? Don't you think we have enough trouble with ShadowClan without antagonizing ThunderClan too?" She whisked her tail decisively. "Finleap will stay here tonight. You can both sleep in the apprentices' den. I expect you to keep an eye on him, Violetshine. If he sneaks away in the night, you will be held responsible."

Finleap glanced apologetically at Violetshine. He clearly didn't want to make trouble for her. "I'm sorry," he whispered.

But Violetshine wasn't ready to give up. "His new Clanmates will be worried about him if he stays out all night."

"He should have thought of that before he came here!" Leafstar turned away, the fur lifting along her spine. Growling, she stalked toward the fresh-kill pile.

Bellaleaf blinked kindly at Finleap and followed the SkyClan leader.

"*I'm* pleased to see you," Harrybrook whispered before he padded away.

Hawkwing shook his head. "I'm afraid you caught Leafstar at a bad time," he told Finleap. "But she's right. You can't just visit anytime you please. Next time, tell Bramblestar your concerns, and, with any luck, he'll send you with a patrol to ask permission to come to our camp."

Finleap dipped his head. "Okay," he mumbled.

As Hawkwing headed away, Violetshine nudged Finleap's shoulder with her own. "At least we get to share a den," she mewed. "It'll be like old times. And you can tell me your gossip." She blinked at Finleap, hoping she'd cheered him up. But worry darkened his gaze.

"Twigbranch won't know where I am."

"She'll find out tomorrow." Were Finleap and her sister mates now? Gently, she guided him across the clearing. "Are you hungry? There's prey left on the fresh-kill pile."

Finleap shook his head. "No, thanks," he murmured.

Gravelpaw and Fringepaw were practicing battle moves beside the apprentices' den. Palepaw and Pigeonpaw were sharing a mouse beside them, while Sunnypaw watched Fringepaw launch a play attack on Gravelpaw.

"Aim for his forepaws, not his hind paws!" Sunnypaw mewed as Gravelpaw easily knocked Fringepaw away.

Blossomheart was sharing a shrew with Mintfur beside the stream. She called out to the apprentices, "You should rest after a meal, not fight! You'll give yourselves bellyaches."

"Warriors get bellyaches, not apprentices!" Pigeonpaw called back.

"Don't say I didn't warn you." Blossomheart's whiskers twitched as she returned to the shrew.

Palepaw looked up as Finleap and Violetshine passed. "Are you going back to ThunderClan tonight?" she asked Finleap.

Violetshine answered for him. "He'll go home in the morning."

"What's it like being a ThunderClan warrior?" Gravelpaw paused mid-crouch and blinked at Finleap.

"It's okay," Finleap told him. "I guess it's the same as being a SkyClan warrior."

Gravelpaw tipped his head thoughtfully. "What if we have a battle with ThunderClan?" he asked. "Will we be allowed to fight you?"

Violetshine flicked her tail sharply. "We won't have a battle with ThunderClan. Not now that we've got Tree to keep the peace." She caught her breath. *Do I still believe that?* Even if Tree stayed with the Clans, she was no longer sure he could help keep the peace. She pictured him alone in the forest and wondered if he was on his way back to camp yet. She felt guilty for leaving him. Perhaps she should have stayed. What if he never came back? Would anyone care except her?

Worry clawed at her heart, but she couldn't leave camp now. She had to watch Finleap. Before the apprentices could ask any more difficult questions, Violetshine nudged Finleap into the bramble den. "We're sleeping here tonight," she told the apprentices as she ducked in after him. "Don't keep us awake by chattering like starlings."

Finleap followed her in and surveyed the nests circled around the central stem. "Where shall I sleep?"

Violetshine sniffed the bedding until she found two nests that smelled stale. "These haven't been slept in for a while." She realized with a pang that one of them was Twigbranch's old nest. Suddenly she missed her sister with a longing she thought had faded. "Is Twigbranch happy in ThunderClan?" she asked as she climbed into it.

"Yes." Finleap hopped into the nest beside her and sat down. "She seems at home there."

"Are you?"

"I'm still getting used to it," Finleap mewed. "But I like being near Twigbranch." He paused, his gaze unreadable as night swallowed the den. "Although I think I was wrong to assume she wanted the same things as me."

"What do you mean?" Violetshine blinked at him. "Aren't you close anymore?"

"We're still close." There was sadness in Finleap's mew.

Violetshine was puzzled. "I thought you'd be mates by now."

"So did I." Finleap shifted in his nest. Violetshine could hardly see him in the darkness. "Twigbranch is just focused on her apprentice. She doesn't want a mate." Bracken crunched as he settled down. "I'm probably being selfish. Maybe I should be focusing on my apprentice too."

"Twigbranch was always serious about being a good warrior." Violetshine kept her mew bright. "I'm sure she loves you."

"Yeah."

As her eyes adjusted to the growing darkness, she could see the silhouette of his ears. "Was Reedclaw glad to see you?"

"Yes." He sounded cheerier. "She's nearly well enough to leave the medicine den."

"I didn't think Leafstar would be so upset about you visiting."

"Harrybrook and Bellaleaf seemed ruffled too, but I don't think it was about me coming back. What did Hawkwing mean when he said I'd caught Leafstar at a bad time?"

Worry crept along Violetshine's spine as she remembered how badly the meeting had gone. They were closer than ever to war with ShadowClan. And Tree had been humiliated. What if he left? The thought made her feel sick.

"Violetshine?" Finleap's mew jerked her from her thoughts. "Is something wrong in SkyClan?"

"No," she answered quickly. It felt disloyal to reveal

SkyClan's problems to a ThunderClan warrior, even Finleap. "Everything is fine." As she blinked into the darkness, her paws pricked anxiously.

She hoped she was telling the truth.

CHAPTER 10

Alderheart's pelt prickled. He still didn't feel all that comfortable in ShadowClan's camp. Even here, alone in the medicine den with Puddleshine, he couldn't shake the feeling he was being watched. He pressed a small morsel of deathberry to Puddleshine's lips. When the unconscious tom didn't stir, he gently pried his teeth open and slipped the dark flesh through the gap. Puddleshine didn't even twitch. His head felt heavy, like dead weight against Alderheart's paws as he laid it back on the edge of his nest.

The sun had set and evening was fast turning to night. Darkness was pressing at the edges of the medicine den. Puddleshine hadn't regained consciousness since Juniperclaw and Sparrowtail had carried him back to the ShadowClan camp that morning. His breathing was shallower, and his fur was damp. Heat throbbed from his pelt and flooded Alderheart with fear. Would Puddleshine make it through the night? What would Tigerstar do if the ShadowClan medicine cat died?

Alderheart blinked the thoughts away. The deathberries *had* to work. The dream had promised that they would. Fire had made way for fresh growth. StarClan wouldn't mislead him, would they? He pushed the thought away. He mustn't doubt StarClan. They'd always been with him, he was sure, even before they'd sent him his very first vision, the one that had led him in search of SkyClan.

And yet worry sat like a stone in his belly as he buried the seeds he'd stripped from the berry. When he was sure they were safely disposed of, he scraped leaves from a small patch of earth he'd clawed up at the other side of the den. He wiped his paws in the crumbly dirt until they were clean and then carefully swept the leaves back to cover the poisoned patch. Finally he wrapped the berries back in their dock leaf and tucked them beneath Puddleshine's nest.

He'd carried the berries to the ShadowClan camp, hidden in a bundle of tansy and marigold. Tigerstar hadn't forbidden Alderheart from continuing with his treatment, but he hadn't given permission either. Alderheart didn't dare ask. He couldn't risk Tigerstar saying no. The deathberries were his only hope. And yet they still showed no sign of working. He could only wait and pray to StarClan.

Frustration itched beneath his pelt. He felt powerless, and Tigerstar's threats had made it worse. Didn't he realize that any cat's death was punishment enough for a medicine cat? Warriors were so rabbit-brained. They missed what was truly important in their scrabble for power and territory. Outside, he could hear Cloverfoot and Scorchfur murmuring to each other in hushed voices as they guarded the entrance. Tigerstar had ordered them not to leave their posts and promised to keep the medicine den guarded day and night. *As if I might run away from a sick cat who needs treatment!*

Growling to himself, Alderheart padded to a crevice in the bramble wall of the den where Puddleshine kept his herb store. He might as well make himself useful and sort through Puddleshine's herbs. Reaching in, he scooped out the dried bundles and separated the leaves, making piles for each herb. Some crumbled in his paws; others were stiff and dry. It had clearly been a while since Puddleshine last collected fresh stores, before he got his infection. Carefully, Alderheart began to strip out the driest herbs—herbs that could no longer hold healing powers—and lay them to one side.

"What are you doing?" Cloverfoot thrust her head into the den. Her nose twitched. "Do you need those?" Her eyes sparked with indignation as she saw the leaves laid out in front of Alderheart.

He met her gaze levelly. "I'm clearing out the useless herbs."

"How do I know you're not destroying Puddleshine's stocks?" she snapped.

"Why would I do that?" Alderheart glared at her. "I'm a medicine cat, not a warrior. I don't want to harm any cat."

Cloverfoot's gaze flicked toward Puddleshine. "What about him? You fed him deathberries."

"To cure him." Alderheart snorted. "Do you seriously think I'd try to kill your medicine cat?"

She narrowed her eyes. "If we lose him, the whole of ShadowClan will suffer."

"That's why I'm trying to *save* him," Alderheart hissed.

"*And* because he's a friend. But you're not a medicine cat. You wouldn't understand the bond we share."

She eyed him wordlessly for a moment, then slid into the den. "Perhaps I don't understand," she meowed, "but I'm going to watch you sort those herbs, just to make sure you don't ruin them."

Scorchfur peered through the entrance. "Is everything okay in there?"

"It's fine," Cloverfoot told him. "I'm just watching Alderheart sort herbs."

Alderheart forced his fur to stay flat as Scorchfur withdrew and Cloverfoot sat down at the edge of the den and stared at him. Slowly he carried on picking out useless herbs. "You need to gather more thyme," he told Cloverfoot without looking up. "These leaves are so dry, there can't be much strength left in them."

"How do I know what thyme looks like?" Cloverfoot mewed testily.

"It looks like this." He pushed a stalk toward her. "Sniff it. The smell is unmistakable." He returned to the other leaves. "Fresh watermint will be sprouting soon. You should gather some of that too. And borage, and nettles . . ." He met her gaze. "You do know what nettles look like, I assume?"

"Of course I know," she snapped. "But I'm a warrior! I don't gather herbs."

"Once Puddleshine's fever has broken, you can escort me into the forest and I can gather some for you." Alderheart unwrapped a dock leaf and sniffed the stale poppy seeds inside. "Puddleshine will be weak for some time, even when the sickness eases."

As he spoke, the den entrance rustled. Stonewing limped into the shadowy den. "Scorchfur said it would be all right to come in." His gaze slid nervously toward Puddleshine. "Is he okay?"

"Does he look okay?" Alderheart snapped.

Stonewing blinked at him uneasily. He lifted up a forepaw. "I've got a thorn in my pad."

Cloverfoot glowered at the white tom. "Can't you get it out yourself?"

"It's in deep." Stonewing shuddered.

Alderheart padded forward. He sniffed the wound. The thorn was firmly embedded in Stonewing's pad. "It will need herbs to stop it getting infected." He touched the hard root of the thorn with his tongue, tasting the blood that welled around it. "I can pull it out," he told Stonewing, "but it will hurt."

Stonewing's whiskers trembled.

"Once it's out, it will feel a lot better." Alderheart caught Cloverfoot's eye. She looked suspicious. "I think I can get it out, if you'll let me try?"

Cloverfoot hesitated.

"I don't want to go lame," Stonewing told her. "Anyway, it's my paw. I say let him try."

Cloverfoot shrugged. "Okay," she agreed. "I just hope you

don't end up like Puddleshine."

Alderheart ignored her and felt gingerly for the thorn with his teeth. He gripped it and tugged, gently at first and then, when he felt it give, more sharply. It slid out of Stonewing's pad with a rush of blood.

Alderheart dropped the thorn on the ground. "Give your paw a good wash while I find some marigold," he told the white tom.

Stonewing was already lapping fiercely at his pad, his pelt smoothing as pain gave way to relief.

Alderheart lapped up a few crumbling leaves of marigold and chewed them; then he padded back to Stonewing and licked the poultice into the wound. "Leave the marigold there for a day; then keep the wound clean."

Stonewing nodded, gratitude brimming in his dark blue gaze.

Cloverfoot shifted at the edge of the den. "I guess you might as well handle Puddleshine's duties while you're here," she grunted as Stonewing limped out.

Alderheart didn't respond, moving instead to check on Puddleshine. The other medicine cat still hadn't stirred. Alderheart washed the damp fur around his neck. *Please get better.* Surely the deathberries had to work soon. He mustn't lose Puddleshine. Even without Tigerstar's threat, such a loss was too dreadful to think about. He'd told Cloverfoot the truth: The ShadowClan medicine cat was his friend. But how long could Puddleshine last with this fever?

"Cloverfoot?" Scorchfur's mew sounded at the entrance.

"Berryheart's outside with Hollowkit. She says Hollowkit has a cough. Shall I let them in?"

Cloverfoot blinked at Alderheart. "Is it safe in here for a kit?"

Alderheart bristled. "Do you think I'd harm a *kit*?"

Cloverfoot nodded toward Puddleshine. "I mean, he's not contagious, is he?"

"Of course not." Alderheart sniffed. "They can come in."

Cloverfoot shifted to one side as Berryheart nudged Hollowkit into the den.

The black-and-white queen blinked hopefully at Alderheart as Hollowkit coughed beside her. "He's been sick for a few days," she meowed.

The black kit's cough sounded dry. "Is your throat sore?" Alderheart asked him gently.

"Only when I swallow." Hollowkit shifted closer to his mother and glanced at Puddleshine. "Is he going to die? Yarrowleaf says you tried to poison him."

Alderheart blinked at the kit. "A medicine cat would never harm any cat." He turned and grabbed a tansy stem between his teeth and dropped it at Berryheart's paws. "This should ease it," he told her. "Get him to chew a mouthful before he goes to sleep and another when he wakes." He sniffed the kit's head. There was no heat there. "Has he had any fever?"

"No." Berryheart pulled the tansy closer. "Just the cough."

"Good." Alderheart looked into Hollowkit's eyes. They were clear. "It's just a cough left over from leaf-bare. It'll be gone in a day or two. Keep him away from the other kits, but if they haven't caught it by now, they'll probably be fine."

"Spirekit and Sunkit are already sleeping with Yarrowleaf's kits," Berryheart told him.

Alderheart blinked approvingly.

Berryheart dipped her head. "Thanks for the tansy." She picked up the stem and led Hollowkit from the den. As she passed Cloverfoot, Alderheart saw the two cats exchange glances. Then Cloverfoot's gaze flicked back to him. For the first time he saw respect there.

He nodded at her and returned to his herb pile.

"Alderheart!"

An alarmed yowl jerked him from sleep. He opened his eyes into darkness. It took a moment for him to remember where he was. The sour smell of Puddleshine told him that he was in the ShadowClan medicine den. He hadn't meant to fall asleep! He glanced quickly at Puddleshine, relieved to see that the tom was still breathing, albeit shallowly. He'd planned to watch him through the night.

Cloverfoot had dropped off ages ago. She lurched awake now, blinking. "What is it?"

As she scrambled to her paws, Yarrowleaf burst through the entrance. "Bring Alderheart!" The ginger she-cat's eyes were wide with concern.

Scorchfur stumbled after her, blinking sleep from his eyes. "What's happened?"

"It's Shadowkit . . ." She stared desperately at Alderheart.

"I'm coming." He raced past her into the cleari. striped the camp.

Tigerstar was outside the nursery, his pelt bristl. fear. "He's in here."

Alderheart pelted past him and burst into the brai. den. Moonlight filtered through the roof, enough for him tell Dovewing's nest from the others. The pale gray she-cat crouched there, staring with horror at a small shape beneath her. Pouncekit and Lightkit cowered with the other kits at the side of the den. As Alderheart leaned over the edge of Dove-wing's nest, Berryheart hustled them outside.

Shadowkit was twitching at the bottom of the nest, his head flicking back and forth as spasms gripped his body.

"How long has he been like this?" Alderheart asked Dove-wing.

"Not long. I sent Yarrowleaf to fetch you as soon as it started."

"We have to hold him still until it passes." He reached quickly into the nest and gripped the kit's legs. "Cradle his head firmly to stop it from moving," he told Dovewing.

Tigerstar pressed beside him. The dark tabby's fur spiked against Alderheart's pelt, and he could feel the ShadowClan leader trembling.

"Hold his shoulders," he told Tigerstar.

As Tigerstar reached into the nest, Alderheart glimpsed Cloverfoot peering into the nursery. Relief swamped him. "Do you remember the thyme I showed you?" he called to her.

es wide.

ordered. "Bring the freshest stalks." He

Dovewing. "Has he been ill? Any fever? A

ould explain such a fit?

shook her head.

ad fits before," Tigerstar growled.

owkit twitched violently beneath Alderheart's paws.

Ve've seen this before." Dovewing didn't take her eyes

m her kit. "When we were on our way back to the lake, he

would have visions—they came with seizures like this. We had

thought they were getting better." Her voice dropped to an

anxious murmur. "But, if anything, they're getting worse . . ."

Beneath the steadying paws, Shadowkit's spasms eased. Alderheart thrust his muzzle close, relieved to feel the kit's breath on his nose. Heat pulsed from his thin pelt. "When he stops twitching, wash him to cool him down." Alderheart felt Shadowkit's legs grow still. He sat back on his haunches. "I don't know how to prevent the seizures, but thyme will ease his shock."

The entrance trembled as Cloverfoot slid through. She dropped two stalks of thyme beside Alderheart. Alderheart bent to nip leaves from the stems so he could chew them into a pulp that Shadowkit could swallow.

"Wait." Tigerstar nudged him away and sniffed the leaves.

Dovewing stared at Tigerstar in disbelief. "Don't you trust him?"

Cloverfoot edged forward. "You can trust him," she mewed softly. "He treated Stonewing and Hollowkit earlier. He seemed to know what he was doing. I watched him. He only wants to help."

Tigerstar narrowed his eyes suspiciously.

Alderheart ignored him. "The thyme will soothe him," he told Dovewing. "When he comes around, chew up a few leaves—"

"And make him swallow them," Dovewing murmured. "I remember Puddleshine giving him thyme before."

Alderheart gave a nod. "If he has fits in the future, just hold him so he's safe and cool him down as much as you can."

With a final twitch, Shadowkit fell limp at the bottom of the nest like a leaf coming to rest after a storm. Dovewing bent to lick him as Tigerstar shook out his pelt. The Shadow-Clan leader smoothed his ruffled fur with a few laps, but Alderheart could still smell the brown tabby's fear-scent. His pelt prickled with frustration. *Until I know what caused the kit's convulsions, I can only treat the symptoms.*

A small mew sounded in the nest. "Dovewing?" Shadowkit slowly opened his eyes and gazed at his mother.

She buried her nose in the soft fur behind his ear. "Are you okay?" she asked, a break in her mew. "You scared us."

"I'll be all right." Shadowkit rolled onto his paws and pushed himself up. Weakly he blinked at Tigerstar. "I had another vision."

Dovewing reached for the thyme and began chewing the leaves. "Eat this." She held her muzzle close to Shadowkit's.

He ducked away from her. "Not until I've told you about my vision."

Dovewing and Tigerstar exchanged anxious glances.

"Go and check on the kits," Tigerstar told Cloverfoot. He flicked his tail, and she dipped her head and left. Alderheart was burning with curiosity. Was StarClan sending a message through Shadowkit? Tigerstar looked at him. "You'd better leave too."

Alderheart dug his claws into the needle-strewn floor. "I'm a medicine cat. I should hear this."

Tigerstar growled. "You're a *ThunderClan* medicine—"

Shadowkit cut him off. "Can he stay? He's a medicine cat— he might know what it means."

Dovewing nodded. "He should stay," she agreed.

Tigerstar shifted his paws. "Okay." His dark gaze fixed on Shadowkit. "What did you see?"

"It was raining on RiverClan land." The kit's mew was weak. Dovewing pressed against him, supporting him with her flank as he went on. "I was in the marshes there, and the rain kept getting heavier and heavier. The sky was black with clouds, and I could barely see the trees for the rain. It got worse until I could feel water pressing against my fur, in my ears, in my nose." The kit shivered, fear showing in his eyes. "It was in my mouth. I couldn't breathe and then" —as he paused again, Dovewing wrapped her tail around him with a sob—"everything went black."

Dread ran like icy water along Alderheart's spine. He stared at the kit, his mouth dry.

"What does it mean?" Shadowkit blinked at him.

"I'm not sure." Alderheart shifted his paws uneasily. "It

might just be a nightmare brought on by the fit."

"Of course," Dovewing mewed brightly. She settled into her nest and pulled Shadowkit protectively against her belly. "It was just a dumb nightmare."

"It didn't feel like a nightmare," Shadowkit whimpered.

"Eat the thyme," Alderheart told him. "And rest with Dovewing. You'll feel better in the morning."

"My head hurts." Shadowkit's eyes were dark.

"I'll fetch some poppy seeds. They'll ease the pain." Alderheart staggered out of the den, his mind swimming and his legs quivering, as if they could barely hold him up. He could think of only one meaning for Shadowkit's vision, and it filled him with dread.

The kit was going to die.

"Was it just a nightmare?" Tigerstar's mew startled him. The ShadowClan leader had followed him out and was staring at him in the moonlight.

Alderheart tensed. "I hope so."

Tigerstar narrowed his eyes. "But you think it meant something else."

Alderheart dropped his gaze. *How do you tell a father that his kit has seen his own death?* "I-I don't know," he mumbled.

"Is he going to drown, like Flametail?" Grief glittered in the ShadowClan leader's eyes, the fur around his neck spiking. Alderheart knew it must be hard for Tigerstar to remember his brother, who had fallen through the ice on the lake and been trapped there.

"I can't predict the future." Alderheart's belly tightened.

"But he did see something dark. Something that must be avoided."

"His own death?"

Alderheart tore his gaze away from the stricken leader. It frightened him to see such a strong cat so scared. "I don't know." How could he tell Tigerstar he might be right? And what if Shadowkit's vision did come true? Tigerstar was already threatening to destabilize the Clans by putting pressure on SkyClan. With a shiver, he wondered what terrible vengeance a grieving father would wreak upon the forest.

CHAPTER 11
❧

Twigbranch glanced anxiously around the trees, hoping to catch a glimpse of Finleap's pelt. Overhead, sunshine flickered between the branches. As she breathed the musty scents of the forest, a soft breeze swirled dead leaves around her paws.

"Have you seen Finleap?" Flypaw looked at her eagerly.

"He went out early." Twigbranch's ears twitched uneasily. It was midmorning and Finleap had still not come home. But Flypaw seemed unconcerned. Her gaze was flitting around the forest, alighting one moment on a leaf fluttering in the morning breeze, another moment on a bird as it hopped along a branch overhead.

"Snappaw says he was supposed to do battle training with Finleap this morning, but Finleap wasn't even in his nest." Flypaw darted forward and slapped her paws down to trap a quivering fern stem.

"He left before dawn." Twigbranch hated lying, but she wanted to protect Finleap until she'd had a chance to find out where he'd gone. She'd brought Flypaw along the beech trail this morning because it still smelled of Finleap's scent. He must have come this way yesterday, before he disappeared.

Her paws pricked with worry. Should she report him missing? Perhaps he needed help. *If we don't find him before sunhigh, I'll tell Bramblestar he's gone.*

She tasted the air. Finleap's scent trail lingered here, but it was stale. Narrowing her eyes, she peered through the shafts of sunshine, which slanted between the trees, and scanned the forest. Her heart ached for a glimpse of his brown pelt. *Where is he?*

"Twigbranch?" Flypaw looked up from the fern stem she'd captured.

"Yes?" Twigbranch dragged her attention back to her apprentice.

"Are we going to practice hunting?"

"Of course." Twigbranch had promised they would. "We're heading for the beeches. There might be mice there." Or fresher scents of Finleap.

"Why do you keep scanning the forest? Are you looking for something?"

Twigbranch hesitated. Flypaw was sharper than she'd thought. "I'm just looking out for squirrels," she mewed lightly.

Flypaw straightened and gazed between the trees. "There's one over there," she mewed, nodding to a tall oak tree on the far side of a dip in the forest floor.

Twigbranch saw gray fur bobbing between leaves high up on a branch. "It's too far to climb."

"But you used to be a SkyClan . . ." Flypaw's mew trailed away. Something else had caught her attention. The gray striped she-cat pricked her ears excitedly. "Look! It's the border patrol! There are more cats with them. They smell like SkyClan."

Twigbranch followed Flypaw's gaze. Brackenfur, Lionblaze, and Cherryfall were heading toward them. The patrol was escorting a group of SkyClan cats through ThunderClan territory. It was hard to make them out between the trees. She glimpsed Sagenose and Macgyver, and excitement fizzed in her paws as she recognized Violetshine's scent. As they came closer she could see that her sister was padding between them, Hawkwing at her side. Her father had come too! Quickly, she hurried to meet them, happiness bursting in her chest as she saw Finleap trailing behind. *He's safe!* She tried to make eye contact, but he avoided her gaze. Unease sparked in her pelt. She wanted to greet him and ask him how he was, but she didn't know if their Clanmates had discovered he'd been missing yet.

"Hi." She greeted Lionblaze breezily. Finleap might have joined the patrol without mentioning he'd been gone. "What's happened? Why are SkyClan cats here?"

"We met them at the border," he told her. "Finleap was with them." His eyes narrowed suspiciously as he stared at her. "But they won't tell us why. They want to speak with Bramblestar."

Her belly tightened. What was Finleap doing with SkyClan? "Is everything okay?" She caught her father's eye, but was disappointed when she saw no answer in his gaze.

"Let's save explanations for Bramblestar," he meowed.

His coldness sliced into Twigbranch's heart. *Aren't we kin anymore? Am I just another warrior to him now?* Did Violetshine feel the same way? She glanced hopefully at her sister. Violetshine blinked at her reassuringly as Flypaw caught up to them.

"What does SkyClan want?" the young tabby asked Lionblaze.

"I think Finleap knows more than I do," he answered pointedly.

Flypaw blinked at Finleap. "There you are! Snappaw was looking for you."

Hawkwing flicked his tail irritably. "Can we hurry up?"

"Suits me." Huffing, Lionblaze headed between the trees.

Twigbranch hurried to Finleap's side. "Are you okay?"

"Yes." He looked away. She saw his pelt prickling self-consciously.

Was he going to explain why he'd stayed out all night? "Where have you been?"

"Let's get back to camp," he grunted. Pushing awkwardly past her, he followed the patrol. Flypaw bounced after them, her tail flicking as happily as if she were returning to camp with a juicy mouse.

Violetshine hung back and fell in beside Twigbranch. "Hi." She rubbed her muzzle along Twigbranch's jaw. Twigbranch purred as her sister's scent infused her. How could she have thought, for even a moment, that Violetshine would stop loving her? They had been apart for so much of their lives and yet their bond was as strong as any littermates'. As relief swamped her, questions tumbled out. "What's going on? Why was Finleap with your patrol?"

Violetshine watched the warriors disappear through a wall

of ferns. "I've been told not to say anything until Hawkwing has spoken to Bramblestar. But don't worry. It's nothing serious. Warriors just like to show their claws once in a while."

Show their claws? Twigbranch stiffened. "Is there going to be a fight?"

Violetshine's eyes suddenly darkened. "Not with Thunder-Clan." Before Twigbranch could ask more, Violetshine darted after her Clanmates. Twigbranch hurried at her heels. What was happening? Her heart lurched as she caught up with Violetshine, but her sister's gaze was fixed on the cats ahead of them. She clearly didn't want to discuss why SkyClan had come to ThunderClan territory.

"Are you okay?" Twigbranch asked tentatively.

"I'm fine." Violetshine glanced at her.

"And Hawkwing?" Twigbranch hopped over a stick that crossed the trail. "He looked at me like he hardly knew me."

"Don't worry," Violetshine told her. "He hasn't even spoken to me since we left camp. He's on a mission, that's all. Once he's passed his message on to Bramblestar, I'm sure he'll be back to normal."

Twigbranch glanced at the camp wall ahead. The patrol had nearly reached it. What was so important that Hawkwing hardly acknowledged her? And what had Violetshine meant when she'd said there wasn't going to be a fight *with Thunder-Clan?*

The bramble wall shivered as the ThunderClan warriors escorted the SkyClan patrol into the camp. Twigbranch slid in after them, Violetshine at her tail.

"What do you think he's going to say?" Flypaw brushed past her excitedly as, around the camp, ThunderClan warriors got to their paws.

"I don't know." Twigbranch nudged Flypaw gently toward the apprentices' den, where Snappaw and Spotpaw were straining to see over the heads of their Clanmates. "Watch with your littermates." She slipped in beside Violetshine.

Bramblestar was already scrambling down the tumble of rocks. Tiny stones cracked beneath his paws and showered the clearing. Lionblaze stopped in front of him and nodded toward the SkyClan patrol. "We met them at the border."

As the ThunderClan leader dipped his head to Hawkwing, Jayfeather padded from the medicine den, his nose twitching hopefully. Was he expecting to hear news of Alderheart? Twigbranch knew he'd been worried about him. Jayfeather's blind blue gaze rested on the SkyClan patrol for a moment; then he turned back inside.

Outside the warriors' den, Poppyfrost peered past Bumble-stripe and Molewhisker.

Cinderheart narrowed her eyes. "Why is Finleap with *them*? I thought he was training Snappaw today."

Graystripe poked his head out of the elders' den.

"Who is it?" Millie called from inside.

"SkyClan has sent a patrol," Graystripe called back.

"What?" Millie sounded irritable. "I can't hear you."

Rolling his eyes, Graystripe headed back inside.

Hawkwing met Bramblestar's gaze evenly. "One of your

warriors showed up in our camp without permission."

Bramblestar's hackles lifted. "Who?"

Hawkwing nodded at Finleap. Sharply, Sagenose nudged the warrior forward with his muzzle. Finleap padded miserably across the clearing as Hawkwing went on. "Did you send him to spy?"

Finleap jerked his head up. "I wasn't spy—"

"You're already in trouble." Hawkwing flashed him an angry look. "Don't make it worse for yourself."

Twigbranch's heart twisted as Finleap flinched. Why was Hawkwing being so hard on him? He had known him since he was a kit. They'd been Clanmates. How could he ever believe Finleap would spy on his former Clan? She glanced at Sagenose and Macgyver. They were standing stiffly, their gazes hard. They looked defensive, as though they were facing a battle patrol, not a peaceful Clan. Had something happened in SkyClan that had put them on edge? She looked furtively at Violetshine. Her sister was as still as a rock, her gaze fixed on Hawkwing.

Bramblestar lifted his chin. "If Finleap came to SkyClan, he did it without my knowledge or permission. I would not send a spy to your camp, and certainly not Finleap. Finleap doesn't have a dishonest whisker on his muzzle. And he certainly would never *betray* anyone, let alone his former Clanmates."

Finleap widened his eyes, as though surprised by Bramblestar's praise. Hawkwing nodded, his ruffled pelt smoothing at last. *He knows Bramblestar is telling the truth.* Relief swamped Twigbranch. *Whatever is troubling SkyClan, he knows that Finleap is a good cat.*

Bramblestar looked sternly at Finleap. "When did you leave?"

"Last night." Finleap stared at his paws.

"Last night?" His gaze flicked accusingly toward Twigbranch. She shrank beneath her pelt. He must have guessed that she'd known Finleap was missing.

"I was going to come back straight away, but Leafstar wouldn't let me leave," Finleap mumbled.

"Don't blame Leafstar for your mistake," Bramblestar snapped. "You shouldn't have crossed the border without permission, let alone gone into another Clan's camp."

"I'm sorry." Finleap's shoulders sagged.

Bramblestar frowned. "I'm surprised no cat reported you missing."

Twigbranch dropped her gaze guiltily.

"It's all my fault," Finleap meowed quickly. "I had to see Reedclaw. I'd heard she was sick and I was worried about her. I'm really sorry."

Bramblestar didn't move. His gaze was stern. "It's natural that you miss your kin. But it's no excuse for sneaking around behind your Clanmates' backs. We have to be able to trust you, and we need to know you're safe. You will clean out the elders' den for the next moon. And Twigbranch can help you. She should have reported you missing as soon as she knew. You might have been in danger."

Twigbranch's ears grew hot as her Clanmates glanced at her.

"Did you know he was leaving?" Violetshine whispered.

"I knew he wanted to see Reedclaw," Twigbranch whispered back. "But I didn't think he would go without telling any cat. I guess I should have reported him when I saw he was gone, but I didn't want to get him in trouble."

Violetshine nudged Twigbranch's shoulder with her nose. "You must love him a lot."

Twigbranch shifted her paws self-consciously. "I guess."

"Why didn't you come with him? You could have visited me and Hawkwing."

Guilt pricked through Twigbranch's pelt. "I didn't want to break the rules. I've got an apprentice now; I can't act like a kit anymore. I've got responsibilities here." She glanced at her paws. "Besides, he didn't ask me," she added ruefully. She glanced at Finleap. Would she have gone if he had?

Violetshine's pelt brushed hers. "We still miss you."

"I miss you too." Twigbranch leaned closer.

"Violetshine!" Hawkwing called across the clearing. "We're leaving now."

Twigbranch looked hopefully at her father. Was he going to speak to her? He blinked at her, affection brimming in his eyes, but Sagenose and Macgyver were shifting impatiently beside him. He dipped his head and turned away.

Violetshine brushed her tail along Twigbranch's spine. "Maybe we'll see you at the next Gathering," she meowed. "We can catch up then."

"Yeah." Sadness welled in Twigbranch's chest as she

watched Violetshine hurry out of camp after Hawkwing and Sagenose. She'd forgotten how comforting it felt to have kin close by.

Bramblestar headed up the rocks back to Highledge as the rest of the Clan returned to their duties.

Finleap caught her eye. He looked apologetic as he padded toward her. "I'm sorry," he meowed. It was the first time they'd spoken since their argument. "You must have been worried."

"I was, but it's okay." She hurried to meet him, pressing her muzzle to his. "I should have realized how important it was for you to see Reedclaw." Violetshine's scent was still in her nose. "Kin don't stop being kin just because they're in a different Clan."

Finleap pulled away. "But I got you into trouble."

"It doesn't matter." Twigbranch gazed at him. It was so good to have him back. "Besides, it might be fun cleaning out the elders' den if we do it together."

"I guess." He looked at her uncertainly.

She frowned. Wasn't he happy to be home? "Did you miss me?"

"Of course."

"I missed you. I wondered where you'd gone."

"I *told* you," he protested.

"You *said* you were worried about Reedclaw. You didn't say anything about sneaking away for the night!"

"I didn't plan—" He stopped and took a breath. "Let's not argue again. Seeing my old Clan and my kin made me think."

"Think?" Twigbranch shifted uneasily as Finleap looked suddenly serious.

"You're the only one I feel truly close to in ThunderClan," he explained. "I miss being around cats I've known all my life."

Her heart began to race. Was he going to tell her he was leaving? "But you'll settle in soon. In a few moons, you'll feel like you've known ThunderClan forever. You heard how much Bramblestar thinks of you." *You can't leave.* Twigbranch didn't even dare say it out loud. Didn't Finleap love her after all?

"I like it here, but I don't feel like I belong." Finleap glanced at his paws. "Which is why I want to start a family. Here, in ThunderClan. Then I'll feel part of the Clan. I'll feel like I have something here that is truly my own. I want to have kits."

"Kits?" Twigbranch's mouth was so dry, she could hardly speak.

Finleap watched her, his gaze expectant.

"But you know how I feel about kits," Twigbranch blurted. "I'm not ready. I want to concentrate on mentoring. I've told you all this."

"I know." Finleap held her gaze. "But I need you to think about it again. I have to feel I belong here—that you want me. If you don't ever want to have kits with me, I'm not sure I'll ever feel at home in ThunderClan."

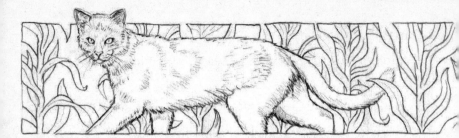

CHAPTER 12

Violetshine's paws trembled. The smooth bark of the pine branch felt slippery beneath her pads. Trying not to look at the forest floor below, she shuffled closer to Hawkwing. What if she timed her jump wrong? What if she landed badly and twisted a paw? This would be the first time she'd fought since Darktail had infiltrated the Clans. Was she ready to face battle again? "Hawkwing?" she whispered. "How long will we have to wait?" Waiting was making her anxiety worse.

He glanced at her reassuringly over his shoulder. "When you see a ShadowClan patrol, get ready. But don't jump down until you hear Leafstar give the order."

The SkyClan leader was crouching in the next tree, on the same branch as Macgyver. Her mottled brown-and-cream pelt was camouflaged among the sun-dappled branches. Bellaleaf and Harrybrook were hunkering down in a pine on the other side of the trail. It would be sunhigh before long. The ShadowClan patrol would come soon, surely? ShadowClan had crossed into SkyClan territory every day since the Gathering. Each time, they'd used this trail to venture deeper and deeper into SkyClan land.

Leafstar's anger had grown. Each ShadowClan incursion had fed her fury. "We have to make a stand," she'd told her Clanmates last night. "At the gorge we were the only Clan. We never had to fight to preserve our boundaries. But things are different here. We have to defend ourselves." No cat had argued. Since the meeting with Juniperclaw, less than a quarter moon earlier, ShadowClan's incursions had become more and more brazen. They'd even left markers to show they'd been there. "Let's teach them that no part of SkyClan land is safe for intruders. After tomorrow, they won't dare set paw here again!"

Violetshine could feel her heart beating. She was proud Leafstar had chosen her for the attack, but she was scared she'd let her Clanmates down. Nervously she scanned the trail. A bird was hopping over leaves there. It froze for a moment, then fluttered into the air and flitted high into the treetops. Hawkwing stiffened as ShadowClan scents drifted through the pine. Violetshine pricked her ears and heard the rustle of leaves, and then paw steps. They were coming.

She stared along the trail, hardly daring to breathe as Snaketooth padded into view. Strikestone was with her, Blazepaw trotting at his side. Grassheart followed, her pale tabby tail flicking like a snake behind her.

Guilt pricked in Violetshine's belly. Grassheart had been one of the queens in the nursery when Violetshine had been a kit in ShadowClan. She'd been kind enough—not exactly motherly, but more caring than Violetshine's foster mother, Pinenose. It seemed strange that they were enemies now, but as long as ShadowClan was trying to steal SkyClan's land, what else could they be? She had to defend her Clan. The ShadowClan cats looked at ease, as though they were patrolling their own territory. How dare they? She glanced toward Leafstar, waiting for the signal to attack.

Leafstar watched the ShadowClan cats, her hackles lifting as they neared. Stiff as an adder waiting to strike, she tracked them until they were padding beneath her. Then she signaled with a hiss: "Attack!"

Violetshine's heart lurched as Hawkwing dived onto the ShadowClan patrol. Yowls of surprise exploded into the air as Harrybrook, Macgyver, Bellaleaf, and Leafstar dropped onto their victims. With a hiss, Violetshine unsheathed her claws and leaped from the tree. She landed squarely on Strikestone's back. The tom collapsed beneath her. Violetshine dug in her claws and clung on fiercely as Strikestone dropped and rolled in a practiced movement.

She grunted as Strikestone rolled over her, but she didn't let go. She remembered her training. *Never expose your belly.* Gripping hard, she clung on while Strikestone staggered clumsily to his paws. Then she sank her teeth into his scruff and began pummeling his spine with her hind legs. He shrieked and bucked beneath her.

Beside them, Blazepaw wailed in pain as Harrybrook battered the young tom's nose with a flurry of swipes. Bellaleaf hooked her claws into Snaketooth's shoulders and flung the ShadowClan she-cat to the ground. Leafstar hissed at Snaketooth, "Did you think you could invade our land whenever you liked?" As the SkyClan leader slashed at Grassheart's nose, Strikestone reared beneath Violetshine. She dug her claws in harder as he staggered backward. *I've got you!* Triumph surged in her chest.

Suddenly her spine slammed against hard wood. Stars flashed in her vision and merged into jagged lightning. Strikestone had shoved her against a tree. With a groan, she let him go and slithered to the ground. Strikestone turned on her, his eyes flashing. Panic flowed through her as the ShadowClan tom lifted his forepaw. He curled his lip and swung a blow at her muzzle. Then dark gray fur blurred at the edge of her vision. Hawkwing lunged at the ShadowClan tom and sent him reeling before his claws could reach Violetshine's nose. Strikestone's blood spattered the forest floor.

Through a haze of shock, Violetshine could smell their fear-scent mingled with the stone tang of blood. The Shadow-Clan cats were outnumbered and fighting for their lives.

"Retreat!" Grassheart's eyes were wild with fright as Leafstar held the she-cat to the ground.

Leafstar's eyes blazed. "Show this to Tigerstar!" She ripped fur from Grassheart's flank, leaving claw marks in her flesh.

Grassheart scrabbled free and fled. Blazepaw ducked away from Harrybrook and raced between the trees. Strikestone grabbed Snaketooth, and together they ran for a stand of bracken. Crashing through it, they disappeared.

"Should we chase them over the border?" Hawkwing glanced at Leafstar.

"Let them run," the SkyClan leader growled. "I think they got the message."

Still winded, Violetshine pushed herself to her paws. She stared at the bloody trail the ShadowClan warriors had left.

"Are you okay?" Leafstar glanced at her.

"Just winded," she puffed.

Leafstar looked at the others. "Anyone hurt?"

"Hardly a scratch." Harrybrook flicked his tail.

"I think only ShadowClan cats got injured," Bellaleaf growled.

Hawkwing blinked proudly at Violetshine. "You fought well."

She dropped her gaze self-consciously. "I should have held on longer."

"Strikestone fought hard." Hawkwing touched his muzzle to her head. "No warrior could have held on longer."

Pride warmed Violetshine's pelt as Leafstar turned toward camp. "I think that's the last we'll see of ShadowClan for a while," the SkyClan leader meowed.

Shrouded in sleep, Violetshine allowed herself a small purr of relief that she could feel Tree lying beside her—that he was still here in SkyClan and had not grown so frustrated with trying to mediate between the Clans that he had left forever. He was here, sleeping but restless, as he had been every night since the disastrous meeting with Juniperclaw. But his quick movement now was more than just restlessness. It jolted her fully awake. "Is something wrong?" Alarm sparked beneath her pelt. He was sitting up in his nest, his body tense as he stared into the darkness. As she pushed herself to her paws, an angry yowl split the cold night air. The den shook as something tugged at the wall. Outside, paw steps thrummed the clearing.

"ShadowClan!" Hawkwing yowled an alarm through the darkness. He raced for the den entrance.

Violetshine's belly tightened. She'd guessed ShadowClan would retaliate, but she'd never thought they'd attack the camp in the dead of night. Sparrowpelt, Bellaleaf, and Plumwillow darted from their nests. Blossomheart and Nettlesplash were already pushing their way outside. Heart racing, Violetshine followed. "Are you coming?" She looked back at Tree.

He froze. "How can I mediate between the Clans if I take sides in battles?"

Violetshine nodded quickly. He was right. If he was their only chance for peace, he couldn't be seen fighting Shadow-Clan.

ShadowClan stench bathed her tongue as she broke into moonlight. The dens were shredded, and SkyClan cats swarmed in the clearing. Two ShadowClan warriors were streaking across the camp. She recognized Snowbird's brilliant white pelt. Sandynose and Nettlesplash dived at her, but Snowbird dodged them skillfully and pelted for the entrance. Scorchfur barged between Cherrytail and Mintfur as they tried to catch his pelt, ducking under Macgyver's belly and flicking his tail clear as Hawkwing dived at him.

They were fleeing, their damage done. The walls of the

dens were tattered; stems scattered the earth.

"Don't let them get away!" Hawkwing gave the order as Snowbird and Scorchfur pelted from the camp entrance. Macgyver led Bellaleaf, Nettlesplash, and their Clanmates after them. Violetshine scanned the clearing. Were there more ShadowClan warriors in camp? As the others disappeared into the forest, movement beside the fresh-kill pile caught Violetshine's eye.

Juniperclaw! The ShadowClan deputy was dragging a vole from the pile. He was stealing SkyClan prey! With a yowl, Violetshine raced across the clearing. "Leave that alone!" She slewed to a halt in front of him, outrage sparking in her pelt. Juniperclaw froze and eyed her spitefully through slitted eyes. She lunged at him, catching his flank in her claws. With a growl, he tore free and fled through the shadows at the edge of the clearing. She pelted after him, but he was fast. Skimming the ground like a bird, he shot from the camp and disappeared into the brambles a fox-length from the entrance.

Violetshine pulled up, panting. There were enough Sky-Clan warriors in the forest. She should stay in camp and make sure there were no more ShadowClan warriors lurking around the dens. She ducked back inside.

Leafstar was standing in the clearing, Hawkwing and Sandynose at her side. The SkyClan leader looked about her, her amber eyes wide. Leaves littered the ground; stems hung from the walls where the ShadowClan cats had torn them. "Is that why they came?" She blinked at the damage, her eyes clouded with confusion. "To destroy our dens?"

Hawkwing frowned. "What's the point? Dens can be rebuilt."

Sandynose lashed his tail. "Perhaps they thought they were giving us a warning."

Violetshine forced her ruffled pelt to smooth as she padded to Hawkwing's side. The thought that ShadowClan could invade the camp while they slept made her nervous. "Perhaps we should post guards at night," she ventured, looking at Leafstar.

The SkyClan leader didn't seem to hear her. She was watching the entrance.

Nettlesplash ducked into camp, his pelt ruffled from his race through the forest. Blossomheart and Sparrowpelt hurried at his heels. "We lost them," Nettlesplash puffed. "They were heading for the border. Macgyver's leading a patrol to track their scent to make sure they don't come back."

Blossomheart stared at the ragged camp. "What a mess!"

Leafstar's pelt twitched. "Let's worry about it in the morning." She nodded to Sparrowpelt. "Help me guard the entrance. The rest of you, get some sleep."

Hawkwing flicked his tail. "I'll stand guard too." He nudged Violetshine toward the warriors' den and padded away.

Tree was standing at the entrance. His eyes were round with dismay. Violetshine stopped beside the yellow tom and shivered. "I can't believe they invaded our camp," she murmured. "They're no better than rogues."

Tree blinked at her through the darkness. "I really thought

I could help keep peace between the Clans." He sounded defeated. "But they seem determined to fight, and there's nothing I can do. I can't stand by and watch ShadowClan destroy you. But I'm not sure I have the power to stop them."

I can't stand by and watch ShadowClan destroy you. Violetshine's heart sank. He'd said *you* and not *us.* He was talking as though he didn't belong in SkyClan. She pressed against him. "You still might get them to see sense." Her words sounded hollow. ShadowClan had crossed the border too many times. And now they'd come right into SkyClan's camp. She didn't see how there could be peace between SkyClan and ShadowClan now. But she had to make Tree believe there was still a place for him in SkyClan.

Tree didn't respond. Instead he tucked his muzzle into her neck fur. The warmth of his breath soothed her, but she knew he felt beaten. She could feel it in the heaviness of his body as he leaned against her. Had the Clans broken his spirit? Her heart ached with grief. If he couldn't bring peace, would he leave? He'd joined SkyClan as a mediator. If he couldn't mediate, why should he stay?

As she woke, Violetshine felt the warmth of newleaf sunshine seeping into the den. She opened her eyes. The den was bright where torn walls let the light in. Her heart quickened as she saw Tree's empty nest. Where was he?

She hopped out of her nest and hurried from the den. Outside, she scanned the ravaged camp, relieved to see Tree. He was helping Harrybrook gather brambles beside the apprentices' den. If he were planning to leave, he wouldn't bother helping the Clan now, surely? Palepaw and Pigeonpaw darted around them, racing each other to snatch up broken stems, while Sunnypaw and Nectarpaw threaded loose tendrils back into the den wall.

Warriors milled in the clearing, pacing restlessly as Hawkwing murmured in Sandynose's ear. Sparrowpelt was hungrily eating a vole beside the fresh-kill pile. Leafstar stalked around the edge of the camp. Her gaze was dark as she sniffed at the torn dens. Was she going to announce a fresh attack on ShadowClan? They certainly deserved it after their raid on the SkyClan camp. The SkyClan leader stopped beside the medicine den, where Frecklewish and Fidgetflake were frowning at a hole ripped in the side. "Was your herb store damaged?"

"No, thank StarClan," Frecklewish told her.

Hawkwing lifted his muzzle and surveyed his warriors. They turned to him expectantly.

"Bellaleaf." He nodded to the orange she-cat. "Choose three warriors to help you mend the elders' den." He flicked his tail toward the clump of bracken where Fallowfern slept. The deaf elder was sitting among the bent stems, her nest open to the sky. Hawkwing went on. "Nettlesplash, take a patrol of apprentices into the forest. Collect as many stems as you can find. Bracken will do. Brambles would be better if you can get them back to camp without pricking your paws."

As Nettlesplash signaled to Sunnypaw and Nectarpaw, Leafstar looked up from the shredded medicine den. "You're wasting your time, Hawkwing," she growled.

Hawkwing looked at her. "What do you mean?"

"Why bother rebuilding?" Leafstar sat down heavily. "Whatever we build, ShadowClan will destroy. And the other Clans won't lift a paw to defend us."

Violetshine stiffened. What was Leafstar saying? They couldn't let ShadowClan defeat them!

Bellaleaf stared at the SkyClan leader. "We can't give in!"

"We must fight them." Harrybrook flexed his claws.

Hawkwing gazed evenly at Leafstar. "We must keep rebuilding until they realize we're here to stay."

"What's the point?" Leafstar stared at him bleakly. "Why did we even come here? The Clans clearly don't want us. We had a good home in the gorge, and with Darktail gone, we can go back there and make it better. Why fight to stay beside the lake when no cat will fight at our side? It we are to be alone, let's be alone where there are no borders to defend and no other Clans jealous of our land."

Nettlesplash blinked at her, his brown pelt twitching. Sagenose and Mintfur exchanged anxious looks.

"Is the gorge far away?" Palepaw whispered to Pigeonpaw.

Frecklewish swished her tail. "You're just downhearted," she told the SkyClan leader. "You're probably tired. Why not sleep and think about it when you're rested?"

As she spoke, Sparrowpelt began to retch. Violetshine jerked her muzzle toward the warrior, who was hunched a tail-length from the fresh-kill pile. His flanks heaved as he convulsed. Eyes round with pain, he vomited a slippery lump of half-chewed vole onto the ground. Frecklewish hurried toward him. She sniffed the vole as Sparrowpelt convulsed again. Her pelt spiked with worry as he vomited again and collapsed, groaning.

Leafstar hurried toward him.

"Stay away." Frecklewish signaled her backward with a flick of her nose. "I don't know what's causing this yet."

"Was the vole rotten?" Hawkwing called across the clearing.

Frecklewish shook her head.

Sparrowpelt let out a low, trembling wail. Violetshine's pelt prickled as she heard it. He must be in a lot of pain. What was hurting him so badly? She caught her breath as a thought struck her. Sparrowpelt had eaten the vole she'd seen Juniperclaw touching last night. That seemed strange. Perhaps the ShadowClan tom hadn't been trying to steal SkyClan's prey after all. Did he have a darker plan? Had Juniperclaw done something to the vole to make it harm Sparrowpelt? Her chest tightened. Destroying the dens could have been a distraction. Had the real plan been for Snowbird and Scorchfur to keep SkyClan busy while Juniperclaw poisoned their prey? Would ShadowClan really do something so fox-hearted?

CHAPTER 13

Alderheart buried the deathberry seeds under the wall of the medicine den with the others. He glanced at the entrance hopefully. The half-moon gathering was tonight. Would Tigerstar let him go? He wanted to be there. He had important news.

Puddleshine was recovering, asleep in his nest now. The ShadowClan medicine cat's fever had broken in the night. Alderheart still felt light-pawed with relief. His remedy had finally worked! The deathberry flesh he'd given Puddleshine this morning would be the last.

He cleaned his paws in the loose earth at the side of the medicine den. Then he carefully covered the crumbled patch with leaves and glanced over his shoulder at Shadowkit. "You have to stay away from this part of the den, remember?"

The gray kit nodded solemnly. Since his fit, Shadowkit had been helping Alderheart with his medicine-cat duties. Alderheart could hardly turn around without tripping over him. Was this how he'd been when he used to help Jayfeather? The thought amused him. He'd found work for the kit, and now Shadowkit was neatening nests, fetching herbs, and chasing spiders out of the den—often without Alderheart instructing him to do it. *He just seems to* know *what to do.*

Alderheart was secretly pleased that Tigerstar had let the kit spend so much time here. The ShadowClan leader had also stopped posting guards. Clearly Tigerstar was starting to trust him.

Paw steps sounded at the den entrance. Lightkit and Pouncekit crowded the doorway, their eyes bright with excitement.

"Shadowkit!" Pouncekit could hardly keep still. "Strikestone and Blazepaw have promised to give us badger rides around the clearing."

"They're going to *race* while we ride them!" Lightkit squeaked. "It's going to be great."

"You have to come!" Pouncekit looked pleadingly at Shadowkit. "You've missed all the fun since you've been helping Alderheart."

"I'm having fun here," Shadowkit told her.

Lightkit looked unconvinced. "How can looking after sick cats be as much fun as badger rides?"

"I've got a lot to learn," Shadowkit told him. "I'm going to be a medicine cat one day."

Alderheart's chest tightened. *He might not live long enough.* The kit's vision flashed in his mind. *I could feel water pressing against my fur, in my ears, in my nose . . . in my mouth. . . .* And yet Shadowkit was planning his future. His own vision did not fill him with any dread. If Shadowkit was destined to be a medicine cat, perhaps he had received not a prediction, but a *warning.*

Alderheart shook out his fur and told himself there would

be time to figure that out. He hoped he was right. "One day you'll be too old for badger rides," he told Shadowkit.

"I don't care." The gray tom puffed out his chest. "I want to stay here and help you."

Pouncekit rolled her eyes and nudged Lightkit out of the den. "We're wasting our time. Let's go and have some fun."

"Are you sure you don't want to go and play?" Alderheart pressed. "You can come and help again afterward."

"I want to stay here," Shadowkit mewed firmly.

There was clearly no arguing with the kit. "In that case, fetch the marigold Cloverfoot gathered yesterday," he told him. "It's nearly time to re-dress Grassheart's wound."

"That's the bright green one that smells like sour nettles, right?"

"Yes."

As Shadowkit trotted to the herb store, Alderheart looked at Grassheart. She was asleep in a nest near the medicine den, where early morning sunshine streamed through the entrance. Alderheart had been treating her since she'd returned the day before with a claw wound on her flank. He'd treated Blazepaw, Strikestone, and Snaketooth at the same time. They had scratches, but Grassheart's wound was so deep he'd kept her in the medicine den. The patrol said SkyClan had ambushed them. Alderheart thought it strange and wondered why SkyClan had provoked ShadowClan with such a bold attack. How would that help the tension between the two Clans?

"Is this it?" Shadowkit nosed a fresh bundle of green stems in front of the herb store.

"Yes." Alderheart blinked approvingly. "Take two stems to Grassheart's nest while I check on Puddleshine." As he spoke, Puddleshine woke up and blinked at him drowsily over the edge of his nest. The medicine cat's gaze was still clouded, and his pelt needed a good wash, but it was good to see him awake again. "Can you manage a mouthful?" Alderheart crossed the den and nosed a morsel of mouse closer to his muzzle.

Puddleshine lapped it doubtfully with his tongue. "It might take a while for my appetite to come back."

"You need to get strong," Alderheart told him.

"It's enough to be awake," Puddleshine murmured.

Alderheart checked his scratches once more. The sour smell had lifted, and the wounds were finally starting to heal. For the first time in days, Alderheart felt a rush of joy. As he sat back on his haunches and purred, Shadowkit trotted past him, a bunch of marigold stems flopping from his jaws, and headed toward Grassheart's nest.

Puddleshine blinked at the fresh herbs, his nose twitching. "Those are too fresh to come from my store. Did you bring them with you?"

"Cloverfoot gathered them," Alderheart told him.

Puddleshine's eyes widened. "It's not like Cloverfoot to help with medicine-cat duties. Did Tigerstar order her to do it?"

"She volunteered."

Puddleshine gave a husky purr. "You've made yourself popular here," he teased.

"I'll be even more popular once I tell Tigerstar that you're recovering." Alderheart hadn't had a chance to share the news with the ShadowClan leader.

Across the den, Grassheart groaned.

"She's waking up!" Shadowkit mewed excitedly.

"I think you'd better go help your apprentice," Puddleshine purred.

"He'll be your apprentice soon." Alderheart crossed the den.

"Shall I chew up the marigold?" Shadowkit picked up a stem in his teeth.

"You're too young to be chewing up herbs," Alderheart took it gently away. "Marigold is quite strong. It might make you feel sick."

"Can I help rub the ointment into her wound then?"

Alderheart didn't answer. Grassheart was lifting her head. She looked at him blearily, pain shadowing her eyes. "My side hurts."

Alderheart checked the wound. "It's not infected," he told her. "It'll feel better once I've put some fresh marigold on it."

Shadowkit fluffed out his fur. "*I'm* going to help," he told the tabby proudly.

Alderheart's whiskers twitched with amusement. "You have a much more important job."

"What?" Shadowkit stared at him.

"Grassheart and Puddleshine need water. I want you to take that moss"—he jerked his muzzle toward a bundle beside the den entrance—"carry it to the puddle next to the elders' den, and give it a good soak. Then bring it back quickly before all the water drips out."

"Okay!" Shadowkit raced to the moss, grabbed it between his jaws, and sprinted out of the den.

Quickly, Alderheart chewed a marigold stem. Then he lapped the pulp gently into Grassheart's wound. She closed her eyes and seemed to drift back to sleep. It felt strange to be treating another Clan's battle injuries. What would Sky-Clan say if they knew a ThunderClan cat was helping to heal their rivals? Would they think he was a traitor? *It's not my battle.* Besides, medicine cats weren't supposed to take sides. They were meant to save lives and ease suffering. If warriors wanted to fight, let them. Alderheart wasn't going to refuse any cat care.

A rustle at the entrance shook him from his thoughts. Was Shadowkit back already? He turned and saw Tigerstar padding into the den.

"I just saw Shadowkit soaking moss in the puddle. It's good to see him looking so happy after—" The ShadowClan leader hesitated as he saw Puddleshine sitting up in his nest. His eyes brightened. "Why didn't you tell me?"

"I wanted to make sure he could eat first." Alderheart padded to Puddleshine's nest. "If he can eat, he's definitely recovering." He noticed with a flicker of satisfaction that the second morsel of mouse had disappeared.

Puddleshine licked his lips and blinked at Tigerstar. "I'm sorry I've been such a worry. It was mouse-brained of me to get tangled up in that Twoleg mesh. But I couldn't resist trying to reach the borage underneath."

"I'm just glad to see you better." Tigerstar lifted his tail. "You see?" He swished it toward Alderheart. "All he needed was proper care in his own den."

Alderheart glanced at the gap beneath Puddleshine's nest where the deathberries were hidden. Should he tell Tigerstar that he'd carried on feeding Puddleshine the deathberry flesh? He hesitated, unease pricking beneath his pelt. And yet, if he had found a new cure, he should share it. Another medicine cat might have need of it one day. He looked Tigerstar in the eye. "I brought the deathberries with me from ThunderClan. I've been feeding the flesh to Puddleshine since I arrived."

Surprise flashed in the ShadowClan leader's eyes. Alderheart stiffened, waiting for anger. But Tigerstar only tipped his head and looked thoughtful. "You're as brave as a warrior," he meowed at last. "What if the deathberries had killed him?"

"It was a risk I had to take," Alderheart told him. "He'd have died for sure if I *hadn't* given them to him."

Puddleshine stretched his muzzle forward. "I owe him my life."

Tigerstar narrowed his eyes. "Then we must thank you, Alderheart. ShadowClan honors your courage."

Alderheart dipped his head, warmed by Tigerstar's praise. "I'm a medicine cat," he murmured. "I had no other choice."

"What can I do for you in return? Do you want to go home?"

"I'll go as soon as Puddleshine is well enough to return to his duties here," Alderheart told him. "ThunderClan can manage without me until then." Tigerstar nodded as he went on. "But tonight I'd like to go to the Moonpool to share with StarClan."

"It's half-moon!" Tigerstar sounded as though he'd forgotten. He dipped his head. "I mustn't stop a medicine cat from sharing with StarClan. And you can tell the other cats that Puddleshine is recovering. ShadowClan is whole again."

And I'm no longer your prisoner. Alderheart blinked politely at the ShadowClan leader. "Thank you."

As he spoke, Shadowkit trotted into the den. He flopped the dripping moss over the side of Grassheart's nest and hurried to his father's side. "Why is Alderheart thanking you?"

"I told him he could go to the Moonpool tonight."

Shadowkit's soft fur fluffed excitedly. "Can I go with him?"

Alderheart shook his head. "I'm afraid not," he told the kit gently. "It's a meeting for medicine cats. We're going to share with StarClan."

"I can share too." Shadowkit lifted his muzzle. "I have visions."

Alderheart saw Tigerstar's gaze darken with worry. Was he remembering Shadowkit's dream too?

"You have to stay in camp," Tigerstar told Shadowkit. "Someone has to look after Puddleshine and Grassheart while Alderheart is gone."

Shadowkit pricked his ears. "I'll be in charge of the medicine den!"

"Yes." Tigerstar purred indulgently. "And Tawnypelt can help you. Just in case you get sleepy."

"I won't get sleepy," Shadowkit promised. He blinked

earnestly at Alderheart. "I'll make sure Puddleshine and Grassheart get the best care while you're away."

"Thank you." Alderheart touched his nose to the kit's head. "That will be a great help."

The bright half-moon hung overhead. The high cliffs encircling the Moonpool reflected its light, sparkling where quartz cut lines through the granite.

Alderheart followed the trail dimpled by ancient paw prints to the bottom of the hollow. Frecklewish sat with Willowshine at the water's edge. As Alderheart approached and dipped his head in greeting, the SkyClan medicine cat stood up. His ears pricked guiltily. Not long ago he'd been treating a wound inflicted by Frecklewish's Clanmates. Did that make him disloyal? And if so, to whom? *It's not my battle.* He pushed the thought away.

Leafpool was already hurrying to greet him, and Jayfeather was blinking at him, his blue gaze expectant.

"Are you okay?" Jayfeather sounded anxious.

"We were worried you might not come." Leafpool pressed her muzzle eagerly to his cheek.

"I'm fine," Alderheart reassured them.

"How's Puddleshine?" Jayfeather's fur twitched.

"He's recovering. The fever broke last night."

"Thank StarClan!" Leafpool lifted her eyes to the glittering sky.

Jayfeather padded closer. "The deathberries worked?"

"I told you they would." Alderheart flicked his tail, relieved to feel certain at last.

"You were taking a risk," Jayfeather grunted.

"You would have taken the same risk if it had been your idea," Alderheart teased.

"Maybe." Jayfeather settled at the water's edge. A faint breeze stirred the water's surface and set it rippling against the tips of the blind cat's paws.

"Congratulations, Alderheart." Leafpool's eyes glistened with relief. "When can you come home?"

"I promised Tigerstar I'd stay until Puddleshine is well enough to return to his duties." ShadowClan needed him.

"Hi." Kestrelflight reached the pool breathlessly and nodded greetings to the other cats. He must have run the last part of the journey. Alderheart hadn't seen him on the trail.

"Is all well in WindClan?" Leafpool asked.

"Yes, thank you." Kestrelflight took his place at the water's edge.

"How is ThunderClan?" Willowshine asked. "Any sickness?"

"The usual coughs and bellyaches," Leafpool told her.

"RiverClan is well," Willowshine reported. "Softpaw got caught in a strong current that carried her close to the rapids. Dapplepaw managed to drag her out in time, but she swallowed a lot of water."

"Was she sick?" Leafpool asked.

"She's getting better now." Willowshine sounded relieved.

"Mothwing's back at camp, keeping an eye on her." She glanced at Frecklewish. The SkyClan cat hadn't spoken. "Where's Fidgetflake?"

Frecklewish gazed into the water. "He stayed behind," she mewed softly.

Alderheart exchanged glances with Leafpool. The Sky-Clan medicine cat was unusually quiet. Alderheart wondered if he should ask if all was well, but Frecklewish turned toward the pool and crouched beside it.

"Let's share with StarClan," she mewed.

Alderheart padded to the water and settled at the edge. As the others took their places around the pool, he closed his eyes and dipped his head.

As the water touched his nose, a vision roared around him. Wind battered his pelt, and he felt himself lifted by a storm that tossed him like a leaf. Rain lashed his face and he fought to see, flailing against the hurricane until, suddenly, the wind dropped him and he fell onto wet grass. He hunkered down while the storm raged above. Against a clouded sky, five saplings stuck up like sharp claws as, around them, the wind streamed through marsh grass and set it rippling like water around their roots. The saplings rattled in the wind, their branches twisting together. Entwined, they stood firm, unbending against the storm. Alderheart narrowed his eyes. Hope flared in his heart when he saw the saplings resist.

Then a fierce gust swept over him and his heart lurched as, with a crack, one of the saplings gave way. It snapped at the roots and in an instant was carried away, tumbling over the grass like a twig. The rain hardened and the wind roared louder. The other saplings untwined and, one by one, the storm tore them from the earth and batted them away. In a moment, Alderheart found himself staring at an empty meadow, where nothing showed against the horizon but an endless sea of grass.

He opened his eyes, snatching his nose from the Moon-pool and shaking water from its tip. He sat up as the other medicine cats straightened and stared at one another, blinking. "The five Clans must stand together!" he blurted.

"I saw saplings," Willowshine gasped.

"When one was uprooted, the others were blown away," Kestrelflight chimed in.

Alderheart's fur pricked along his spine. *We shared the same vision!*

Jayfeather sat up and gazed blindly around the pool. "It sounds like we all saw the same thing. If that's true, then StarClan is telling us that no Clan must fail. If one fails, we all fail."

"But which Clan will fail?" Kestrelflight looked puzzled. "ThunderClan and WindClan are as strong as ever. Shadow-Clan has a leader now and has returned to its home, and RiverClan is one of the five again."

Frecklewish's hackles lifted. "All of you! You're so complacent that you don't see what's happening!" Anger sparked in her pale green eyes. "ShadowClan wants to drive SkyClan from the lake! Didn't you hear Tigerstar's threat at the last Gathering?"

"We heard it," Leafpool told her. "But it's just a territory dispute, isn't it? Clans have them all the time. We thought you and ShadowClan were going to work it out."

"How?" Frecklewish stared at them. "Did you think Leafstar could create new territory? Or that Tigerstar could be persuaded to settle for less?"

"Tree said he would help you," Kestrelflight meowed.

Frecklewish lashed her tail. "Did you really think an outsider could bring peace within the Clans?" She didn't wait for an answer. "You act like this is not your problem. But StarClan has sent this vision to show you that it is! If the Clans don't stand together to settle this fight, then SkyClan will be driven from the lake."

Alderheart stared at the SkyClan medicine cat. She was right. They had ignored the dispute between SkyClan and ShadowClan. *It's not my battle.* Shame washed him. He'd acted like the problem would go away if he ignored it. Now StarClan had made it clear that it wouldn't.

Leafpool gazed evenly at Frecklewish. "Surely it's not that bad?"

"ShadowClan attacked our camp last night," she told them.

Alderheart stiffened. It was the first he'd heard of an attack on SkyClan. He wasn't surprised Tigerstar hadn't told him, but he had been awake in the night, caring for Puddleshine. Why hadn't he heard the battle patrol return? Had no cat been injured?

"They shredded our dens while we slept," Frecklewish went on. "Worse, Leafstar doesn't want to rebuild. She wants to leave and return to the gorge."

"Leave the lake?" Kestrelflight's fur rippled nervously. "You can't. Not after all we've done to bring you here."

"Why can't we?" Frecklewish challenged. "You're doing nothing to keep us here."

Alderheart shifted his paws uneasily. It was possible that SkyClan could return to the gorge. Darktail had driven them out, but Darktail was dead now and his rogues disbanded. There was nothing to stop SkyClan returning to the home they'd made moons ago.

"We must speak to our leaders," Leafpool mewed quickly. "We must find a solution."

Frecklewish's gaze darkened. "No solution can repair what ShadowClan has done."

Jayfeather narrowed his eyes. "If you need help rebuilding your camp, I'm sure Bramblestar will send a party to help with the work."

"I'm not talking about the damage to the camp. Shadow-Clan poisoned our prey. They want to kill us!" Anger sharpened Frecklewish's mew.

"Poison?" Unease wormed beneath Alderheart's pelt. "What do you mean?"

"When the ShadowClan cats were in our camp last night, Violetshine saw Juniperclaw near the fresh-kill pile. She chased him off, but when Sparrowpelt ate a vole from the pile, it made him sick."

"Perhaps it was an old vole," Willowshine mewed hopefully.

"*Really* sick," Frecklewish growled. "He was in agony. I gave him yarrow to get rid of whatever was hurting him, and he vomited seeds." She turned her icy gaze on Alderheart. "*Deathberry* seeds."

Alderheart felt the chill of the night pierce his fur as the other medicine cats turned to stare at him.

"You took deathberries to ShadowClan to treat Puddleshine, didn't you?" Frecklewish mewed accusingly.

Alderheart's thoughts raced. It was true. He'd kept a store of deathberries. But they were hidden. No one knew about them, surely. And yet it seemed strange that Sparrowpelt would get sick so soon after a ShadowClan raid. Had poisoning SkyClan prey been part of a deadly ShadowClan plan?

Jayfeather bristled. "Are you saying Alderheart is behind the poisoning?"

"I'm saying that ShadowClan had access to deathberries because of him."

"That's not true!" Alderheart fluffed out his fur indignantly. "I kept the berries hidden. Even Tigerstar didn't know they were there." He hoped it was true.

"Did anyone see you give deathberries to Puddleshine?" Leafpool asked.

Alderheart paused. Had Cloverfoot or Scorchfur seen him when they'd been guarding the entrance to the medicine den? "I don't know! But I know how many berries were wrapped in the leaf, and none are missing." He was sure he hadn't noticed any berries missing when he'd given Puddleshine his last dose that morning. "None are missing," he repeated, meeting

Frecklewish's gaze. "If Juniperclaw did poison your fresh-kill pile with deathberries, they didn't come from me."

Leafpool whisked her tail impatiently. "Who cares where the berries came from? Every cat knows about deathberries. We're all taught as 'paws to stay away from them. What's important is that the dispute between ShadowClan and Sky-Clan is growing worse. We have to stop it before Leafstar decides SkyClan must leave the lake."

Jayfeather nodded. "We saw the vision. If SkyClan leaves, we will all be destroyed."

"We must tell our leaders," Kestrelflight agreed.

"They must hold an emergency Gathering," Willowshine mewed.

Alderheart's shifted anxiously. "The last Gathering didn't help solve this problem. Another Gathering might make the situation worse."

Leafpool stared at him. "If Bramblestar knows what's at stake, he will do whatever it takes to make SkyClan stay beside the lake."

"Harestar will follow the wishes of StarClan, and StarClan clearly wants SkyClan to stay," Kestrelflight guessed.

"What about Mistystar?" Alderheart looked anxiously at Willowshine.

The gray tabby hesitated. "Her faith in StarClan's wisdom is still shaken since Darktail nearly destroyed us. But I will do my best to persuade her that we must stand together to keep SkyClan from leaving."

Alderheart saw worry flash in Willowshine's eyes. Did she

doubt Mistystar's commitment to the Clans? It had not been long since she closed RiverClan's borders, even to medicine cats, refusing to engage with the other Clans. She might see sense in SkyClan doing the same.

"What about Tigerstar?" Jayfeather was staring at Alderheart, his milky gaze more piercing than any sighted cat's. "You've been living in their camp. Do you think Tigerstar can be persuaded to cooperate?"

"I d-don't know." What could he say? Tigerstar hadn't spoken to him about the dispute with SkyClan, but with one of his warriors lying injured in the medicine den, he doubted the ShadowClan leader would feel much compassion for his neighbors. Besides, Tigerstar had started the dispute with his claim to SkyClan territory. And he'd actively encouraged his warriors to cross the border time and time again. The ShadowClan leader would never give up his claim, even if StarClan wanted SkyClan to stay beside the lake.

Jayfeather got to his paws. "We will just have to persuade him." He nodded to the others. "Tell your leaders they must meet. The Clans must make peace and stand together." A chilly wind spiraled around the hollow as he went on. "Or the coming storm will tear us all away."

CHAPTER 14

♣

Stones jabbed into Twigbranch's pads as she followed Sparkpelt and Larksong along the shore. Bramblestar and Squirrelflight headed the patrol. Flypaw, Snappaw, and Eaglepaw chattered excitedly at the back. It felt strange to be traveling to the island when the moon was barely more than half-full, but after Jayfeather and Leafpool had returned from the Moonpool, Bramblestar had sent word to the other Clans that there would be a special Gathering.

Finleap's fur brushed Twigbranch's flank and she glanced at him, wanting reassurance. "Do you think SkyClan will really leave the lake?"

"I don't know." Finleap wouldn't meet her gaze.

"But if StarClan sent a message saying there has to be five Clans, surely the other Clans will try to persuade them to stay?"

"I don't think *ShadowClan* wants them to stay." He sounded weary, as though he thought reasoning with ShadowClan was pointless.

"But surely, if the other Clans want them to stay . . ." Her mew trailed away hopefully.

"Who says they do?" Finleap stared ahead.

Twigbranch's belly tightened. Would the other Clans refuse to support SkyClan? After all, no one had offered them land. *What if they do leave?* She'd lose Violetshine and Hawkwing forever! Her thoughts quickened. Would Finleap go with them? She hadn't decided about kits yet.

The other Clans won't let them go! They can't! Twigbranch knew that Bramblestar was taking Leafstar's threat seriously. He was clearly determined to stop her. He'd said as much to Squirrelflight and Lionblaze that morning, and his gaze had been dark as he'd chosen warriors for the patrol.

She glanced at Finleap, wishing he would say something encouraging. "I'm glad Bramblestar picked us. What if it's the last chance I get to see Violetshine and Hawkwing?" *Please tell me everything will be okay.*

"I thought kin wasn't important."

There was bitterness in his mew. Twigbranch flinched. Since he'd told her he wanted to have kits, Finleap had been distant. She always seemed to be the one to start conversations, while he only replied in short, vague phrases. Her heart ached, but what could she do? Promise to be his mate? Give up mentoring Flypaw so that she could have his kits? Anger pricked at her belly. He was pressuring her into something she didn't want yet. But she loved him, and she could understand that he was acting out of unhappiness. If only he could find his place in ThunderClan. She'd planned to keep stalling—refusing to give him a straight answer—to give him time to adjust. But what if SkyClan left? It would force him to make a decision. Clan or kin?

She changed the subject. "I hope Reedclaw has recovered from her cough."

Finleap didn't respond.

Ahead, Lilyheart stopped at the lake's edge to take a drink. As Twigbranch passed her, she glimpsed ShadowClan across the water, trekking along the far shore.

Sparkpelt must have noticed them too. "ShadowClan will be glad to see SkyClan leave," she mewed to Larksong.

Larksong followed her gaze. "Leaf-bare must have been hard for them. How could they hunt properly when SkyClan had taken half their land?"

"I hope they get it back." Sparkpelt fluffed out her fur. "If ShadowClan goes hungry, it means trouble for all the Clans."

"No cat wants a hungry Clan on their border," Larksong mewed.

Sparkpelt swished her tail. "With SkyClan gone, everything can go back to normal."

Twigbranch could hardly believe her ears. Sparkpelt *wanted* SkyClan to leave. What about StarClan? Didn't she care that the five Clans were meant to be together?

She blinked at Finleap. "Did you hear that?"

Finleap's pelt was prickling. "I guess she's worried the conflict between ShadowClan and SkyClan might spread."

Twigbranch was unnerved. Sparkpelt had been her mentor. Had she *always* wished SkyClan would leave? *Why didn't I realize?* "Do you think the other Clans feel the same way?"

Finleap shrugged. "If they do, then SkyClan will *have* to leave."

Her mouth grew dry. Hearing Finleap say those words out loud made her realize that she hadn't truly thought it was possible until now. But he was right—SkyClan would have no choice but to leave if none of the Clans were on their side. "I really might never see Hawkwing and Violetshine again."

Finleap didn't speak. Didn't he care?

"Will you go back with them?" She stared at him, her heart pounding.

"I don't know." He avoided her gaze.

Was she going to lose her kin and her love at the same time? What would be left if they went? Feeling sick, Twigbranch followed her Clanmates to the tree-bridge.

She crossed silently, pulling away from Finleap as she reached the far shore and hurrying to catch up to Flypaw.

Flypaw glanced at her. "I hope Harepaw and Dapplepaw are at the Gathering. I've got so many new moves to show them."

Snappaw swished through the grass beside them. "Wait till they see all the battle skills we've learned."

As they emerged into the clearing, Flypaw whisked her tail. "They're here!" WindClan and RiverClan moved beneath the trees, moonlight dappling their pelts. Flypaw darted toward a knot of apprentices at the far side. As Snappaw chased after her, Twigbranch hesitated. Her Clanmates were nodding greetings to the other warriors. She scanned the clearing.

SkyClan and ShadowClan hadn't arrived yet. Sparkpelt was talking with Breezepelt and Mallownose. Twigbranch narrowed her eyes. Was she telling them that she *wanted* SkyClan to leave? Were they agreeing with her?

Nervously, Twigbranch padded to the shadows beneath the Great Oak. Bramblestar was already waiting beside the wide, gnarled trunk. The ThunderClan leader's gaze was unreadable.

Twigbranch's paws pricked as she smelled SkyClan scent. The long grass swished, and SkyClan spilled into the clearing. Leafstar and Bellaleaf flanked Frecklewish. Sandynose and Plumwillow were at their heels. *Hawkwing! Violetshine!* Relief swamped her as she saw her father and her sister pad into the moonlight. She hurried to meet them. "Is it true?" She blinked at Hawkwing, her heart pounding. "Is SkyClan going to leave?"

Hawkwing's gaze was solemn. "We're not sure yet." He glanced toward Leafstar, who was heading for the oak.

Violetshine pressed her muzzle to Twigbranch's cheek. "I hope this Gathering will mean we can stay." She stiffened as the long grass swished again and Tigerstar stalked into the clearing. Juniperclaw followed, his eyes narrow and watchful. Stonewing, Cloverfoot, and Scorchfur streamed out behind the skinny deputy. Strikestone and Tawnypelt brought up the rear. Wordlessly, the ShadowClan warriors moved around the edge of the clearing, keeping their distance from the other Clans.

"They haven't brought any apprentices," Violetshine whispered.

Twigbranch swallowed. "I guess it's not an ordinary Gathering."

Tigerstar padded toward the Great Oak. He nodded curtly to Bramblestar, then leaped onto the lowest branch.

"You'd better join your Clanmates," Hawkwing whispered to Twigbranch. "The meeting's about to start."

"Will I see you afterward?" Twigbranch blinked at him expectantly. "You won't leave without talking to me, will you?"

"Of course not." He touched his nose to her ear.

Violetshine flicked her tail along Twigbranch's spine. "Whatever happens, we'll see you before we leave." She hurried after Hawkwing as he joined the SkyClan cats clustering beneath the Great Oak. *Before we leave.* A shiver ran along Twigbranch's spine. Did she mean leave the Gathering or leave the forest? *Don't be rabbit-brained!* She shook out her fur. *It's all going to be fine.* She watched Bramblestar leap into the Great Oak and take his place beside Tigerstar. Leafstar, Mistystar, and Harestar followed. The leaders *had* to come to an agreement. It was what StarClan wanted.

Across the clearing, Flypaw was chattering excitedly to Harepaw. "Twigbranch is going to show me how to catch a buzzard one day." Dapplepaw crouched beside them, copying a hunting crouch Snappaw was demonstrating.

"Hurry!" She beckoned them with a flick of her tail. They scurried after her as she slipped between her Clanmates and stopped beside Finleap.

Bramblestar lifted his muzzle. "You know by now that our medicine cats have received a message from StarClan." He looked down to where Jayfeather stood beside the other medicine cats, and nodded to Leafpool.

Leafpool's moonlit gaze swept the gathered cats. "Last night, at the Moonpool, we shared a single vision." A breeze swished through the branches overhead as she went on. "We saw five saplings standing together. A fierce wind raged around them, but each sapling wove its branches into the others'. The wind could not bend them. But when one broke away, the storm ripped them all from the earth."

Kestrelflight leaned forward. "The message seems clear: The five Clans must support one another."

"Or every Clan will be lost," Willowshine chimed in.

Alderheart lashed his tail urgently. "We must put an end to conflict."

"How?" Mallownose yowled. "There has always been conflict between Clans!"

"And there always will be." Breezepelt called from the other side of the clearing. "We are five Clans, not one."

Brackenfur's eyes flashed in the moonlight. "The Gathering was once the only truce we obeyed."

"We must protect our borders," Cloverfoot growled.

Twigbranch shifted her paws uneasily. She gazed across the sea of pelts, which bristled beneath the stars.

Alderheart lashed his tail. "You speak as though peace were impossible!"

"We are *warriors*!" Tigerstar's growl sounded from above.

"We are warriors!" Stonewing echoed the cry, repeating it like a cuckoo. "We are warriors! We are warriors!"

His Clanmates lifted their voices beside him, and the cry spread throughout the Clans. Twigbranch's pelt spiked as she saw the yowling faces. This was not what StarClan wanted.

"We may be warriors," Bramblestar called out from beside Tigerstar, "but we are not fools! Do we seek conflict for conflict's sake? Sacrifice your life for your Clan, but don't sacrifice your Clan for the sake of tradition!"

The yowling faded into an uneasy silence.

"Bramblestar." Tigerstar curled his lip in disgust. "You're always so smart with words. You want us to give up conflict, but what else must we give up for the sake of peace?"

Stonewing flattened his ears. "He wants ShadowClan to give up land."

Bramblestar's tail twitched as he stared back at Stonewing.

Tigerstar's eyes narrowed. "This peace would suit ThunderClan very well. You keep your land and we lose ours. You grow fat while we grow thin."

Below, Juniperclaw flattened his ears. "Why should ShadowClan alone suffer?"

Leafstar's eyes blazed. "How dare you say ShadowClan is the only one to suffer! We have suffered as much as any Clan, and we go on suffering because of ShadowClan." She nodded at Frecklewish. "Tell them what ShadowClan has done!"

The SkyClan medicine cat narrowed her eyes. "Sparrowpelt has been poisoned."

"So?" Scorchfur stared at her from the crowd. "What does that have to do with us?"

"He vomited deathberry seeds," Frecklewish answered

evenly. "I recognized them at once. Some cat must have given them to him."

As the Clans shifted uneasily, Tigerstar gazed from the Great Oak. "Are you accusing ShadowClan of feeding your Clanmate deathberries?" He snorted scornfully. "He clearly ate them by accident."

Harestar narrowed his eyes. "Would any cat eat deathberries by accident?"

Mistystar tipped her head. "Had SkyClan ever seen deathberries before they came to the forest?" She eyed Frecklewish inquiringly.

Frecklewish shifted her paws. "No. They didn't grow near the gorge."

"Then isn't it possible a SkyClan cat could eat deathberries by mistake?"

Hawkwing bristled beside Juniperclaw. "Why would any cat eat a berry when they are surrounded by warm, juicy prey?"

Tigerstar met his indignant gaze. "Sparrowpelt must have eaten one. How else could he have swallowed the seeds?"

"He was poisoned!" Sandynose lashed his tail.

Plumwillow's hackles lifted beside him. "We know that Alderheart was treating Puddleshine with deathberries. There were deathberries in the ShadowClan camp. And now one of our warriors has been poisoned by them."

Around her, the SkyClan cats murmured angrily.

"It's just a coincidence!" Tigerstar's gaze flicked to Alderheart. "Did any of your berries go missing?"

"No . . ." Alderheart's fur prickled along his spine, his eyes darting this way and that. He was clearly walking through his memory. "I kept a close eye on all of them, but . . ." He began shifting uneasily, his claws digging into the earth.

Leafstar leaned her head toward him from her perch. "But what?"

"I can't be sure that none of the seeds I buried were taken."

Tigerstar's hackles lifted. "Are you accusing ShadowClan of using your seeds to poison Sparrowpelt?"

As the Clans whispered nervously to one another, a small voice sounded at the edge of the crowd. "I saw Juniperclaw near our fresh-kill pile."

Twigbranch's whiskers twitched with surprise as she saw Violetshine meet Tigerstar's gaze.

"He was there on the night before Sparrowpelt got sick." Violetshine's mew trembled as she called out across the heads of her Clanmates.

"But you have no proof that Juniperclaw poisoned him!" Outrage hardened Tigerstar's yowl. He glared venomously at Violetshine. Twigbranch's heart lurched as Tigerstar raged on. "A cat becomes sick and you blame us? Grassheart is lying in our medicine den now, injured by a wound inflicted by SkyClan. She was attacked! She didn't just happen to get sick after one of your patrols passed by."

"'Passed by'?" Leafstar bristled. "You *invaded* our camp!"

"And you attacked our patrol!" Tigerstar shot back.

"You were on our territory!" Leafstar showed her teeth to the ShadowClan leader.

Bramblestar slid between them. His gaze flashed toward

Tree. "Can you do nothing to mediate here?"

The yellow tom shifted in the shadows at the back of the crowd. He padded into the moonlight and met Bramblestar's gaze. "How can I mediate? No cat will listen to me. I have tried to make peace between ShadowClan and SkyClan, but neither side is willing to compromise." He looked around at the cats gathered in front of him. "Tigerstar was right when he said you were warriors. I don't think there can ever be peace between you."

Twigbranch saw defeat in the loner's eyes. Had he given up? Violetshine was staring at Tree, her eyes glittering with fear. *She's scared he'll leave the lake.* He'd admitted that he was powerless to bring peace to the Clans. Surely he had no place here now?

Leafstar snarled beside Bramblestar. "I don't know why we ever came here! We suffered enough because of Darktail and his rogues. We should have guessed that you were hardly better. The lake Clans are only loyal to their bellies, and their hunger for territory means more to them than any warrior code." Bramblestar's ears twitched indignantly, but Leafstar went on. "All of you act as though you're doing SkyClan a favor by letting us hunt beside the lake. We've done nothing but try to help the Clans. We made our camp where you chose and kept to borders you marked. We took in Shadow-Clan and even offered to let them become SkyClan warriors. Then, without complaint, we let them leave to re-form their own Clan. And now they steal our prey and mark our territory as though it's their own. And the rest of you don't object.

You are so scared of sharing your own territory, you let ShadowClan treat us like outsiders. And now, after Shadow-Clan has tried to murder one of our Clanmates, you make excuses. ShadowClan can steal our land and kill us one by one and none of the other Clans will lift a paw." The SkyClan leader curled her lip in disgust as the gathered cats watched her silently. "That is why we are leaving the lake and returning to the gorge."

Twigbranch caught her breath. *They're leaving . . . they're really leaving!* She looked across the crowd to Violetshine, grief tugging at her heart.

"You belong beside the lake," Bramblestar insisted.

"You mustn't leave." Harestar got to his paws. "You were driven from the Clans once before, long ago. It must not happen again."

Mistystar narrowed her eyes. "Why not? Things have been complicated since they came. Wouldn't it simplify everything if they returned to the gorge?" She blinked apologetically at Leafstar. "Even if you are far away, you'll still be one of the Clans. You can still follow the warrior code and honor Star-Clan. And you might be happier there."

Leafstar stared at her, then dipped her head. "At least you are honest."

Tigerstar snorted. "ShadowClan has been nothing but honest. We have told you we want our territory back. What is more honest than that? If you must go, then go."

"But what about the vision?" Jayfeather's panicked mew sounded from below the oak. He padded forward and stared blindly up at the leaders. "StarClan has told us that the five Clans must stand together. How can we stand together if Sky-Clan is at the gorge?"

Frecklewish whisked her tail anxiously. "StarClan showed the vision to all of us."

"They know a storm is coming." Leafpool stood at the Sky-Clan medicine cat's shoulder.

"We must face it together!" Kestrelflight called.

Alderheart stared beseechingly at Bramblestar. "You can't let SkyClan leave, or we are all lost."

Twigbranch shivered. She could hardly believe this was happening. How could the Clans allow this? The cats of WindClan and ThunderClan shifted nervously. Fear flashed in their eyes as they exchanged glances. SkyClan moved closer together, like hunted prey, while RiverClan gazed uneasily at Mistystar. ShadowClan watched silently, muscles taut beneath their pelts.

Bramblestar lifted his chin. "ThunderClan will give up territory for SkyClan!"

Squirrelflight jerked her muzzle toward him. Lionblaze's hackles lifted while his Clanmates blinked at each other in surprise. Hope flared in Twigbranch's chest. "Do you think he'll really give up land?" she whispered to Finleap.

"I hope so." He was watching Bramblestar through narrowed eyes. "SkyClan mustn't leave."

Bramblestar looked urgently at Harestar. "Is WindClan willing to sacrifice land to keep SkyClan beside the lake?"

Harestar hesitated. He looked toward his Clanmates who

stared back, pelts prickling. "We will give up territory if the other Clans give up territory too. If SkyClan needs land, all must provide it, or none. No one Clan must have an advantage. It's the only way to keep peace."

Bramblestar blinked hopefully at Mistystar.

She stared back at him coldly. "I've made RiverClan's position clear. We think it's better for everyone if SkyClan returns to the gorge."

"What about the vision?" Bramblestar's tail flicked.

Tigerstar growled. "We've survived prophecies before. We'll survive this one. ShadowClan is taking back their land. SkyClan can live on it at their own risk or they can leave."

Leafstar curled her lip. "So, no Clan is willing to make space for SkyClan?"

Around the Great Oak, heads dropped and paws shifted uneasily.

The SkyClan leader's amber eyes shone like fire. "I see how it is. . . . Every cat wants *other* cats to be the ones to help. Some of you talk so much about uniting, about your wish for us all to live peacefully side by side, as if you care as much about the other Clans as you do your own. But it's clear to me now that that is all lies! No wonder StarClan sees storms in your future. We've seen and heard enough. We're not part of the lake Clans, and I think we can all agree on that by now. SkyClan doesn't belong here. We never will."

"Please," Bramblestar pleaded, "don't make a rash decision. We can still find a solution, I know it."

Leafstar eyed him coldly. "If it will make you happier, I will

consult with my warriors tonight and decide in the morning."
She leaped from the branch, and the crowd opened below to
let her pass as she headed toward her Clanmates. Sagenose
and Bellaleaf met her silently, their eyes dark.

Twigbranch felt Finleap move beside her. He was trembling. "They're really going to leave," he mumbled. She hardly
heard him. Her heart was racing. *I have to speak to Hawkwing and
Violetshine before they leave.* As she darted across the clearing,
threading between her Clanmates, she heard Finleap calling.
"Twigbranch!"

She ignored him. Didn't he understand? This might be
the last chance she had to speak to her kin. "Hawkwing!" She
reached her father, breathless.

He pressed his muzzle to her head.

Violetshine stared at her. "We're leaving." Grief glistened
in her gaze.

"You can't go!" Twigbranch looked at them desperately.

"We must follow our Clan," Hawkwing told her.

"I'm sure Bramblestar will let you join ThunderClan. You
can stay by the lake with me." Twigbranch stared desperately
at her father. "You mustn't leave. I'll be alone!"

Violetshine glanced at Hawkwing uncertainly. He blinked
back at her and turned to Twigbranch. "We are SkyClan," he
told her. "Where SkyClan goes, we go."

"You could come with us," Violetshine mewed eagerly.
"Leafstar would take you back. And Finleap too. We could
all be together." Twigbranch hesitated. Perhaps she *should*
leave with them. "You've been SkyClan before. You could be

SkyClan again," Violetshine pressed. "All your kin are in Sky-Clan."

Twigbranch's fur prickled. What about ThunderClan? It had taken her so long to discover she truly belonged there. But her ThunderClan Clanmates weren't kin. How could she live without kin? As her thoughts whirled, her heart seemed to crack. She took a breath and met Violetshine's hopeful gaze. She knew what she must do. "I'm ThunderClan now." Twigbranch dropped her gaze. "I never belonged in SkyClan. I'm not sure I ever could."

She felt Hawkwing's breath on her muzzle as he leaned closer. "You have to do what you feel is right. And so do we."

She looked up, a lump in her throat. "Please don't leave me."

Hawkwing's eyes rounded with sorrow. "There's nothing I can do. I'm SkyClan's deputy. My Clan needs me. I can't leave them."

Anger surged in Twigbranch's chest. "But you can leave *me*!" She glared at Violetshine. "How can you go after all we've been through?"

Violetshine stared back at her in surprise. "But you left me, over and over."

Twigbranch froze. It was true. She'd abandoned her sister, first to ShadowClan and then to SkyClan. Guilt washed over her. Was this what it felt like for Violetshine?

"SkyClan!" Leafstar called to her Clanmates from the long grass. Harrybrook and Macgyver hurried after her.

"We must go," Hawkwing mewed huskily. He turned away.

Twigbranch gazed frantically at Violetshine. "Is this the last time I'll see you?"

"I don't know." Violetshine touched her muzzle to Twigbranch's. Her breath was warm in the chilly night air. "It's up to Leafstar now."

"Good-bye." Twigbranch could hardly speak. Her throat tightened as Violetshine pulled away and headed after Hawkwing. As she turned back to her Clanmates, she saw Finleap. He was watching Plumwillow and Sandynose disappear into the grass. She hurried to his side. "Did you say good-bye?"

He didn't answer. The sorrow in his gaze pierced her heart.

"Are you planning to go with them if they leave?" She felt numb.

He stared at her. "I love you, Twigbranch. But if you don't want to have kits, I should go with my kin. At least I'll be somewhere I belong, instead of chasing a dream that might never come true."

Twigbranch stared at him. "Don't you care what *I* want?" Anger cut through her grief. "Having kits isn't just *your* choice. It's *our* choice. And just because I don't want to have kits now doesn't mean I never will."

Finleap's ears twitched self-consciously. She didn't wait for him to respond.

"You're meant to love *me*," she snapped. "Not the family I might give you. If you won't wait until I'm ready, then I guess you weren't the cat I thought you were. Maybe you *should* leave."

Pushing past him, she headed into the long grass.

CHAPTER 15

Violetshine followed Hawkwing across the tree-bridge and jumped down onto the shore. They were heading home to the pine forest, probably for the last time. Clouds were drifting across the moon, and a breeze rippled the surface of the lake. The weather was changing. She landed next to him, the gravel shifting beneath her paws. "Will Twigbranch be all right without us?"

Hawkwing hesitated. "She has ThunderClan. They are her family now."

"And I guess she has Finleap," Violetshine mewed hopefully.

"Yes." She heard a catch in Hawkwing's mew as he turned and hurried to catch up to his Clanmates. She tried not to picture Twigbranch's expression as they had said good-bye. *I'm sorry for leaving you.* Twigbranch was the only cat she'd known her whole life, since the moment she was born. This fresh separation rekindled the loss she'd felt as a kit, when Shadow-Clan had taken her to live in the dark pine forest, while her littermate was in ThunderClan. Her heart ached as Tree fell in beside her. She felt his warmth next to her.

"Twigbranch will be okay," he murmured softly as they padded along the shore.

"I'll miss her."

"I know." Tree gazed at the SkyClan cats ahead.

An owl hooted in the woods on the far side of the lake, its cry echoing over the water before a gust of wind snatched the sound away. The breeze carried the scent of rain. Violetshine fluffed out her fur.

"If we go to the gorge, do you think I'll ever see Twigbranch again?" She looked at Tree, but he seemed distracted. His gaze had slipped away. What was he was thinking about?

Ahead, Macgyver walked beside Leafstar. Hawkwing trailed a little behind with the others, matching Plumwillow's pace. Macgyver flicked his tail crossly. "I hope Bramblestar hasn't made you change your mind."

"I promised to think about it overnight." The SkyClan leader steered the patrol closer to the shelter of the trees.

"We have to leave." Harrybrook hurried closer to Leafstar.

Behind him, Bellaleaf's ears twitched. "We don't *have* to do anything."

"We shouldn't let the Clans push us around." Sagenose bent his head against the wind. "If we leave, they will always remember us as weak."

"We should stay and fight for our place beside the lake," Bellaleaf pressed. "It's what StarClan would want us to do."

Leafstar snorted. "StarClan has only ever made life difficult for us."

Frecklewish pricked her ears. "StarClan can see further

than we can. Perhaps we must bear a little hardship before we can find peace."

"We'll find peace at the gorge," Macgyver meowed.

"And we'll see old friends," Harrybrook chimed in. "The daylight warriors will be pleased to see us."

"We don't need daylight warriors," Dewspring huffed. "We're real Clan cats now. I like living in a forest. I don't want to live somewhere strange."

"It won't be strange once you're used to it," Macgyver mewed.

Sagenose grunted. "We can't go back to the gorge. Our life is here now. There's plenty of prey in the forest, and there won't be trouble from rogues anymore. Once we've shown the Clans that we can't be pushed around, SkyClan can thrive beside the lake."

"I don't want to leave Finleap." Plumwillow's tail fluttered nervously over the stones. "How will he cope without his kin close by?"

"He's got Twigbranch," Macgyver told her. "He'll have kin of his own before long."

Harrybrook scrambled over a rock jutting beneath the trees. "You promised we'd go home to the gorge, Leafstar. You can't change your mind. You saw the hostility from the other Clans. They only think of themselves. They don't care about us. Why should we care about them?"

Leafstar kept walking, her gaze fixed ahead while her warriors argued. Violetshine watched her father as he followed them. Was he going to speak? Suddenly, she felt Tree's fur bristling against hers. She glanced at him and saw his pelt bushing. Could he scent danger? She stiffened and tasted the air. There were only prey-scents from the forest. She realized that Tree's ears were pricked; he seemed to be listening intently. His gaze was fixed, as though someone were walking beside him, but no cat was there. A chill reached through Violetshine's pelt as she recognized the glazed look in Tree's eyes. He was seeing a dead cat! Her heart quickened. Was she surrounded by ghosts?

Tree suddenly quickened his pace. She hurried after him as he caught up to the others. "Leafstar!" His mew was urgent.

The SkyClan leader stopped and faced him. Worry flashed in her eyes. "What's wrong?"

"A dead cat is with us." Tree dipped his head respectfully to the empty space beside him.

Harrybrook and Sagenose backed away, their pelts spiking. Hawkwing narrowed his eyes.

"Who is it?" Leafstar tipped her head.

"I don't know her name." Tree spoke quickly, as though he had important news to share. "But I've seen her before. She says I must remind you of Echosong's vision. It led you to the lake. She says you belong here. You must stay."

Macgyver whisked his tail. "He's imagining it! He's just scared of leaving the forest."

Tree didn't take his eyes off Leafstar. "She says you must stay."

Leafstar glared at him. "Echosong's vision may have led us here, but it will not keep us here. I must do what's right for

SkyClan now, not what was right for us when Echosong was alive."

Tree glanced anxiously to the empty space beside him. "She says SkyClan *must* stay," he told Leafstar. There was urgency in his mew.

Leafstar shifted her paws. "I've heard from every cat now, both living and dead." She dipped her head to Tree. "Thank you for your concern, but I can't risk my Clan on the visions of loners. You don't truly understand what it means to be a Clan cat. No one voice can be louder than another. Only the good of the Clan counts." Leafstar turned away and began heading along the shore. Her Clanmates followed, silent now.

Violetshine stopped nervously beside Tree. "Is the dead cat still here?"

"She's gone." The yellow tom gazed at her dejectedly.

"I'm sorry Leafstar didn't listen to you." If she had, then SkyClan wouldn't have to leave the lake. Violetshine wouldn't have to leave Twigbranch.

"The Clans will never listen to me," Tree murmured. "They don't want my help."

"*I* listen to you!" Alarm flashed through Violetshine's fur. Was he planning to leave? "I'll *always* listen to you. You're wise and kind and good."

He blinked at her slowly. "I wish things could have been different. I wish I could have made a place for myself in the Clans. But there's no role for me here."

Desperation clawed at her chest as she realized what he was saying. "You could be a warrior. I could train you."

Tree shook his head. "I have to stay by the lake. The dead cat was so sure we should stay. And besides, I was meant to be a loner. Being with your Clan has made me realize that. There's no place for me in SkyClan, or any Clan. If SkyClan leaves, it must leave without me."

Her breath caught in her throat. This was what she'd feared all along. How could she be happy without him? "Don't you want to be with me?"

"Of course I do." His gaze was full of warmth. "We belong together. But I can't be a Clan cat." He reached his muzzle close to hers. "Why don't you come and be a loner with me? We don't need a Clan. We can be happy on our own."

Violetshine swallowed. She'd been afraid he would suggest that, because she knew she would be tempted to go with him. Should she? The thought of spending every day with Tree thrilled her. But how could she turn her back on her father and her Clan? They meant everything to her. But Tree loved her. Not because she was kin, but because she was special to him. She could see that in the way he was looking at her, his eyes glistening with hope. *He wants me to stay so much.*

"We could remain by the lake," Tree went on. "You'd be near Twigbranch and you'd be with me."

Violetshine wanted to bury her nose in his fur and say yes. She wouldn't have to leave the lake and abandon her sister, and she'd be able to stay with the cat she loved. But she couldn't imagine life without Hawkwing. She'd grown up without him; she couldn't risk losing him again. Not like this.

And she could tell from the claw she could feel in her chest at the thought of turning her back on her Clan, that SkyClan was where she belonged.

She steadied her breath. The patrol was disappearing into the forest. "Come on," she mewed lightly. "Let's catch up to the others. It's late and I'm tired. Maybe Leafstar will decide to stay and we won't have to make a choice."

Hurrying past Tree, she followed her Clanmates. Her whiskers trembled. Was Leafstar really going to lead SkyClan away from the lake? *I can't leave Tree and Twigbranch behind.* Every hair on her pelt seemed to spark with dread. *But I have to!* How could she choose? Her only hope now was that Leafstar would decide to stay. As she padded into the forest, she glanced up. Where the canopy met the sky, stars glittered like dewdrops. *Please, StarClan, let Leafstar make the right choice.*

Violetshine opened her eyes. Dawn light was seeping into the den. She sat up, relieved to feel Tree still snuggled in the nest beside her. They were the last cats left in the den, and she could hear paw steps outside. She nosed him softly. "The Clan is awake."

Yawning, he got to his paws. "Has Leafstar made her decision?"

"I don't know." As Violetshine hopped out of the nest, hope fluttered in her belly. Had Leafstar changed her mind in the night? Would she announce that they would stay and fight for their place beside the lake? She headed out of the den and waited as Tree caught up to her.

Leafstar was already standing in the clearing. Dewspring and Reedclaw huddled close by. Around them, warriors picked their way over the tattered remnants of the torn dens. A cold wind tugged at Violetshine's fur. She moved closer to Tree as rain began to drip from the branches overhead.

Hawkwing sat at the far edge of the clearing, his paws tucked under his tail, while Sandynose paced beside him. Palepaw, Gravelpaw, and Nectarpaw clustered outside their den, their fur pricking with excitement.

Dewspring leaned closer to Reedclaw. "Are we leaving?"

"Leafstar hasn't spoken yet," Reedclaw whispered back.

Frecklewish peered from the shelter of her den, narrowing her eyes against the wind.

Leafstar glanced around the ravaged camp, determination in her gaze. Violetshine held her breath. *Don't make us leave.* A fierce breeze rustled the young leaves overhead as Leafstar spoke.

"I've thought hard about what is best," she meowed slowly. "I've decided that SkyClan will leave the lake. We are returning to the gorge."

More claws seemed to rake Violetshine's gut. She stared at Leafstar, wishing she'd misheard, hoping wildly that perhaps the SkyClan leader would see the disappointment in her eyes and change her mind. But Leafstar stared resolutely at her Clanmates. She was being so strong, and yet it was clear that she needed her Clan's support. Violetshine knew suddenly that she couldn't stay if her Clan left. She turned to Tree and saw grief glittering in his eyes. He knew what she was going to say. She swallowed. "I have to go with them." Her mew was no more than a whisper.

"I know." Tree pressed against her. "I'll miss you. But I must stay."

Hawkwing dipped his head respectfully to Leafstar. "When do we go?"

"Now." The SkyClan leader flicked her tail. "There's no reason to hesitate. Gather what you need. We leave immediately."

Frecklewish's eyes widened. "I don't know if Sparrowpelt is strong enough to travel."

"His Clanmates will help him," Leafstar told her. "The poison is out of his belly. He'll grow stronger on the journey."

Frecklewish hesitated. "If he grows tired, we must rest."

Leafstar nodded. "All right."

Frecklewish ducked inside her den and began tossing bundles of herbs into the clearing. They were neatly wrapped in leaves and tied with grass. Fidgetflake darted out and picked up a bundle. "Carry this, please." He dropped it at Harrybrook's paws and darted back for another as Frecklewish guided Sparrowpelt from the den. The dark tabby tom's amber eyes were dull, and he moved slowly. Mintfur and Macgyver hurried to help, slipping to either side of him and pressing against him as he headed toward the entrance.

Plumwillow padded to the fresh-kill pile. Sadness darkened her gaze as she picked up a mouse left from last night and began to head for the entrance. Sagenose grabbed a sparrow and followed her.

Violetshine's paws felt frozen to the earth. She pressed her muzzle against Tree's cheek. "Please keep an eye on Twigbranch."

"I'll do what I can," he promised.

"We must always remember each other."

"I could never forget you." His eyes clouded with grief.

"I love you." As she tore away from him, Violetshine's heart seemed to split. She hurried after her Clanmates as they headed out of camp. Hawkwing gently took the mouse from Plumwillow. She nodded her thanks and caught up to Sandynose.

"Don't dawdle." Reedclaw hurried Quailpaw and Sunnypaw onward as they paused to look back at the camp.

Nectarpaw bounced around Harrybrook. "Is it far?" she mewed excitedly.

"Far enough," he told her. "Calm down. You'll need your energy for the journey."

Violetshine blinked back sorrow. She was following her Clan away from the two cats she loved best. A lump lodged in her throat as she pictured Tree alone in the deserted camp, but she didn't look back. She had made her decision.

SkyClan was leaving the lake.

CHAPTER 16

The wind had changed. In the hours since dawn the sky had grown darker. Now rain pattered softly on the roof of the medicine den. Peering from the entrance, Alderheart looked through the haze at the empty clearing. The cats of ShadowClan were sheltering in their dens. Damp pine scent washed his muzzle as he watched rivulets running around the edge. The puddle beside the elders' den had swollen.

He fluffed his fur against the cold and turned back inside. Crossing the den, he sniffed the patch where he'd buried the deathberry seeds. He'd sifted through it while Puddleshine and Grassheart had been sleeping and had found seeds mixed with the soil, but it was impossible to tell if any were missing.

"Are you still worrying about them?" Puddleshine sat up in his nest. His pelt was slick from a thorough wash.

Alderheart had told him about the Gathering. "Frecklewish said they'd poisoned Sparrowpelt."

Grassheart shifted stiffly in her nest. "A ShadowClan warrior would never poison another cat. We're warriors, not fox-hearts. We settle arguments with our claws."

"I know." Alderheart couldn't believe that ShadowClan

would use poison to harm another Clan. The warrior code wouldn't permit such slyness, and he'd spent long enough in the ShadowClan camp to see for himself that they were as honorable as any other Clan. And yet the coincidence nagged at him.

"Is SkyClan really going to leave?" Grassheart's question distracted him from his thoughts.

"Leafstar promised she'd think about it, but the Clans didn't say anything to make her want to stay." His belly tightened. *Please, StarClan. Let her decide to stay.*

"I can't believe the leaders didn't take your vision seriously." Puddleshine climbed out of his nest.

"Nor can I." Alderheart sniffed the ShadowClan medicine cat's wounds. They were healing fast, and there was no sign of fever. "Five medicine cats shared the same vision. How much more proof do they need before they will act?"

"What can they do?" Grassheart looked puzzled. "Tigerstar can't abandon our claim to territory. We need more space to hunt. As long as SkyClan keeps our land, ShadowClan will always face the threat of hunger."

"*Some* Clan has to give SkyClan territory," Puddleshine argued. "Is it too much to ask each of us to donate a little? At least the burden will be shared."

Alderheart wasn't sure Leafstar would like to hear Sky-Clan called a burden, but he agreed that it wasn't fair to ask ShadowClan alone to give land to SkyClan. "If only the other leaders were willing to compromise."

"Leafstar could have compromised," Grassheart pointed

out. "She could have agreed to let ShadowClan hunt on Sky-Clan's land."

Puddleshine frowned. "Two Clans chasing the same prey could never work."

Alderheart's paws felt heavy. There seemed no way to find space for SkyClan beside the lake *and* keep peace between the Clans.

A shadow moved at the entrance. Alderheart's paws sparked with anxiety as Tigerstar padded into the den. *Are you accusing ShadowClan of using your seeds to poison Sparrowpelt?* Tigerstar's words rang in his head as he dipped his head in greeting. "Hi." Was the ShadowClan leader still angry with him?

"Hi." Tigerstar shook rain from his pelt and glanced around the den. "How are your patients today?"

Alderheart shifted his paws. "Grassheart's wound is healing well. There's no sign of infection, and Puddleshine—"

Tigerstar cut him off. "I can see Puddleshine is looking much better. You've done great work here, Alderheart. ShadowClan will always be grateful to you for tending to our medicine cat and taking such good care of our Clanmates while he's been ill." Tigerstar's piercing gaze swung toward him. There was no sign of anger, but the dark tabby's tone was brisk as he went on. "I think it's time you went home. Puddleshine looks well enough to take up his duties once more."

"I am." Puddleshine lifted his chin.

"Good." Tigerstar kept his gaze on Alderheart. "Are you ready to leave?"

"Yes." Alderheart blinked at him. Was Tigerstar throwing him out?

"Your Clan must miss you. I'm sure they'll be glad to have you back." Tigerstar glanced toward the entrance, where rain dripped from the brambles. "You can wait out the rain if you like."

"Thanks, but I'd like to get home as soon as possible." Alderheart didn't care whether Tigerstar wanted him to leave. His heart felt suddenly light as he realized that he was no longer responsible for ShadowClan. He was going *home*. He nodded to Puddleshine. "Take care of yourself."

Puddleshine dipped his head. "Thanks, Alderheart. You saved my life."

"You would've have done the same for me."

As Puddleshine gazed at him warmly, Grassheart sat up. "Thanks for taking care of me."

"I'm glad I could help." Alderheart signaled to Puddleshine with a flick of his tail. "I put marigold on Grassheart's wound this morning. She'll need fresh ointment tonight."

"I'll see to it."

Tigerstar didn't move as Alderheart padded to the den entrance. "Do you need a patrol to escort you?"

"No, thanks." Alderheart slipped outside. There was someplace he wanted to go before he headed home, and he didn't want a ShadowClan patrol watching. He hurried through the rain, surprised as he saw Berryheart duck out of the nursery.

"Are you leaving?" She blinked at him, raindrops collecting on her whiskers.

"Yes." Alderheart halted. "Puddleshine's well again."

Dovewing slid out. "Thank you for taking care of Shadow-kit."

"And Hollowkit," Berryheart chimed in.

"Keep him out of this rain," Alderheart told her.

"I will." As Berryheart spoke, Shadowkit hurried from the den.

"Are you leaving?" He stared at Alderheart with round eyes.

"Yes." Alderheart tipped his head, disappointed at leaving the young tom.

"But I was going to help you in the medicine den later."

Sadness pricked Alderheart's belly as he saw the kit's eyes dull. He hated letting Shadowkit down. "You can help Puddleshine," he told him. "I'm sure he'll appreciate it."

Shadowkit looked crestfallen. "But I like helping you."

Dovewing scooped the kit close with her tail. "Alderheart has to go. His Clan needs him."

"But what if I have another vision?"

Alderheart saw Dovewing's eyes darken. "Your mother knows what to do," he soothed, hearing his voice sound confident, while feeling a faint tingle of uncertainty in his belly. He still hadn't gotten to the bottom of Shadowkit's last vision, but it certainly sounded ominous. "Be careful," he called as he headed for the camp entrance. "Stay in camp. Don't forget that visions are sent to guide us."

He ducked through the thorn tunnel and hurried into the

forest. If the young tom had developed a connection to Star-Clan, that surely meant that everything was going to be fine. *So why don't I feel more at ease?* he asked himself as he headed for the SkyClan border.

By the time he crossed it, rain had seeped deep into his fur. Raindrops collected on his whiskers as he followed a rabbit trail toward the SkyClan camp. He had to find out what Leafstar had decided. No cat would stop him. It would be easy to persuade a patrol that he was on his way to see Frecklewish. Even the toughest warrior would think twice about sending a medicine cat away.

SkyClan's scent was faint. Perhaps the rain had washed away their markers. He tasted the air as the bramble wall of the camp appeared beyond a rise, hoping to find stronger SkyClan scents here, but he could barely detect their musk through the damp tang of the forest. Worry wormed beneath his pelt. Surely they wouldn't leave without saying good-bye? He'd known Violet-shine longer than anyone else had known her. He'd been the one to find her as a kit and bring her to the Clans. He liked to think she wouldn't go without seeing him first. He pressed back grief and pricked his ears hopefully as he listened for the sounds of Clan life. He heard the pattering of paws. An apprentice? He halted and scanned the forest. A squirrel flashed across the trail and disappeared among the brambles. He frowned. It was unusual to find such easy prey close to a Clan camp. He hurried to the entrance and ducked inside.

The clearing was empty. Were the SkyClan cats sheltering from the rain? He padded quickly to the warriors' den and peered inside. Stale scent washed his nose. He ducked out and scanned the camp, unease creeping in his belly. The dens were torn. Brambles scattered the ground. The camp was in ruins. The ShadowClan raid had been thorough. The vision of saplings standing against the storm flashed in his mind. SkyClan wasn't hiding from the rain; they were gone.

His heart lurched. The vision was coming true. Fear flashed beneath his pelt. He remembered how angry Leaf-star had been at the Gathering. *And now, after ShadowClan has tried to murder one of our Clanmates, you make excuses.* Had Shadow-Clan really tried to kill a SkyClan cat? Surely not. They were honorable warriors, not fox-hearts. And yet Frecklewish had found deathberry seeds in Sparrowpelt's vomit. And Violet-shine had seen Juniperclaw tampering with SkyClan prey. Neither cat would lie.

Thoughts whirling, he scurried through the rain to the medicine den and ducked inside. Herb smells mingled with the stale scent of sickness. He glanced around, not sure what he was looking for. Violetshine had seen Juniperclaw beside the fresh-kill pile. Alderheart hunched his shoulders against the rain and padded around the edge of the clearing. He sniffed the ground, searching for fresh-kill scents, stopping when he smelled traces of a mouse. They were faint, half washed away by the rain, but blood stained the earth here, and deeper musky prey-scents seeped from the soil. This must be where SkyClan stored fresh-kill. He scouted the ground around the patch, looking for clues. *ShadowClan scent?* He halted and opened his mouth, drawing the smell over his tongue. Focusing, he followed the faint trail toward the camp wall. Here, sheltered from the rain, the scent was stronger. It was definitely ShadowClan. He ran his paw over the wet earth. It was smoothed by paw prints. Crouching, he peered beneath the tangled stems of the bramble. His paws pricked as he saw seeds scattered on the ground. Reaching in, he pulled them out. He recognized them at once. *Deathberry seeds.* He smelled ShadowClan scent on them. His hackles lifted.

It was true.

ShadowClan had brought deathberry seeds to the SkyClan camp!

Juniperclaw? Surely not . . . he was the ShadowClan deputy. Violetshine must have been mistaken. Or perhaps she'd seen Juniperclaw after another warrior had planted the seeds. A chill reached through his fur. Had Tigerstar ordered one of his Clanmates to leave deathberry seeds here? Was this his plan to drive SkyClan away?

Alderheart straightened, shock pulsing beneath his pelt. Tigerstar wouldn't be so cruel. He was fierce, but he was a *warrior.*

But they're all *warriors.* Alderheart had lived among Shadow-Clan. They were not so different from ThunderClan. He couldn't believe any of them capable of such malice. And yet some cat had brought deadly seeds into SkyClan.

Quickly he buried them so that no creature could pick them up accidentally, and headed back to ThunderClan. Bramblestar should know what he'd found.

* * *

"Alderheart!" Sparkpelt was the first to see him as he ducked through the ThunderClan camp entrance. She raced across the clearing, her paws sending up spray as she splashed over the slick earth, and rubbed her muzzle along his cheek. "Are you back for good?"

"Yes." Alderheart blinked at her distractedly, barely seeing his littermate. His thoughts were racing. He had to tell Bramblestar about SkyClan and the seeds.

She stiffened. "What's happened?"

"SkyClan is gone."

Sparkpelt shrugged. "Leafstar said they were leaving."

Had she forgotten the vision? Why wasn't she upset? "Don't you know what this means?"

"Peace, of course." She tipped her head, as though she didn't understand why this bothered him.

"You're home!" Jayfeather called from the medicine den before Alderheart could respond to Sparkpelt. He beckoned Alderheart from the rain with his tail.

"I'll be there soon. I have to speak to Bramblestar first!" Alderheart told him.

"Alderheart!" Molewhisker poked his head out of the warriors' den. "It's good to see you!"

Thriftkit, Bristlekit, and Flipkit scrambled from the nursery, raindrops glittering in their fluffy pelts.

Bristlekit raced toward Alderheart. "What was it like in ShadowClan?"

"Was Tigerstar scary?" Flipkit followed.

Alderheart nosed them gently away as they crowded his

paws. "I'll tell you about it later." He began to head toward the tumble of rocks.

"Come back at once!" Ivypool yowled from the nursery. "You'll all get greencough out there."

"It's not fair." Thriftkit scowled at her.

"Cats on hunting patrols don't worry about greencough," Bristlekit grumbled.

As they headed back to the nursery, Alderheart bounded onto the Highledge and stopped outside Bramblestar's den. He tasted the air. Bramblestar was inside, and Squirrelflight was with him. He ducked through the trailing vines and shook the rain from his pelt.

"You're home!" Bramblestar blinked at him.

Squirrelflight thrust her muzzle to his cheek. "It's good to see you."

"I have to talk to you." Alderheart stared at them urgently. "SkyClan is gone."

Squirrelflight and Bramblestar glanced at each other, as though recalling a previous conversation.

"You don't seem surprised." Alderheart searched Bramblestar's gaze.

Bramblestar shrugged. "Well, Leafstar seemed pretty certain last night."

Frustration surged in Alderheart's chest. Why was no one else as upset about this as he was? "But she said she'd think about it!"

Squirrelflight's eyes rounded with sympathy. "She was just being polite."

"Of course, we wish it hadn't come to this," Bramblestar meowed gravely, "but we were out of options."

Squirrelflight moved closer to her mate. "Your father did what he could. He offered them territory."

Bramblestar's ears twitched. "Without the support of the other Clans, we couldn't make SkyClan stay."

Alderheart stared at them. Were they ready to accept Sky-Clan's loss? Didn't they remember the vision? "What will happen to the rest of the Clans?"

"StarClan will guide us," Bramblestar told him.

"Why would they bother when no cat listens to them?" Anger jabbed at Alderheart's belly.

Squirrelflight ran her tail along Alderheart's spine. "We listen," she murmured. "But we can't change what has happened."

"You can tell the other Clans the truth!" Alderheart shook his mother off.

"The truth?" Bramblestar echoed.

"ShadowClan drove SkyClan away." Alderheart was trembling with rage. "When they invaded SkyClan's camp, they put deathberry seeds in the prey."

"I know that's what Frecklewish told us at the Gathering," Bramblestar mewed soothingly. "But we have no proof. Sparrowpelt might have picked the seeds up anywhere."

Alderheart lashed his tail. "I have proof! I found seeds beside the fresh-kill pile at SkyClan's camp. They had ShadowClan scent on them." He stared in triumph at his father.

Bramblestar's eyes widened for a moment. Concern darkened his gaze.

"You have to do something!" Alderheart pressed.

"Do what exactly?" Bramblestar shook out his fur. "Sparrowpelt survived. And SkyClan has already left. Accusing ShadowClan of poisoning their fresh-kill pile won't bring them back."

"It would only stir up trouble," Squirrelflight chimed in.

"We are four saplings now," Bramblestar added. "But we can still stand together."

"It's more important than ever that the remaining Clans unite," Squirrelflight agreed.

Alderheart stared at them in disbelief. "But the vision said that when one sapling goes, the storm destroys us all."

"We did what we could!" Bramblestar snapped; then more softly he added, "StarClan won't desert us." He looked away, his gaze flitting toward the shadows at the edges of his den. Alderheart could see his father's pelt prickle. *He's scared.*

Fear tugged deep in Alderheart's belly. *The Clans are in danger, and there's nothing he can do.*

CHAPTER 17

❧

"Hurry up!" Narrowing her eyes against the rain, Twigbranch stopped at the top of the rise and waited for Flypaw to catch up. She wanted to take her apprentice hunting near the farthest ThunderClan border. Finleap and Snappaw were at the bottom of the rise. They'd decided to stay at the training ground and practice battle moves.

"Is Finleap all right?" Flypaw glanced back at the brown tom as she padded toward Twigbranch.

"I guess he misses his kin." She knew it was more than that, but she didn't want to talk about Finleap. Especially not with her apprentice. Twigbranch began to follow the trail deeper into ThunderClan territory.

Flypaw bounded after her. "It's like he's nervous when he's around you. Have you had an argument?"

"No." Twigbranch ducked beneath a branch. There was fresh mouse dung on the other side. Maybe the scent would distract Flypaw from questions.

In the days since SkyClan had left, Finleap had seemed uneasy. They'd talked after the Gathering and he'd decided to stay in ThunderClan. Twigbranch had been relieved. Of course Finleap was upset at losing his kin, and at first she'd tried to be supportive, but it was like he was clinging to the loss. He'd started to act as though he'd made the wrong choice. He'd begun to eat alone and go to his nest early instead of sharing tongues with the Clan. He was acting like an outsider. Frustration itched beneath Twigbranch's pelt, growing stronger each day. How could Finleap ever feel like part of ThunderClan if he didn't try to fit in? At least he'd stopped talking about having kits. Had he really accepted that they wouldn't have kits until they were *both* ready? Twigbranch wasn't sure the matter was settled. Part of her wondered if Finleap wished he'd left with SkyClan after all.

Flypaw stopped to sniff the mouse dung. "Shall we hunt here?" she mewed.

"I want to show you somewhere new." Twigbranch felt a flicker of satisfaction as Flypaw's eyes flashed excitedly. She'd learned that her apprentice worked better when they were in an unusual part of the forest. Fresh stimulation seemed to keep her focused, and so, whenever she could, Twigbranch challenged Flypaw with tricky battle moves or prey that was hard to catch.

She veered away from the SkyClan border. The rain had almost washed the scent line clean, and the fading scent renewed her longing for Hawkwing and Violetshine. She pushed them from her mind and broke into a run. "Come on," she called to Flypaw. "I want you to see the very edge of Clan territory. It's a long way." She fluffed her fur and followed the winding trail. Her paws slithered on the wet ground as she zigzagged between trees and ducked through gaps in brambles.

By the time they neared the border, Twigbranch was out of breath.

Flypaw raced past her. "Is this the right way?" She disappeared over a rise.

"Slow down!" The path was slippery where the trail had turned to mud. She followed Flypaw over the rise and blinked through the rain at the forest beyond. A damp haze hid the border. Beyond it, the land belonged to loners and Twolegs. Warriors didn't often come this far, and there would be plenty of prey here.

Flypaw was already sniffing around the roots of a beech. Her wet pelt was spiked with excitement as she circled the trunk. "I smell mouse." She backed away, crouching.

Twigbranch was impressed. Flypaw had found the scent even through the rain. And she was keeping her distance from her quarry. Twigbranch crouched beside her and followed the young cat's gaze to the shadow between the roots.

"It's a hole," Flypaw whispered. "Should we wait until a mouse comes out or try to dig down?"

"What do you think?" She was testing Flypaw.

Flypaw frowned thoughtfully. "It's nearly sunhigh. Mice sleep through sunhigh." Her ears pricked excitedly. "The mouse will be sleepy. We should dig. Even if it tries to run, it will be slow."

"Let's try it." Twigbranch knew that Flypaw would learn more if she experimented for herself. She let the striped tabby start to scrape at the soil in front of the hole, then hopped onto the root beside her and helped. The rain had made the earth soft, and it was easy to dig. Mud squished between Twigbranch's claws as she hauled out dirt.

"I can smell it!" Flypaw started scrabbling more eagerly at the hole. Suddenly her paw broke through into a tiny cave hollowed out beneath the root. A mouse darted out, slipping past her paw. Flypaw hesitated, then lifted herself onto her haunches and twisted. In a single fluid movement she threw herself at the mouse, catching it nimbly between her forepaws. She tugged it toward her and killed it with a single bite.

Twigbranch shook the mud from her paws. "Great catch." Her chest swelled with pride.

Flypaw blinked at her happily. "Can we eat it now?"

Twigbranch shook her head. "Save it for the fresh-kill pile."

"But I'm hungry."

"So's your Cla—" Twigbranch broke off. A familiar scent was drifting from the forest beyond the border.

Flypaw narrowed her eyes. "Your nose is twitching. Can you smell something?"

"Bury your mouse under some leaves and follow me." She picked her way through a patch of ivy, heading for the border.

Flypaw pushed her catch quickly beneath a root and scraped leaves around it. "Are we allowed outside Clan territory?" She hurried after Twigbranch.

"Of course." Twigbranch glanced at her, barely listening. It was Tree's scent, she was certain. But what was he doing here? Hadn't he left the lake with SkyClan? Hope quivered in her belly. If he'd stayed behind, perhaps Violetshine had stayed with him. She quickened her step, crossing the scent line into the forest beyond.

The brambles grew closer here, and pines sprouted between the oaks. She knew the land here stretched right to the mountains, too far to patrol and too wild to hunt. Lilyheart had told nursery tales about foxes and badgers that prowled here. Twigbranch tasted the air nervously as the forest floor sloped upward. She could smell blood mingled with Tree's scent. Was he hurt? As she scrambled up the slope, her paws slid on wet leaves. Rocks jutted from the ground. She squeezed between them, climbing higher as the land sloped more steeply.

"What are we looking for?" Flypaw was at her tail.

"I just want to check something." Tree's scent was stronger. He must have been here for days. Her heart quickened as she tasted for her sister's scent. Surely Tree wouldn't have stayed without Violetshine? She must be with him. She clambered over the last rock as the land evened out. A holly bush sprouted between the trees. Twigbranch padded around it, sniffing the ground. The muddy earth had been smoothed by paw prints. "Tree?" she called out softly. Fur brushed leaves inside. She glimpsed movement between the branches. "It's me. Twigbranch."

"Tree?" Flypaw sounded surprised. "Didn't he leave with SkyClan?" She slid past Twigbranch and began sniffing the bush.

"Careful." Twigbranch nosed her away. "Can't you smell blood?"

"It's just fresh-kill." Tree pushed his way from the bush and halted in front of her. His thick yellow fur was fluffed out against the rain.

Twigbranch's heart leaped as she met the tom's gaze. "Is Violetshine with you?"

His eyes darkened. "She's with SkyClan."

Disappointment dropped like a stone in her belly.

"Come out of the rain." Tree led her through a gap in the branches. She pushed her way in. The prickly leaves scraped rainwater from her pelt. Flypaw squeezed in after her.

A half-eaten rabbit lay beside a nest of bracken at one edge of the makeshift den. Rainwater dripped through the roof, but it was warm.

"What are you doing here?" Twigbranch searched his gaze. Had SkyClan refused to take him to the gorge?

"I wanted to stay beside the lake." Tree sat down, while Flypaw sniffed the rabbit.

"Why?" Twigbranch frowned.

"I don't belong in SkyClan. And I figured the lake must be important. A dead warrior made me beg Leafstar to stay."

Twigbranch blinked at him. "What about Violetshine? I thought you were mates!"

"I asked her to stay with me," Tree told her. "But she wanted to go with her Clan."

Twigbranch knew how much her sister loved Tree. But what was the point of love, she wondered, if it wasn't strong enough to keep cats together? She thought, with a pang, of Finleap. Love had kept them together, but were they happy? Her heart ached, and she pushed the thought away.

Flypaw poked the rabbit. "Can I have a mouthful?" she asked Tree,

Tree shrugged. "Eat as much as you like. There's more prey in this part of the forest than I can hunt."

Her fur bristling happily, Flypaw took a bite.

I don't belong in SkyClan. Twigbranch gazed quizzically at Tree. "So are you a loner again?"

"I guess." Tree shifted his paws.

"But I thought you were the Clan mediator." Had he given up on the Clans altogether?

"The Clans never listened to me." Tree shrugged. "I was wasting my time."

"Wasting your time?" Twigbranch didn't understand how time with the Clans could be wasted. But then, she'd never known any other way of living. "Is sleeping under a bush by yourself any better?"

"Not really." Tree looked at her sadly. "I thought I'd enjoy going back to my old life. But it's not the same. I miss Violet-shine. I miss having other cats around. Hunting for myself isn't as much fun as it used to be."

Twigbranch blinked at him sympathetically. He didn't seem to feel he belonged anywhere. "I guess this weather doesn't help."

Tree frowned. "It's rained ever since SkyClan left. And the wind has been getting stronger. Have you noticed?"

Twigbranch pricked her ears. The soft swish of leaves had risen to a roar.

"It's like the vision," Tree went on. "The medicine cats said the saplings were destroyed by a storm."

Alarm pricked through Twigbranch's pelt. "Do you think this is the storm they saw?"

"I don't know. But if it is, SkyClan should be here. They are the fifth sapling, aren't they?" Worry glittered in Tree's amber gaze. "If they're not here, the storm will destroy all the Clans."

Flypaw sat up and licked her lips. "Perhaps, when SkyClan sees how bad the weather is, they'll come back."

Twigbranch glanced at her. Would the storm make Leaf-star rethink her decision to leave? Her paws pricked. It might be enough to make the SkyClan leader realize that her Clan belonged beside the lake. "We could go after them." She looked at Tree. "We could make her change her mind."

"How?" Tree narrowed his eyes. "SkyClan still doesn't have a home beside the lake."

"Look at the storm," Twigbranch pressed. "Surely now the other leaders will see that SkyClan needs to live here. I bet RiverClan territory is already starting to flood. Mistystar must be wondering if she made the right decision. All the leaders have to change their minds if the rain keeps getting worse. Perhaps they'll realize they have to share some of their land."

Tree looked unconvinced. "The weather might not be enough to make them change their minds. They were pretty stubborn at the Gathering, despite the vision."

"We need other cats to speak out. There must be cats in every Clan who are worried about the vision and want Sky-Clan to stay."

"Plumpaw and Eaglepaw think SkyClan should have stayed," Flypaw told them. "So do Dapplepaw and Harepaw in RiverClan. It's only the leaders who want them gone."

Hope surged in Twigbranch's chest. "If we can persuade cats in every Clan to speak out, we could get the leaders to change their minds."

Tree tipped his head. "It's no use convincing the other leaders until we've convinced Leafstar."

"Surely she'll see sense?" Twigbranch pictured SkyClan trudging though the pouring rain.

Flypaw looked thoughtful. "We could take cats from each Clan to *find* SkyClan and persuade them that we want them beside the lake."

Twigbranch nodded eagerly. "And when we've brought them back, we can persuade the other Clans to let them stay."

Tree looked thoughtful. "I guess if enough cats support SkyClan, the leaders will *have* to change their minds."

Twigbranch purred. For the first time in days, she felt hopeful. Hawkwing and Violetshine could return to the lake and the Clans would be safe. "This is going to be great," she mewed. "But there's one thing I have to do first."

Tree looked at her. "What?"

"I'm going to do this the right way." Twigbranch puffed out her chest. "I'm not running off like a newleaf hare this time. I'm going to go to Bramblestar and tell him about our plan. I'm going to ask for his permission."

CHAPTER 18

Violetshine padded after her Clanmates, her head bowed against the driving rain. Her ears were flat against her head and her eyes narrowed. She'd felt nauseous since she woke this morning. The sodden mouse Hawkwing had brought her had just made her feel worse. She'd lost track of how long they'd been traveling and hardly glanced along the trail anymore. Sparrowpelt had slowed them down at first, but he was recovering, and they'd picked up speed despite the weather.

Her Clanmates didn't seem much happier. She was aware of them trudging around her, their pelts slick against their frames as they pushed onward.

Harrybrook grumbled behind her. "If it gets any wetter, we're going to drown."

"We should find shelter," Plumwillow called out.

"We'll find shelter at the gorge," Leafstar yowled from the head of the group.

Irritation jabbed Violetshine's belly. Did Leafstar even remember the route to the gorge? They'd been walking for days, the weather worsening with each new dawn, and still Leafstar couldn't tell them how much longer they'd be traveling. No cat complained. They simply followed Leafstar without question. *Because* they're *leaving less behind,* she thought resentfully. The pain in her chest hardened. She might never see Twigbranch again. And Tree. Her paws grew heavier. If only he'd come. This journey would be an adventure they'd share together. She would hardly feel the rain if he were beside her.

"Can we explore the trail up ahead?" Sunnypaw's mew cut into her thoughts. The ginger she-cat was looking eagerly at Plumwillow, while the other apprentices were turning to their mentors.

"I suppose that would be okay," Plumwillow purred.

When all the mentors nodded, the apprentices raced ahead.

"Don't go far!" Sagenose called as they disappeared around jutting rocks that marked a bend in the trail.

Violetshine shook out her fur as her thoughts returned to Tree. Why had he stayed behind? If he'd truly loved her, he'd have come. The thought clawed at her belly. Pushing it away, she braved the rain and looked up at the hillside. The storm lashed her muzzle as she recognized the gorse-covered slope. Alder trees dotted the hillside, and, halfway up, a dip opened in the heather. *This is where I first met him!* Her heart ached. She remembered how cocky he'd first been, flirting with her even though she'd been distracted by her search for Needletail. And then he'd reunited her with her dead friend, before she'd gone to StarClan. Nostalgia gripped her heart. She suddenly felt overwhelmed by loss. Was every cat destined to leave her?

Reedclaw nudged her shoulder with her nose. "Violetshine?"

"What?" Violetshine wanted to be alone with her thoughts.

Reedclaw flinched. "Sorry to disturb you." Raindrops streamed from her whiskers. "But we're heading up the slope."

Surprised, Violetshine saw that her Clanmates had veered from the muddy track at the bottom of the valley and were heading toward the heather.

"Hawkwing persuaded Leafstar that we should rest for a while in that dip." Reedclaw eyed her nervously. "I just thought you should know."

"I'm sorry I snapped," Violetshine mewed guiltily. "I'm just in a bad moood." Thinking about Tree was making her sad. She glanced toward the jutting rocks. "We should tell Sunnypaw and the others that we've changed route."

"I'll go." As the small tabby she-cat hurried away, Violetshine caught up to her Clanmates on the slope. She wondered whether Tree's scent would still be on the heather here. *Don't be rabbit-brained.* His scent would have disappeared moons ago.

"Violetshine! Plumwillow!" Reedclaw's terrified yowl cut through the wind.

Plumwillow jerked her muzzle around. Violetshine turned, alarm sparking through her pelt.

Reedclaw was racing through the rain, her fur on end. "Sunnypaw is stuck in the mud! She's sinking!"

Tinycloud and Sparrowpelt broke from the group. They raced downslope, their paws slithering over the wet grass. Violetshine pelted after them. She was hardly aware of the rain now. Sunnypaw was in trouble. "Are the other apprentices safe?" she called as she caught up to Reedclaw. Tinycloud and Sparrowpelt ran on, their paws splashing through puddles as skidded around the rocks.

"I think so." Reedclaw's eyes were wide. "They're trying to reach her, but the mud's too deep."

"Come on." Violetshine hared after Sparrowpelt. Tinycloud had already disappeared. As Violetshine slewed around the corner, the valley opened into a wide stretch of mud. She could see Nectarpaw and Quailpaw teetering at the edge, their pelts bristling. Gravelpaw and Palepaw were standing just behind them, tiny claws digging into the earth.

"Help!" Sunnypaw's terrified wail echoed around the valley. Violetshine could make out her ginger head straining above the slick brown surface. She reached a muck-covered paw upward, her claws outstretched as she grabbed at air. Violetshine's heart lurched. The apprentice was sinking deeper as she struggled. Tinycloud had reached Quailpaw and, pushing past him, plunged into the mire.

"Stay back!" Sparrowpelt grabbed her tail with his teeth. The tom was still emaciated after his illness, but strong enough now to drag Tinycloud away from sucking mud.

"We have to save her!" Tinycloud turned on him, eyes wild.

Violetshine scanned the valley. There had to be some way they could reach the drowning apprentice safely.

Paw steps thrummed behind her. Hawkwing pulled up and shook the rain from his fur. He followed her gaze, his tail twitching. "Find a stick!" he yowled. "A long one that can reach her."

Nectarpaw blinked at him for a moment, then hared up the

slope to a small grove of trees clinging to the hillside. Quail-paw and Sparrowpelt raced after her, Hawkwing at their tails. Violetshine hurried to where Tinycloud was leaning over the mud. She squeezed in beside the white she-cat, feeling with her paws for firm ground beneath the mud slick. Digging her claws into hard earth, she ventured forward, fixing Sunnypaw with her gaze. "Don't struggle!" she ordered.

"But I'm sinking." Terror sharpened Sunnypaw's mew.

Tinycloud pressed beside her. "Stretch your paws out wide," she called. "Make yourself big as though you're facing a fox."

Sunnypaw stared desperately at her mother. Slowly she reached out a forepaw and rested it on the mud. She gritted her teeth as she struggled to lift another free.

"Sparrowpelt is fetching a stick," Tinycloud called. "We'll have you out of there soon. Try to stay calm."

Violetshine could see the young cat struggling against panic. Determination glittered in her frightened gaze. "You're doing great!"

Plumwillow and Bellaleaf charged around the jutting rocks. They reached the edge of the mud, their Clanmates at their heels.

Leafstar pushed past them and stared in panic at Sunny-paw. "Can you reach her?"

"The mud is too deep," Violetshine reported.

Tinycloud looked at the SkyClan leader. "Hawkwing's looking for a stick!"

"We found one!" Nectarpaw bounded down the slope. She flicked her tail toward the trees. Sparrowpelt and Hawkwing were hauling a stick over the wet grass.

"Hurry!" Tinycloud didn't take her eyes from Sunnypaw. The young cat was slipping deeper into the mud. As it reached around her throat, she lifted her muzzle, her paws flailing as she tried to keep her nose above the surface.

Bark brushed Violetshine's hind paw, and she hopped out of the way as Hawkwing slid the stick past her. As Sparrowpelt guided it over the mud, Violetshine steadied it with her paws.

"Quick!" Tinycloud leaned farther out, straining to get closer to her kit as Sunnypaw's ears slid beneath the surface. The apprentice whimpered as the mud covered her eyes and her muzzle began to disappear from sight.

"Grab the stick!" Sparrowpelt thrust it closer.

Can she hear? Violetshine's breath caught in her throat as Sunnypaw's flailing paw knocked against the stick. Desperately, the apprentice hooked her claws over the end and began to haul herself higher. Her muzzle pushed free of the mud and, with a jerk, she bit onto the stick and wrapped both paws around it.

"Pull!" Hawkwing gave the order. Violetshine dug her claws deep into the bark and tugged as Sparrowpelt and Hawkwing hauled the stick toward firm ground. The mud pulled at Sunnypaw like a hungry fox, but she clung on blindly, her eyes plastered shut. Nectarpaw and Quailpaw grabbed the stick and began pulling. Rain beat mud from Sunnypaw's fur, her flanks, and then her hind legs, slowly sliding free. Sunnypaw gave a choking sob as, with a squelch, the mud lost its grip. As soon as she was in reach, Tinycloud grabbed her bedraggled scruff and dragged her onto the grass. Sunnypaw collapsed, trembling, as Tinycloud lapped the mud from her eyes.

The Clan murmured anxiously as they stared across the mud slick, their wet pelts bristling.

Leafstar hurried around the edge. "Is she okay?"

Frecklewish darted past her and pressed her ears to Sunnypaw's chest. She sat back on her haunches, her eyes glistening with relief. "She'll be fine."

As Sunnypaw pushed herself to her paws and coughed up muddy water, Plumwillow hurried to her side. Alarm prickled through her dripping pelt. "Why did you go so far out?"

Tinycloud nosed the dark gray she-cat away. "This is strange territory. How was she to know that the mud was so deep?"

Plumwillow met Tinycloud's gaze, fear brimming in her amber eyes. "What are we doing here? We're far from the lake and nowhere near the gorge. And no cat should be traveling in weather like this. No wonder StarClan wanted us to stay." She swung her head toward the Clan as they crept closer.

Hawkwing blinked at her evenly. "We'll be at the gorge soon. We'll be safe then."

"Soon?" Harrybrook snorted. "I remember how long it took us to reach the lake, and how many warriors we lost! Who knows how many dangers we'll meet on the way this time!"

"And who knows what we'll find when we get there?" Plumwillow added. "We've been gone for moons. Foxes might have moved in."

"Or badgers!" Macgyver pushed his way to the front.

Sunnypaw looked at him, trembling. "I want to go home."

Leafstar, who had been listening thoughtfully, lashed her tail. "We *are* going home!"

"Not *our* home." Quailpaw blinked at her.

"We don't want to live anywhere but the lake," Nectarpaw mewed.

Sunnypaw shook mud from her ears. "We were born there."

Leafstar's hackles lifted. Violetshine heart quickened as she saw rage burn in the SkyClan leader's eyes. "That doesn't mean you should *die* there!" she snapped. "There was nothing for us at the lake. No land! No prey! No respect! We would have had to fight for every morsel. Is that really how you want to live? Treated like rogues? Have you forgotten who you are? You're SkyClan. The lake was *never* home. StarClan only wanted us there for some prophecy that was never to do with us. Why should we sacrifice ourselves for Clans who don't even respect us?"

Plumwillow shifted uneasily as Harrybrook and Macgyver exchanged looks. Behind them, Bellaleaf and Nettlesplash glanced nervously around.

Violetshine's chest tightened as she watched her Clanmates. Sunnypaw was filthy. Tiredness dulled Frecklewish's eyes. Fidgetflake was shivering. "Everything's going to be okay." She lifted her voice, surprised to find herself speaking out. "Remember, we are SkyClan. It doesn't matter where we are or what problems we face. We will face them together." Leafstar blinked at her as Violetshine went on. "You are the first true Clan that I've known. I was raised in ShadowClan when it was falling apart. The cats there turned on one another. When they faced problems, they were no better than rogues. But SkyClan is different. You took me in and welcomed me. You taught me how cats can overcome even the worst times. You lost your home, you lost one another, but you found one another again and kept on going. I'm proud to be a SkyClan cat. I would never want to belong anywhere else." She looked around at the faces of her Clanmates. Warmth rose beneath her pelt as she saw hope spark in their weary gazes.

"Let's go." Leafstar flicked her tail, less with anger now and more with determination. She padded up the grassy slope beyond the mud pool and headed toward the stretch of heather.

Hawkwing bounded after her as the rest of the Clan followed. Tinycloud rested her flank against Sunnypaw and guided her up the slope. Violetshine glanced back at the wide stretch of mud. The stick that had saved Sunnypaw's life had been washed clean by the rain already.

As she padded after her Clanmates, Frecklewish fell in beside her. "Do you think the rain will stop tomorrow?" Violetshine murmured, glancing at the heavy gray sky.

"I've never seen the sky this dark." Beyond the hilltop, the gray clouds stretched into black. "It looks as though the rain will get worse before it gets better."

Violetshine stifled a shiver. Rivulets streamed over the grass as she climbed. The storm wasn't going to lift anytime soon. But she'd meant what she'd said. She could get through anything as long as she had her Clan around her. Tree was far behind them now, and though his loss sat in her heart like a stone, she knew that she had to keep moving forward.

Even if it meant never seeing Tree again.

CHAPTER 19

❧

Alderheart was glad to reach the ShadowClan border. There would be better shelter on the other side, where oak turned to pine and the canopy grew thicker. The rain was harder than ever, streaming along branches and down trunks so that the springy forest floor squelched beneath his paws.

He paused and glanced along the scent line. When he didn't see a patrol, he crossed it. If any cat challenged him, he would tell them he was on his way to check on Puddleshine's wounds. There was no need to admit that he wanted to ask the ShadowClan medicine cat a few questions about his Clanmates.

Bramblestar had dismissed his worries about how Sparrowpelt had come to be poisoned, but Alderheart couldn't forget it so easily. Even though the victim had recovered and was gone, there was still a cat living among them who was willing to murder another cat. That was dangerous. Alderheart had brought deathberries into the ShadowClan camp, and the trail seemed to lead from there to SkyClan. Had Puddleshine seen anything suspicious while he was ill? Had he heard gossip since SkyClan had left? Some cat in ShadowClan must know more than they were saying.

The ditches that cut into the earth here like claw marks were brimming with water. Alderheart had never seen them full before. He shuddered. If parts of ShadowClan territory were underwater, what must RiverClan be like? Yesterday, the evening patrol had brought news of flooding around the river. After another night of heavy rain, the flooding must be worse now. *StarClan, protect them,* he prayed, but he couldn't shake the feeling that StarClan would have little sympathy for the stricken Clan. *They tried to warn us.* Alderheart picked his way past the flooded ditches. *Five saplings must stand together.* Mistystar had chosen to ignore the warning. Did she expect to be unaffected by the storm now that SkyClan had gone?

Pelts, slicked by rain, moved in the shadows ahead. Alderheart halted and lifted his tail. If it was a patrol, they would pick up his scent and come to question him. He waited as eyes flashed through the gloom.

"Alderheart?" Cloverfoot hailed him through the rain. "What are you doing here? Is everything all right?"

She hurried toward him. Berryheart and Juniperclaw were with her.

"I've come to check Puddleshine's wounds," he called.

Berryheart blinked at him warmly as she reached him. Cloverfoot dipped her head in greeting. "Puddleshine is doing great," she told him.

"That's good to hear, but I'd still like to see his wounds," Alderheart insisted. "He had an infection I'd never seen before. I'd like to see how it's healing."

"That's kind of you." Cloverfoot looked at Juniperclaw.

The ShadowClan deputy narrowed his eyes. "I'm sure Puddleshine can take care of his own wounds."

"Some are hard to reach," Alderheart meowed lightly. "Since I've come this far, I might as well take a look."

Cloverfoot and Berryheart looked at Juniperclaw expectantly. The black tom nodded curtly. "Okay."

"Thanks." Quickly, Alderheart padded toward the camp. He didn't want Juniperclaw to change his mind. He glanced back as he neared the bramble wall. Berryheart and Cloverfoot were heading away, but Juniperclaw was still watching him, his eyes slitted.

Alderheart shook out his pelt and ducked into the camp.

Rain drenched the clearing where the trees opened to the sky. Snaketooth and Grassheart huddled outside the nursery. Stonewing was hurrying Cinnamonpaw around the edge of the camp, keeping to the shelter of the bramble wall. Strikestone was carrying a robin toward the warriors' den. The brown tabby eyed him with surprise. He dropped the robin on the wet ground. "What are you doing here?"

"I've come to check on Puddleshine," Alderheart told him quickly. "I saw Juniperclaw outside. He said it was okay."

Strikestone nodded. "You'll probably be welcome there." He jerked his muzzle toward the medicine den. "Shadowkit's had another fit."

Alarm flashed beneath Alderheart's pelt. He remembered Shadowkit's last fit and the prophetic dream that had accompanied it. Shadowkit had seen himself drown. And Dovewing had told Alderheart that her kit's seizures were only getting worse. Could that mean his vision was about to come to pass? Alderheart tried not to think about the flooded ditches so close to the ShadowClan camp as he raced across the clearing and pushed his way into the den.

Puddleshine leaned over a nest at the far end. Tigerstar and Dovewing crouched beside him, their eyes dark with worry. They turned as Alderheart entered.

"Is Shadowkit okay?" Alderheart hurried to the nest and looked in. Shadowkit was limp at the bottom. His pelt was wet where Puddleshine had swabbed him with moss.

"The seizure's just passed." Puddleshine met Alderheart's gaze. The ShadowClan medicine cat looked relieved to see him.

"I brought him here as soon as it started," Dovewing told him.

"I'm glad I was in camp." Tigerstar's pelt was spiked with worry.

"Shadowkit will need thyme for the shock," Alderheart meowed, but Puddleshine had already turned toward his herb store. He fetched a few sprigs and laid them on the side of the nest as Dovewing took the moss and ran it gently over Shadowkit's flank.

The kit stirred and opened his eyes. He looked up weakly and tried to purr as he saw Dovewing.

"It's okay." She reached her nose to his cheek softly. "You're safe."

Puddleshine beckoned Alderheart away. "What do you

think? Will he always have these fits?" he whispered.

Alderheart glanced at Dovewing and Tigerstar. They were leaning into the nest, comforting Shadowkit. "I don't know," he admitted, his head drooping. "Hopefully, he will grow out of them."

Puddleshine shifted uneasily. "He told me about his last vision."

"About the rain?" Alderheart stifled a shiver.

Puddleshine's gaze was dark. He clearly understood the vision's deadly meaning. "Do you think it will come true?"

Before Alderheart could answer, Shadowkit called to him weakly from the nest.

Alderheart hurried to answer. "I'm here."

Relief showed in Shadowkit's gaze. "I'm glad." As he struggled to sit up, Dovewing hopped into the nest and tucked him against her flank. "It was the same vision," he breathed. "Just like before."

Alderheart swallowed. "Sometimes nightmares come back," he mewed gently.

He avoided Dovewing's gaze, but he could tell by the pricking of her pelt that she didn't think it was a nightmare any more than he did.

Tigerstar puffed out his chest. "It's just a dream, Shadowkit," he meowed brightly. "Nothing bad is going to happen."

"But I've had visions before and they've come true," Shadowkit mewed.

"This one won't," Tigerstar promised. "I won't let it."

Alderheart glanced at the ShadowClan leader and glimpsed

dread in his eyes. He changed the subject. "Have you been helping Puddleshine since I've been gone?" he asked Shadowkit.

"Yes." Shadowkit lifted his chin. "Grassheart's wound is better. She's back in the warriors' den now."

"I'm glad to hear it."

"Tawnypelt had a bellyache," Shadowkit told him. "And Scorchfur twisted his paw. And Puddleshine has been collecting fresh herbs and I've been helping him sort them." The kit was brightening quickly. "Puddleshine says I'm more help than a whole patrol of warriors."

"I expect you are," Alderheart purred, relieved to see Dovewing relax a little too.

Shadowkit's ears twitched. "Cloverfoot has been collecting herbs for us. She says she likes to be useful. She even made Scorchfur join her. But Juniperclaw hasn't come back to help."

Come back to help? Alderheart stiffened. He didn't remember Juniperclaw helping in the medicine den while he'd been in the camp. "Did Juniperclaw help before?" he meowed lightly.

"He came into the den one time while you'd gone to make dirt," Shadowkit explained. "I woke up and he was digging over there." Shadowkit nodded toward the edge of the den, where Alderheart had buried the deathberry seeds. "When I asked him what he was doing, he said he was getting rid of the seeds so they wouldn't hurt anyone. He must have gotten rid of them all, because he hasn't been back since."

A chill ran along Alderheart's spine. Had Violetshine been right? Was ShadowClan's deputy responsible for Sparrowpelt's poisoning? He glanced at Tigerstar. The ShadowClan leader looked uneasy. Alderheart poked the thyme sprigs. "Shadowkit seems much brighter," he told Puddleshine. "But he should swallow these, just to be sure."

"I was thinking the same thing." Puddleshine began to strip the leaves from their twigs. Dovewing dabbed them onto her paw and held them close to Shadowkit's muzzle. As the kit wrinkled his nose, Alderheart padded away from the nest. He beckoned Tigerstar with his tail. "We need to talk," he whispered.

Tigerstar eyed him distrustfully, but he followed as Alderheart led the way out of the den, fluffing his fur out against the rain.

"This way." Tigerstar padded past him to a sheltered spot where a rowan stretched low branches over the camp wall.

Alderheart hurried after him. "Remember the Gathering!" he hissed urgently. "Violetshine said she saw Juniperclaw by the SkyClan fresh-kill pile. Now Shadowkit says he saw him digging up deathberry seeds." He stared at Tigerstar. Surely the ShadowClan leader had to take Sparrowpelt's poisoning seriously now?

Tigerstar squared his shoulders. "No ShadowClan cat would do something so fox-hearted!" Anger sharpened his mew.

"Not even Juniperclaw?" Alderheart pressed. "He turned rogue once, remember?" Juniperclaw had left ShadowClan to follow Darktail and his rogues when he'd been an apprentice. He'd returned only after Darktail had revealed himself to be a ruthless enemy of the Clans.

"Are you questioning my judgment?" Tigerstar's hackles lifted.

"No." Alderheart stood his ground. Even if Tigerstar was covering for his deputy, he wouldn't be frightened into silence. This was too important. "You're probably right to believe he's loyal now. But did you think about how far he might go to prove his loyalty?"

Doubt flickered for a moment in Tigerstar's eyes. Alderheart felt a glimmer of relief. He felt sure that the ShadowClan leader hadn't known about Juniperclaw's plan. Tigerstar blinked. "I don't care what you think Juniperclaw might or might not have done. It's a question of trust. ShadowClan cats *trust* their Clanmates. Besides, this is between SkyClan and ShadowClan, and SkyClan is gone. The matter is closed."

"But if Juniperclaw is capable of doing something—"

Tigerstar cut him off. "What does it have to do with you?" He thrust his muzzle closer to Alderheart. "Why is a Thunder-Clan cat sticking his nose into ShadowClan's affairs?"

Alderheart held his gaze. "Don't you care that you may have a murderer in your Clan?"

"No cat has been murdered." Tigerstar pulled back slowly. "Did Bramblestar put you up to this?"

"Bramblestar told me to forget it, just like you," Alderheart told him.

But Tigerstar wasn't listening. "Bramblestar has always been an interfering old buzzard. ThunderClan should learn to keep its whiskers out of other cats' prey."

"Even if it means letting a cat break the warrior code?"

Alderheart stared at him. Tigerstar couldn't let Juniperclaw get away with this.

"I think you should leave now." Tigerstar's mew was cold.

"But I haven't checked Puddleshine's wounds."

"Puddleshine is fine. You saw that for yourself." Tigerstar signaled to Snaketooth and Grassheart with a flick of his tail. As they hurried across the clearing, he jerked his nose toward Alderheart. "I want you to make sure Alderheart reaches the border," he told them. "It's time he went home."

Alderheart searched Tigerstar's gaze. Was he really going to ignore this? His heart sank as Tigerstar looked away. Tail drooping, he followed Grassheart and Snaketooth to the entrance.

Grassheart glanced at him. "What did you say? Tigerstar looked pretty angry."

"I thought he was going to claw your pelt off," Snaketooth mewed.

"It was nothing," Alderheart mumbled. Frustration itched beneath his fur. Why wouldn't any cat take the poisoning seriously? As he reached the entrance, the brambles trembled.

Juniperclaw emerged from the tunnel. He looked at Alderheart. "Are you leaving already?" There was a suspicion in his gaze.

Alderheart glared at him without answering.

"Tigerstar asked us to escort him to the border," Grassheart told the ShadowClan deputy

"Really?" Juniperclaw narrowed his eyes.

"He wants to make sure I'm safe," Alderheart grunted.

"Cats are always safe on ShadowClan land." Juniperclaw looked away. "As long as they're allowed to be there."

Alderheart reached camp, his paws itching to tell Bramblestar that Shadowkit had seen Juniperclaw take the deathberry seeds. His father would have to do something, surely? A Clan's deputy mustn't be capable of cold-blooded murder.

As he hurried through the dripping tunnel, he scanned the camp. Bramblestar was crouched in the shelter of the camp wall, sharing a mouse with Brackenfur. Twigbranch was pacing beside them, her eyes glittering excitedly. She glanced urgently at Bramblestar, as though willing him to finish eating. Beside them, Thornclaw was nosing through the bedraggled fresh-kill pile, while Ivypool called to Thriftkit, Flipkit, and Bristlekit from the nursery.

"Come inside!" she ordered.

They looked at her from the edge of the puddle beside the clearing.

"We're pretending to be RiverClan cats!" Flipkit waded into the muddy water.

Bristlekit splashed after him. "Look! I can swim!" The water barely covered her paws.

"Me too!" Thriftkit squeaked.

"You look like drowned mice!" Ivypool ventured a little way into the rain, her pelt prickling as the rain touched it. She hurried to the puddle and grabbed Bristlekit by the scruff. Lifting her off her paws, she carried her to the nursery, whisking the other two along with her tail.

Water streamed down the cliff behind the medicine den. It dripped from the Highledge. Graystripe looked out miserably from the elders' den and turned back inside with a snort.

"Bramblestar." Alderheart hurried toward his father.

As Bramblestar looked up from his mouse, the camp entrance rustled and Lionblaze raced in. Cherryfall and Bumblestripe were on his heels. They hurried past Alderheart and stopped, panting, in front of Bramblestar. The Thunder-Clan leader scrambled to his paws.

"We traveled around the lake, as you ordered," Lionblaze puffed. "RiverClan has been flooded out of their camp. They're sheltering with WindClan."

Twigbranch darted forward and stared imploringly at Bramblestar. "That makes it easy!" she mewed. "You have to let me fetch them back!"

Bramblestar waved her away with his tail and nodded to the patrol. "How are they all doing?"

Alderheart padded closer, curiosity prickling in his pelt, as Lionblaze carried on with his report. "They're wet and miserable, but they seem safe. Mistystar was very upset, though."

"She says StarClan was right and we should have listened to them," Cherryfall told him.

"Actually, both she and Harestar say the same thing," Bumblestripe chimed in. "If we're to survive this storm, we need SkyClan back."

Bramblestar narrowed his eyes. "Are they willing to give up

land, then, as I've said ThunderClan would do?"

Cherryfall twitched her whiskers anxiously. "Not exactly," she said.

"But they both said they would be willing to discuss it further," Lionblaze added. "I think they might be convinced."

Twigbranch pushed herself forward again. "We have an opportunity, then," she urged. "StarClan clearly wants all the Clans to stay together. What if I take cats from each of the Clans, and we try to persuade SkyClan that they *are* wanted here?"

Hope soared in Alderheart's chest. "It can't hurt," he urged. "But . . . the biggest obstacle remains: Tigerstar."

"Tigerstar will have to accept StarClan's will," Bramblestar growled.

"What if he still refuses to give up land?" Bumblestripe asked.

"Then he will have to answer StarClan alone." Bramblestar nodded to Twigbranch. "Take the warriors you need from ThunderClan, and recruit as many cats as you can from the other Clans. Find Leafstar and persuade her to come back."

Twigbranch's eyes shone. She lifted her muzzle, ignoring the rain, and purred. "I'll bring SkyClan back," she promised.

As she headed toward the warriors' den, Alderheart tried to catch his father's eye. He still had to speak to him about Juniperclaw.

"Go with Twigbranch," Bramblestar told Lionblaze. "Help her recruit volunteers for her patrol and tell Mistystar and Harestar what we've decided."

As Lionblaze dipped his head and turned away, Alderheart padded forward. "I need to talk to you." He blinked expectantly at his father.

Bramblestar narrowed his eyes. "You look worried. Do you think it's too late to bring SkyClan home?"

"It's not about SkyClan." Alderheart jerked his nose toward the Highledge. "Let's talk over there." He led Bramblestar away from the crowded fresh-kill pile, relieved to find shelter beneath the jutting rock.

Bramblestar gazed at him anxiously.

"We have to help ShadowClan," Alderheart told him.

"Help them?" Bramblestar looked puzzled.

"Shadowkit saw Juniperclaw take deathberries from the medicine den," Alderheart told him quietly. "Violetshine says Juniperclaw was beside the SkyClan fresh-kill pile just before Sparrowpelt got sick."

"So you really think Juniperclaw poisoned Sparrowpelt?"

"I know he did," Alderheart insisted. "He told me that every cat is safe on ShadowClan territory as long as they're allowed to be there. As far as ShadowClan is concerned, SkyClan *wasn't* allowed to be on ShadowClan land. It's obvious—he poisoned Sparrowpelt as a warning. He wanted SkyClan gone, and he saw a way to drive them away without a battle."

Bramblestar's gaze darkened. "Tigerstar should never have trusted him," he growled.

"But he did!" Alderheart blinked expectantly at his father. What was Bramblestar going to do about it?

Bramblestar looked away. "This is Tigerstar's problem. We

can't interfere with another Clan."

"But you must! I spoke to Tigerstar. He won't accept that one of his warriors would break the warrior code. He's not going to do anything."

"And what would you have me do? Accuse his deputy of murder?" Bramblestar shifted his paws uneasily. "It's not my place to interfere."

Alderheart held his father's gaze. "ShadowClan is in danger. Juniperclaw was a rogue once. We saw what happened last time ShadowClan let a rogue tell them what to do. They could abandon the warrior code again—and once a Clan abandons the warrior code, it stops being a Clan."

CHAPTER 20

❧

Twigbranch's paws were numb with cold. She'd been trudging beside
Tree across muddy fields since dawn. Nightcloud, Flypaw, and
Willowshine trekked after them with the rest of the patrol,
and she wondered if they regretted now having agreed so easily to join her on this quest. She stopped and shook out her
fur, then glanced at the woods beyond. She couldn't wait to
reach the trees. They would offer a little shelter. "I'm tired of
being wet and cold."

Tree looked at her. "Get used to it. This weather doesn't
look like it's going to let up."

Twigbranch eyed the dark sky ahead. "Let's hope we can
persuade SkyClan to come back, or it might never stop."

They'd left the day before at dusk and trekked half the
night before resting in a makeshift camp outside Clan territory. Tree remembered the route he'd followed when SkyClan
had led him to the lake. He'd suggested they follow it now,
since it was the most likely path SkyClan had taken.

It had been easy to find volunteers from WindClan and
RiverClan. Cats had hurried forward, alarmed by the worsening weather and eager to put an end to it by bringing SkyClan

back. But Tree had insisted they take only cats who had always wanted SkyClan beside the lake. Twigbranch had agreed and had chosen Nightcloud, Hootwhisker, and Gorsetail from WindClan, and Willowshine, Icewing, and Lizardtail from RiverClan.

She glanced back at them now, their heads down and tails drooping. Flypaw padded between them. Finleap was at the back with Lionblaze and Cherryfall. Twigbranch hoped to catch Finleap's eye, but he didn't look up. She'd been pleased when he'd volunteered to come and hoped that the journey would bring them closer. But he was keeping his distance, the same way as he had back at camp, and she was finding it hard to shake the nagging worry that, when they found SkyClan, he'd ask to join them again. Sadness tugged at her belly. Perhaps they weren't meant to be together. She was sure that, in a different life, their love would have flourished. But here, perhaps love wasn't enough to overcome the troubles they faced. She blinked at Tree. "You must be looking forward to seeing Violetshine again."

"I can't wait." He flicked rain from his ears. Worry darkened his gaze. "I just hope we can reach them in this weather."

The wind was picking up, rocking the trees at the edge of the meadow.

Willowshine fell in beside Twigbranch. "How much worse can the storm get?" She raised her voice to make herself heard over the wind.

Twigbranch narrowed her eyes against the rain. "I don't know, but we have to keep going."

Willowshine nodded and hunched her shoulders harder.

The wood sheltered them for a while, but they were soon out of the trees and crossing wetlands, picking their way through sedge, their paws sinking into the waterlogged ground. Twigbranch could see a Thunderpath on the far side of a valley. She pointed her muzzle toward it. "Is that where we're heading?" she asked Tree.

"Yes. We follow it toward moorland. But we have to cross a stream first."

She heard the stream before she saw it. Water thundered beyond the sedge. Her pelt prickled nervously. "It sounds more like a waterfall than a stream."

Willowshine hurried ahead and disappeared between the bushes. She returned a moment later. "It's a torrent." Her eyes glittered with fear. "I don't know how we'll cross it."

Twigbranch followed as the small gray she-cat beckoned her though the sedge. On the other side, white water roared past. It was too wide to leap. It swirled and frothed and slapped angrily at the muddy banks. "How in StarClan do we cross *that*?"

"It's too wild to swim across." Willowshine eyed Icewing and Lizardtail as they followed Tree through the sedge. "Even for a RiverClan cat." Her Clanmates stopped on the bank and stared in dismay at the foaming water as Nightcloud led the rest of the patrol out.

Lionblaze padded to the edge. "Could we make it across if we hang onto one another and let the strongest swimmers lead?" He looked at Icewing.

The RiverClan cat's ears twitched. "Those currents would sweep us away."

"Look." Tree nodded to a young alder farther along the bank. It bent over the water. A worn crack where the trunk had snapped moons ago showed fresh, pale wood where the storm had torn it wider. The tree rocked in the wind, yielding at the crack so that its branches dipped toward the river. "If we climb past the broken wood, our weight will bend the tree more," he mewed. "Its branches will reach the far bank, and we can use it to cross."

The alder looked fragile, creaking as the wind tugged it. It wouldn't take much weight to snap the trunk so that it collapsed into a makeshift bridge.

Nightcloud shivered. "It looks dangerous."

Hootwhisker's eyes glittered with fear. "The water might wash the tree away, too."

Twigbranch blinked at Tree. "Perhaps we look for another place to cross."

He shook his head. "This is the only place. The water will be wilder if we head downstream, and upstream the banks are too steep."

Flypaw's eyes were wide. "What if I fall in?" she breathed.

"I won't let you." Twigbranch ran her tail along Flypaw's spine. She glanced at the others. "Let's try to snap the trunk first. We can decide after that."

Tree nodded and led the way. He leaped past the splintered wood and balanced on the sloping trunk. Then he reached along it with his paws and pushed. "Help me."

Hootwhisker and Lionblaze leaped up beside him. Together they pressed against the trunk. Cherryfall slipped around the other side and, keeping clear of the water's edge, reached up and hooked her claws into the bark. She pulled the trunk as the others pushed. Twigbranch hurried to help her, rearing onto her hind legs and digging her foreclaws into the wet wood. She heard a snap and felt the tree give. Cherryfall dodged away. Twigbranch ducked as its branches crashed onto the far bank. Wood splintered around Tree as Lionblaze and Hootwhisker leaped clear, and the alder trembled and fell still like fallen prey.

Triumph surged in Twigbranch's chest. It had lodged clear of the water, and the river slid beneath it. "We can cross!" The tree was narrow, but smooth. They could easily pick their way across it and scramble through the branches onto the far shore. She leaped onto the trunk and blinked at the others.

Lionblaze's fur was ruffled, but his eyes shone. He jumped up and headed across, curling his claws into the bark as the wind ruffled his pelt. Finleap followed. Twigbranch blinked at him reassuringly as he brushed past her, but he avoided her eye. Lizardtail and Hootwhisker went next, and the others followed. As she waited for them to cross, Tree nudged Flypaw past her onto the trunk.

The apprentice's ears were twitching anxiously. Twigbranch ran her tail reassuringly along the young she-cat's spine. "I'll be right behind you," she promised. As Flypaw padded cautiously forward, Twigbranch followed, keeping close enough to grab her if she lost her footing, but not crowding her. The river churned below, spray breaking over the bark. Flypaw was taking her time, but Twigbranch resisted the urge to hurry her on. She knew that the young she-cat did best when she was allowed to go at her own speed. Slowly Flypaw padded along the trunk, her tail quivering and her pelt bushed. She quickened as she neared the end, darted forward in a rush, threw herself among the branches, scrabbled through them, and fought her way to solid ground.

Twigbranch followed the trunk onto the thickest branch and picked her way among the jutting twigs until she could see earth beneath. She leaped down and looked back for Tree. The yellow tom had already crossed the trunk. She was impressed to see how at ease he seemed, as though he crossed raging rivers every day. He followed Twigbranch's path nimbly and leaped down beside her. "That was a great plan," she told him, swishing her tail happily.

Lionblaze nodded respectfully to Tree. "I didn't know loners were so resourceful."

Tree's whiskers twitched with amusement. "Warriors aren't the only smart cats in the forest."

Finleap scowled. "Let's go," he mewed briskly. "We can't waste time congratulating one another. We have to catch up." As he padded away, Tree glanced at Twigbranch questioningly.

She looked away. "Finleap is right. We should keep moving." This patrol had been her idea. These cats were relying on her. She wasn't going to let Finleap upset her.

They trekked through the afternoon, following Tree as he

led them to the Thunderpath and then following it until it turned toward the flat land. They left it then, and their path grew steeper, lifting onto moorland, which rose and dipped until the patrol was lost in a sea of heather. The rain was relentless and the wind seemed to strengthen as evening drew closer. Drenched to the skin, Twigbranch tried to ignore the growling hunger in her belly. She followed Tree, hardly seeing or feeling, aware only of the rain streaming over her face and the wet earth beneath her paws.

"That's where I met SkyClan." Tree's mew took her by surprise. She looked up and found him gazing toward a stretch of heather on the hillside. "I don't know which route they might have taken from here."

She glanced at him anxiously. "Do you think we'll be able to pick up their scent?"

"It might be hard in this weather," Tree meowed. "We'll have to guess where they went next. If we're lucky, there might be a loner who saw them."

"I hope so." Twigbranch's heart quickened. Had they come this far only to lose SkyClan's trail? She saw a sheltered dip among the bushes. "We could make camp there for the night."

Tree shook his head. "The earth will be too boggy," he told her. "I know this place. There's shelter farther up." He nodded to the trees, which grew where the slope steepened.

Twigbranch looked at them wearily. They seemed a long way off. "Is there anywhere closer?"

"Come on." Tree's mew was gentle. "It'll be worth the climb."

Twigbranch glanced back at the others. Their eyes were dull with exhaustion. "We're heading for shelter," she told them.

Lionblaze pricked his ears. "Is it far?"

"Beyond those trees," Tree told him. "There's good hunting and a cave."

Lionblaze trudged past her. Hootwhisker and Icewing followed him, lifting their heads for the first time since sunhigh. Flypaw stumbled and Twigbranch hurried to her side. "It won't be long until you can rest," she mewed encouragingly.

Finleap hurried ahead with Cherryfall, and Tree took the lead while Twigbranch stayed close to Flypaw. The young she-cat was struggling to keep her footing on the uneven grass. Pushing into the wind, Twigbranch pressed her flank against her apprentice and guided her forward as the slope steepened. She felt Flypaw relax as they reached the woods. Sheltered from wind and rain, the patrol quickened its pace. Darkness was falling, and soon they were following Tree through shadow. At last the trees opened into a clearing where a wall of rock cut into a steep bank. It made a shallow cave against the dark hillside, and Tree padded inside and turned to face the others.

Flypaw was shivering as Twigbranch nudged her into the cave. It was hardly more than an overhang, but with its back to the wind, it provided shelter.

Once inside, Flypaw sat down heavily. "I'm hungry."

"Rest while I hunt," Twigbranch told her.

Flypaw shook her head. "If you're hunting, so am I."

Determination flashed in her eyes.

Twigbranch felt a rush of pride. She touched her nose to Flypaw's head. "Okay."

Nightcloud was sniffing the back of the cave. "It's dry here." Her mew echoed against the stone.

Lionblaze shook rain from his pelt. "Take Gorsetail and fetch some bedding," he told her. "The rest of us will hunt." He glanced at Twigbranch. "Is that okay?"

Twigbranch nodded. It felt strange to have such an experienced warrior ask her permission. She noticed Finleap gazing at her and met his eye hopefully. He dropped his gaze and hurried from the cave.

"Are you ready to hunt?" She blinked at Flypaw.

"Yes." The young tabby got to her paws.

Twigbranch led her among the trees, following a rabbit trail through the undergrowth. Night swathed the forest. She opened her mouth, tasting for prey, but even here the rain had washed the scents away. She pushed deeper into the woods. Wind roared through the branches. Rain pierced the canopy. She scanned a stretch of brambles but there was no sign of prey. Weariness pulled at Twigbranch's bones. She felt suddenly dizzy and realized that she was too tired to hunt. She could be more help to the patrol if she built warm nests for the night.

Finleap's pelt flashed beyond the brambles. He looked as though he was stalking something.

"Go and help Finleap." She waved Flypaw toward him with her tail. "I'm going to help Nightcloud."

As Flypaw hurried toward Finleap, Twigbranch headed back to the cave. Had SkyClan sheltered here? How far ahead were they? She paused as she reached a clump of brambles and tore out as many fronds as she could carry. Grasping the stems between her jaws, she dragged them to the cave and dropped them beside Nightcloud.

The WindClan warriors had already heaped piles of ferns at the back to the cave. Nightcloud nodded thanks to Twigbranch and spread the bracken with the rest of the bedding. "We'll be cozy tonight."

"Good." Twigbranch purred. "We'll need our strength if we're going to catch up to SkyClan."

"Do you think we'll find them tomorrow?" Nightcloud's eyes shone in the gloom.

"I hope so." Twigbranch wondered if it was possible to find SkyClan so quickly. The journey had been hard going, and the storm showed no sign of easing. She padded to the lip of the cave and gazed at the dark woods.

Tree padded from between the trunks. A fat rabbit hung from his mouth. Twigbranch licked her lips. She could smell its warm scent as he padded toward her.

He laid it on the ground at her paws. "Do you want to share this one?"

"Yes, please." She blinked at him gratefully.

They settled down and took turns ripping flesh from the carcass. The sweet musky flavors sang on Twigbranch's tongue, and at last she began to feel warm. As her fur dried, it fluffed out against the chill of the night.

Tree swallowed a mouthful and stretched happily. "I haven't been so hungry in a long time."

"That's because you've been living with a Clan," Twigbranch told him, still chewing.

"Maybe," he conceded.

"Were you always a loner?" Twigbranch tore another strip of flesh from the rabbit.

"Yes." Tree's eyes were round in the darkness. "My mother left me when I was a kit. I taught myself how to hunt and find shelter."

"That must have been hard."

"I guess." He shifted onto his belly. "It's so long ago I hardly remember."

Twigbranch swallowed her mouthful. "Did you like living alone?"

"I liked the freedom," Tree told her. "The only thing I worried about was my next meal. I liked having no responsibilities. But then I met Violetshine." He sounded faintly annoyed, even though his eyes were clouded with wistfulness. Twigbranch swallowed back a purr of amusement. Violetshine had clearly disrupted his beloved loner life. "For the first time, I started thinking about having a family. I *wanted* responsibility. I miss her so much." Twigbranch's heart ached for him as he stared blindly into the forest. He blinked. "But we're going to find her and I'm going to tell her how I feel."

Twigbranch followed his gaze. "I can't imagine having kits," she mewed guiltily. "Finleap wants to already, but I'm not ready to give up being a warrior."

"You don't have to give it up," Tree reminded her. "Queens only stay in the nursery until their kits are weaned, don't they?"

"I guess." Was she being selfish, wanting to focus on herself? "But I don't want to worry about that yet. I like being a mentor. I'm learning so much every day."

"You're young," he mewed gently. "There's no rush."

"Violetshine's young too."

"Yes." Tree's gaze softened. "But she's always wanted a family. I think she'll make a great mother."

"So do I." Twigbranch suddenly missed Violetshine with a piercing grief she hadn't felt since her sister left. As silence settled between them, Flypaw burst from the ferns at the edge of the trees. Her eyes were bright and a shrew dangled from her jaws.

She hurried toward Twigbranch and dropped it on the ground. "I caught it first try," she mewed proudly.

"Well done!" As Twigbranch purred admiringly, she saw Finleap padding toward them. He was carrying a bedraggled sparrow. It was skinny and looked more like crow-food than fresh-kill.

He stopped beside Flypaw and laid it on the ground. "I was thinking that we could share this . . ." He eyed the fat rabbit lying, half-eaten, between Twigbranch and Tree. "But I guess you don't need it." Anger hardened his mew.

Twigbranch shifted uncomfortably. "I didn't realize you were bringing me food. Tree just offered and I was hungry."

Finleap wasn't listening. He was still staring at the rabbit.

"I guess he knows where the best prey lives. This used to be his home. It's easy to hunt when you know the territory."

Tree stared at Finleap coldly. "I could catch a rabbit anywhere."

"Did you used to catch rabbits to impress Violetshine?" Finleap mewed pointedly. "Or have you forgotten Violetshine?"

Tree's hackles lifted. "I don't have to impress any cat."

"Really?" Finleap's ears twitched. "You seem to be trying pretty hard to impress Twigbranch."

Tree glanced scornfully at Finleap's scrawny catch. "Harder than you. You ignore her for the whole journey and then you bring her *that*."

Finleap curled his lip. *"Loner."* Hissing, he stalked away.

Flypaw blinked at Twigbranch. "What was that about?"

Twigbranch ignored the question and scrambled to her paws. Was Finleap jealous? Hope flickered in her belly. *Maybe he still loves me.* "I'd better go and see if he's okay."

Tree had been hard on him, but Finleap had picked the fight. She couldn't help feeling sorry for him, even though he was acting like a fox-heart. She hurried across the cave. Finleap was sniffing at the bedding, his pelt bristling. "Oh, so you can tear yourself away from Tree?"

Twigbranch blinked at him. "What are you talking about? Tree loves Violetshine!"

He glanced at her angrily and padded out of the cave.

"Where are you going?" She hurried after him. "We have to talk."

He began to climb the steep bank beside the cave.

"Don't walk away!" Frustration flared beneath her fur. She scrambled after him.

At the top, the forest opened and moorland fell away. Heather crowded the dark hillside. Twigbranch followed him across the windswept grass, narrowing her eyes as rain battered her face.

He stopped as he reached a swath of heather and turned on her. "I bet you don't even want to find SkyClan! You're probably happy to see Violetshine gone now that you've made Tree notice you."

Shock froze Twigbranch. "Do you have you bees in your brain?" She stared at him. "How could you say something like that? I would never betray my sister. And I'd *never* make Tree try to notice me. I told you! He's just a friend. And he wouldn't do that to Violetshine, either!"

"You haven't left his side since we left camp," Finleap snarled.

"I'm leading the patrol, and he knows the way!" Twigbranch snapped.

"Every time I look at you, your muzzle's in his ear."

"We were just talking! I've got to talk to *some* cat. Ever since SkyClan left the forest, I feel like I can't talk to you." Grief pressed in her belly. "I don't know why you stayed with me. You've made it pretty clear that you wish you'd left with Sky-Clan."

"I stayed because I love you!" Finleap spat.

"You've hardly *looked* at me. If that's love, I don't want it!" She lashed her tail.

"You don't know what love is!" He glared at her accusingly.

"Of course I do!" Why was he being so mean? "I love you!"

"Not enough to have my kits."

She stared at him, wind tugging at her fur. "Is that it? If I won't have your kits, you don't want me?"

"I want you to love me enough to have kits." Hurt sharpened his gaze.

"And I want you to love me enough to wait." She felt suddenly weary. She was tired of having this argument. "Forget it, Finleap." Rain streamed from her whiskers. "We'll find Sky-Clan soon. And then you can go back to them." As she turned away, a shadow moved at the edge of her vision. She narrowed her eyes.

A black tom was pushing through the heather. The rain had slicked his pelt, and he'd flattened his ears against the wind. "Hi!" he called out as he neared them.

Finleap arched his back warily. "Who are you?"

"I'm Spider." The tom stopped in front of them. He seemed unfazed by Finleap's hostility. "I live around here."

"Alone?" Finleap asked.

"Of course." Spider blinked at him.

Finleap let his hackles smooth. "Why aren't you hiding from the storm?"

"I was," Spider told him. "Then I smelled cat scents. Are there others with you?"

Twigbranch nodded. "We left them at the cave."

"I thought so." Spider sat down and hunched his shoulders against the weather. "I don't usually have much company up here. It's weird you should show up so soon after the other group."

Twigbranch stiffened. "The other group?"

"Did you meet SkyClan?" Finleap leaned forward eagerly.

"SkyClan . . . ," Spider mewed thoughtfully, as though remembering. "Yes, that's what they called themselves."

"How long is it since you saw them?" Twigbranch's heart seemed to skip a beat.

"They passed here yesterday." The tom was vague. "Then they headed that way." He jerked his muzzle toward the stretch of moorland. "I hope they're okay. I heard there's been flooding over there. It'd be a shame if they got caught in it."

Finleap's eyes widened. "We're getting close!" He headed toward the cave. "We have to tell the others."

Twigbranch raced after him. "Thanks, Spider!" she called over her shoulder.

"Happy to help!" The black tom was already disappearing into the heather.

She followed Finleap down the steep slope beside the cave, half scrambling, half falling on the slippery grass.

"We know where SkyClan has gone." Finleap was already inside the cave, sharing the news with Lionblaze. "And we're closing in on them. They passed through here yesterday."

Tree was sitting beside the remains of his rabbit while

Flypaw shared her shrew with Nightcloud and Gorsetail. The yellow tom was staring into the forest. As Twigbranch hurried to tell him about Spider, she noticed that his eyes were glazed. He was murmuring, as though talking to someone.

She stopped beside Flypaw. "What's wrong with Tree?"

Flypaw shrugged. "I don't know. He's been like that since you left." She took another bite of shrew and chewed it thoughtfully. "I thought he was talking to me at first, but he must be talking to himself. Maybe the weather's getting to him."

Twigbranch padded closer to Tree and sniffed him warily. "Tree?" she ventured softly. "Is everything okay?"

He turned to her, blinking. His gaze cleared and he stiffened. "Not exactly. I was talking to a dead warrior."

Twigbranch stiffened. Was the warrior still here? Her pelt prickled uneasily. Was it the same cat who'd told him to stay beside the lake? "Who was it?"

"The same cat who told me SkyClan should stay beside the lake."

She noticed alarm in his eyes. "What did they say?"

"SkyClan is in trouble." For the first time, Tree looked worried. "We can't stay here tonight. We have to go and help them."

Twigbranch's belly tightened as she remembered Spider's warning about the flooding. "Did the warrior tell you what the trouble was?"

Tree shook his head. "She didn't know."

She? Was it Needletail? Twigbranch knew that Violetshine's old friend had spoken to Tree before. "What was her name?"

"I don't remember. She's a cat I've seen before . . . I mean, when I was a loner. We met when she was alive." Tree's gaze suddenly widened. "But actually . . . she looks like you. Not her pelt. She had white fur, with brown speckles. But her eyes . . ." As he hesitated, the fur lifted along his spine. "Her eyes were just like yours."

A chill ran through Twigbranch's pelt. "Green?" she whispered.

"Just like yours," he breathed again.

She knew who it was. A dead warrior who was worried about SkyClan, who had Twigbranch's eyes. There was only one cat who fit that description. Her heart seemed to skip a beat.

"Pebbleshine." Twigbranch's mew caught in her throat. "Oh, Tree—you were speaking to my mother."

CHAPTER 21

❧

Violetshine was dreaming.

Tree. The rain was over, and he was beside her in the nest. She smelled his scent and pressed closer.

He nuzzled her ear with his nose. "I missed you."

Warmth reached her bones for the first time in days, and she snuggled deeper into the bracken. Her heart ached with happiness. They were safe in the SkyClan camp once more. She could hear the lake lapping against the shore. *How strange.* The lake didn't used to be so close to the camp.

"Never leave again," Tree murmured.

I won't. She tried to speak, but the words wouldn't come. Instead water trickled from her mouth. It dripped into Tree's fur. He leaped up, his pelt bristling in surprise. *I'm sorry.* She tried to apologize, but more water bubbled from her lips. Tree backed away, disgust darkening his gaze. As he turned away, Violetshine felt a chill in her fur. Alarm sparked in her belly.

"Wake up!" Dewspring's yowl jerked her from sleep. She opened her eyes into rain and remembered with a stab of disappointment the hill where SkyClan had made camp last night. Weak dawn light showed the bristling pelts of her Clanmates.

"Flood!"

At Plumwillow's shriek, Violetshine scrambled to her paws. Fear shrilled beneath her fur. Where the hill had once been surrounded by muddy fields, now a great lake swirled around it and lapped at their nests.

"The water's still rising." Hawkwing hurried around the Clan, nudging them higher up the slope. At the top, a great elm rocked in the wind. The Clan had camped beneath it because it was the tallest tree as far as the eye could see. A maple grew nearby, but it was smaller and had promised less shelter. Saplings sprouted around its roots where they'd wanted to build nests. Violetshine stared at it now, wishing they'd made their camp there. The land where it grew sloped upward, beyond the reach of the flood, but there was no way to reach it. Water cut it off, and they were trapped on a rapidly shrinking island.

Violetshine's paws seemed to be rooted to the spot. She stared at the water. It washed over the grass. Currents churned the muddy torrent.

"Get back." Hawkwing steered her toward the elm as the flood lapped higher and the grass where Violetshine had stood disappeared.

Leafstar stared across the drowned landscape. Her eyes were round with disbelief. "StarClan help us."

Bellaleaf swung her muzzle toward the stricken leader. "They tried to warn us, remember?"

"We were meant to stay with the other Clans!" Sagenose hopped clear as the water lapped higher.

Dewspring flattened his ears. "This is what happens when you ignore StarClan."

Leafstar blinked at him, fear showing in her eyes. Her voice was tight. "There was no place for us beside the lake."

"We should have fought harder to make one," Bellaleaf snapped.

"Instead we're going to drown in the middle of nowhere!" Dewspring's pelt bristled.

Hawkwing glared at his Clanmates. "Don't blame Leafstar! She has always done what she thought was best for the Clan. How could she know the future?"

Sagenose grunted. "StarClan knew it." He nodded toward the saplings. "Look!"

Violetshine followed his gaze and counted five saplings growing in the shadow of the maple.

"They warned us," Plumwillow whispered.

"They knew what would happen if we left." Sandynose paced frantically.

Frecklewish pushed her way to the front of her Clanmates. "The saplings are all healthy." She flicked her tail toward them. "None have been broken by the storm."

Hawkwing lifted his muzzle. "She's right. The saplings are surviving the storm, and so will we."

Quailpaw shrieked and leaped backward as water lapped his paws. "We're going to drown!"

Hawkwing glanced up at the elm. "We're SkyClan," he yowled. "We can climb!" He leaped up the trunk, scrambling easily onto the lowest branch.

Leaning over, he called down. "There's plenty of space up here."

Violetshine nudged Sunnypaw toward the trunk as her Clanmates hurried toward it and swarmed into the branches.

Frecklewish waited at the bottom while Fidgetflake clawed his way up. Violetshine pressed beside her. "Do the saplings mean we'll be okay?"

Frecklewish looked at her, hollow-eyed. "For now."

Fear tightened Violetshine's belly. She glanced back toward the maple as Frecklewish climbed into the tree. The stretch of water between the elm and the maple was as wide as a river. If only they could cross it, they could escape the flood.

"Violetshine!" Hawkwing called down.

Violetshine realized she was the last cat left on the ground. Water swirled higher around the hilltop. A wave washed over her paws. As the last trace of grass disappeared, she scrambled upward and heaved herself onto the branch beside Hawkwing.

Harrybrook and Macgyver had leaped to higher branches. They helped haul the others up. Violetshine glanced at her Clanmates, dotted along the branches. They populated the tree like crows waiting out the night.

Leafstar sat resolutely on the end of Hawkwing's branch and gazed into the churning water. "Perhaps we should have stayed beside the lake," she murmured.

Sagenose leaned over the branch above her. "I wish you'd decided that earlier."

Violetshine glared at him. "Leafstar is our leader and she would die to protect us," she growled. "If she brought us here, she did it with good reason. How can you be sure we wouldn't have faced danger if we'd stayed?"

Harrybrook peered down through the leaves. "We're safe for now," he called. "We should be grateful for that."

Violetshine looked at her father. "How long until the water goes down?"

His gaze was dark. "Not until the rain has stopped."

Plumwillow called from a branch overhead. "That's not going to be anytime soon!" She jerked her muzzle toward the sky. "Look at the clouds."

They darkened toward the horizon. The rain swept down in great shadows, obscuring the distant hills.

Nettlesplash curled his tail over his paws as he hunched against the storm. "If we don't drown, we'll starve."

Violetshine's belly was hollow with hunger. Nettlesplash's words frightened her. She shifted closer to her father. "We'll find a way to escape, won't we?"

He touched his muzzle to her head. "StarClan won't let us die here."

She wanted to believe him, but StarClan had warned them not to leave the lake. Had StarClan known that this flood would be waiting for them? In the medicine cats' vision, a storm had ripped the saplings from the earth. Would it destroy SkyClan just as easily?

* * *

Has sunhigh passed? Violetshine couldn't be sure. The clouds were unreadable. She only knew that her claws ached from gripping the bark as rain battered her face and wind tugged her pelt. She fought to stop her teeth from chattering.

The Clan had fallen silent around her as they waited out the storm. Even Hawkwing's shoulders sagged.

She pressed closer to him. "We'll be okay," she whispered, hardly able to believe it.

He looked at her, his eyes round with pity. "I'm just glad I had a chance to know you and Twigbranch."

Her heart lurched. *He thinks we're going to die!* "We'll see Twigbranch again," she mewed desperately. "This isn't the end."

Farther along the branch, Leafstar's ears twitched. She looked at Violetshine. "You're right," she mewed firmly. "This isn't the end." She sat up and raised her voice. "SkyClan will not die here." Faces peered from the branches above as she went on. "We have come too far and survived too much to die here." Leafstar got to her paws. "I may have been wrong to lead you here, but I won't let anyone die because of my mistake. We are SkyClan. We have relied on our courage, strength, and intelligence since the Clans began, and we can rely on them now. If we work together, we can find a way to safety!" She looked up at her Clan, her eyes shining with determination.

Macgyver hopped onto the next branch down. "Why don't we swim for it?"

"Too dangerous." Leafstar flicked her tail. "SkyClan cats aren't swimmers, and the currents look strong."

The floodwater had stopped rising, but it swirled menacingly around the trunk of the elm. Broken branches floated past.

"We could leap onto one of those." Violetshine nodded toward one as it sailed beneath them.

"How do we know it will ever reach land?" Hawkwing cautioned.

"I'd rather be stranded in a tree than on a log," Sagenose called.

I wish Tree were here. Violetshine longed for his reassuring presence. *He'd be able to come up with a good idea.*

"Perhaps we could jump from here." Plumwillow slithered down the trunk and landed on a long thick branch that jutted toward the maple. She padded along it. "It almost reaches the far bank."

Leafstar slid past Violetshine and jumped nimbly onto Plumwillow's branch. She padded past the gray she-cat and picked her way to the end.

Violetshine held her breath. Had Plumwillow found an escape route?

Leafstar stopped as the branch began to dip under her weight. She peered through the leaves. "It's not long enough."

Plumwillow hurried to her side. "It's only a short jump."

"A fox-length," Leafstar countered. "That may be too far for some cats. And we'd need a firmer jumping-off place to be sure of covering a gap that wide." The branch quivered as she moved.

Plumwillow looked into the maple, which stretched

tantalizingly close. "If only its branches reached a little lower. They'd bridge the gap."

Hawkwing padded to her side. As Violetshine followed, her paws pricked with agonizing hope. The far bank suddenly seemed closer, and yet it was still too far away. "The maple branches are young," Hawkwing commented as he peered among the leaves. "They would be easy to bend."

Plumwillow swished her tail impatiently. "How can we bend them? We can't even reach them."

Leafstar narrowed her eyes. "If one cat could make it across," she mewed softly, "they could bend a branch."

"Two would be better." Hawkwing didn't take his eyes from the maple.

"Or three," Plumwillow chimed in.

"I'll go," Sagenose meowed.

"I'll go too," Macgyver called from above.

"I should go first." Hawkwing squared his shoulders.

"No!" Violetshine's fur spiked. Hawkwing mustn't leave her! "What if you drown?" She felt sick as she stared down at the muddy water.

Leafstar lifted her muzzle. "I'll go." She eyed her Clan. "I brought you here. I'll lead you out."

"You're our leader." Hawkwing blinked at her. "You mustn't risk your life."

"I have nine lives to risk," she countered. "You only have one."

"Let's wait and see if the rain stops!" Nectarpaw's frightened wail sounded above.

"If you drown, it won't help any cat," Harrybrook called.

"I won't drown." Leafstar fluffed out her wet fur. "We have to find a way out. We can't live in this tree forever." She picked her way closer to the end. The tip dipped precariously beneath her weight.

The Clan watched in silence as Leafstar fixed her gaze on the maple branches. She crouched and bunched the muscles in her hind legs. Then, trembling, she leaped.

Violetshine felt the branch shake. Time seemed to slow as Leafstar flew through the air. Violetshine willed her on. *Please make it!* Her pelt spiked as Leafstar fell. Thrashing the air, the SkyClan leader snatched at the maple, but it was out of reach. She hit the water with a splash and disappeared below the surface.

Shock pulsed through Violetshine. She stared at the swirling water, blood roaring in her ears.

Dewspring leaned over the edge. "I'll save her!"

"No!" Hawkwing ordered. "She has more lives to lose than you. You'd be dead in four breaths."

Violetshine's throat tightened. "Where is she?" The SkyClan leader had still not surfaced.

"Wait." Hawkwing stared down, every muscle taut.

A shape appeared in the muddy water. Leafstar's head bobbed up. Terror flared in the SkyClan leader's eyes as she blinked up at the Clan. With a gasp, she disappeared. The water frothed as she fought her way back to the surface. She opened her mouth and then slid under once more.

"We have to save her!" Wild with panic, Violetshine lunged

forward. Teeth pierced her scruff as Hawkwing jerked her backward. Violetshine turned to glare at him. "What? We can't just watch her die!"

Brown fur flashed on the far bank, a blur behind the driving rain. She gasped as a shape plunged into the water. *A cat!* What was it doing? It could drown! She watched the cat dive beneath the surface, bob up, and then dive again. She glimpsed broad shoulders and a wide forehead before they disappeared again. It was a tom. Would he be strong enough to survive the flood? He broke the surface once more. This time he dragged Leafstar with him. Flailing against the current, he tugged Leafstar toward the bank.

With a gasp, Violetshine recognized his pelt. She struggled free of Hawkwing's grip. *Finleap?* What was he doing here? She stared in amazement as more cats streamed to the edge of the water and began to haul Finleap and Leafstar from the flood. Tree was with them! And Twigbranch. Even through the pouring rain, she recognized them. Her heart soared.

Excited yowls rang from above.

"ThunderClan sent a patrol!"

"Lizardtail's with them."

"And Gorsetail."

"Have all the Clans come?"

Harrybrook and Macgyver leaped down and crowded close to Violetshine. Nectarpaw and Quailpaw strained to see from the branch above them.

Violetshine's gaze was fixed on Leafstar. Was she moving? Had Finleap dragged her from the water in time? She recognized Willowshine's pale tabby pelt. The RiverClan medicine cat was pumping Leafstar's chest with her paws.

The SkyClan leader lay lifeless on the shore as Willowshine worked on her. Violetshine held her breath. *Let her live!* Then Leafstar twitched. With a violent jerk, the SkyClan leader's head rose, and she vomited muddy water.

"She's alive!" Sagenose yowled triumphantly overhead as Leafstar stared groggily around.

Jubilant cries rang from the tree, and the group of cats on the shore turned to look.

Finleap's face fell in dismay as he saw his former Clanmates trapped, but Tree padded to the edge of the water and called across. "Don't worry!" he called. "We'll find a way to rescue you."

Violetshine pushed past her father, desperate to speak to Tree. "You came!" Joy pulsed beneath her pelt. She thought she'd never see him again.

His eyes widened as he saw her. "You're safe!"

"Not yet." Violetshine lifted her muzzle. "We need you to bend the branches of that maple so we can climb across."

He nodded at once and turned to his patrol. In a moment, Tree, Twigbranch, Hootwhisker, and Lionblaze were climbing the maple. They moved among the branches to one that was already dipping toward the water. Clustering around it, they stretched up and pushed with their forepaws. As it began to bend deeper, Tree signaled to Lionblaze and Hootwhisker with his tail. They clambered over the others and balanced on the branch. Under their weight, it dipped further. Gingerly, they crept along it until it was bobbing over the surface of the water.

Violetshine blinked. It was going to work. She could see where the tip of Plumwillow's branch and the maple overlapped.

Plumwillow was the first to cross. Macgyver and Harrybrook followed, the branches trembling beneath them. One by one, the SkyClan cats scrambled to safety.

Hawkwing nudged Violetshine forward. "Go on," he murmured.

"You go first." She didn't want to let him out of her sight.

"I'll be okay," he told her. "Trust me."

She padded along the branch, her heart quickening as she neared the end. Water swirled beneath, but she fixed her gaze on the maple and slithered onto the branch. She felt it quiver as she landed and scurried toward the trunk. Heart pounding, she leaped to the ground and looked back in time to see Hawkwing dart to safety.

Relief washed over her like warm sunshine. She almost didn't notice the rain.

A moment later, Tree was nuzzling her while Twigbranch wove happily around Hawkwing.

"It's great to see you." Purring, Tree rubbed his muzzle over every part of her face. She pressed against him, joy flooding her pelt. "I never want to be a loner again," he told her. "From now on, I go wherever you go."

Violetshine pulled away and looked deep into his eyes. Love bubbled inside her. "Never leave me again."

"I won't."

"Even if a whole patrol of dead warriors tells you to."

"I promise."

She touched her nose to his cheek and turned to Finleap. "Thank you!"

Finleap's eyes shone as Violetshine hurried toward him. "It looks like we arrived just in time."

"You were so brave!" Violetshine blinked at him. "Where did you learn to swim?"

"That wasn't swimming," he joked. "It was drowning."

"You saved Leafstar."

As she spoke, Twigbranch hurried to her side and thrust her muzzle against her ear, purring. "I was worried I was never going to see you again."

Violetshine breathed in Twigbranch's scent. "What are you doing here?"

"I persuaded Bramblestar to let me bring a patrol to beg Leafstar to return to the lake."

"But RiverClan and WindClan cats are with you." Violetshine was confused.

"We wanted to show Leafstar that we *all* want SkyClan beside the lake," Twigbranch explained. "We thought it was the only way to convince her to come back."

Violetshine lifted her muzzle to the sky. Rain washed her face. "I think she knows now that we shouldn't have left."

"Let's hope so." Twigbranch glanced at Leafstar, who was looking dazed beside Willowshine. "We can talk to her when she's recovered."

Violetshine blinked at Finleap again. "I still can't believe you risked your life to save her."

Finleap shrugged. "Any cat would've done the same."

"But you're the only one who did." Violetshine caught Twigbranch's eye. "I can see why you love him so much. He's a great warrior."

Twigbranch looked at Finleap. Was that sadness in her eyes? "He is," she murmured. "And I do love him. Very much."

CHAPTER 22

Alderheart stifled a shiver and paced along the scent line. He'd been waiting with Bramblestar at the ShadowClan border since sunhigh. The storm rocked the trees and rain trickled through the canopy. "Can we just cross it?"

"No." Bramblestar shook drops from his whiskers. "We'll wait for a patrol to take us to the camp. I don't want to start the meeting on the wrong paw."

It had been two days since Alderheart had told Bramblestar that Juniperclaw had stolen deathberry seeds from the medicine den, and Bramblestar was finally willing to travel to ShadowClan and discuss the matter with Tigerstar. "There needs to be peace between the Clans," he had told Alderheart that morning. "And you were right. How can that happen when a rogue-hearted cat is a deputy? How could he ever be trusted? What if he becomes leader?"

Alderheart had greeted the news with relief. He could see from his father's face that Bramblestar wasn't optimistic about their mission but that, with the storm worsening by the day, he clearly felt he couldn't ignore the problem any longer.

Now Alderheart peered into ShadowClan territory, hoping

to glimpse a patrol. "Tigerstar will have to listen," he mewed.

"Tigerstar is young," Bramblestar cautioned. "And he has a lot to prove after running away and then returning with a ThunderClan mate and half-Clan kits. It will be hard for him to admit that he chose badly when he made Juniperclaw deputy."

"But he has to face it," Alderheart pressed. "Juniperclaw tried to murder another cat. Tigerstar can't let him get away with that."

"Tigerstar can do what he likes." Bramblestar's eyes were dark. "I don't know whether he will admit his mistake or cover it up."

"He can't cover it up!"

"Why not?" Bramblestar scanned the ShadowClan forest. "He's ambitious, and he has the unquestioning loyalty of his Clan."

Paw steps thrummed beyond the brambles. Bramblestar pricked his ears.

"Here they come." Alderheart fluffed out his fur and watched as Strikestone, Blazepaw, and Snaketooth burst from the bushes.

They pulled up at the border. Snaketooth's pelt bristled as she saw Bramblestar. "What are you doing here?"

"I want to speak with Tigerstar." Bramblestar gazed at her calmly.

Strikestone narrowed his eyes. "Why?"

"Isn't the storm keeping you busy?" Snaketooth growled. "We thought you'd be preparing for a flood."

Blazepaw tipped his head. "Perhaps the sun is shining in ThunderClan territory."

Strikestone curled his lip. "The sun always shines on ThunderClan," he mewed sarcastically.

Bramblestar flicked his tail impatiently. "I don't have time for this," he told them. "Take me to Tigerstar."

Strikestone and Snaketooth exchanged glances.

"Okay." Strikestone lifted his muzzle. "But hurry up. We have *so* much territory to patrol now that SkyClan is gone."

"And plenty of prey to hunt." Snaketooth beckoned Bramblestar across the border with her tail.

Alderheart's pelt prickled nervously as he followed. Had ShadowClan forgotten the vision? "Aren't you worried now that SkyClan has left?"

"Why?" Snaketooth began to head toward the Shadow-Clan camp. "It's what we wanted."

Alderheart was surprised by her indifference. "What about the storm?" Surely they could see that the vision was coming true?

"Storms pass," Strikestone grunted. "We've survived worse."

Alderheart glanced at Bramblestar. His father was staring ahead, his gaze unreadable. Only the faintest prickle along his spine betrayed his unease. Alderheart padded beside him as Strikestone, Snaketooth, and Blazepaw flanked them. His optimism was fading. ShadowClan clearly didn't regret driving SkyClan away. Perhaps they wouldn't care what Juni-perclaw had done.

They ducked into the camp after Strikestone. Blazepaw

and Snaketooth followed them in. Cloverfoot and Scorchfur were sharing a mouse beside the fresh-kill pile. Rain pounded their pelts. The overhanging alder and pine gave little shelter, and the wide clearing was slick with mud. Tawnypelt sat at the edge. Her fur was wet, but she made no effort to move, even when she saw Bramblestar.

Scorchfur looked up, chewing. He blinked at the patrol and jumped to his paws. "Bramblestar's here with Alderheart," he called as he hurried to Tigerstar's den.

Tigerstar padded out, with Dovewing just behind him. The leader's gaze was wary. *He's clearly wondering why we've come,* Alderheart thought.

The dark brown tom stopped at the edge of the clearing and stared at Bramblestar. "Welcome."

Bramblestar stopped a tail-length from the ShadowClan leader. He shifted his paws uneasily. "Have you heard about RiverClan's flood?" he began.

"We've seen it for ourselves," Tigerstar told him.

"RiverClan is sheltering with WindClan," Alderheart told him.

"They could have come to us," Tigerstar meowed evenly. "We have enough prey now to spare for a Clan driven from its home."

But not SkyClan. Alderheart swallowed back the words. Instead he glanced toward the medicine den. "How is Shadowkit?"

"Still having the same vision." Tigerstar stood unflinching

in the rain. "But the fits have eased. It comes as bad dreams now."

"You must be worried." Alderheart blinked at him sympathetically.

"Nothing will happen to him." Tigerstar swished his tail. "I don't intend to let him out of my sight."

How could he be so sure that the kit's vision wouldn't come true? "But with the flooding, aren't you—"

Bramblestar cut him off. "I'm sure Tigerstar knows how to take care of his own kit."

As he spoke, Pouncekit and Lightkit came bounding out of the nursery. Dovewing raised her tail at them, to tell them to settle down. Then she looked to Bramblestar. "Is that all you came to speak to us about?"

Bramblestar shook his head. "No . . . There's something else we need to discuss."

"Alderheart!" Puddleshine appeared at the medicine-den entrance. He blinked happily across the clearing. Alderheart dipped his head to his friend but didn't move. The damp air seemed to crackle with tension. Puddleshine's eyes darkened as though he sensed it.

Tigerstar's gaze was fixed on Bramblestar. "What?"

He knows. Alderheart shifted his paws uneasily. He'd accused Juniperclaw when he'd visited last, and the Shadow-Clan leader must have guessed what they had come to discuss. *But he's going to make Bramblestar say it out loud.*

"Alderheart has told me that Juniperclaw was seen taking

deathberry seeds from the medicine den, and that Violet-shine saw him afterward beside the SkyClan fresh-kill pile." Bramblestar spoke slowly.

Dovewing pricked her ears, clearly surprised. Tawnypelt padded closer, while Cloverfoot stopped chewing the mouse she'd been eating.

Strikestone showed his teeth. "Are you accusing my litter-mate of poisoning Sparrowpelt?"

Tigerstar signaled silence with a sharp flick of his tail. He didn't take his eyes from Bramblestar. "I thought I'd made my position clear," he growled softly. "SkyClan has left. The matter is closed."

"Tigerstar?" Dovewing hurried to his side. "Is this true? Did Juniperclaw use *poison*?" Her pelt bristled anxiously. Alderheart felt a pang for his former Clanmate. It must be a shock to find that her new Clan was capable of such ruthless-ness.

Tigerstar looked at her. "Alderheart has convinced himself that it's true."

"Is it?" Dovewing's mew trembled.

Tigerstar hesitated.

"SkyClan may be gone, but Juniperclaw is still your dep-uty." Bramblestar spoke evenly. "Aren't you worried that a cat capable of such a rogue trick might one day take your place? Is that the future you see for ShadowClan?"

Doubt glistened in Tigerstar's eyes.

"You can't ignore this," Dovewing pressed. "You can't let

ShadowClan become rogues again. Don't you remember what happened last time?"

Tigerstar blinked at her. "Do you expect me to turn on my Clanmate because of ThunderClan gossip?"

"It's more than gossip!" Alderheart's paws pricked with indignation. "We have evidence."

"Juniperclaw's not far away." Dovewing glanced toward the camp entrance. "He's hunting beside the ditches. Send someone to fetch him; have him explain."

Tigerstar held her gaze for a moment, then nodded to Scorchfur. "Fetch Juniperclaw."

Alderheart watched the tom race from the camp. Rain dripped from his whiskers as he waited beside Bramblestar. No cat spoke until, at last, paw steps sounded outside.

Juniperclaw's eyes were dark as he padded into camp.

Strikestone hurried to his littermate's side. "Tell these ThunderClan cats that it's not true!"

Juniperclaw didn't look at his Clanmate. Instead he glared at Alderheart.

"You knew where I'd buried the seeds!" Alderheart growled. "Shadowkit saw you digging them up. And Violetshine saw you beside the fresh-kill pile. You poisoned SkyClan's prey!"

Strikestone pressed against Juniperclaw, but the other ShadowClan cats didn't move.

"Well?" Tigerstar growled. "Is it true?"

Juniperclaw flattened his ears. "I saved ShadowClan from countless battles. We got our land back, and Grassheart was the only cat seriously injured."

"Not the only one." Bramblestar's tail twitched angrily. "Sparrowpelt nearly died."

Juniperclaw's gaze flashed toward Tigerstar, doubt showing for the first time. "I did it to protect my Clan!"

"It's true, then?" Strikestone shrank from his brother.

Relief washed Alderheart's pelt. *Juniperclaw acted alone.* ShadowClan's warriors still had honor. He watched as Strikestone curled his lip.

"Only a rogue would use poison!" the brown tabby snarled. "Did you learn nothing from Darktail?"

Dovewing lashed her tail angrily. "It looks like he learned too much!"

"I'm loyal!" Juniperclaw glanced frantically around his Clanmates. "I saved you from fighting."

"We are warriors." Tigerstar stared at his deputy. "We fight. We don't murder. Did you never learn the warrior code?"

"I protected my Clan!" Juniperclaw backed away.

Pity pierced Alderheart's chest. How could any warrior be so misguided?

"You are no longer ShadowClan's deputy." Tigerstar's dark gaze fixed on Juniperclaw. "I'm not even sure if you are worthy of being a ShadowClan warrior." He jerked his muzzle toward Tawnypelt and Scorchfur. "Take him to the warriors' den and guard it. I will decide his punishment later."

Juniperclaw's shoulders sagged as the two warriors escorted him to the den. Silently, he slunk inside.

"I was mistaken." Tigerstar looked bleakly at Bramblestar. "I shouldn't have chosen him for deputy. I thought his experience with Darktail would have strengthened his faith in the warrior code, not weakened it."

"I understand why you did it," Bramblestar told him. "You wanted to unite your Clan by including those who once betrayed you. It was a noble gesture."

"But wrong." Tigerstar dipped his head.

Dovewing pressed against him. "You couldn't have known that."

"I wasn't just wrong about Juniperclaw." Tigerstar lifted his muzzle to the driving rain. "The storm StarClan warned us about is here, and I drove SkyClan away. I was so focused on rebuilding ShadowClan that I ignored the warning of my ancestors."

He regrets SkyClan's leaving! Hope sparked in Alderheart's belly. But before he could ask whether Tigerstar would let them return, Pouncekit peered from the nursery. "Dovewing, we're hungry! Can we have fresh-kill?"

"I'll bring you some," Dovewing told the gray tabby she-kit. As she turned toward the fresh-kill pile, she called to Pouncekit. "Will the two of you share a shrew with Shadowkit?"

"Shadowkit's not here." Pouncekit blinked at her mother.

Dovewing's eyes darkened. She hurried toward the nursery. "What do you mean?"

Tigerstar was at her heels. He pushed past her and raced inside. "Where is he?" Pouncekit and Lightkit crowded around him as he ducked out again.

"He was playing a game," Lightkit told him. "He was pretending he had an important mission to save his Clan. Pouncekit wanted to go with him, but he said it was something he had to do by himself."

"Search the camp!" Tigerstar's desperate gaze flashed toward his Clanmates.

Dovewing wove frantically around Lightkit and Pouncekit. "Did he say where he was going?"

Pouncekit looked frightened. "No."

"He just said he had to save us and then he sneaked out of the den," Lightkit told her.

Bramblestar was already searching the dripping grass at the edge of the camp. Scorchfur had hurried into the elders' den while Blazepaw hunted behind it. Tawnypelt and Strikestone left their post outside the warriors' den and began sniffing the ground.

Alderheart stared toward the entrance tunnel. Could the kit have left the camp without anyone noticing? He remembered with a jolt the dirtplace tunnel and hurried to check it. Dodging around the back of the warriors' den, he saw black fur disappear into shadow. His eyes widened with surprise. The fur was too dark to be Shadowkit's. Who was sneaking out? He hurried to the narrow tunnel entrance and smelled Juniperclaw's scent. The former ShadowClan deputy smelled frightened. "Juniperclaw's escaped!" Alderheart raced back to the clearing.

Tigerstar glanced at him distractedly. "Let him go," he

snapped. "We don't need rogues like him in the Clan." He pushed his way past Strikestone and sniffed the muddy path to the entrance. His pelt spiked. "Shadowkit went this way." He followed the trail through the tunnel before darting back. "He's left the camp!"

"I didn't see him leave!" Dovewing's eyes were round with guilt.

"Perhaps we should send a cat to WindClan," Bramblestar suggested.

Tawnypelt bounded over to her son. "I'll go!"

Tigerstar nodded at the tortoiseshell. "Yes . . . Go to Wind-Clan and tell them that Shadowkit is missing. Tell Harestar and Mistystar that he must be found. He's in . . ." His voice was now barely a whisper. ". . . he's in great danger."

As Tawnypelt raced from the camp, Alderheart watched his father. Bramblestar was gazing at Tigerstar. The Shadow-Clan leader's eyes were bright with fear. "We will find him," Bramblestar promised. Tigerstar stared wordlessly back, and Alderheart's throat tightened with pity. "Have faith, Tiger-star," Bramblestar went on. "If the Clans work together, we will save him."

CHAPTER 23

Twigbranch *stared through the rain. The* sky darkened as night drew in. SkyClan scents filled her nose. Behind her they crowded into Tree's shallow cave, thankful to be out of the rain and to be heading back to the lake. She shifted her paws uneasily. She and Finleap hadn't spoken on the journey back from the flooded moor. His former Clanmates had clustered around him as they'd traveled, praising him for saving Leafstar and sharing stories of their adventure.

When they'd reached the cave, the nests they'd made were still there, and dry, thanks to the shelter of the overhanging rock. They'd needed to make more. But there was enough space, and even though the fresh bedding they dragged from the woods was wet, there would be a chance to get dry and warm while they rested overnight.

"Hey."

Fur brushed her flank, and she turned her head to see Finleap beside her. Her heart ached. Would she ever be able to stand this close to him again? "Hey."

He gazed at her, his yellow eyes glittering with uncertainty. "I'm sorry."

"Sorry?" She blinked at him. "What for?"

"For saying you were getting too close to Tree." He glanced back to where Violetshine was making nests for the SkyClan apprentices. Flypaw was helping, excitedly showing Nectarpaw how to shape the ferns with her paws. "I was just angry. I never really thought—"

"It's okay." She cut him off. "It doesn't matter now."

He tipped his head questioningly. "Now that Violetshine's back?"

"Now that we've found SkyClan." She turned her face to the woods. "You'll be going back to them, I guess."

"Back to SkyClan?"

"If I'm not going to have your kits, you might as well return to your kin." Sadness pricked Twigbranch's eyes. Should she change her mind? Having kits now might not be so bad.

"But I thought you loved me." He sounded surprised. "You told Violetshine you loved me very much."

"I do," she mewed softly. "But not enough to have your kits. Not now. Maybe not ever."

Finleap glanced at his paws. "Let's forget about kits, huh?"

She blinked in surprise. "Forget?"

"I was wrong, Twigbranch. Seeing SkyClan again made me realize . . . however much I love my kin, I love you more. I don't want you to have kits if you don't want to. I can live without them. But I can't live without you."

Twigbranch stared at him. "Do you mean that?"

"Yes." Finleap's eyes shimmered with love. "I've been so wrapped up in feeling hurt, I didn't realize how much I was hurting you—or how much I was hurting our relationship."

"And what happens next time you're upset?" Twigbranch's mouth was dry. "Will you stop talking to me again?"

"No. Next time we'll discuss things properly. No more arguments." Finleap met her gaze solemnly. "Watching you over the past few days has reminded me how amazing you are, Twigbranch. You persuaded Bramblestar to let you bring a patrol here. You found a way of getting SkyClan back to the lake. I'm lucky to have you. I promise I'll never hurt you again."

She stared at him, hope surging in her chest. "So you're really okay with me not having your kits yet?"

"Yes." He leaned closer. "I'm so sorry I put you through that. I guess it was harder leaving SkyClan than I expected. It took me a while to realize I had no kin in ThunderClan, and then I couldn't stop thinking of everything I'd left behind. I forgot to value what I had. Look." He jerked his nose toward SkyClan once more. Tree was holding the side of a nest firmly while Nectarpaw wove an extra bracken stem between the fronds. Violetshine was leaning over the edge to press moss inside. "I know now that having kin isn't the only way to fit in. I'll find another way to feel part of ThunderClan."

"Does that mean you're not going back to SkyClan?" Her paws trembled.

"Why would I, when you're in ThunderClan?" He blinked at her. "Let's enjoy being warriors and mentors for now."

"If I have kits with any cat, it will be you," she murmured. Would she ever be ready?

"Okay," he purred. "But only if we both want them."

Twigbranch pressed her muzzle against his, happiness warming her pelt for the first time in days. "I love you so much, Finleap."

"And I love you."

Tree padded from the woods, a squirrel between his jaws. Macgyver and Sandynose followed him, each carrying a pigeon. They dropped them inside the cave entrance.

Macgyver blinked at Twigbranch. "There's good hunting here."

"Harrybrook and Dewspring are bringing more," Sandynose told her.

Finleap sniffed one of the pigeons. "It smells good."

Macgyver pushed it toward him. "Take it."

"We can hunt for ourselves," Twigbranch told him quickly. She didn't want to take his catch when there were so many mouths to feed.

"Why bother? By the time both patrols are back, there'll be enough for everyone," Tree purred.

Macgyver winked at her. "Besides, it looks like you two have more talking to do."

Twigbranch looked away, her ears burning.

Macgyver purred. "Don't be embarrassed. . . . We've all been in love before."

"Are you teasing my sister?" Violetshine padded from the back of the cave and gave Macgyver a stern look.

"Just a little." Macgyver picked up his catch and nudged Sandynose away.

Tree shook the rain from his pelt and settled beside the pigeon they'd left behind. "It would be a shame to waste it."

Violetshine lay down and leaned against him. She tugged the pigeon closer with her paw and took a bite. "I'm too hungry to argue."

Finleap caught Twigbranch's eye. "Let's eat," he told her. "I think we've both earned our meal tonight."

"Do you think we should?" Twigbranch glanced guiltily toward SkyClan.

"Of course." He followed her gaze. Harrybrook and Dewspring were back from their hunt, and the Clan looked happy, giving out prey. Leafstar lay on a pile of bracken, her eyes weary but content as she watched. Flypaw was demonstrating a hunting crouch to some of the other apprentices. Hawkwing was hurrying up the slope, three mice hanging from his jaws. Reedclaw and Plumwillow followed, carrying more.

Relieved to see every cat so relaxed, Twigbranch settled beside Finleap. He tore a wing from the pigeon and passed her the carcass. Her mouth watered as she smelled its warm scent. She sank her teeth into its soft breast and tore away a juicy mouthful. Chewing, she looked at Tree. "Finleap was right. You do know where all the best prey lives."

Tree's eyes sparkled. "There's a difference between knowing where it lives and being able to catch it." He glanced teasingly at Finleap. "Do you want to catch another scrawny sparrow? Twigbranch might get hungry in the night."

Finleap huffed. "I was having a bad day."

Tree purred. "Perhaps you should try fishing instead of

hunting. You're a natural swimmer." He glanced at Leafstar. "I don't know how you managed to pull her out of that flood. You were amazing."

"I guess StarClan guided my paws." Cheerfully, Finleap tore a bite from the pigeon wing.

Violetshine flicked a feather from her nose with her paw. "How did you find us? We were so far from the lake."

"We still are," Tree grunted, his mouth full.

"The search patrol was Twigbranch's idea," Finleap explained.

"Tree led the way," Twigbranch chimed in. "We'd never have known which trail to follow without him."

"He's smart for a loner." Violetshine's eyes flashed playfully.

"He'll make a good Clan cat." Twigbranch took another bite of pigeon.

Violetshine pricked her ears. "You sound as though you approve."

Twigbranch swallowed. "I do."

They finished their meal in contented silence. As they began to wash afterward, Hawkwing padded toward them. He was licking his lips. "There's good hunting around here." He stopped beside them. "I haven't tasted squirrel that delicious since the gorge."

Violetshine rolled her eyes. "Don't talk about the gorge. We're not going back there. You'll have to get used to lake squirrels."

He touched his nose to her head and settled beside her.

The woods were dark now. Night had fallen. Behind him, the other SkyClan cats were climbing into their nests. Harrybrook was already snoring.

Violetshine stared into the shadows beyond the cave, her gaze thoughtful. "How did you know which route to follow after the hollow?" she asked. "Tree wouldn't have known which way to go."

"A loner had seen you," Twigbranch told her.

"Spider!" Violetshine seemed to remember him.

"Yes." Twigbranch purred.

"You caught up with us pretty quickly," Hawkwing commented. "And just in time."

"We knew you were in trouble." Finleap washed his ear with a paw.

Hawkwing looked at him. "How?"

Finleap and Tree exchanged glances.

"Pebbleshine told Tree," Twigbranch mewed softly.

Violetshine jerked her muzzle toward Twigbranch. Amazement flashed in her eyes.

"Pebbleshine?" Hawkwing stared at her, confusion clouding his gaze.

"Yes." Twigbranch's mew was no more than a whisper.

"She spoke to Tree?" Grief thickened his mew.

"Yes." Twigbranch's heart ached with pity as she realized how much her father still missed her mother. "While we were making camp here for the night."

Violetshine's pelt prickled. "Are you sure it was her?"

Tree brushed his tail along her flank. "She had Twigbranch's eyes," he murmured. "I should have guessed it was her mother."

"Have you seen her before?" Violetshine blinked at him.

"Yes, we met briefly when she was alive. And she's the war-rior who told me that StarClan should stay by the lake."

"Why didn't you tell me it was Pebbleshine?" Violetshine sat up.

"I didn't realize until I described her to Twigbranch," he explained. "I had forgotten her name. But suddenly it was obvious."

Hawkwing's eyes had clouded. "Is she happy?"

"You can ask her yourself," Tree mewed, looking up. "She's here with us."

Twigbranch's heart lurched. "Here?"

Violetshine jumped to her paws. "Where is she?"

Hawkwing stared at Tree. "Can you see her right now?"

Tree nodded. "I can help you see her, too—like I did with the lost ShadowClan cats at the lake." He got to his paws and closed his eyes. As he stood, still like a rock, the air around them seemed to shimmer. Twigbranch got shakily to her paws as a dark shape moved on the slope in front of the cave. A warm scent touched her nose, and her heart ached with joy. "Pebbleshine," she whispered.

A white she-cat stopped a tail-length away. Her soft green eyes shone in the darkness. Her pelt was specked with brown, like owl feathers, and there was a sleekness to her fur that reminded Twigbranch of Violetshine. How familiar she looked, and yet Twigbranch had never seen her before.

Violetshine leaned forward, sniffing.

Hawkwing padded past them and touched his nose cautiously to Pebbleshine's muzzle. "My love." He closed his eyes, as though drinking in her scent. "I thought I would never see you again."

"I'm so sorry I left you alone," Pebbleshine whispered. "I was trapped in the monster. I could feel it taking me farther and farther away. I fought to get out, but there was nothing I could do."

"I wish I'd been able to find you." Hawkwing's mew caught in his throat.

"Losing you was unbearable, but then . . ." Pebbleshine's gaze drifted from Hawkwing's. She blinked at Twigbranch and then Violetshine. "Then our kits came." Love flooded her mew. She padded forward and wove around them. Twigbranch shivered as her mother's fur brushed hers, no more than a breeze and as cool as stone. "I've been with you both since you were born," Pebbleshine murmured. "Even after I died, I couldn't leave you. I couldn't go to StarClan, not while you faced life with only each other."

"They have me now," Hawkwing mewed softly. "And their Clans."

Pebbleshine's gaze flitted to Tree and then Finleap. "And they have cats who love them." There was a purr in her mew. "Thank you for letting me speak to them, Tree—just for a moment."

Tree stared at her, his ears peaked in concentration. "It's my pleasure. I'm sorry I didn't realize the connection earlier.

I knew you were a Clan cat, but . . ."

Pebbleshine purred. "You are a good cat, Tree. You have always helped me when I needed help. I'm glad they are loved. They don't need me anymore."

Panic flared in Twigbranch's belly. "We will always need you!"

Violetshine stared frantically at her mother. "We've only just found you."

"You have much more now than I could ever give you." Pebbleshine backed away toward the shadowy woods.

Violetshine darted forward, but Hawkwing waved her back with his tail. "Let her go," he breathed. "Let her take her place in StarClan, where she belongs. She must be lonely here."

"She has us!" Twigbranch flashed him an angry look. Hawkwing returned it, his gaze soft. Shame washed her pelt. She was being selfish. She dipped her head. "I'm sorry. Of course she must go."

"I will still be able to see you from StarClan," Pebbleshine promised.

"But you won't be close." Grief pressed in Twigbranch's throat.

"I will always be in your heart, just as you are in mine." Pebbleshine blinked at her fondly. "You will be a great warrior, Twigbranch. I can see that already. And you." She turned her gentle green gaze on Violetshine. "You'll be a wonderful mother to those kits."

"Kits?" Violetshine tipped her head, puzzled.

Pebbleshine glanced at her belly. "Don't you know?"

Shock showed in Violetshine's eyes. "I'm going to be a mother!"

Twigbranch pricked her ears. *A mother!* She lifted her tail happily. Violetshine was going to have the family she'd always wanted. She heard Tree purring loudly. He rubbed his muzzle against Violetshine's cheek. "I can't wait to be a father."

Hawkwing's eyes shone. "Is that why you've been so tired and irritable?" he mewed. "I thought it was just the weather getting you down."

"So did I!" Violetshine purred at him.

Twigbranch glanced at her mother. Pebbleshine was turning away. "Wait!" Twigbranch hurried after her into the rain. She wanted to drink in her scent once more, but by the time she reached her, the scent had vanished. Her mother moved like a shadow toward the trees.

"I will always love you!" Hawkwing called after her.

"Good-bye!" Violetshine wailed.

"Good-bye, Pebbleshine." Twigbranch's words were hardly more than a whisper as she watched her mother disappear into darkness. Her heart ached with loss as she felt the rain pound against her pelt. And then she saw, on the grass where Pebbleshine had walked, that stars seemed to sparkle in her paw prints.

CHAPTER 24

As they crested the hill, Violetshine narrowed her eyes against the rain. It swept up from the lake, carried on a wind that seemed hungry for fresh bones to chill. She thought of her kits, warm and safe inside her, and felt protective. She was happy to bear the brunt of the storm if it sheltered them from its fury.

Tree was at her side. He hadn't left her as they'd trekked back from the cave. Last night, SkyClan had decided to approach the lake through RiverClan territory, staying clear of the flood and making straight for ShadowClan's camp. Tigerstar was the only leader left to convince. Leafstar had already dispatched messengers to WindClan and Thunder-Clan territory, begging them to send patrols to support them as they faced the ShadowClan leader.

"Go to WindClan," Leafstar had told Macgyver and Plumwillow. "Ask Mistystar and Harestar to send cats to ShadowClan. We don't intend to fight, but we need voices to support our claim." She'd told Nettlesplash and Sandynose the same as she'd sent them to ThunderClan.

Now, as they headed down the slope into RiverClan territory, Violetshine's heart pricked with hope. Perhaps, at last, the question of land for SkyClan could be settled. Tigerstar couldn't hold out against four Clans, could he?

Hawkwing followed them, Leafstar at his side. Frecklewish and Fidgetflake trailed behind with their Clanmates. Nectarpaw was limping. A clumsy jump had twisted her paw. Sandynose and Bellaleaf pressed beside her, helping her to walk.

Tree led the group toward the river, which tumbled downhill. It was swollen by rainwater but still narrow here. As it flowed to the lake, it grew wider. Where once it had gently encircled RiverClan's camp and spread idle streams through their land, now it churned angrily. The camp had disappeared beneath the muddy torrent.

Violetshine halted. She stared down at the shore, shocked by how high the lake had risen. "The rain must stop soon, or *every* camp will be lost!"

"The five Clans are together," Tree reminded her. "We will survive this storm."

"We're not together yet." Doubt pricked at her pelt.

Leafstar padded to her side. "Have faith," she mewed gently. "We didn't come this far to fail."

Violetshine met the SkyClan leader's gaze, relieved to see her so determined.

Tree stopped at the river's edge. He nodded to the fallen tree that bridged the water. "Let's cross here."

"Okay." Leafstar went first, Hawkwing and Sparrowpelt at her tail. Violetshine waited for Bellaleaf and Sagenose to guide Nectarpaw over. She held her breath as the injured apprentice limped haltingly over the slippery wood, relieved as she stumbled onto the far shore. Frecklewish followed.

Twigbranch stopped beside Violetshine. "You go next." She nosed Violetshine toward the branch.

Violetshine resisted. "Let's make sure Flypaw gets safely across first." She nodded toward the young she-cat.

Flypaw was staring round-eyed at the tree-bridge. Muddy water frothed beneath. "After this journey," she mewed, "I'll never be anxious about crossing the tree-bridge to the island again."

"Don't worry, Flypaw." Twigbranch blinked sympathetically at her apprentice and nudged her forward with her nose. "This will be the last river we cross for a while."

Flypaw climbed onto the bridge and Twigbranch followed. Gingerly, the young she-cat crept along it. Her wet fur prickled with fear.

Finleap jumped up after them. "Stay close to each other," he warned. "Watch where you're putting your paws."

"We'll be okay," Twigbranch told him.

Violetshine stifled a shudder as she watched them cross, then relaxed as first Flypaw and then Twigbranch and Finleap jumped down the other side.

"Come on." Tree hopped onto the log and looked back at Violetshine. "Stay close to my tail."

Violetshine blinked, relieved he was with her, and climbed after him. Her heart lurched as her pads slipped on the wet bark. She wobbled. *Having a bellyful of kits is throwing off my balance,* she realized. Digging her claws in, she steadied herself. She fixed her gaze on Tree and began to follow. Her heart lurched again as the bridge trembled. Lizardtail and Hootwhisker had leaped on behind. Violetshine stopped and looked back, bracing herself against the wind, as she checked to see if they'd found their footing. In single file, they padded after her, their whiskers stiff with concentration. She looked forward once more, swallowing as she glimpsed white water thundering beneath her.

Tree had already reached the other side. He watched her from the far bank, his eyes wide with worry. "Be careful."

She blinked at him reassuringly. "I'll be okay—"

A sudden roar made her freeze. Thunder seemed to rumble upstream. She jerked her muzzle around. A wall of water and debris crashed toward her. She stared at it, terror shrilling through every hair on her pelt. It slammed into the bridge, knocking Hootwhisker and Lizardtail away before sweeping her downstream with such force she thought it would smash her to pieces. A moment later, she was swirling. Water churned around her. It filled her nose and her ears and pressed its way into her mouth. Something hard hit her hind leg. Something else thumped the side of her head. Blinded by water and terrified, she flailed against the torrent. As the water lifted her up, she threw out her forepaws, hope flashing as they hit something hard. She dug in her claws, clinging on for dear life as the deluge surged past her. It dragged at her limbs, trying to haul her downstream. The sudden flood subsided and her head emerged. She took a desperate gulp of air and blinked water from her eyes.

She was gripping a root that jutted from the bank. She struggled to drag herself along it to the safety of the shore, but the force of the water held her in place. She felt as though the lake was sucking her toward it and clung on harder. She wouldn't let it swallow her into its crow-black depths.

Staring upstream, her heart flashed with relief as she glimpsed Hootwhisker and Lizardtail clinging like wet rats to a rock in the middle. They were stranded, but she could see them hauling themselves clear of the water. She looked past them, fear gripping her once more as she wondered if a second wall of water might sweep down and knock them all away.

"Violetshine!" Tree slewed to halt on the bank beside her. He strained to reach her, but she was too far away, streaming like a weed in the powerful current. The root was sinewy, too thin to walk along, but strong enough to hold her for as long as she had strength to cling on.

I won't let go, she promised her kits. The muscles in her fore-legs screamed with the strain. She ignored the pain. She was going to save her kits.

On the other bank, Lionblaze and Gorsetail leaned over the edge, calling out to Lizardtail and Hootwhisker.

"We'll find a way to get you off!" Lionblaze yowled.

Gorsetail looked around frantically, as though searching for something they could use to reach the stranded cats. Cherryfall, Nightcloud, and Willowshine clustered around her, their eyes wide with panic. Dewspring and Quailpaw stared in horror toward Violetshine.

She tried again to haul herself along the root. If only the

current would let up for a moment, she'd have the strength to pull herself to safety. She tried to ignore Tree's terrified face. Leafstar and Hawkwing had caught up to him now, Twigbranch and Flypaw at their heels. Violetshine steadied her breathing and hung on. *The flood will ease in a moment,* she told herself. *I can get to safety then.*

Something small and dark bobbed in the water upstream. It slid past the rock where Hootwhisker and Lizardtail shivered. Violetshine knew at once that it wasn't debris. As it swirled closer, she made out the shape of a head. Ears twitched as it spun. *A kit!* She stared at it. There was no kit that young in SkyClan. Had a kit been left behind when RiverClan fled their camp? It spun closer and she recognized the gray pelt. *Shadowkit!* Why was he in RiverClan territory? His eyes were wild with fear and his paws flailed uselessly in the torrent. Tree followed her gaze, his eyes sparking with horror as he saw the kit. On the far bank, Willowshine and Dewspring were staring at Shadowkit, their fur spiked.

"StarClan, help him!" Willowshine raced to the edge, wailing frantically. Shadowkit glanced at her desperately as he spun past, out of reach.

I have to save him! Violetshine let go with one paw and prepared to lunge toward him.

"Don't let go!" Tree shrieked in panic. His gaze flicked toward Shadowkit once more. He'd guessed what she was planning.

Shadowkit hurtled closer. He would be within reach any

moment. She would have to let go. She'd grab him and try to swim. If she could just keep their heads above the surface for long enough, she'd get them to shore. She had to. As she bunched her muscles, timing her dive, shadow flashed at the edge of her vision. A black tom leaped from the other bank. Diving into the rapid water, he grabbed Shadowkit and swirled past.

Juniperclaw! Violetshine's heart seemed to stop as she recognized him. What was the ShadowClan tom doing here? Water washed her muzzle. Spluttering, she flung both paws around the root once more and looked behind her.

Juniperclaw was swirling in an eddy of calmer water behind her. Shadowkit dangled by his scruff from the tom's teeth, water streaming around him. He churned at the water and whimpered with terror. Juniperclaw's face was twisted with determination as he swam. The backwash from the eddy carried him a little way upstream. Violetshine stuck out her hind legs, felt him grasp them, and braced herself as he hauled himself closer. With a desperate growl, he dragged himself along the length of her flank and reached out for the root. He grabbed it and clung on; then, grunting with the effort, he pushed Shadowkit onto the root with his muzzle.

Gasping, the kit scrabbled onto the gnarled bark. He was trembling, his eyes screwed shut. Tree leaned out. "I can reach him!" Leafstar and Finleap gripped his pelt as, gingerly, he grasped Shadowkit's tail in his teeth and, with a jerk, snatched him onto the bank.

Violetshine turned her head. Juniperclaw clung on between her and the bank. "You saved him," she gasped.

He stared at her, his eyes glazed with shock.

"Juniperclaw!" Tree yowled to him from the bank. "Can you help Violetshine get to the bank?"

"Climb over me," Juniperclaw grunted. Water streamed into his mouth and he spluttered.

"No!" Violetshine stared at him, horrified. She couldn't risk knocking him away. "What if you lose your grip?"

"I can hold on," he promised.

"Do what he says!" Tree strained at the edge of the water. "He's stronger than you! And he's not carrying kits!"

Juniperclaw's eyes widened. "Kits?" His gaze grew more urgent. "Climb over me! You mustn't die." More water filled his mouth. She saw him stiffen as he tightened his grip on the root. His eyes pleaded with her frantically.

Her heart in her mouth, Violetshine let go one of her paws and gripped onto Juniperclaw's shoulder. He grimaced as she dug her claws in. She reached her hind legs around him and clung on like a tick as she let go her other paw and eased herself over his back. The water dragged at her. She heard him growling as he fought to cling on. Reaching up on his other side, Violetshine caught hold of the root again. She was closer to the bank now. The current softened here. Released from its grip, she managed to work her paws along the root until she was only a muzzle-length from land. As she reached for the bank, she felt teeth in her scruff. Tree had lunged down and grabbed her. He hauled her from the water and pulled her, dripping, onto the shore.

She collapsed. "Save Juniperclaw." She lifted her head, straining to see the black tom.

He was hanging on to the root by his claw tips. "Tell Tigerstar I'm sorry." He glanced up at her, relief in his eyes, and then he slid away. The water carried him down into the churning straits below, and he disappeared from view.

"No!" Rage surged through Violetshine. StarClan couldn't let him die! *He saved Shadowkit.* Tree was nuzzling her, but she could barely feel it. She was numb with shock and grief.

"Look! Look!" Shadowkit yowled beside them. He was staring upstream.

On the far shore, Willowshine had plunged into the water. Lionblaze held on to her, grasping her flanks with his claws. Gorsetail and Nightcloud gripped Lionblaze from behind. SkyClan clustered at their backs, each cat gripping the one in front until they formed a long chain that stretched out into the flood. At the tip, Willowshine swam toward the rock, where Hootwhisker and Lizardtail stared with wide, frightened eyes. With a final push, she reached them and pulled herself onto the stone.

Violetshine's breath slowly eased. Calm seeped into her. She felt suddenly exhausted. She had to sleep.

"Keep her warm." Frecklewish's mew sounded far away. "She's in shock."

She was vaguely aware of Tree and Twigbranch pressing

against her. They were warm. She could feel their hearts beating beside hers.

"Violetshine." Hawkwing's mew reached through the haze that enfolded her. "Wake up. You need to wake up. For your kits."

Alarm flashed beneath her pelt. Her kits! She couldn't sleep now. She shook herself awake. "Hootwhisker! Lizardtail!" She remembered Willowshine's desperate swim.

Tree blinked at her. "It's okay. They're safe now."

She looked upstream. Lizardtail and Hootwhisker were shivering on the far bank as Gorsetail and Leafstar hauled Lionblaze and Willowshine from the water.

She gazed into Tree's eyes. "You saved me." Love flooded her heart, and she reached her muzzle to his.

As his warm breath touched hers, Shadowkit fluffed out his pelt beside them. "I did it!" he yowled, triumphantly. "I did what my vision told me and I brought the Clans together!"

She pulled away and stared at him. "What exactly did your vision tell you to do?"

"I had to drown to make the Clans help one another." The kit's eyes shone excitedly.

"You threw yourself in on purpose?" Violetshine pricked her ears. "Do you have bees in your brain?"

"It worked, didn't it?" Shadowkit looked proudly around at the cats. Violetshine followed his gaze and realized that cats from every Clan had come to help them. Could the kit be right?

He must have been touched by StarClan. She drew him close and looked up. The clouds were beginning to lighten. Excitement fluttered in her belly as the wind dropped. The landscape around them seemed to quiet, and she pricked her ears, her heart quickening as suddenly the rain stopped.

CHAPTER 25

Alderheart looked up at the clear, black sky. He narrowed his eyes against the brightness of the moon. Countless stars glittered above the island. For the first time in days, his fur was dry, and a warm wind promised newleaf once more.

The island clearing was crowded. Across the sea of pelts, Alderheart could see Twigbranch and Violetshine sitting with Hawkwing, Tree, and Finleap. Their eyes were round and their fur fluffed. They were clearly happy to be reunited. He whispered in Jayfeather's ear, "It looks like every cat has come."

Jayfeather grunted. "After what we've been through, who would be mouse-brained enough to miss this Gathering?"

Alderheart purred softly. Tigerstar had called the emergency Gathering when SkyClan arrived in his camp. Now the Clans looked up at the Great Oak, where Bramblestar, Harestar, Tigerstar, Mistystar, and Leafstar sat side by side on the lowest branch. Their deputies sat below them on the roots. Only Juniperclaw was missing. Alderheart felt a pang. He knew he'd been right to speak out, but he wished his investigation hadn't ended in Juniperclaw's death.

As Puddleshine shifted beside him, Alderheart blinked at him warmly. The tom's fur was sleek once more. His scars were hidden beneath his thick pelt. His eyes were bright, and he was staring eagerly at the Great Oak.

Tigerstar got to his paws and looked around at the gathered cats. "We come to speak of change," he meowed. "Change that must come if the Clans are to survive. But first I have news of Juniperclaw. Many of you will know that he is dead. But you may not know the whole story. Juniperclaw admitted to poisoning the SkyClan fresh-kill pile. He saw an easy way to drive SkyClan from the lake and he chose to go through with it, even though he knew he was breaking the warrior code. He believed he could protect his Clan best by saving us from fighting for our land. But a Clan that won't fight for their land when they have to is no Clan at all. And Juniperclaw paid dearly for his crime. He lost his deputyship and his life."

The Clans watched him in silence as he went on.

"But he died a courageous death. He died saving lives. Shadowkit was caught in the flood on RiverClan land. Juniperclaw pushed him from the water before being swept into the lake. He could have saved himself, but he chose to help Violetshine get out of the flood. He saved the SkyClan warrior, at the cost of his own life. I hope that he finds peace in StarClan." The ShadowClan leader looked down at Cloverfoot. She shifted on the oak root as she sat beside the other deputies. "Cloverfoot will be ShadowClan's deputy now. Like Juniperclaw, she once turned her back on the Clans . . . But I believe that, like Juniperclaw, she is ready to serve her

Clan honestly and in good faith."

"Cloverfoot!" Scorchfur was the first ShadowClan cat to call her name.

Snowbird chimed in. "Cloverfoot."

"Cloverfoot." Her name rang through the clearing as her Clanmates yowled their approval and their yowling spread among the other Clans.

Alderheart dipped his head to her, pleased that she'd been chosen. She puffed out her chest proudly, and her eyes reflected moonlight as she looked back at him.

Bramblestar lifted his muzzle. "Twigbranch led a patrol of cats from ThunderClan, RiverClan, and WindClan to find SkyClan and persuade them to return to the lake." Twigbranch glanced at her paws as the Clans turned to look at her. Finleap moved closer to her as Bramblestar went on. "Despite the storm, the patrol managed to bring SkyClan back—"

He broke off as cheers erupted from the watching cats. Surprise showed in his eyes. He pricked his ears, clearly delighted, and waited for the yowling to die away. "We still must settle on where they will live, but we know that their place is beside the lake with the other Clans."

Strikestone called from among the ShadowClan cats, "Land must be given equally."

"Every Clan must help!" Lizardtail called from among the RiverClan cats.

Bramblestar dipped his head. "Yes. This time, each Clan will give up some of its territory to make them a home."

Harestar glanced apologetically at Leafstar. "We should have agreed to this sooner."

Leafstar eyed him. "You should have." Her gaze flitted reproachfully to him and Mistystar. "If the other leaders had taken responsibility in the first place, a lot of suffering could have been avoided."

Mistystar dipped her head. "RiverClan will not turn our tails on you again."

"Next time, WindClan won't wait for others to decide before doing what is right," Harestar promised.

Leafstar looked satisfied and turned to Tigerstar. "And what about ShadowClan?"

Tigerstar met her gaze evenly. "ShadowClan only ever wanted fairness. If I hadn't stood up for what belonged to ShadowClan, nothing would have changed. You would have kept half our land, and my Clanmates would have faced countless moons of hunger."

Leafstar's ears twitched. "That's one way of looking at it."

Anxiety pricked Alderheart's paws. Was the gathering going to descend into an argument? He quickly searched the SkyClan leader's gaze. Had Tigerstar's refusal to admit the part he'd played in her Clan's suffering insulted her? He tipped his head, surprised. Was that amusement in her eyes? It only lasted a moment. Leafstar blinked it away and turned back to Bramblestar. Alderheart relaxed. Clearly, she was willing to indulge Tigerstar's arrogance for now.

"The past is the past," Bramblestar meowed. "We must

work together and decide a future where we can all thrive."

"How will the land be divided?" Mistystar asked.

"SkyClan knows the forest well," Bramblestar began. "They could take a stretch of land between ThunderClan and ShadowClan, from the mountain border to the lake."

Leafstar narrowed her eyes. "What will RiverClan and WindClan give?"

"We can shift our border," Harestar suggested, "so that ThunderClan can take from us part of what they give to Sky-Clan." He looked expectantly at RiverClan. "You could do the same for ShadowClan."

Mistystar tipped her head. "Five territories beside one another with the lake at their heart," she murmured thoughtfully.

Below, the Clan cats exchanged anxious glances. Alderheart tensed. Would the leaders agree to Bramblestar's plan?

Mistystar nodded. "I think it could work."

Bramblestar looked hopefully at Tigerstar. "What do you think?"

Tigerstar glanced at his Clanmates. Moonlight shone in his dark gaze.

Alderheart nudged Puddleshine anxiously. "Why's he hesitating?"

"Hush." Puddleshine quieted him with a wave of his tail.

Tigerstar blinked slowly at Bramblestar. "Are you suggesting that SkyClan become our neighbors again?"

Leafstar bristled. "Do you have a problem with that?"

Tigerstar's whiskers twitched. "I can't think of anything

better. We've put up with ThunderClan long enough. It'll be good to have a new Clan on our border." He eyed Bramblestar mischievously.

Bramblestar huffed. "ThunderClan will enjoy a break from ShadowClan as well."

"You'll miss our scent markers!" Strikestone called from the gathered cats.

Amused purrs rippled through the Clans.

Hootwhisker yowled from the back of the crowd. "What will Gatherings be like without ThunderClan and Shadow-Clan bickering like starlings?"

Mistystar purred. "I'm sure they'll still find things to bicker about."

Bramblestar flicked his tail impatiently. "Are the territories settled?"

"Yes." Tigerstar dipped his head.

"From now on, each Clan will have equal land and an equal voice," Harestar meowed.

"And SkyClan can start building yet another camp." Leaf-star rolled her eyes dramatically.

"We'll send warriors to help," Bramblestar offered.

"And ShadowClan will send warriors to help RiverClan rebuild their camp," Tigerstar chimed in.

Happiness washed Alderheart's pelt. He'd never seen the Clans cooperating like this before. Was this the beginning of a new era of peace? He glanced at Tree. They might even learn to listen to a mediator when they had disputes from now on.

Tree touched his muzzle to Violetshine's ear. She buried

her nose in his neck fur. Her pelt looked lustrous in the moonlight. Carrying kits clearly agreed with her.

Beside her, Twigbranch's eyes brimmed with joy as she watched the leaders. She seemed bigger than usual, and Alderheart wondered if she'd grown. She looked every bit as much as a warrior as Squirrelflight now. Flypaw nosed in between her and Finleap. Twigbranch glanced at her apprentice warmly and shifted to make room.

A rush of pride warmed Alderheart's belly. It seemed only a few moons since he and Needletail had found the tiny kits and brought them back to the Clans. If only he'd been able to see the future. He could never have imagined what a difference they'd make. He glanced again at the stars. Was Needletail there now, watching? Was she proud of what the kits had become? *Thank you for helping me find them, Needletail.* His heart ached with fondness. *I hope you're happy in StarClan.*

Breathing the soft night air, he prayed that this peace between the Clans would last. *From now on, let us face new threats as StarClan intended—five Clans united.*

ENTER THE BRAVELANDS

Heed the call of the wild in this action-packed series from **Erin Hunter.**

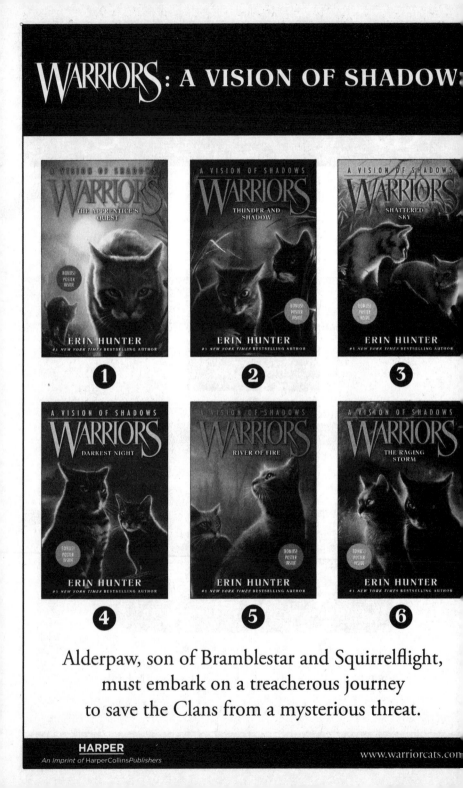

Alderpaw, son of Bramblestar and Squirrelflight,
must embark on a treacherous journey
to save the Clans from a mysterious threat.

WARRIORS: SUPER EDITIONS

These extra-long, stand-alone adventures will take you deep inside each of the Clans with thrilling tales featuring the most legendary warrior cats.

HARPER
An Imprint of HarperCollinsPublishers

www.warriorcats.com

WARRIORS: MANGA

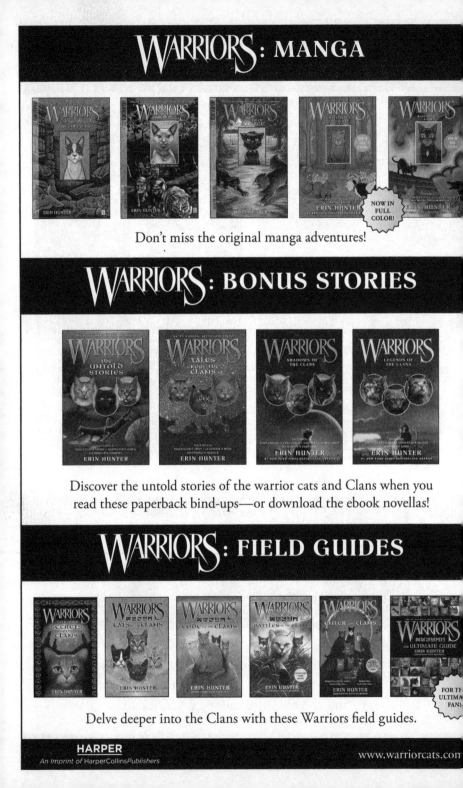

Don't miss the original manga adventures!

WARRIORS: BONUS STORIES

Discover the untold stories of the warrior cats and Clans when you read these paperback bind-ups—or download the ebook novellas!

WARRIORS: FIELD GUIDES

Delve deeper into the Clans with these Warriors field guides.

HARPER
An Imprint of HarperCollinsPublishers

www.warriorcats.com